HOUSE
OF GLASS

ALSO BY SARAH PEKKANEN

The Opposite of Me
Skipping a Beat
These Girls
The Best of Us
Catching Air
Things You Won't Say
The Perfect Neighbors
The Ever After
Gone Tonight

WITH GREER HENDRICKS

The Wife Between Us
An Anonymous Girl
You Are Not Alone
The Golden Couple

HOUSE OF GLASS

SARAH PEKKANEN

ST. MARTIN'S
PRESS

NEW YORK

First published in the United States by St. Martin's Press, an imprint of
St. Martin's Publishing Group

HOUSE OF GLASS. Copyright © 2024 by Sarah Pekkanen. All rights reserved.
Printed in the United States of America. For information, address St. Martin's
Publishing Group, 120 Broadway, New York, NY 10271.

ISBN 9781250283993

For Jamie Desjardins, with gratitude

Children's games are hardly games.
Children are never more serious than when they play.

—Montaigne

CHAPTER ONE

Tuesdays at 4:30 p.m. That's her routine.

I stand on a grimy square of sidewalk near the busy intersection of 16th and K Streets, scanning the approaching pedestrians.

My new client will arrive in seven minutes.

I don't even need to meet her today. All I have to do is visually assess her to see if I'll be able to work with her. The thought makes my shoulders curl forward, as if I'm instinctively forming a version of the fetal position.

I could refuse to take on this client. I could claim it's impossible for me to be neutral because the media frenzy surrounding the suspicious death of her family's nanny has already shaped my perceptions.

But that would mean lying to Charles, who is the closest thing I have to a father.

"You know I hate asking for favors, Stella," Charles said last week from across the booth in his favorite Italian restaurant. He unfolded his heavy white napkin with a flick of his wrist, the crisp snap punctuating his words.

Perhaps a reminder that in all the years I've known him, he has never asked me for a single one?

"I'm not sure if I can help her," I'd told Charles.

"You're the only one who can. She needs you to be her voice, Stella."

Saying no to the man who gave me my career, walked me down

the aisle, and has provided a shoulder during the dissolution of my marriage isn't an option. So here I wait.

My new client won't take any notice of me, a thirty-eight-year-old brunette in a black dress and knee-high boots, seemingly distracted by her phone, just like half the people in this power corridor of DC.

Two minutes until she's due to arrive.

As the weak October sun ducks behind a cloud, stealing the warmth from the air, a nasal-sounding horn blares behind me. I nearly jump out of my skin.

I whip around to glare at the driver, and when I refocus my attention, my client is rounding the corner a dozen yards away, her blue sweater buttoned up to her neck and her curly red hair spilling over her shoulders. Her expression is wooden.

She's tiny, even smaller than I expected. She appears to be closer to seven years old than nine.

Her mother—tall, brittle-looking, and carrying a purse that costs more than some cars—holds my client's hand as they approach their destination: a gray stone building with its address discreetly displayed on a brass plaque. Inside is the office of DC's top child psychiatrist.

In another few moments, they'll disappear through the doors and be swallowed up by the building.

She's just a kid, I remind myself. One who has been through more in the past month than some people endure in a lifetime.

I'm good at my job. Maybe the systems and strategies I've developed will carry me through. I can put a favor in Charles's bank for a change.

A few steps away from the entrance of her therapist's building, little Rose Barclay stops. She pulls her hand out of her mother's and points down to her shoe. Mrs. Barclay nods, busying herself by removing her oversized sunglasses and placing them in a case while Rose bends down.

I squint and crane my head forward.

People stream past Rose like water around a rock, but no one seems to notice what she's doing.

Rose isn't adjusting the buckle on her shiny black Mary Janes, as I'd assumed.

Her left hand is stretching out to the side. Seeking something.

I'm drawn forward. Closer to her.

It happens so quickly it's almost over before I realize what she has done. If my angle had been off—if I'd been watching from across the street or inside the building—I never would have noticed.

Rose straightens up, her left hand slipping into the pocket of her sweater as her right hand reaches up for her mother's.

The evidence is gone now, tucked away.

But I saw it. I know what this shy-looking girl collected off the sidewalk and concealed to keep.

A shard of broken glass, shaped like a dagger, its end tapering to an evil-looking point.

CHAPTER TWO

My first rule for meeting a new client: It's always on their turf.

Sometimes that means at a skateboard park, or in side-by-side chairs at a nail salon, or in their backyard while they throw a tennis ball for their golden retriever. Food is typically involved. My clients rarely want to confide in me early in the process, and eating pizza or nachos provides space for silence.

I never press hard during the first meeting. It's all about establishing trust.

By the time I see them, any trust my clients once held in adults has been shattered.

When divorce court judges are presented with the most brutal, complicated custody cases—ones in which no resolution seems possible—they appoint someone like me: a best interest attorney, or guardian ad litem. We represent the children.

My particular area of expertise is teenagers. I never take on clients younger than twelve. But Charles—or Judge Huxley, as he's more widely known—wants me to break that rule. One of his colleagues is the presiding judge on the Barclay case, and she is having trouble finding the right attorney for Rose.

I take a last glance up at the gray building Rose disappeared into only moments ago. She's in a safe space, being tended to by a highly trained professional. Her mother is present.

So who does the girl think she needs to protect herself from with a shard of glass that could double as a knife?

My Uber pulls up to the curb. "Stella?" the driver asks as I slide into the backseat, and I nod.

He turns up the radio, and an NPR reporter's modulated voice pours out of the speakers. I'm relieved the driver doesn't want to make conversation. I need to gather myself before reaching my next destination, another office building close to the National Cathedral. This appointment is a personal one.

I stare out the window as the driver winds his way north through clogged streets, muttering under his breath when he gets stuck behind an illegally parked Tesla.

My mind feels overly full, a dozen discordant thoughts buzzing through it. I reach for my phone to send a text to Marco, my soon-to-be ex-husband, then discard the idea. He knows I'm coming, and he won't be late. Like all the partners in his prestigious law firm, he parcels out his days in six-minute billing increments, which makes him acutely aware of time.

I step out of the Uber at the stroke of five o'clock, heading for a nondescript brick building that holds more than its share of heartbreak.

I bypass the elevator and climb the stairs to the fourth floor, then walk into the small reception area of suite 402. Marco is waiting, leaning back in a chair as he smiles at something on his phone.

The sight of him still takes my breath away. His Italian roots show in his glossy dark hair, tan skin, and eyes that turn to amber when the sun hits them. Our coloring is so similar we've been asked more than once if we're related.

"Just one of those old married couples who start to look alike," Marco used to joke.

He rises now, placing a hand on my shoulder as he leans in to brush a kiss across my cheek. I start to wrap my arms around him, but he pulls back before I can embrace him in a real hug.

We both speak at the same time, our words entwining instead of our bodies.

I aim for a joke: "Fancy meeting you here."

Marco pulls out a DC cliché: "How was traffic?"

He gestures to the coffee table where two sets of documents topped by identical blue pens await. "Lakshmi already brought out the paperwork."

I blink hard. This is happening fast. "So all we have to do is sign?"

He nods and hands me one of the slim stacks of paper.

Unlike the divorces I encounter through work, the one Marco and I are going through is as amicable as it gets. Our biggest disagreement came when Marco insisted on giving me the little row house we'd bought together near the DC line. We both know why: He makes twenty times as much as I do now. I accepted the house. But I insisted he take our fancy espresso maker. It was a bigger sacrifice than it sounds; I love a good cup of coffee.

I hesitate, then scrawl my name across the bottom of the final page of our divorce agreement. When I look up, Marco is recapping his pen.

Lakshmi steps into the waiting room. "Hey, Stella. You guys all set?"

I nod, my eyes skittering away from her sympathetic ones. This is the final step in the dissolution of our marriage. After Lakshmi files the papers, I'll get a letter in the mail notifying me our uncontested divorce has been granted.

My gaze roams across the box of tissues on the coffee table. Next to it is a sculpture of an eagle in flight, its wings outstretched. I recognize the symbolism: tissues for grief at an ending, the bird an image of hope for the future.

Marco and I wed on a crystalline winter day nearly ten years ago, just as the first snow of the season began to fall. Even before I said the vows I meant with my whole heart, I knew we'd end up here.

It was only a question of when.

CHAPTER THREE

Marco and I claim two stools at the bar of a casual Mexican place in Tenleytown. Always the gentleman, he pulls mine out before seating himself.

Ever since we met in law school at George Washington University, we've been cultivating a list of our favorite restaurants around town. This one didn't make the cut, but the margaritas are good and it was convenient. Besides, Marco has let me know he can't linger for dinner.

We order a pair of spicy margaritas on the rocks, no salt. A bartender delivers a basket of crispy chips and a dish of warm salsa along with our drinks.

I watch as a barback cuts limes with a small knife, the blade easily slicing through the fruit's green skin. The knife is only a little bigger than the piece of glass Rose Barclay put in her pocket.

"It's always the husband," Marco says, continuing the conversation we began while we walked here. "Ian Barclay knocked up the nanny. She was two months pregnant, right?"

"Closer to six weeks."

"So he tried to eliminate the problem."

"The wife had plenty of motive, too," I counter. "Jealousy. Rage. Plus, Beth Barclay is the one with all the money. What if the nanny came after her for blackmail or child support?"

"So why didn't Beth kill her husband *and* the nanny?" Marco asks. "They both betrayed her."

I shrug and swirl a chip into the salsa. "Crimes of passion defy logic. If she did it, she probably didn't plan it out. There are subtler ways to murder someone than by pushing them through a third-story window."

I pause, regretting the flippancy of my words as I recall Rose's vacant expression. Rose was in the backyard helping her grandmother pick tomatoes from the vegetable garden when it happened. Rose might have seen her nanny tumble through the air. She would have heard the fatal crack of skull against the stone patio.

"Both parents were in the house, right? So whose alibi is stronger?" Marco wants to know.

In the month since the nanny's death, media coverage has tapered off, but there is no shortage of old news clips on what police termed a "suspicious death." I've spent the past few days digging into research, so I tell Marco what I know: Beth Barclay claimed to be in her second-floor office, writing an email to her fellow members of the board of the Kennedy Center. She had classical music playing through her computer speakers, as she typically did when she worked, and she insisted it masked the sound of the window glass breaking a floor above. Police verified Beth transmitted an email around the time the nanny fell.

Beth's husband, Ian, was on the phone with an employee of his landscaping company; his home office is down the hall from Beth's. He uses noise-canceling AirPods for his calls, and claims he didn't hear a thing until he ended his call and heard his mother screaming. That phone call was also verified.

Both Barclays lawyered up the moment it became clear the police considered them suspects and refused to take lie detector tests, multiple press outlets reported. Police recently closed the active investigation, so it's now considered a cold case.

And both Barclays are fighting for sole physical and legal custody of Rose.

"Let's say you pushed the nanny. How fast could you make it from that third-floor window back down to one of those second-floor offices?" Marco wonders. Then he smiles. "Who am I asking? I know you're going to find out."

I smile, too, the sorrow I felt in our mediator's office beginning to fade. I've always bounced my cases off Marco. His even temperament and contemplative nature are two of his many wonderful qualities. We no longer share a home or life together, but we still have this: A deep friendship. An enduring connection. A different kind of love.

"Another?" the bartender asks.

I look down and see I've drained my margarita. "Sure."

Marco's glass is almost full.

That's unlike him. Marco loves a good cocktail.

I frown and take in more details. I do what I've learned to do in my cases, when just about everyone I encounter lies to me to further their own agendas—or delusions. I look for the unspoken messages. His tell.

His fingertips are drumming on the wooden bar. He hasn't loosened his tie, like he typically does at the end of a workday. Instead of leaning back against the curved, welcoming backrest of his stool, he's sitting up straight.

Marco's body language reveals what his words don't: Something is weighing on his mind.

I probe for the source of his unease. "Everything good at work?"

He shrugs. "Fine. You know, the usual."

Marco doesn't derive his sense of self-worth from the eight-figure deals he navigates. He takes more pride in volunteering pro bono hours to battered women and donating a chunk of his salary to charities that serve underprivileged children. His heart is with people—with family.

It's one of the things I love most about him. It wasn't only Marco I gained when we wed. From the start, his big, Italian-American family folded me into their gatherings: everyone talking over one another, the table laden with food, someone always topping off your wineglass, friendly arguments and laughter swelling like waves.

If Marco isn't troubled by something at work, maybe it has to do with his family. His older sister is pregnant with her fourth child—a high-risk pregnancy due to her diabetes. But last I heard, all was going well. His mother experienced chest pains recently. The doctors ran tests and told her it was just gas. But doctors aren't infallible.

"Mom's seventieth is coming up fast," I venture. "Is the plan still the Inn at Little Washington?"

Marco's fingers speed up their rhythm. Bingo.

"Ah, yeah . . . Actually, I was hoping we could talk about that."

My heart accelerates, echoing the staccato rhythm of Marco's fingertips.

Marco's mother has long talked about celebrating her milestone birthday at the coveted kitchen table in the only three-star Michelin restaurant in the DC area. A reservation was secured nearly a year ago. Though Marco's father passed away shortly after we wed, Marco's four siblings, along with their spouses, will all be there.

I was invited, too. They still consider me family.

I brace for Marco's next words.

"I've met someone," he says. I flash to the memory of him smiling down at something on his phone when I walked into the mediator's lobby and the way he deflected my invitation to dinner tonight.

Marco wouldn't be telling me this if his new relationship weren't serious—serious enough that the woman he wants to bring to that long-awaited family dinner isn't me, an ex-wife who still calls her former in-law "Mom."

It isn't hard to do the math. No matter how many chairs the table holds, there won't be enough room for both of us.

Marco has already found the hope the eagle statue in the mediator's office promised.

I can't blame him. We've been separated for more than a year.

I do what needs to be done. I smile and maintain eye contact. I don't allow myself to give away a single tic or clue. My work has taught me to lie convincingly.

"I'm happy for you." I lift my glass in a toast. "She's a lucky woman. Bring her to the dinner. I'll drop off my gift for your mom some other time."

Marco smiles, his posture finally relaxing. "Thank you for under-standing."

On our wedding day, I was so in love I thought we could overcome anything. But there was one thing neither of us could compromise on. A dividing line that only grew deeper and wider with time.

Marco wanted kids.

I didn't. More than that, I couldn't. Not physically but emotionally.

People who endure childhoods like mine tend to go one of two ways, a therapist once told me. Either they try to give their kids the kind of parenting they wish they'd had, or they avoid children alto-gether.

Marco hoped I'd change my mind about motherhood. I hoped our love would be enough.

I turn my gaze away from his, watching the knife cleave through another lime.

CHAPTER FOUR

The tall iron gates swing open, and I gently press down on my gas pedal, easing along the curving private road toward the Barclay estate in Potomac, Maryland. This historic Colonial and its twenty acres of land were purchased for $12 million, according to public records. And that was before the Barclays renovated the mansion and added a reclaimed-wood barn and two-story shed.

The property is in both Ian and Beth Barclay's names, but Beth's inherited fortune made the buy possible.

I take another swig of hazelnut coffee from my travel mug. I feel a bit off my game—I didn't sleep well last night after Marco's news—and I need to be sharp.

As of today, I'm officially the best interest attorney for Rose Barclay.

It's time to meet my newest client.

I crane my neck as I approach the house, trying to glimpse the area where the nanny was pushed—or fell. But my view is blocked by a big excavator parked by the side of the house, its giant metal claw waiting to smash and grab.

I shift my gaze to the house. It's like something from a place time forgot, with its gray-green serpentine-stone construction and wide front porch. The house is ringed by sprawling oak and cedar trees, but not a single fallen branch or brown patch mars the emerald expanse of lawn. Lush blue hydrangea bushes, with flower clusters as big as bowling balls, line the beds surrounding the front porch.

I park my Jeep in front of the garage and double-check that I have everything I need. My phone is fully charged and has a good camera, since I never know when I'll need to document something. In my shoulder bag I've tucked my laptop and a new yellow legal pad. My cherished Montblanc pen—a gift from Marco—is in an interior pocket.

I step out and inhale the clean air. It's hard to believe this place is less than thirty minutes from the hustle and grime of DC. Instead of the rush of traffic and bleating of horns, all I hear is birdsong.

I climb the porch steps and press my finger to the bell. Beth Barclay opens the door a moment later, like she was hovering nearby.

Police never officially deemed her a suspect in the murder. But I can't help assessing her ballerina-lean, five-foot-nine frame. Strong enough to push her petite young nanny through the fragile single-pane glass of a hundred-year-old window?

Absolutely.

"Ms. Hudson?" she asks, even though I gave my name at the gate intercom.

"Call me Stella." I extend my hand.

She takes it. Her grip is firm.

"Welcome. I'm Beth."

She has the same pale skin, delicate features, and red hair as her daughter. But the years have sloughed away some of the vibrancy of Beth's coloring.

I step across the entryway and feel my eyes involuntarily widen.

It's as if I've landed in another time.

From the narrow-planked, dark wood floors to the steel-gray steam radiators and pocket doors with skeleton keyholes, it's as if this house has been perfectly preserved for a century, waiting for the Barclays to move in.

Most major renovations of old homes involve tearing down walls to create an open floor plan and using architectural tricks to bring in light and flow.

The Barclays didn't do any of that. They went backward in time, not forward.

The floor is slightly sloped, and the ceilings are low. The hallway is papered in a flowery ivory pattern, and the console table looks like an antique, with its rickety legs and brass fixtures. Above it hangs a watercolor in an ornate gold frame that could have come off the wall of a museum.

"Would you care for some coffee, or perhaps sparkling water?" Beth offers.

Despite all she has been through—a double betrayal, a death in her home, a public scandal, and a looming divorce—her manners are impeccable, her voice soft and cultured. She wears slim-fitting, camel-colored pants and a cream sweater with a scarf that looks like vintage Hermès knotted around her neck. But I can read the deep strain in her eyes, and in the faint lines around her mouth.

Beth looks like a woman on the brink—of an eruption or a collapse. Maybe both.

I shake my head. "No thanks."

"So." Beth's hands twist together. "I'm not quite sure how this works."

I smile in a way that I hope reassures her. "All I need to do today is meet Rose. You can remain with us the whole time."

Beth doesn't look happy. Then again, most people aren't when faced with a lawyer who may decide the best thing for their child is to have minimal contact with them.

"I'm going to be around a lot during the next few weeks, so it's important Rose feels comfortable with me," I continue. My job requires me to assess everything in Rose's world and get multiple perspectives from people she knows before I give the court my custody recommendation.

"I understand." Beth nods toward the staircase, with its intricately carved, thick wooden banister. "She's in her room."

"Just one question first. How much does Rose know about the divorce?"

"She's aware her father and I are divorcing, and that we both want her to live with us."

I can't help thinking that's a huge emotional burden to place on the shoulders of a small child.

As I follow Beth to the stairs, I pause and peer into a formal living room to my left. Furniture is grouped around a simple brick fireplace—it looks like another original feature of the house—and a large black piano awaits, sheet music resting on the ledge above its keys. Rose plays, I remember. She's supposed to be remarkably good for her age. There's a silver tea set on the coffee table, and the rug is woven in dark blue and maroon shades. The room feels sterile, as if it has been staged but not truly lived in.

Something else feels off about this house, but I can't put my finger on it. There's a heaviness to the air, as if gravity is somehow stronger within the confines of these walls. Maybe the rage and turmoil and pain swirling around are affecting me.

We climb the stairs, the hundred-year-old wood creaking under our weight. Rising in symmetry with each step is a series of photographs of Rose, from infancy through the present. I'm struck by the fact that Rose is smiling in only two of the pictures. There's something eerily adult in her eyes, even as a toddler.

I want to pause and study the photographs—there's another off detail tickling my brain—but Beth is moving quickly. It's a struggle to catch up to her; my limbs feel leaden.

As we approach the second-floor landing, my gaze is pulled to the rear of the house. A window overlooks the grounds. The nanny would have tumbled past that pane of glass, her face filled with terror, her arms outstretched.

I suppress a shudder. If I were the Barclays, I'd move out as quickly as possible. It seems strange that given the ugliness of their pending divorce, they're still living under the same roof.

But Charles explained why: The Barclays have agreed to sell the house, and Ian Barclay is honoring the prenup he signed by not angling for alimony or a piece of Beth's inheritance, so their standoff has nothing to do with money. Each will leave the marriage with the same assets they brought into it.

But neither Beth nor Ian wants to give up their chance at winning full custody of Rose—and they see moving out as a losing chess move.

My chest tightens. The fate of a helpless young child rests in my hands, and I have no idea if I'm equipped to fix what seems like an unwinnable future for her.

More than a half-dozen doors with round brass knobs line the second floor, and all are closed. I wonder what lies behind them. There are no other visible windows in the hallway, and the space is dim.

Beth passes two doors, then pauses at the third and taps her knuckles against it. I inhale a deep breath into my pinched lungs. This is my first chance to look beyond the surface, to see what all the tabloid articles and TV clips couldn't.

Beth opens the door to reveal a tidy bedroom with walls painted soft pink. A wooden rocking chair occupies one corner, and on the canopy bed is a large cloth doll that appears to be formed in Rose's image—down to her wide blue eyes and freckles.

"Rose? I have someone I'd like you to meet."

I don't love Beth's choice of words. There's an implication of owner-ship to them, like I'm here as Beth's guest. In order for me to do my job, Rose can't think I'm in the corner of either of her parents. I'm here to serve her, not the adults in her life.

Rose twists around from her white wooden desk, where she's reading a book. I glimpse the title on the jacket: *Anne of Green Gables*.

"Hi, Rose." I keep my tone light. "My name is Stella Hudson."

Rose's eyes are downcast. She doesn't give any indication she has heard me.

"I'm a lawyer, Rose. And guess what? I'm here to work for you."

She doesn't react.

Sometimes my clients are glad I've arrived. They're desperate for someone to finally listen to them. Others are resistant. This year alone I've had a fifteen-year-old girl slam a door in my face, narrowly missing catching my hand in it, and a seventeen-year-old boy curse me out, a vein bulging in his forehead and his voice rising into a deep-timbred shout—just before he fell to his knees and burst into tears.

I have no idea how Rose feels about my presence.

"I know there's a lot going on for you right now, and it's probably pretty confusing," I continue. "I'll be spending some time with you and your parents over the next few weeks to help figure out what will make you happiest."

Rose is wearing a green velvet dress today, with her loose red curls pulled back in a matching headband. Up close, I see a sprinkling of freckles across her nose and cheeks. Again, I'm struck by how young and innocent she appears—and by how formally she is dressed.

I wonder where she put the shard of glass.

"I like your room." I glance around, spotting a blue ribbon from a horse show, a tall bookshelf in white wood, and a painting of a garden scene in another large, ornate gold frame.

"This painting is so pretty and peaceful. It must be nice to look at."

I keep my tone gentle and pleasant as I admire the pink flowers and the little dog peeking out from behind a tree. "I didn't see the dog at first . . . It's almost like he's playing hide-and-seek."

I don't ask a single question because I know Rose won't answer.

She can't speak.

CHAPTER FIVE

It's as if Rose split into two people when she watched her nanny die: The little girl of before—a gifted student with the vocabulary of a much older child.

And the expressionless child who sits before me now, suffering from traumatic mutism.

Rose has seen the top doctors in the region. None can say when she will talk again. It could be in a day, or in six months.

Beth sits on the edge of her daughter's bed, twisting her hands together again. I catalog it as a nervous tic.

Beth probably thinks I don't understand what her daughter is going through.

But I'm one of the few people who does.

There are different kinds of mutism that afflict children. Some kids can't speak in certain environments, such as at school. That's called selective mutism.

Mutism can also occur after brain trauma or surgery.

Rose suffers from a condition that's far rarer and not well understood: traumatic mutism. The onset is swift and overwhelming, and as the name suggests, it occurs after a severe trauma. One documented case involved a girl who was mauled by a dog and didn't speak for six weeks. Another case—not documented—occurred when a girl discovered the body of her mother.

That girl was me.

I was a little younger than Rose when I experienced the sensation of my throat closing up around my words, sealing them away. I couldn't speak for months after I saw my mother's lifeless form on our living room floor.

Charles knows this; it's why he asked me to work with Rose. He believes I'm in a unique position to understand her.

Back when I was a child, traumatic mutism wasn't understood at all. Some people believed I was being defiant, that I was perfectly capable of speech. Perhaps being punished would remind me how to talk.

I push away the memory fast.

I spend the next few minutes talking about a horse I once met named Pacino who loved peppermints, then admire the row of perfect little origami cranes decorating the top of her bookshelf.

"Rose made those," Beth tells me.

When I thank Rose for letting me see her room, she doesn't give any indication she has heard me.

"I'll be back tomorrow to talk with your dad, so I'll probably see you again then," I tell Rose.

Beth takes my cue and stands up. I watch as she walks over and drops a kiss on Rose's forehead, telling her daughter she'll be back in a moment.

Rose picks up her book again. But the jacket gapes away from the book cover, and I glimpse the title printed on the spine.

The first word isn't *Anne.*

It's *The.*

It's an old trick to hide books beneath different books' jackets to camouflage what you're reading. I had a friend in junior high school who did it with Judy Blume books to fool her strict mother.

If the book Rose is so engrossed in isn't *Anne of Green Gables*, what is it?

I can't linger any longer. Beth is in the doorway, looking at me expectantly.

I follow her as she retraces our path downstairs. When we reach the entryway, she begins to head for the front door. I quickly ask, "Actually, can I take you up on that glass of water now?"

I'm not thirsty. I want to get a look at more of the Barclays' home. Plus, it will give me a chance to talk more to Beth.

The kitchen is in the rear of the house. We walk down the narrow hallway, passing a small library with an exposed stone wall and floor-to-ceiling shelves, as well as several other rooms with closed doors. I see activity going on in the backyard through the clear panes of the sliding kitchen doors that lead to the patio.

Parked to one side of the yard is a work truck with the name of the company in big letters—*TRINITY WINDOWS*—and beneath it, a line of script that reads *Plexiglass: The Safe, Clear Choice for Today's Homes*.

Out of the corner of my eye, I see Beth open a dark wood cupboard and pull out a blue tumbler, filling it with filtered water from a small tap on the side of the deep sink.

I clock the cement countertops, the copper cabinet handles, the stone floor. Modern luxury renovations tend to incorporate products like solar panels or glazed tiles on the walls, but all the materials I've seen in this house were available a century ago.

I turn my focus onto two men unloading a pane of what looks like glass—but must be plexiglass—from the back of their truck, carrying it down the ramp toward the house.

"Stella?"

I look over to see Beth holding out the glass of water.

When I take it, it feels strange in my hand. Much lighter than I expected.

I examine it more closely and realize it isn't glass, even though it looks identical. It's the sort of acrylic that is shatter-proof. I know because Marco's sister, the one who is pregnant with her fourth child, switched to those when her kids knocked one too many drinks off the kitchen table.

It's a discordant modern detail in a home that seems frozen in time.

My eyes flit to the truck again. It's filled with large, rectangular shapes. Dozens of sheets of plexiglass.

Enough for every window in this enormous house.

"Well, it's a busy morning. And Rose needs to get back to her schoolwork."

"Her schoolwork?" I echo. It's a Saturday, and I can't imagine a third-grader has much homework.

"My mother-in-law has been homeschooling Rose. We thought it would be best to take her out of school temporarily, given everything . . ." Beth's voice trails off. "Thank you for coming."

She is dismissing me. She smiles, but the expression doesn't reach her eyes.

Her behavior is unusual. Typically, parents are desperate to curry favor with me, to show how competent and kind they are. Or to sneak in a bad word about the other parent.

Beth reaches for the tumbler in my hand, even though I've only taken a few sips. I relinquish it.

Then she begins walking to the front door. I reluctantly follow. There's something nagging at the corner of my mind. A series of clues I've filed away that add up to something just beyond my grasp.

Right before we reach the front door, I glance back at the grand curving staircase. When I climbed it, I was distracted by Rose's somber expression in the pictures.

That prevented me from noticing the other detail I'd tucked into my subconscious—until now.

My skin prickles as the realization hits me.

The photos are bare in their frames. Unprotected by a layer of glass.

I rub my fingertips together, still feeling the surprising lightness of the acrylic water tumbler.

Now I look beyond my initial observations, taking in the details I *didn't* see: There are no crystal chandeliers hanging from the ceilings. No mirrors in Rose's room or in the hallway. No china cabinets with clear panes.

And workmen are replacing all the antique windows with sheets of clear plastic.

Nothing in this house is made of glass.

CHAPTER SIX

I'm heading down the road toward the security gate when an old Nissan Sentra tears around a curve, its muffler popping like a gunshot.

I jerk my steering wheel to the right to avoid a collision, braking hard. The other driver does the same, but since he's going double my speed and he overcorrects, he skids at a forty-five-degree angle onto the grass before coming to a stop.

I'm tempted to flip him off. But the driver may have information I need. So I turn off my engine and step out with a smile.

"You okay?" I call, noticing his tires have dug deep channels into the grass.

He doesn't answer. His head is resting on the steering wheel and his eyes are shut. For a second, I fear he's injured. Then his head rises.

I quickly assess him: He's a young guy, maybe twenty-five. Handsome in an edgy way. Dyed-blond hair with black roots and a couple of tattoos on his arms. His car and clothes tempt me to peg him as working class, but in my line of work I've learned to avoid drawing conclusions.

He meets my eyes, then revs his engine. He's preparing to leave.

The urge to stop him seizes me, and without thinking, I leap in front of his car.

He meets my gaze through the windshield, and I almost flinch when I see the fury burning in his red-rimmed eyes.

But if anger scared me away, I'd never be able to do my job.

I hold up my palms and force another smile. "Got a second?"

His right hand lifts up and then slams down. Instead of blaring the horn, though, he hits the steering wheel so hard his fingers must sting.

Then he rolls down the window. "What?"

He isn't Rose's piano teacher—not with that treatment of his fingers. I can't imagine the Barclays employing a guy with this kind of attitude as a contractor. So who is he?

I walk over to his side of the car. "Hi, I'm Stella Hudson. I'm here because of Rose. The judge overseeing the divorce hired me to help her."

He tilts his head back, listening.

"Do you mind if I ask you a couple questions?"

He doesn't say yes, but he doesn't decline, either.

"What's your connection to the Barclays?"

"To *them*? None."

Scorn sharpens his tone. I ask the next obvious question.

"So why are you here?"

"Look, I didn't exactly get invited for dinner. I showed up because they've still got Tina's stuff and her family wants it."

I've never seen a picture of him, but I'm now certain it's the nanny's boyfriend. I scour my memory for his name: Pete.

"You were dating her? The nanny?"

He pounds his steering wheel again, this time with both fists. "She has a name! Why doesn't anyone ever say her name?"

He's right.

"Tina de la Cruz." Hearing me acknowledge her seems to blunt the razor-sharp edge of Pete's anger. But it must still be festering beneath the surface.

Anger is a natural part of the grieving process, but for Pete, it's obviously more layered: Tina was his girlfriend, but she was also sleeping with Ian Barclay—and carrying Ian's baby.

I catalog Pete's heavy breathing and tense, muscular body. His affect is at odds with our bucolic surroundings. In the distance, two horses—one a lush sable brown, the other a dappled gray—are grazing in a field surrounded by a wooden fence. The smell of freshly cut grass wafts through the gentle early-fall air.

The juxtaposition hits me: Every detail of the Barclays' seven-bedroom home and manicured gardens is flawlessly curated. And every person I've encountered here is deeply damaged.

"You're here to get her things?" I echo, stalling because I'm working something out.

He nods curtly.

"Will it all fit in your car?" His Nissan doesn't have much of a trunk.

"It's just a couple bags and boxes," he said. "That's what they told Tina's mom."

Probably her clothes and toiletries, maybe a few books and personal tokens. A family like the Barclays would furnish the nanny's room. They wouldn't want her bringing in an old mattress and mismatched dresser and nightstand.

I need to keep him talking. He knew Tina well. Even though she kept secrets from him, maybe she occasionally confided in him.

"It must be difficult for you to be here," I say. "Would you like my help?"

He considers it for a second, then shakes his head.

"I'm going to get in and out of that house as fast as I can," he tells me. I see a muscle twitch in his jaw. "And Ian better not get in my way."

I throw out another question, hoping to strike a nerve. "Do you blame Ian for the affair?"

"Are you for real? Tina wasn't like that—she didn't sleep around. He's twice her age and her *boss*. He probably came on to her and she was scared he'd fire her if she said no."

I edge closer and take in the brown rosary beads hanging from his rearview mirror, and the McDonald's drink in his cupholder. The interior is neat but worn; the vehicle must be ten years old. The only thing in the car that looks new is the T-shirt Pete is wearing with a logo that looks like a guy jumping over a park bench.

I dig in another direction. "Do you think Tina wanted to quit?"

His eyes darken. "Yeah. She hated it here. The house creeped her out. She was going to get a Taser."

"Why?"

"Stuff started happening to her here."

The hair rises on the back of my neck. "What happened to Tina here?"

He looks at me, incredulous. "What happened? They killed her."

"Who, Pete? Who do you think killed Tina?"

He shrugs. "If I knew that, I would've already done something about it."

He puts his hands on the wheel. I notice a few curious items in the front seat: a pair of thin gloves and sneakers with Velcro straps instead of laces. I take a closer look at Pete. He's wearing long, baggy shorts that have ridden up to reveal bruises on his knees, and there are scrapes on the knuckles of his right hand, as if he had been punching someone. There's also an Ace bandage around his left wrist. Either he's terribly accident-prone, or something else is giving him injuries.

"One last thing—you said the Barclays didn't invite you here," I blurt.

"Yeah. They don't know I'm coming. They'd probably just put her stuff out on the porch, and I want to see her room one last time."

I reach into my pocket for one of the business cards I carry on me at all times. "Please call me if you think of anything else. Anytime."

I give it to him and step back, staring after him as he drives off. He has no idea how much information he provided.

The Barclays aren't aware he's coming. But Pete made it through the gate. That means he knows the security code. Tina must have given it to him at some point.

Most security gates have an alert that sounds inside the house when the gate is opened. Perhaps because the Barclays are having work done at the house, they aren't concerned about vehicles arriving today.

What I'm more curious about is Pete's past visits to the estate. I can't see Beth allowing Tina to entertain Pete in the house, but perhaps Tina snuck him in when the Barclays were out. Clearly Pete has been in her room before, or he wouldn't have said he wants to see it one last time.

Anger was pulsing off Pete when we spoke.

Was he angry enough by Tina's betrayal to push her to her death?

Marco's words echo in my mind: *It's always the husband.*

Unless it's the boyfriend, I think.

CHAPTER SEVEN

People grieve in different ways. Pete is stewing in rage. When my father died after swerving off the road to avoid a deer and smashing into a tree at the age of thirty-six, my mother turned to alcohol and then drugs.

As for me, I stay busy. That makes it harder for my demons to catch me.

Right now, going home isn't an option. Marco moved out last year, but memories of him linger like a ghost. Last night I kept seeing him lift his head off the pillow next to mine, his eyes sleepy and his longish hair rumpled. This morning, I flashed to an image of him leaning against the kitchen counter, a tiny bit of espresso foam on his upper lip as he sipped from his cup.

I reach for my cell phone and call Charles.

It's five o'clock on a Saturday, but chances are Charles will be free. He's been married for forty years, but it's a hollow union. He and his wife share a home and not much else. Charles has a cordial but distant relationship with his two adult sons, too, for reasons I don't fully understand.

It's one of the threads that links us—we're two loners who long for connection.

"Free for dinner?" I ask when he picks up.

He hesitates. "Of course."

"Are you sure?"

"How does Old Angler's sound? Say, 6:30."

"Perfect."

I disconnect the call, but can't shake the sense that Charles isn't being entirely truthful. That brief hesitation hinted of other plans he is probably now canceling in order to see me.

If I were a better person, I would've pressed Charles harder to be honest about whether he had a conflict. But I need him too much right now.

He's the only adult in my life who has always been there for me.

I met Charles when I was seventeen, the day after I discovered a briefcase filled with cash.

I was a high school senior, working as a sandwich maker for minimum wage at a deli on Western Avenue, the street that divides DC and Maryland. I took as many shifts as I could, and not just because I was broke. I'd been living with my aunt ever since my mother died of a drug overdose when I was seven, and having a job got me out of the house.

By the time I'd been employed at the deli for a week, I'd memorized the ingredients of all thirty-two sandwiches listed on the big overhead menu. I worked the grill, lining up chopped vegetables and meats in neat, sizzling rows, then topping them with cheese and scooping up each row with my long, flat spatula before slipping it into a freshly sliced baguette.

My first paycheck was for seventy-four dollars. I remember staring down at that slim rectangle of paper in my hands, thinking of all the things I yearned to buy. My aunt prohibited makeup, and bought me only a few cheap, sturdy items of clothing from Sears every year—navy slacks and shorts, and a couple of plain T-shirts and sweaters.

It didn't make high school any easier.

I would've loved to have used some of my earnings to buy a tube of mascara or lip gloss, and maybe a pair of jeans with rips at the knees and chunky Steve Madden wedges like the other girls wore.

Instead, I walked to the bank next door and opened a savings account and deposited every cent.

Even back then, I knew the most valuable thing money could buy was a way out.

Legally, I needed to stay with my aunt until I was an adult in the eyes of the courts that had assigned her to be my guardian. But when I turned eighteen—the week after I was scheduled to graduate high school—I'd be on my own. My aunt had made it crystal clear she wasn't going to pay for college. While other seniors talked about college or gap years, I kept my head down and worked double shifts on the weekends.

I was under no illusions about what life on my own would be like—a rental in someone's moldy basement, peanut butter sandwiches and oatmeal for meals—but that would still be better than living with my aunt, breathing the air that always seemed filled with her resentment toward me. I was counting the days until I could leave.

I found the briefcase late on a Saturday night. It was just me and one other employee closing up, and I was flipping chairs on top of tables to clear the floors for vacuuming.

I almost didn't see the briefcase at first. It was tucked beneath a chair, its dark walnut color blending in with the wood of the tables.

It didn't have any identifying characteristics. No ID tag or monogram.

Without giving it much thought, I opened it.

When I saw the stacks of twenties, I sucked in my breath.

I spun around, but my coworker was mopping the kitchen floor, loudly singing along to the Bon Jovi song playing over the deli's speakers.

I closed the briefcase quickly and left it exactly where I'd found it.

I suspected it belonged to a thin, jittery guy who'd come in late for a Pepsi. His pupils were so huge his eyes looked black—like my mother's used to get when she was high. He was worse than the customers who undressed you with their eyes, or the ones who sent back their food because they hadn't bothered to read the menu and didn't realize their sandwich contained onions.

This guy felt like danger.

The only people who would carry around that kind of cash had to be criminals. He'd be back for it, I was certain.

A half hour later, our doors were locked and I'd finished vacuuming. The briefcase was still there. So I picked it up and carried it into the small storage room. I tucked it behind a box of the clamshell containers we used for carry-out orders. I was opening the deli tomorrow morning, so when the guy realized his briefcase was gone, I'd be here to return it.

I hesitated, then checked to make sure my coworker wasn't nearby before I opened the briefcase again.

I reached forward, thumbing through the bills and tallying the total in my head.

It was more money than I'd ever seen.

That night I lay in the twin bed in my aunt's spare room—even after ten years, it never felt like my bedroom—watching the shadows from an oak tree play across my wall. I kept feeling those bills slipping past my thumb, like poker cards I was shuffling.

Ten thousand dollars. A small fortune. More than enough to buy a used car and put down the first month's rent and security deposit on a cheap room.

It would give me a running start.

But the man with black eyes would come back. I was sure of it.

At a few minutes before 6 a.m., I unlocked the doors of the deli and stepped inside. Two of my coworkers and our manager trickled in as the smell of the coffee I was brewing filled the air. I was unpacking the delivery of croissants and muffins from a local bakery, arranging them in the glass case by the cash register, when our first customer arrived: a tall, elegant man. He looked around, then walked toward me.

"Good morning."

I couldn't return his greeting. My mouth was full because I'd swiped a blueberry muffin and I'd been pulling off chunks to nibble while I worked.

"I'm wondering if you can help me," the man continued. "I left my briefcase here last night. I figure someone took it, but I thought I'd check anyway. Did anyone happen to see it?"

I'd been wrong about the owner of the briefcase; it didn't belong to the man with black eyes.

For a split second, I considered lying. This man didn't look like he could hurt anyone. I clocked his expensive-looking pin-striped suit and fancy watch. He didn't expect to get the money back. He probably wouldn't even miss it.

I wanted to lie so badly.

But I couldn't.

Not because I was a scrupulously honest person—the swiped muffin was evidence of that—or because I felt bad for the guy.

The only reason I didn't keep the money was because I figured I'd get caught. Life didn't usually break my way. This could only end badly.

I swallowed my muffin and nodded. "I found it." Then something made me ask: "Can you describe it?"

He raised an eyebrow. "Smart of you to check. It's dark brown. A couple years old."

"Be right back."

I went into the storage room and grabbed the briefcase and brought it out. I handed it across the counter to the man, who was smiling by now.

"I can't believe it. Thank you so much." He opened the briefcase and looked inside, then pulled out five of the twenties and slid them across the counter to me.

"Here. I insist."

I wasn't going to argue. "Thanks." I folded up the bills and tucked them in my pocket.

"It's so rare to meet someone with integrity these days. I'm a defense lawyer, and you have no idea how many liars and thieves I encounter in my line of work. Did you look in the briefcase when you found it?"

Something about him inspired me to be honest. Maybe because I wanted to be the kind of person he imagined I was. So I nodded.

"You could've kept the money. It's from a client who paid in cash yesterday, and I had no way to trace it."

"Don't remind me." I wasn't completely joking, but he threw back his head and laughed.

Then he leaned closer, his eyes narrowing as they traveled over my face. He was assessing me, but not in a creepy way.

"You found this last night. And you're back working again this early?"

I shrugged. "Yeah."

"Are you still in high school?"

Normally I'd bristle at personal questions from a customer. But something about this guy's manner put me at ease.

"I'm a senior. Graduating in June."

"How are your grades?"

"Honor roll," I replied truthfully. I'd harbored a fantasy about getting a scholarship to college, so I'd worked hard in all my classes.

"And what are you doing after graduation?"

"I—I, ah—"

I have no idea.

He nodded, like he'd registered my unspoken words.

"You're obviously a hard worker. Do you like it here?"

I shrugged. Does anyone like working at a place for minimum wage where they get burn marks from the grill and always smell like fried onions? "Sure."

He nodded again, just once, like he'd come to a decision. Then: "Too bad."

"Why?"

I held my breath, waiting for his answer. Somehow I already knew finding that money was going to provide me with a way out after all.

"My receptionist is expecting her first baby and just gave notice. She's leaving in May. And it's almost as difficult to find a smart, hard worker as it is to find an honest person these days. So if you like this job, it'll be harder to convince you to come work for me."

He smiled and held out his hand. "I'm Charles."

CHAPTER EIGHT

The beer garden at the Old Angler's Inn is an oasis in the DC area. On pleasant evenings, you can order a veggie burger and a cocktail and sit on a tree-lined patio under the stars. Sometimes a musician strums a guitar and sings old Carly Simon or new Ed Sheeran songs, and there are always a few dogs by their owners' feet, praying for a dropped French fry.

Charles is waiting at a table when I arrive. He rises, and I lean into the hug he offers, holding on for a beat longer than usual.

"Wonderful to see you, sweetheart," he murmurs in my ear.

I settle into the chair opposite him, taking in his dear, familiar face. His thick hair is silver now, and lines crease his face, but his blue eyes are as sharp as they were the day we met.

He's only a few years older than my father would be.

"I'm glad you called, Stella. I've been wondering how things are going with the case."

I wait until the approaching waitress has taken our order before I answer.

"I met Beth and Rose Barclay today."

"And?"

"Beth was a little aloof. Cold."

"Perhaps she was nervous?"

I shake my head. "More uncomfortable, I'd guess. Maybe she wanted to be in control of the process and didn't like the fact that she wasn't. She practically kicked me out after I met Rose, as if she wanted to assert her authority somehow."

Charles nods. He doesn't know the Barclays personally, but he has dealt with similar situations as a family law judge. "People with that kind of money are used to running the show."

"True."

Charles leans forward. "And you saw Rose, too? How was that?"

I tell him the truth, like I've done since the day we met. "Mixed. She's so young, Charles. And she must be suffering terribly . . ."

The emotions I suppressed in order to do my job threaten to pour out now. Tears prick my eyes as the memory that's been haunting me most of my life envelops me again: *There's a heavy knock on the door. My mother ushers me into the only closet in our little efficiency, whispering, "Don't make a sound." I hear her conversation with a man who has a deep voice. Then she says, "No . . . please." It grows quiet. Too quiet. I pull my mother's coat from a hanger and wrap myself up in it. It smells like her—the good smells from before, like a hint of the sweet perfume she used to wear, nearly overpowered by the way she smells now, sweaty and unclean. I wait for my mother to open the closet door and let me out. But she never comes. I finally fall asleep and awaken with my foot painfully tingling. When I creep out of the closet, I have no idea what time it is. The apartment is dark, but the glow from the nearby streetlamp seeps through the cheap curtains. My mother is on the floor. Her eyes are open and blank, like all the light has drained out of them.*

I dial 9–1–1, but when the dispatcher comes on, I don't make a sound.

I can't.

I swallow hard and pull myself back into the present. "It was strange . . . to see what I was like at around her age. I've never known anyone else who had it."

"Traumatic mutism." Charles was the one who gave me a name for my condition. In a voice filled with compassion, he told me it wasn't my fault. That I should have received help instead of shame and punishment from my caretakers.

"How am I going to figure out what's best for Rose when she can't tell me anything?" I ask him.

The waitress brings over our drinks, setting down my beer and Charles's martini and saying she'll be back with our veggie burgers soon. Charles thanks her and waits until she is out of earshot before speaking again.

"Stella, when I heard about this case, I knew it was meant for you. Not just because you're in a unique position to understand Rose. Your heart is still in your work. You've never gotten numb or jaded, like so many do. Little Rose deserves someone like you fighting for her."

As always, Charles's faith in me is a tonic and incentive. My pulse slows and my breathing evens out.

I thank him and reach for my beer, the glass cold in my palm, tasting the tangy hint of lemongrass in the microbrew.

I note the heaviness of the thick glass in contrast to the tumbler I held at the Barclays'. Tomorrow I'll go back to the plastic house, as I've begun to think of it. The place that scared the nanny.

What else happened to Tina there? I wonder.

"Do you think one of the parents could have done it?" I ask Charles. "That's the part that worries me the most. That I could end up sending Rose to live with a killer."

His hand reaches up and briefly massages his jaw. "The police conducted a thorough investigation and no one was arrested. I think you need to consider the possibility the nanny tripped and fell. I understand that the window was so close to the floor it wasn't up to code, but it was grandfathered in because of the age of the house. Maybe this was a tragic accident, nothing more."

"It's certainly possible," I concede.

"Are you going to talk to the police?"

I nod. "I've already put in a request. I gave your name as a reference."

"As you should have. Who else is on your interview list?" he asks.

"Ian and Beth Barclay, of course. His mother, Harriet. Rose's piano teacher and schoolteacher. Maybe some of Tina's friends . . ."

Charles must pick up on how overwhelmed I feel. "One by one," he tells me, "the pieces of the story different people provide will start to fit together and form an image. And then you'll know what to do."

I wish I could believe him. Both Ian and Beth's sides will call witnesses at the divorce trial, but in a case as hostile and divisive as this one, my report will hold enormous sway with the judge. I need to get it right.

When the waitress delivers our meals, we order a second round of drinks and move on to lighter topics: a jazz concert Charles recently attended at Strathmore Hall, and whether I should trade in my Jeep for a Bronco. Charles doesn't mention his wife, or the two sons who live in faraway states and are raising children Charles rarely gets to see. I don't bring up Marco and his new relationship.

We finish our burgers and sit in companionable silence, listening to the guitar player. He finishes a Jimmy Buffett song and launches into an Ellie Goulding cover, "Bittersweet." I recognize it because it was a favorite of one of the teenage clients I worked for last year.

"Baby, don't forget my name when the morning breaks us," he sings.

At a nearby table, a baby with a headful of dark curls has fallen asleep against his mother's chest. She strokes light circles on his little back with her fingertips, a contented smile playing at the edge of her lips. Her husband's arm is curled around her shoulders, enveloping his little family in a cocoon.

This will be Marco soon, I realize. He wants children. This time, he will have picked a woman who shares his desire.

My mother's descent into addiction always occupies a warning place in my mind. It's why I typically stop at two drinks.

Tonight, though, I signal the waitress and order a third.

CHAPTER NINE

At 10 a.m. sharp, I pull my car into the now-familiar spot in front of the Barclays' garage. Several other vehicles are here, including a van with the logo *Perfectly Seasoned* on the side.

Loud, mechanical noises vibrate through the air, signaling construction at the back of the house. But I can't see it from my vantage point.

I'm tempted to walk around and take a look, but it's too early in the process for me to veer from my established protocol. First I need to meet with Ian and ask him some provocative questions. He won't like them, but his reaction will give me some measure of how well he manages his emotions.

I climb the porch steps and ring the front bell, but this time it takes a minute for the door to open.

When it does, I catch my first glimpse of Ian Barclay.

My initial impression: He's even better-looking than in photos, with his tall, rangy frame, blunt features, and strong jawline. His thick, sandy hair is a little rumpled, like he recently ran a hand through it, and he's wearing a simple black Henley shirt and worn Levi's.

One of the tabloid headlines flits through my mind: *Blue-Blood Heiress vs. Blue-Collar Gardener!*

"Hey there. Stella, right?" His easy smile crinkles the corners of his eyes and elevates him to another level of attractiveness.

"Yes. Nice to meet you, Ian."

"Come on in." He opens the door wide, and as I step into the entryway, I notice he's wearing socks but no shoes. He's less formal than his wife, that's for sure.

"Thanks for coming out," he says. In this way, he is like Beth. It seems he's claiming ownership of our encounter—as if I'm here at his invitation.

"It's my job." My tone is light, but my meaning is anything but. I work for Rose, and no one else.

"So." He opens his arms wide in a gesture that feels like a question. "Do you want to talk in my office?"

That's exactly what I want. I need to get a handle on his supposed location when Tina died.

"Perfect."

He turns and leads me up the staircase. I can't help but stare at the progression of photos of Rose again as I pass them. Who removed all the glass from the frames, and why?

Again, I'm enveloped by a sense of heaviness, the suffocating descent of claustrophobia. I try to swallow, but my mouth has dried up.

Ian reaches the upstairs landing and turns right, toward the window overlooking the backyard. If the pane has been replaced with plexiglass, I can't tell. But I read up on plexiglass windows last night— they're far more common than I thought—and now I realize there's a clue in the fact that I can barely hear the mechanical noises from outside. Old, thin glass wouldn't be able to buffer those loud sounds as effectively.

I'm tempted to ask Ian about the new windows, but instinct cautions me to wait.

All the doors are closed again in the dim, narrow hallway. It's another peculiar detail about the house.

Ian pauses before one, but instead of opening it, he reaches into the pocket of his jeans and pulls out a leather key chain.

He wiggles a silver key into a new-looking lock above the antique knob and the tumblers click.

When did Ian install the lock? I wonder.

In a divorce as contentious as the Barclays', it's possible Ian wanted to safeguard his computer and business files from Beth's prying eyes. But my mind flits to another, darker explanation: He needed a secure place for trysts with his daughter's nanny.

Ian opens the door, and I walk in slowly, taking in the rectangular room. There's a desk in the middle that looks like it's been fashioned from an old barn door, and in one corner are two fabric-covered swivel chairs separated by a small round table. Across from the desk is a dark blue couch.

I don't see any framed photographs or pictures. No paperweight on his desk. No clock on the wall.

Nothing made of glass.

My pulse accelerates.

I force myself to tamp down on my unease. I need to register every nuance of this encounter.

"I, ah . . ." Ian gestures to the chairs. "Do you want to sit down?"

"Sure." I walk over and take one, but Ian doesn't follow. He remains by the doorway, like he's preparing to bolt. I assess his long legs and athletic physique. Sprinting down a flight of stairs to his office would only take him seconds.

"Would you like some water?" he offers.

"Love some." My mouth is still dry; plus, I want to see what he serves it in.

He moves to a mini-fridge at the bottom of a shelving unit and opens it, taking out two cans of flavored seltzer.

"Grapefruit or lime?"

"Grapefruit, please."

It feels like he's stalling. Anyone might, in his position.

In the court of public opinion, Ian has been covered in mud: the handsome landscaper from a humble background who married an heiress and had an affair with their twenty-six-year-old nanny—oh, and potentially killed the nanny, who was carrying his baby.

But one thing I've learned during the years I've navigated the intricacies of divorces is that the breakdown of a marriage is rarely sourced entirely in one individual. Both parties usually contribute to it, to one degree or another. I'm in no way excusing affairs, but I also believe they can be symptoms of a deeper marital problem.

Plus, for all I know, Beth might have had a dozen affairs before Ian slept with Tina.

I crack open my seltzer and take a long sip, then begin. "I know this isn't a fun process. But I need to do the best possible job I can for Rose, and that means getting to know you."

The muscles in Ian's jaw twitch, like he's clenching his teeth. But it works. He finally takes a seat.

I start off gently.

"How would you describe your daughter's personality?"

Ian blinks. Maybe he thought I'd be like the paparazzi who camped outside the gate to his house in the days after Tina's death, shouting questions like *Did you push the nanny?*

"I always say Rose fits her name. Delicate and sweet."

I nod encouragingly, noting his body language relaxes a fraction when he describes his child.

"She's incredibly smart. Much smarter than I was at her age. She started to read when she was three. At first I thought she'd memorized all the Dr. Seuss books—but no, she could actually read them. She loves music, too, but get this—she's into classical. Mozart and Beethoven. She even likes Wagner, and he's not for everyone. She's always been an old soul, you know?"

I think of her solemn expression in the photographs, and the velvet headband matching her high-necked dress. She does seem like an old-fashioned child, as if she could have been plucked out of a previous century and set down in this one.

I lob a few more softball questions to Ian, asking what he and Rose do together for fun, her favorite foods, and her routines on school nights. He answers without hesitation, telling me she adores breakfast for dinner, especially waffles and strawberries, and likes to read herself to sleep. It sounds as though he knows his daughter well and enjoys spending time with her. It could be the truth, or it could be what he wants me to believe.

I hit him with the question I know he's dreading. "Tell me what happened between you and Tina."

The truth is, I'd rather not hear the sordid details. Like most affairs, this one spewed shrapnel, injuring everyone in the vicinity. I think of Beth's brittle smile, Pete's rage, and how Rose has folded into herself.

Ian closes his eyes. Pain washes across his face. It looks genuine.

"I still can't believe Tina is gone."

I wait for him to gather himself and continue.

"I told Detective Garcia everything a couple times, but if you need me to repeat it, I will."

"I'd rather hear it directly from you," I prompt.

The homicide detective in charge of this case—Natalia Garcia, who I also intend to meet—would've made Ian repeat his story in an effort to pinpoint any contradictions or discrepancies. I'm taking a different tack. My gut is pretty reliable. I want to weigh what it tells me against Ian's words.

"Tina and I clicked from the start." Ian's eyes grow faraway. "She was fun and happy, and she lightened up Rose a bit, too. Beth isn't a fan of silly. She never liked it when I made funny faces around Rose, or pretended to be a monster chasing her on the playground."

I'm curious to know how attached Rose was to Tina, but I don't want to interrupt Ian's flow. He hasn't even begun to answer my question.

"Beth never allows Rose to have fast food, or any kind of sugar except on special occasions. I feel like a Hershey's bar or a few fries isn't a big deal, so Tina and I got her treats sometimes, and neither of us mentioned it to Beth. Sometimes it felt like Tina and I were conspiring a little against Beth. That sounds awful, but it wasn't in a destructive way. I guess it was nice to feel like I wasn't being a horrible parent if I bought my daughter a milkshake when she got a good report card."

So the affair wasn't the first secret Ian and Tina kept from Beth. Infidelities often begin with a slow blurring of boundaries, until crossing the final one doesn't seem as momentous.

Ian slumps, as if resigned to the fact that he can't delay this any longer.

"One night Beth was out at one of her charity things, and when I got home from work, Tina was making Rose dinner. I told Tina I could take over, but she ended up hanging out. It was nice. Easy. There was music going—Tina was trying to turn Rose into a Beyoncé fan—and the water boiled over in the pot of pasta because no one was watching it, and guess what? It wasn't a crisis. We all laughed and got some sponges and cleaned it up. It would've been a big deal with Beth. I would've gotten blamed for it. Anyway, it had been a long day, so I opened a bottle of wine. I offered Tina a glass, too."

I can picture the scene now, but I'm seeing it from Beth's perspective. She must have felt violated. Marginalized. Replaced. I've talked to plenty of people who have been victims of affairs in my line of work, and what pains and outrages most isn't just the physical act. It's the emotional betrayal. The fact that Rose was twisted up in it would make it far worse for Beth. I recall again the sinewy strength in Beth's hand when she shook mine. I've read that Tina was five foot two. Beth had seven inches on her. Plus the element of surprise if Tina had her back turned and didn't see Beth racing toward her, hands outstretched, preparing for a shove hard enough to propel Tina through the delicate old window.

Ian rubs his eyes, like he's trying to erase the image his words are drawing. "I went upstairs and tucked Rose into bed, and when I came back, Tina had done the dishes. It wasn't her job—she'd been working all day since Rose had a school holiday. It made me feel . . . good. Like she was taking care of me, too. I topped off our glasses. There was still music playing. A John Mayer song now."

Ian's hands grow still. He lifts his head and looks directly at me, his expression earnest.

"I didn't plan it. Tina was a beautiful young woman, but I'd never looked at her that way. I'm not that guy."

I nod: *Of course.* I have no idea what kind of guy Ian is, but I need him to continue.

"Beth and I have been in separate bedrooms for more than a year." Ian tilts back his head to take a sip of seltzer. "Not a lot of people know that. You don't exactly advertise it when you send out holiday cards. We'd stopped doing things as a couple. She has all her boards and charities, I have my company. Rose is the only thing that connected us, and even how to raise our daughter turned into a battleground.

"So when Tina kissed me . . . At first I tried to pull back. To stop it. But she leaned in again and smiled. Told me she'd been thinking about this moment for a long time. Then, ah, we went up to her room . . ." Ian cringes. "It was stupid. Self-destructive. And it never should have happened."

"Did you sleep together again after that night?" I ask, making sure there is no judgment in my tone.

He clears his throat. His face flushes.

He doesn't want to answer me. And technically, he doesn't have to, even though his divorce lawyer, like Beth's, urged him to meet with me because it wouldn't look good if he refused. But this is the peculiar power of my position: Ian knows he needs to answer my questions, even the invasive ones. Losing face is nothing compared to what else he could lose.

Ian nods. "One more time a few weeks later . . . I was in my office and she was up in her room. She asked me to come look at the sink in her bathroom because it was leaking, and when I got there . . . Well, that was the only other time. But I guess Tina imagined it was more."

"More?" I prompt.

"After the second time, she told me she thought she could fall in love with me. She knew Beth and I didn't have a real marriage. Tina asked if I could see myself loving her."

Few things surprise me at this point. The families that look the strongest are often the ones hiding the darkest secrets.

"I told her we could never do it again, but she kept texting me. It would freak me out—I'd be at dinner with Rose and Beth and my mom, and Tina was two floors above, blowing up my phone with heart emojis. Once she sent a selfie in lingerie and I had to snatch up my phone off the table . . . I mean, I was trying to ask my daughter if she wanted more green beans, and Tina's posing in her bed and asking me to come join her!"

"That does sound stressful," I comment.

He swallows hard. "I didn't know she was . . ." He doesn't want to say the word. So I do.

"Pregnant."

"Yeah. She never said anything to me about it. I only found out after they did an autopsy. As soon as Tina died, I told Beth and the cops everything. I figured the police would find the texts and I knew how it might look. And I don't have anything to hide."

I don't respond to that assertion. Ian is obviously accomplished at hiding things since he had an affair under the roof he shares with his wife and child and mother. "Were you considering a future with Tina?"

"What?" Ian shakes his head firmly. "No. It was . . . physical. Nothing more."

It was more for Tina, I think, but I hide my disdain.

His shoulders slump. "What I liked the most about Tina was that she liked me."

I've heard this before from people who have been unfaithful. They don't cheat because they're wildly attracted to someone else. They do it because someone else made *them* feel attractive.

Ian drops his head into his hands. "I've lost just about everything. My marriage, my reputation, business is down . . . I can't lose my daughter, too. And Beth seems to want that to happen, one way or another. I know Beth told the police I could have done it. Her office is right across from mine, but she keeps her door closed when she's in there. Detective Garcia told me Beth gave a statement saying it was possible I could have slipped upstairs, pushed Tina, and gotten back into my office before my mother started screaming."

I think about the heavy carpeting lining the stairs and hallway—thick enough to swallow the sound of footsteps. Especially if the person running wore socks and no shoes.

I look down at Ian's feet in his dark athletic socks.

"What did you say when Detective Garcia told you about your wife's statement?"

Ian lifts his head and looks me directly in the eye. That's when I see what I've been looking for. Gone is the easygoing, occasionally self-flagellating guy Ian initially presented to be. Now his narrowed eyes are flinty with anger.

"I told the police I work with my door shut, too. Beth could have slipped upstairs just as easily as me."

CHAPTER TEN

A sharp ringing sound cuts through the air.

Ian reaches for his cell phone, which is facedown on the table between us. "Sorry, it's one of my workers."

I hear a man's voice come through the line, but his words are unintelligible. I know Ian, who started working as a landscaper straight out of high school, now runs his own company. It isn't the business you call to get your leaves raked or side garden weeded. The Great Outdoors handles big-budget hardscaping projects—from swimming pools to outdoor kitchens.

"Hang on, I'll come take a look."

Ian disconnects. "We're doing some work in the back and I need to run down there. Should only take a minute."

The call broke our flow, but I've gotten enough from Ian today. I'm far more curious about the noises coming from the backyard. I stand up and reach for my purse. "Mind if I tag along?"

Ian blinks. He doesn't immediately reply, so I up the stakes.

"It's for my report." This isn't untrue. "I need to get a sense of Rose's environment. It'll help me when it comes time to make my recommendation to the court."

I'm strong-arming Ian by reminding him I've got the main say in how custody of Rose will be awarded. Unlike Beth, Ian seems eager to remain in my good graces.

"Oh, of course." But he can't completely quash the edge in his tone that tells me he doesn't like it.

We head down the long hallway. Ian steps aside for me to travel down the staircase first, and instead of waiting for him at the bottom, I turn and walk directly through the arched doorway into the kitchen. There's a woman in a white chef's coat rinsing a head of lettuce at the sink, but she doesn't acknowledge us.

"I see you already know your way around," Ian comments.

I can use this to my advantage.

"Beth showed me yesterday," I say, hoping to ignite a competitive spark in Ian. If he thinks Beth is giving me free access to the house, he may wonder what else she is being open about—and try to one-up her.

I look around the kitchen, visualizing the scene that set every-thing in motion—the first domino to tip. Tina and Rose making dinner, the pot of water for the pasta beginning to boil, Beyoncé singing in the background. Ian coming in, his shoulders relaxing as he took in the happy scene. The cork easing out of the wine bottle. The lingering look between Tina and Ian; the spark igniting.

I pull myself back into the present. Ian slides opens one of the doors and bends down to put on a pair of work boots that are waiting just over the threshold, revealing the source of the mechanical noises: The excavator is digging up the patio, collecting stone and dirt in its giant claw before swiveling and tossing the contents into a dumpster.

It's demolishing the area where Tina landed after crashing through the window.

Erasing the scene.

I follow Ian outside. The excavator stops mid-swivel as a guy wearing a long-sleeved shirt with the logo of Ian's company hurries over, holding an open laptop. I take advantage of Ian's momentary distraction to wander away, to the far edge of the now-broken patio. The yards are breathtaking, with the season's last roses spreading their orange and cream petals and pansies adding bright splashes of purples and yellows to the flower beds. An inviting stone pathway leads to a tiered fountain in the middle of a small pond.

In the distance, I can see the wooden barn by the fenced pastures where the horses are grazing in the gently rolling fields again. There's a two-story shed that complements the style of the barn, with hydrangea bushes flanking its doorway. It isn't hard to imagine the gushing copy the real estate agent selling this house will write: *Picturesque. Timeless. A tranquil oasis.*

My skin prickles as the eerie sense of being watched sweeps through me. I swivel and catch Ian staring at me, his arms folded across his chest, while his employee points at something on the laptop screen. Ian quickly breaks into a smile, but not fast enough to hide the fact that his expression was grim. Because he doesn't like the news his worker is delivering, or because he doesn't like me being here?

I turn back around and find what I've been looking for: the vegetable garden where Rose and her grandmother were picking tomatoes when Tina crashed through the window. The vegetable beds are raised higher than others I've seen—they'd come to my waist. They're set back forty yards or so from the patio, near an old-fashioned rope swing tied to a low branch of a golden oak tree.

Ian steps away from his worker and approaches me.

"What are you building out here?" I ask.

"We're putting in an outdoor fireplace with a pizza oven. It'll increase the resale value of the house."

Does he actually think he's fooling me?

"Nice. Is Rose a fan of pizza?"

Ian smile. "She loves it. Even with anchovies. I told you, my little girl is one of a kind."

"Why did you replace all the glass windows in the house with plexiglass?"

I hit him with the question hard and fast so he doesn't have time to prepare.

Ian flinches. "Beth—she, ah, developed a phobia right after Tina died . . . It's called nelophobia . . . the fear of glass."

I've never heard of it. But I know people suffer from all kinds of unusual phobias—intense fears not just of spiders or germs, but also of sunlight or laughter. The human mind tries to protect us in all kinds of mysterious ways, but some of its strategies do more harm than good.

"It's been . . . difficult," Ian continues. "She's scared of anything that can shatter. We had to replace all our dishes. Mirrors. That sort of thing."

Is he telling the truth? He's avoiding my eyes. He could be embarrassed by his wife's extreme fear. Or he could be covering up for something else entirely.

"You don't have a single mirror in the house?" I ask, wondering how Beth does herself up. When I saw her the other day, her makeup was flawless.

"We put polycarbonate ones in the bathrooms, like they use on boats. They're unbreakable. She's okay with that."

I wrap my arms around myself, feeling chilled even though it's a balmy day for early October.

Tina was right when she told Pete something about this house is deeply off. Whatever she felt is still happening.

I feel it, too.

I pull my mind back to the questions I need answered in order to do my job correctly.

"Did Rose see Tina? After she fell?"

Ian closes his eyes. The excavator jerks into motion again, its claw tunneling several feet into the earth. I suppress a shudder. I can't help thinking it's almost as if it's digging a grave.

"We all saw her." His voice is hoarse, his eyes faraway. It's as if he is looking at the broken body of the young woman who claimed she loved him splayed out on the stones all over again. "My mother was in the vegetable garden with Rose. At first she thought the noise was a tree branch falling. Then she came closer to the patio and saw Tina. I'd just gotten off a call when I heard my mom scream. I came racing down the stairs. Beth was a few seconds ahead of me. I thought something had happened to Rose . . . There was glass everywhere. Beth didn't have on shoes, and she stepped on a shard from the window. Her blood . . . Tina's blood . . ."

Ian's voice is a monotone. He's so pale I'm worried he might pass out.

I reach out and hold his arm. "Do you want to go back inside?"

He swallows hard. "Yeah, okay."

When he sits down to remove his boots, I see his hands are trembling. It takes him two tries to undo the bow on his right.

As we step back into the kitchen, I see the chef is still working at the sink.

Ian doesn't seem to notice her, but perhaps that's because I'm between them and I'm blocking his view. His gaze is drawn toward the living room, the source of the deep, rich piano notes filling the air.

"Rose is having her lesson. Sometimes I like to watch. She doesn't mind."

I could be listening to a classical station on the radio. It's almost unbelievable that she plays so well. Rose isn't merely talented.

She's a prodigy.

Ian walks ahead, through the arched opening to the hallway, and I follow. From our vantage point in the entryway, Rose's back is to us. She sits up ramrod straight, her long hair hanging down her back, her arms bent at perfect ninety-degree angles. I watch her fingers sail up and down the octaves, touching the notes with a speed and dexterity that awes me. The song soars through the air, rich and vibrant.

Sitting next to Rose on the piano bench is a very thin, balding man in a black shirt and black slacks. I initially peg him as being in his sixties, but when he turns his head to follow the path of Rose's dancing fingers, I glimpse his unlined face and realize he's quite young—in his mid-to-late twenties. It's his thinning hair and frail affect that age him.

Rose plays for another minute, and I watch Ian watching her. Whatever else his failings, it's clear he prizes his daughter—or at least her accomplishments. When she lifts her hands off the keys, Ian claps softly, and Rose turns around.

"Hi, Rose," I say softly. "You're really good."

The piano teacher turns around and frowns, then raises a finger to his lips.

I look at Ian, who shrugs.

The teacher speaks softly to Rose; then her fingers rise to the keyboard. Her body still marionette-like, she begins to play.

A high-pitched shout erupts from the kitchen.

The music halts.

Ian spins on his heel and runs. I'm right behind him.

Beth Barclay is standing in the middle of the room, staring at the woman in the chef's coat. The woman's mouth is rounded in shock as she stares back at Beth. In her hand, hovering over a stainless steel pot, is a large glass measuring cup filled with broth.

Gone is the cultured, restrained heiress who met me at the front door only yesterday. Beth is trembling, her body rigid. Despite her expensive-looking outfit and sleek hairdo, she looks completely undone. There's a wildness in her eyes.

"How could you be so careless?" Beth snaps. "I told you we don't allow glass in this house!"

CHAPTER ELEVEN

Three things happen in quick succession: The chef murmurs an apology, then hurries out the front door, still holding the glass measuring cup.

Then Ian reaches for Beth's arm, which she wrenches away before he can touch her. "You need to calm down!" he demands.

And I hear a slight creaking sound, like metal gears moving, just before a panel slides open behind me.

I spin around and see a gray-haired, sixty-something woman leaning on a cane as she limps out of an elevator that was concealed by a kitchen panel I'd assumed led to a pantry.

"Ian! I was just coming up to listen to Rose play. Why is everyone yelling? What did you do?"

There's no resemblance—Harriet is short and a bit heavyset, with plain features—but her familiar tone tells me she can only be Ian's mother.

Ian bristles. "Why do you always assume it's me? I didn't do anything. Beth's the one—"

"Oh, I'm the one?" Beth whirls on him. "*I'm* the one who destroyed everything?"

Harriet's face falls. At first I think she's going to apologize for fanning the flames; then I realize she's looking down the hallway, to the sight of Rose standing alone.

Rose looks so tiny and vulnerable.

"Maybe you should have this discussion out of earshot of your daughter," Harriet whispers.

She's right: Rose's eyes are downcast, and her body is straight and unyielding. I can almost feel the anxiety radiating off her.

Harriet makes her way down the long hall to Rose, her cane tapping the floor with every other step.

"Rose, I'm sorry your lesson was interrupted. Do you want to keep playing?"

Rose doesn't answer. Her grandmother puts her hand on Rose's shoulder. "It's okay, sweetie. I promise everything will be okay."

My chest twists. I'm unable to get enough air. Rose is so innocent, and so utterly alone. *This is too much for her,* I think. *Witnessing a death and having her family fall apart—it's too much for any child.*

I'm starting to hyperventilate. The walls feel like they're closing in, suffocating me.

My vision swims as my mind spins backward, reeling me thirty years into the past again, taking me to the place I dread most, the night of my mother's death: *I'm seven years old, peering out from the closet by the front door, my right foot full of pins and needles because I spent all night curled in a cramped position. The room is dim and still. There's a shape on the floor. A person. Electricity sparks up my leg as my foot touches the ground. I draw closer to the inert form. My voice, high and scared, calling for her for the final time: "Mommy!"*

My lungs are so pinched it's hard to breathe. I need to get out, to run away from this creepy, suffocating house as fast as I can. I'll tell Charles it's too much for me. Another attorney can take over. I take a step forward into the hallway.

Then my blurry vision clears and I see Rose standing in my path.

She's so still. It's as if she's made of plastic, just like everything else in this house.

She looks like she doesn't feel emotions. But I know she feels too much.

Rose is the most vulnerable thing I've ever seen.

The tightness in my chest eases a bit. I relax my shoulders, breathe into my belly. All the tricks a therapist once taught me.

I watch as Harriet takes Rose's hand, speaking gently to her. "Let's go out onto your swing. A little fresh air will feel good, won't it? You can finish your lesson another time."

Harriet leads Rose toward the sliding doors in the back of the kitchen. Toward us.

"After you swing, maybe we can do an art project," Beth tells Rose as she passes.

"And tonight you and I can watch a movie—anything you want," Ian calls after her.

Rose doesn't acknowledge either of them.

I slide my purse strap off my shoulder and set it down on the kitchen counter. Physically I'm still weak and shaky after my near panic attack. But my mental resolve is strengthened.

When Rose was standing in the hallway, listening to her parents argue, she reminded me of a fawn in the woods that freezes when danger is near.

I know what it's like when the person who is supposed to protect you is the one who scares you the most.

Whatever I need to go through to help Rose is nothing compared to what she is now enduring.

I turn and face Ian and Beth. They look shamefaced.

I can never forget one of them may be a killer.

"Look, I'm sorry about all that." Ian exhales loudly. "My mother's a good person. But she blames me for—well, for what happened with Tina and how it ruined everything." He hangs his head. "She's right."

"Harriet moved in for a couple of weeks after she had knee surgery." Beth's mouth tightens. "That was four years ago."

"You said you wanted her to stay—"

"I did, at first." Beth seems to wrestle with her emotions. When she speaks again, her voice has lost its raw edge. She's smooth and in control again.

"Ian's mother is a good person. She raised Ian alone after his father left them. She cleaned houses to make ends meet. She worked so hard all her life and never complained."

"We asked her to move in because she lived in a fourth-floor apartment that didn't have an elevator," Ian continues. "It was painful to watch her limp up and down those stairs with her cane. We've got this huge house with all these empty bedrooms—"

"And Harriet is wonderful with Rose," Beth picks up.

"She's a much softer grandmother than she was a mother," Ian agrees. "And Mom doesn't intrude in our lives. She has the whole lower level with a kitchen and living room, and she spends a lot of time there or tending her garden. She joins us for dinner several times a week, but that's it."

I'm struck by the way Beth and Ian seamlessly pass the conversation baton, the way many married couples do. Breaking old patterns is difficult, as I know too well. I still only sleep on the left side of the bed, as if I'm keeping the other half free for Marco.

"My mother is also homeschooling Rose," Ian continues. "Rose is taking a leave from school."

"Excuse me." The piano teacher is standing in the hallway now, occupying the spot Rose just vacated, holding a black music case with silver hinges. He's so thin he looks concave. His pallor is alarmingly colorless, and I wonder if he is ill. His voice is discordant with his physique; he has the deep, powerful voice of a much more robust man.

"Would you like to reschedule?"

"Phillip, I'm sorry. Yes, please. Add this session to your bill, of course."

The piano teacher nods so deeply it almost looks like a half bow. "I'll see myself out."

I shift slightly so that I can keep an eye on Rose and Harriet walking toward the swing, but still look at Beth and Ian.

"I understand you've developed a phobia of glass," I say.

Beth nods, her mouth a trembling, tight line.

Ian steps closer to Beth, murmuring, "The impact from the fall was what killed Tina, but the window glass . . . When it broke, it was as sharp as a knife and it cut her. Beth can't stand to be close to anything that reminds her of the way Tina died."

His eyes stay fixed on mine. He doesn't move or blink.

Then a sudden movement catches my attention.

Rose is running toward the field where the horses are grazing, her fiery red hair streaming out behind her.

Harriet leans on her cane, looking after her granddaughter.

"Where is Rose going?" I ask.

Beth turns around. "To see Sugar and Tabasco. The mares. They soothe her."

When Rose reaches the gray dappled horse, she throws her arms around her leg. The horse stands still, letting Rose hug her.

"Animals are the only things that seem to make her happy these days," Ian murmurs.

And with those words, he gives me a key to reaching my young client.

CHAPTER TWELVE

I've borne witness to some of the worst things family members can do to one another.

The mother who faked a letter from a doctor stating her child showed signs of abuse after a visit to her father's house.

The father who poured sugar in his own car's gas tank and tried to pin it on the mother to illustrate her alleged mental instability.

The parents who nearly went bankrupt during a two-year custody battle that constantly snagged on minutiae, such as which parent's home would hold their child's saxophone. The saxophone war ended up costing them thousands in legal fees—far more than the price of buying a second instrument. The child's resulting stress and intensive therapy cost them even more.

Never before has a case consumed me like this one.

So I'm breaking yet another rule.

I'm not taking on any other clients until I finish the Barclay case. Rose will get my full focus; I'm going to fast-track all of my interviews. Everything else in my life will be put on hold.

I owe it to Rose to make sure she gets into a safe environment as quickly as possible. I *need* to get her to safety. I think of the oppressive, eerie heaviness that descends whenever I step through the Barclays' door and suppress a shudder.

I still need to interview Beth, Harriet, and the piano teacher I'm calling the Thin Man in my mind, and I want time alone with Rose.

But first I need to talk to Rose's psychiatrist, Dr. Gina Markman.

As dusk descends upon the city, I stand outside Dr. Markman's building, scanning the area where Rose picked up the shard of glass. The sidewalk has been swept clean by now.

I pull open the heavy door to the lobby and bypass the elevators to take the stairs, as is my habit, to the seventh floor. It's not for the exercise; elevators make me deeply claustrophobic.

The reception area of suite 726 has a few soft-looking chairs and a rack of glossy magazines. But it's empty. Dr. Markman told me she had a full day and couldn't meet me until 6 p.m., when the office closed.

I'm a bit early, so I take a seat.

Ten minutes later, she is nowhere to be seen.

She's a busy woman. But I bet that's not the only reason why she's making me wait.

Therapists are typically bound by confidentiality unless their client is a danger to themselves or others.

I'm one of the few people who can get an order from a judge to force therapists to divulge information about clients who are minors.

I had to send one to Dr. Markman to get her to agree to meet with me. This is her countermove.

At 6:15 p.m., the sound of heels against the wooden hallway floor announces her arrival before she comes into view. Even her quick, sharp footsteps sound annoyed.

When she rounds the corner, I rise and offer my hand. "I'm Stella Hudson. Thanks for meeting with me." As if she had a choice.

She's strikingly beautiful, with flawless black skin and hair cropped as close as a knit cap. She looks young enough to be a grad student, and I briefly wonder if she's a prodigy, like Rose.

"Gina Markman."

She gets points for not introducing herself as Doctor, and for her stylish outfit—wide-legged black pants and a hot-pink wraparound silk blouse that I immediately covet.

"I can give you thirty minutes. Let's chat in my office."

Technically, I can ask her as many questions as I want. But I know her heart is in the right place. She's trying to protect her client.

I need to make her understand I am, too. That we're on the same team.

Dr. Markman leads me into her office, which is smaller than I'd expect. She takes a seat behind her desk, and I claim the chair opposite her. Her desk is enviably neat, with just a laptop and wireless mouse, a silver letter opener, and a crystal candy dish on the surface. There's a Degas print on the wall, and a painting of the ocean at sunrise. Her diplomas—from Columbia for undergrad and Tufts for medical school—are in side-by-side frames. A window overlooks the city, and through it, I can see the light gray-white peak of the Washington Monument.

Aside from the dish of individually wrapped hard candy, there's nothing in this room for children. I wonder how she can work with kids in such a sterile environment.

"This isn't where I meet my patients," she tells me, as if she can read my mind. "But I let their parents wait here in order to preserve privacy. There's an art therapy room down the hall where I hold sessions. It's much more child-friendly."

"I'm trying to learn as much as I can about Rose and her parents," I tell Dr. Markman, plunging right in. "The divorce proceedings have reached an impasse. I need to make sure the custody arrangements serve Rose's best interests, and no one else's."

She nods, her lovely chiseled features softening a fraction.

"Rose Barclay is an unusual patient. Unfortunately, I can't say I know her well at all. Clearly she's in a trauma state."

"What can you tell me?"

"I haven't formally tested her IQ yet, but I'm certain it's extraordinary. She's brilliant. I gave her some puzzles early on, just to get a sense of her cogency. She aced them, even the ones intended for much older children. Her mind is something to behold."

"Has she given you any indication of how she feels about her parents?"

Dr. Markman considers my question, then shakes her head. "She expresses herself through art. If there is a clue about her wishes in those pictures, I haven't been able to find it."

"I'd like to see some of Rose's pictures."

She hesitates, then rises to her feet. "Follow me."

Dr. Markman leads me down the hallway and opens the door, flicking on the lights. Here is the therapy environment I expected: It's warm and homey, the walls and furnishings decorated in bright primary colors. There are beanbag chairs and stuffed animals, baskets of toys and dolls, stacks of books, a big dollhouse, an easel and mason jars full of paintbrushes and colored pencils.

Dr. Markman walks to a closet and taps in a code to unlock the door. She reaches inside and finds a large folder. Instead of handing it to me, she clutches it to her chest.

"Art is subject to interpretation," she tells me. "People can look at the exact same image or read the same book and come away with very different impressions."

"I understand."

"Often, what we see in art is a reflection of us. Of our optics. Our mindset. Have you ever tried to read a novel and not enjoyed it, then gone back at another point in time and loved it? The story didn't change. But you did. This is an insight into who we are at any given moment and what we bring to our unique intersection with art."

She's preparing me for something. What am I going to see in that folder?

"Rose has been through so much," Dr. Markman continues, still clutching the folder.

"May I?" I hold out my hand with a warm smile.

"Rose has drawn a number of pictures. They're all variations of the same scene."

In what feels like slow motion, Dr. Markman finally relinquishes the folder. I open it.

The first picture is a death scene.

A long-haired woman—Tina—is splayed out on the stone patio, her limbs at sharp angles to her body. Looking down at her are two figures that can only be Rose and her grandmother Harriet. They are holding hands.

The scene isn't horrific.

It looks peaceful.

Rose has drawn flowers surrounding Tina, a rainbow of pinks and yellows and purples and blues.

It's as if she wanted to make her nanny's death pretty.

I look at the two figures holding hands and suck in a breath.

I recoil as my mind registers what I'm seeing.

Rose's grandma is drawn in simple strokes. She's looking down at Tina's body, her mouth a round shape of surprise.

But Rose has no eyes.

Above her nose are two black circles. They look like holes.

"What does this mean?" I ask Dr. Markman. My throat is so tight my voice sounds strangled.

"At this point, anything we want it to mean. Pick your interpretation. She doesn't want to have seen Tina like that. She doesn't want to be asked about what she has seen. A dozen other possibilities. Depending on the beholder. Depending on the mindset of the artist."

I pull my phone from my purse and snap a picture of the drawing.

I flip to the next page. It's the same image. Tina, broken on the stone. Harriet wearing a shocked expression. Rose with black holes for eyes.

I force myself to channel my thoughts into the clear questions I need to answer: Which parent does Rose belong with? Is one a danger to her?

"How does her mother interact with Rose during the sessions?" I ask.

"Oh, no. I don't allow parents in here." Dr. Markman shakes her head briskly. "This space is for the child only. Beth waits in my office while I work with Rose. My patients need to be able to express themselves freely."

The room is warm, but I feel as if I've been plunged into ice.

"I'm sorry," Dr. Markman tells me. "I have a dinner engagement. I need to go."

She leans in closer. "Are you okay?"

I can't answer.

"Are you a trauma survivor?" she whispers.

It's like she is reading my thoughts again. As if she truly sees me, and knows what I've endured.

She nods, confirming her own question. "I thought so. From the moment we met. I have a sense about these things."

She lays a warm hand on my forearm. It's as if she is willing me strength. Giving me a transfusion from her own reservoirs.

I close my eyes. Inhale it in.

My arm suddenly feels cold again. I open my eyes and see her standing at the doorway, waiting for me to follow. "I'm going to lock up. Can you see yourself out?"

I manage to thank her for her time. I walk down the hallway and take the stairs back down. I step into the lobby and push through the doors onto the street.

Rush hour grips the city. Traffic is snarled and people clog the sidewalks. Beams of light from cars and taxis and buses cut through the gray dusk. A police car futilely wails its siren, but there's nowhere for the cars ahead of it to move.

It's trapped.

There's a bus shelter a few feet ahead. I make my way to it and sink onto the bench, my legs weak.

Of all the things I learned and saw when I was with Dr. Markman, the one I can't get out of my mind is the crystal candy dish.

Beth Barclay brought Rose here only a few days ago. She waited in Dr. Markman's office while Rose drew a self-portrait: the girl with no eyes.

Beth must have seen the candy dish.

And the framed diplomas. The Degas print behind glass. The silver letter opener, shaped like a knife. The window framing the Washington Monument.

It's hard to imagine Beth agreeing to wait in a small room surrounded by objects that supposedly torment her.

And as soon as that thought hits me, another realization lands:

Beth would have needed to travel in a car to take Rose to the appointment. She'd be surrounded by glass windows and shiny mirrors during the duration of that ride.

I need to consider the possibility that both Ian and Beth lied to me. That there's another reason why they've removed all the glass from their house.

CHAPTER THIRTEEN

When the world seems dangerous and angry, I look for the counter-balance of goodness.

It comes in the form of a seventy-nine-year-old widow who lives down the block from me.

Lucille Reed's house is the opposite of the Barclay mansion. There's a crocheted blanket on the back of the old brown couch in the living room, and the avocado-green kitchen hasn't been updated in decades. A stack of *Reader's Digest* sits on the coffee table by a slightly wilted bouquet of pink chrysanthemums. A few dust bunnies reside under the carved wooden TV hutch.

When Marco lived with me, we invited Lucille to dinner every now and then, and he shoveled her walk after snowfalls. When he moved out, I took over the shoveling. Lucille always invites me in for hot chocolate afterward. She makes it from Swiss Miss packets, the kind with mini-marshmallows. Few things taste as good to me as Lucille's hot chocolate on a snowy day.

Lucille spent her adult life as a homemaker. Her husband died years ago, and her children are grown. For a while, she lost her purpose.

Now she tends to wounded souls. It's her passion. Her calling.

I'm desperate to reach Rose, to find a way to connect with her. Her life may depend on it.

So our first outing won't be for pizza or mani-pedis. What Rose needs is a baby squirrel.

Lucille is caring for two at the moment. After a storm shook their nest from a tree, Lucille watched over them, hoping the mother would come back to retrieve them. But a dog or a car must have gotten her because she never did.

"When an injured animal comes to me, I try not to handle it so I don't stress it," Lucille tells Rose as she bustles around her kitchen, preparing a formula that includes goat milk and egg yolks. "But these two are so little they need to be held while I feed them."

Rose is sitting on Lucille's couch, staring at a plastic bin filled with fleece bedding. Beneath the bin is a heating pad. The tiny squirrels are mostly hidden, burrowed into the warmth. But the light brown tip of a tail peeks out from beneath the soft fabric.

I'm sitting on the couch with Rose, but I'm careful not to crowd her.

Three wounded souls are being tended to now.

It was surprisingly difficult to convince Beth and Ian to let me take Rose on an outing. At first both insisted they wanted to come along. When I reminded them I'd been hired to get to know Rose, not spend time with them, I had to promise I'd bring her home within two hours. Beth wanted to know the address and phone number of the neighbor we'd be visiting, but my instinct told me to keep Lucille's personal information private. I merely told Beth she had my cell phone number in case she needed to reach me, and that I'd bring Rose back well before dark.

"She's fragile," Beth said.

"I'm not sure this is a great idea," Ian chimed in.

Even Harriet stood on the front porch, watching us walk to my Jeep and calling after Rose that she'd help her with her math when we got back.

I took note: None of them tried to find out what Rose wanted.

"Lucille is putting the syringe of food into a mug of water to warm it," I tell Rose now, keeping my tone warm and unhurried.

Rose's body language is shifting. At first she sat up straight as a soldier in the pink cloth coat she kept buttoned despite the warmth of the room, her hair in twin braids, her hands folded in her lap. Now she has one leg curled beneath her. A hint of animation is warming her expression.

"I also need to set up my new heating pad for the squirrels. My old one has been acting funny." Lucille slices through the tape holding together a package with a box cutter. "Can you plug it in for me, Stella? There's an outlet to the side of the couch."

I stand up and take the heating pad from Lucille. Then I hesitate.

"Rose, can you do it?"

I hold my breath, watching Rose lift her eyes from the plastic bin. *Take it,* I will her, holding out the pad.

After a moment, she does. Relief pours through me. It's a tiny, vital step. The first time we've directly communicated.

Rose finds the plug, then places the heating pad next to the bin.

"Thank you," I say. "That will keep the squirrels cozy."

Lucille tests the formula by squeezing a drop onto her inner wrist. "I could use some help feeding them, if one of you would like to hold the babies. They're too small to support their own heads and necks."

I look at Rose. She makes full eye contact with me for the first time. I can read her yearning.

"Rose, would you like to?" I ask.

She nods eagerly.

I exhale. I wanted to connect with Rose today, to help her begin to feel safe with me. I've achieved my first goal.

"Put on these gloves." Lucille hands Rose a pair and slips another pair onto her own hands. Then she lifts out the first baby squirrel, keeping it snuggly wrapped in a scrap of flannel.

Rose's eyes widen. Palpable excitement vibrates off her. I smile at her, and I swear I see the flicker of a smile in return.

The squirrel is the size of Lucille's palm. Lucille briefly opens up its wrapping to reveal its furry little body with big feet and ears the size of peas.

For the next fifteen minutes, Rose comes alive. She helps feed the squirrels, then nestles them back into their cozy beds. I quietly pull out my phone and snap a few pictures of Rose, capturing what I hope will be a happy memory for her.

Lucille asks Rose to wash her hands at the kitchen sink as a precaution, even though she had on gloves, and when Rose leaves the living room, Lucille leans close to me.

"Poor girl."

I nod, swallowing the lump in my throat.

Rose returns a minute later, and after Lucille washes her own hands, she shows us an album of pictures of other animals she has taken in—sparrows, starlings, more squirrels, an owl, and baby racoons.

For the first time since I've met Rose, tranquility softens her face. When Lucille shows a picture of a hawk that was hit by a car and could never fly again, Rose reaches out with a fingertip to touch the image of the broken wing, staring at that photo for a particularly long time.

"When wild creatures are hurt, some people say nature should take its course. But there's a better way," Lucille says softly. "People can call their local wildlife rehabilitation center, and sometimes the center will ask someone like me, who has been certified, to help."

I let Lucille's words linger in the silence, hoping Rose can intuit a larger meaning. Help is available to her. She isn't alone.

After we bid Lucille goodbye, I drive Rose home. Since she's too small to sit in my front seat, I occasionally glance at her in the rearview mirror while I make gentle comments about the pink tummies of the baby squirrels, and the noises they made while they ate.

At one point my phone vibrates, but I ignore it.

As we pass through the security gate and head up the drive toward her house, Rose's body language changes. Her arms fold across her stomach. She stares straight ahead, the animation draining from her face.

It's as if she's building a fortress around herself.

"Rose, I was thinking I could take you out for dinner later this week. Your dad mentioned you like waffles for dinner, and I know a great place. Would that be okay?"

She gives me the tiniest nod. But she doesn't meet my eyes.

Beth is waiting on the front porch. She leaps up from the settee and waves as Rose and I step out of my car. I'm seized with the urge to grab Rose's hand, to keep her close to me so I can protect her.

I know what it's like to be delivered to a house you want to escape from. When I was seven, after my aunt was given custody of me because no one tried to find out what I wanted, I walked up the steps to her house, my head hung low and my suitcase in hand, knowing I was leaving a bad environment and heading into a worse one.

My mother, for all her faults and struggles, loved me.

My aunt resented me. Judged me. Hated me.

A sick sense of dread fills my gut as I watch Rose walk through the front door, her hands now tucked into her jacket pockets. I'd given Rose one of my business cards and told her to call anytime, that if I ever heard silence on the line I'd know it was her and I'd rush to the house right away. She'd nodded again, but her eyes were vacant.

The little girl who came alive around the orphaned baby squirrels had vanished.

"We had a nice time," I tell Beth. "I'll be back tomorrow to chat with Harriet." I'm eager to get a sense of the grandmother who came to stay for a few weeks and never left.

Beth smiles and nods. "Of course. See you then." Again, I experience the strong feeling she doesn't want me around.

She wishes I could vanish.

Like Tina vanished, my mind whispers.

When I return to my car, I wait until I'm through the security gate before I check to see who called. Lucille. I hit the callback button.

"Are you alone, Stella?" Lucille asks.

My skin prickles at her question. "Yes. I just dropped off Rose."

"It's the strangest thing. I noticed it right after you left."

I dread what's coming.

Or maybe I sense it.

"I put down my box cutter right next to the package I opened; I'm certain of it. Did you happen to move it?"

"No, I didn't touch it."

"Hmm. I can't find it anywhere. My little grandsons are coming to visit tomorrow, so I wanted to make sure to put it away since they get into everything. Well, maybe it'll turn up." Lucille still sounds puzzled, but she's letting it go.

I can't.

The box cutter was close to the sink. Rose walked into the kitchen alone to wash her hands while Lucille and I remained on the couch.

I flash to an image of Rose, her face vulnerable and innocent.

And her hands tucked into the pockets of her coat.

CHAPTER FOURTEEN

Quick conclusions are the enemy of my work. I can't jump to any.

I need to talk to Marco. He'll listen to me discuss the complexities of this case and reassure me I'm going to find answers. My mind is swirling with dizzying possibilities. Every person I've met who is connected to this case seems to be hiding something.

I reach for my phone, then withdraw my hand.

This past year has been a slow slicing of the ties that once bound Marco and me; a series of painful snips.

Marco is moving into a future that puts me on the sidelines of his life. I need to let him.

I force myself to go to a place where I'll be alone with my racing thoughts. I drive to my house near Friendship Heights, easing into a tight spot on the street. I climb the front steps and unlock the door and walk in, standing in the emptiness.

When Marco and I separated, everyone told me to get a dog.

I listed reasons why I couldn't. I work too much. I like to travel. It wouldn't be fair to the animal.

The only bad thing about dogs is that they leave us much too soon.

I had a dog when I was four. He was gone three years later.

I know what a therapist would say. The one I used to go to said it more than once: *You can't protect yourself against loss, Stella. It's part of living a full life.*

I went to see her a few times after Marco and I separated.

The therapist was about my age, and she had a welcoming smile. She introduced herself as Dr. Chelsea Schneiders, but told me to call her Chelsea. Her office was in her home, and there were a few dog toys in her front yard.

Maybe that's why I told her about Bingo.

Or maybe it's because Bingo is my very first memory.

My dad brought him home on Christmas Eve and somehow kept him hidden and quiet until the next morning. My old memories are fragmented, as long-ago memories tend to be, but I remember his floppy ears and comically long tail and the red bow tied around his neck. He was small, and his gray fur felt wiry instead of soft, but I loved to pet him. At night he slept curled in the crook behind my knees.

After Dad died, it was just me and Mom and Bingo in the house.

Then Mom began to drink. She lost her job. She lost our house.

The first apartment we moved into allowed dogs. Bingo hated it there. It smelled strange, and there were no kids my age.

Did Bingo hate the apartment, or did you, Stella? Chelsea asked.

We both did.

But we should have appreciated the apartment. It was the last good place we lived because it was the last place we were together.

Mom started hanging out with the couple in the next apartment over. When I got home from school and couldn't find her, I knew to look there. That apartment was always filled with people and music and smoke and sour-smelling bottles. Visitors came and went at all hours.

Mom started acting funny. She slept a lot. Laughed too much. Zoned out when I was talking to her. Stopped showering as often. Sometimes she scoured our apartment, scrubbing the insides of cabinets and moving out the stove to clean behind it. Other times she let trash pile up in the kitchen and dirty dishes fill the sink and counters.

She cried often, too, stroking my hair and telling me she was sorry, that she'd get it together and we'd have a house again with a yard for Bingo. But it was hard to believe her. She had aged two decades seemingly overnight. My mom had been so pretty, with glossy dark hair and pink cheeks. Now the skin looked tightly stretched over her bones. Her clothes hung on her.

One afternoon, Mom fell asleep on the couch and she looked cold, so I covered her with a blanket.

When she woke up, she looked at me and blinked; then her whole face collapsed. She stared down at rings she wore—my father's gold wedding band, loose on her left fourth finger but held in place by her smaller, matching band. "My dream was so real. I thought he'd come back," she sobbed. "I miss him so much, Stella."

One evening she didn't come home at all. Bingo and I huddled together in bed, flinching at the strange noises a building makes at night.

The next afternoon my mother was back, smelling unclean, wearing only one of her flip-flops. I heard her ranting to the neighbors about being held in a jail cell.

Things get a little blurry for me then.

We often repress periods in our life that are too painful to acknowledge, Chelsea told me. *What can you remember about that time?*

Mom got even skinnier. Our phone was cut off. The landlord came by, and Mom said we had to hide and pretend we weren't home.

Then Mom told me we were leaving that apartment and going to a new place. She'd get her head on straight. We'd have a fresh start.

Shortly after she said this, I came home from school to discover Bingo was gone. Mom told me our new place didn't allow pets, so she'd given him back to the rescue group where my dad had gotten him. I believed her. My mother had a kind heart. She'd never do anything bad to an animal; in that way, she was like my father, who'd lost his life trying to avoid killing a deer. "I thought it would be easier if you weren't here to see Bingo go," Mom told me.

You never got to say goodbye to your dog, Chelsea had said gently. *Just like you never got to say goodbye to your father. Or your mother.*

You're right, I'd snapped, feeling a flash of anger. *What am I supposed to do with that? I can't change it. No one can change the past.*

I'd sobbed for the next fifteen minutes on her couch while Chelsea looked at me steadily and occasionally offered me tissues. *Now you're starting to do the hard work,* she told me.

At those words, I walked out her door and never went back.

My house is small, but I've done everything I can to make it feel pretty and cozy. It's filled with layers of light from lamps and sconces and ceiling fixtures. I invested in well-built, comfortable pieces of furniture, and although the art on my walls isn't expensive, it's colorful and intriguing.

I keep clutter to a minimum. I make my bed as soon as I get up, and I can't stand to have dirty dishes in the sink. I'm a neat freak; I guess it's a by-product of my early upbringing.

Another one of my personal rules: I keep music playing at all times, even when I sleep.

I can't bear to be alone in the quiet.

As I walk into the living room, though, I realize my house is absolutely silent. I check the stereo and press a few buttons, and the familiar acoustic rock from my favorite station fills the room.

An electrical glitch, or perhaps my neighborhood briefly lost power.

I reach for the volume and turn it down a few notches, keeping it lower than usual. Then I sink down onto my big gray couch and unzip my ankle boots.

I need to sit in my unease, and let my troubling thoughts try to untangle themselves.

Every time I close my eyes, I see Rose.

Rose is losing everything, just as I did. Her voice is gone. Her family as she knew it has split into fragments. She left her school. Soon she'll lose her house.

Those are the tangible things.

She has also lost her joy. Her sense of safety has vanished.

I drop my head into my hands, massaging my forehead.

Why doesn't Beth allow glass in the house?

And why is Rose secretly collecting sharp things?

I need to get into Rose's bedroom, alone. I have to see the title of the book she was concealing.

And I need to know if she has the box cutter.

The more time I spend with Rose, the less I understand her.

I'm still on my couch, my feet propped up on my coffee table, when my cell phone dings with a text from an unfamiliar number. Attached is a video.

The message is brief: It's Pete. Tina sent me this a few days before they killed her.

CHAPTER FIFTEEN

Tina leans toward her phone's camera. The video is shaking, as if it were filmed during an earthquake.

Which means Tina's hand is shaking.

The pictures I've seen didn't do Tina's beauty justice. They didn't capture her charisma or husky voice. Her brown eyes have impossibly long lashes, her full lips are glossed in cherry red, and her sleek hair is highlighted with streaks of gold.

The pictures also didn't show what she looked like when she was frightened.

"Babe? I just got another one."

She holds up a flowered envelope. Her name is printed on it in block letters, and I recognize the address as the Barclay home.

It looks like a party invitation.

Tina pulls out the card and holds it up to the camera.

It's a cartoonlike image of a person staring up at a house. The house appears to be completely empty—the front door and windows are thrown open, revealing the lack of furniture.

It's a farewell card, the kind a friend might send to someone who is moving.

But Tina had no plans to leave the Barclay home. She'd only been working there for six months.

Tina opens the card. There's a preprinted stock message: *I'm sorry to see you go.*

And below that, in block letters written in black ink: *GET OUT, TINA.*

"Who's doing this to me?" Her voice quivers as it rides the edge of anger and fear.

Then she whirls around. When she turns to face the screen again, the whites of her eyes are visible.

"Thought I heard something. But they're all out. Even the grandma." She swallows. "I hate the noises this creepy house makes."

The camera reveals a slice of Tina's third-floor quarters: I see a bed with a blue-and-white patchwork quilt, and a knotted rug on the wood floor. The window Tina tumbled through—the tall, wide one that is only a foot or so off the ground and would never pass code today—isn't visible in the shot.

"I think—" Tina's voice abruptly cuts off. Her head whips around again. *"Someone's up here."*

An instant later, I hear a voice call out: "Boo!"

Tina flinches. "Rose! You scared me."

Rose comes into the video frame, peering at the camera. "Sorry. What are you doing?"

I'm transfixed. This is the Rose of before. Her voice is clear, her eyes bright and alive.

"Don't sneak up on me like that, okay?"

Tina's hand reaches out for the camera. The video stops.

I stare down at the final image, frozen on my screen.

Tina, unsmiling. The remnants of fear twisting her features.

Rose, looming over her nanny's shoulder. Smiling.

CHAPTER SIXTEEN

Detective Garcia's eyes manage to appear simultaneously weary and sharp. She leans back in her chair, her jacket slipping open to reveal the badge hooked on the waistband of her navy slacks.

She takes her coffee black, and we've barely sat down across from each other at a deli's corner table when she has drained her mug and signaled the waitress for a refill.

When I reached out to request a conversation, I gave the detective my bona fides and provided two judges as my reference—Charles as well as Judge Cynthia Morton, who is presiding over the Barclay case. The detective took a day and a half before agreeing to talk to me. I'm certain she used that time to check me out.

"I will keep anything you tell me confidential," I promise. "I could get disbarred if I don't. All I want is to do right by Rose. And that means not sending her to live with a murderer."

She nods. "The truth? Any of them could have done it."

"When you say any of them—"

"Either parent. The grandmother. The boyfriend. At first I liked Ian for it, but we can't get anything to stick to him. Trust me, I've tried."

Dark circles rim her big brown eyes. It isn't hard to guess what keeps her up at night. The same thing that keeps me up: ghosts.

"And it could be none of them," she continues. "Maybe Tina just tripped and fell."

"The press seems to think Ian did it," I offer.

Her lip curls. "The only reason the press cares is because Tina was young and beautiful and the Barclays are rich. If they'd all been nobodies, Tina's death would've gotten two lines in the paper's police blotter."

I see my mother's lifeless body on the floor, her eyes vacant.

I wonder if my mom merited even two lines.

No one ever bothered to find out if she died from an overdose or if someone killed her. Not even me, the daughter she cherished until her addiction consumed the loving mother I once knew.

My throat thickens, and I quickly pull my attention back to the detective.

"We looked at grandma for it, but that's a stretch," she is saying. "The elevator only goes between her lower-level suite and the first floor. They installed it for her when she moved in. Grandma would've had to climb two flights of stairs, push Tina, and race back down and get outside before anyone noticed. With that bad knee? Plus, she was watching Rose."

She drains her coffee again, and the waitress swings by to refill it. The detective waits until she is out of earshot before continuing.

"The boyfriend, Pete, has an alibi. Not an ironclad one, but he was with a friend who vouched for him. We traced his phone records from that night. He would've had to leave his phone at his friend's house since it didn't ping off any other cell towers, then get to the Barclays', climb the fence, get into the house, push Tina, and escape without being seen. Again, it's a little hard to fathom. Even though the alarms weren't activated during the day because so many people came and went to work in the house or grounds."

She exhales, looking exhausted despite the caffeine pumping through her system.

"Is there any way you can tell me if you think you'll make an arrest?" I ask. "Because I can delay giving my recommendation to the court."

"If I had enough evidence, I'd charge someone. But I don't. That's why it's a cold case. It will always be open, but we couldn't justify keeping it active."

My body sags. That's it, then. "So what happened to Tina may never be known?"

The detective's cell phone vibrates. She glances at it, then sets it back down on the table. Her voice is a little hoarse. "People think the worst part of my job is seeing dead bodies. But it isn't. The worst is seeing the living. When I tell someone their brother or mother or daughter is gone and we may never know why or who did it?"

She closes her eyes and shakes her head. It's then I see her fingernails are bitten to the quick.

"Do you think Tina was murdered?" I ask.

Detective Garcia opens her eyes. She looks around the nearly empty deli, then leans in closer. "Two things I keep thinking about. One is this, and it goes no farther than our table: Tina was on the phone with a friend just before her death."

I've devoured coverage of this case, and I never heard that detail.

"We held a few things back from the press," she continues. "Tina was talking about Ian, about her fantasy of running off with him once she told him about the baby. The next sound was breaking glass. That's how we can pinpoint the exact time she fell."

My pulse quickens. "So the friend didn't pick up any other voices in the background?"

Detective Garcia shakes her head. "Tina barely even paused in conversation. The only thing she did was suck in a breath. She was talking fast and pretty excited; it could've just been a loud inhale. Or she could've been startled by someone sneaking up on her. Or it could've been a gasp as she tripped. But here's the thing: We never recovered Tina's phone from the scene."

I frown. "Someone took it?"

Her eyes darken. "The phone has been powered off since the accident. We can't trace it. So there's no way to tell who grabbed it. There were a lot of responders on the scene. And all the Barclays, of course."

I reach for my pen. "What's the friend's name?"

The detective frowns. "That I can't say. I need to hold back a few parts."

I nod, as if conceding. Then I move on.

The detective had said there were two things she kept thinking about.

"What's the second thing?"

"Rose loved to pick vegetables, right? Even had a little wicker basket she always used. She was outside with grandma, gathering the last of the season's baby tomatoes when Tina fell. They'd been out back for about ten minutes when Tina hit the patio, according to grandma."

I nod; this computes with what I've read and heard.

"We found the basket. Crime scene photos show it was back by the vegetable beds."

I can't track where she's going. "Rose probably dropped the basket when Harriet screamed."

The waitress comes over with a pot of coffee, but without breaking eye contact with me, the detective covers the mug with her hand and waits until the waitress moves on.

"It was the end of summer, but there were still plenty of tomatoes on the vines. So why was the basket empty? If the girl loved picking vegetables so much, what was she doing during those ten minutes right before Tina died?"

Ice floods my veins.

"Rose isn't— Do you think she's involved?"

The detective shrugs. "I never rule anything out, but again, it seems like a stretch. The kid can't talk, so we can't ask her anything."

Detective Garcia's eyes travel over my face. She opens her mouth to say something; then her phone buzzes insistently.

"I've got to go." She stands up, reaching for her purse. Then she hesitates.

"Did you hear Ian and Beth both walked out when they were asked to take lie detector tests?"

I nod.

"That's what the press thinks. But that isn't exactly how it happened."

I wait, my stomach twisting.

"They both walked out when I asked them about their daughter."

CHAPTER SEVENTEEN

Something evil lurks in the plastic house.

Whenever I'm there, its tendrils creep out and twine around me, making me feel as if I'm moving through quicksand. I don't know the source of it, but a sense of urgency tears through me, compelling me to search Rose's room.

She is at the epicenter of whatever is happening.

I'm driving down River Road toward the Barclay estate, struggling to keep from speeding. I've texted Harriet to let her know I'd like to stop by for a chat. Though I haven't received a response, I'm planning to wait in the area for as long it takes.

I need to see what Rose is hiding behind the *Anne of Green Gables* book jacket.

And I need to see what she did with the shard of glass and the box cutter I'm certain she stole.

A stoplight ahead of me turns red and I slam on my brakes, stopping just before I skid into the intersection.

Harriet spends most of her time at home, since her damaged knee prevents her from driving all but short distances. If she isn't there now, she will be soon.

I've just crossed into the Potomac suburbs when her reply pings on my phone: That's fine. I'm free all afternoon.

My stomach twists.

I can't shake an image of Tina, terror filling her soft brown eyes, smashing through the glass as jagged shards cut into her skin.

And I can't help wondering why, when no detail or expense was overlooked in renovating the Barclay estate, the death trap of the low window was never considered worthy of attention.

I drive another half mile, and the familiar imposing iron gate comes into view on my left. There's no name on it, just the house number. If you were passing by, you'd never know this was the entrance to the Barclays'.

I press the intercom button. It's answered by a woman whose voice I don't recognize.

"This is Stella Hudson. Harriet is expecting me."

"One moment, please."

I presume she's a housekeeper or another employee, and that she's checking with Harriet. I stare at the intercom speaker and notice just to the left of it is the tiny, unblinking eye of a camera.

Is someone watching me right now?

I pull my gaze away to assess the fence. It would be possible to climb it if someone was fairly athletic and determined to do so.

The gate begins to sweep backward. As soon as the opening is wide enough, I drive through.

I pass the grazing horses and notice the deep groove marks Pete's wheels made in the grass have already been repaired, like he was never even here.

I steer around another curve, and the grand stone house comes into view, its front porch with four pillars accenting its proud bones. The Barclay estate reminds me of a beautiful rock that you turn over to reveal wet, rotting leaves teeming with wiggling bugs stuck to the underside.

My heart flutters in my chest. I want to turn around and drive away from this strange place and its deceptive occupants, but I force myself to pull into my usual parking spot.

I check to make sure I have everything I need. After I met with Detective Garcia, I swung by home to change into thick, soft socks and slip-on sneakers. Then I stopped at a CVS kiosk to print out the photograph of Rose tending to the baby squirrels, which I tucked into an envelope.

Just as I lift my hand to knock on the front door, Harriet opens it. She's wearing navy slacks and a cable-knit turtleneck sweater. Her polished wood cane is in her left hand, as always.

"Stella. I'm glad you texted. Come in."

I step into the foyer.

The heavy darkness folds in on me like weighted shadows. I suppress a shudder. I don't want to be here; my instincts are shrieking at me to leave.

"I've been wanting to apologize for the scene you witnessed between my son and Beth," Harriet says. "And we didn't even properly meet. I don't know where my manners were. I just wanted to get Rose away from the argument as quickly as possible."

I take a deep breath, hoping my voice doesn't shake.

"You did the right thing. Divorce is difficult, and it isn't uncommon for me to see parents have disagreements," I tell her truthfully. "But I'm glad you and I have a chance to meet now."

"Would you like to sit down?" she offers. "I can make us some tea."

I've prepared for this. I need to get Harriet as far away from the house as possible for my plan to work.

"I understand the vegetable garden is your pride and joy. I was hoping you could show it to me while we talk."

Harriet's eyes sharpen. I can't read her thoughts.

She's an independent woman, stoic and hardworking. Devoted to her granddaughter. Despite her physical limitations, she exudes a kind of steely strength.

"Of course. It's a beautiful day, and it'll be nice to go outside."

I follow Harriet down the long hallway to the kitchen, glancing in various rooms as we pass them. The house seems empty, other than a housekeeper I see dusting in the living room. Harriet moves more slowly than my natural pace. But even with her jerky gait, her posture is upright and proud.

When we reach the doors to the backyard, I touch my Apple Watch. It starts ticking off the seconds.

Construction is ongoing, but the patio demolition is now done.

Several workers, all in long-sleeved shirts with Ian's company logo, are busy leveling the land. Harriet calls out a friendly hello as we pass by, greeting the workers by name. I wonder if she's always this pleasant to the employees, or if she wants me to think she is.

"Have you always been interested in gardening?" I ask Harriet as we head toward the vegetable beds. The stopwatch on my wrist hits the one-minute mark.

"It's more of a recent hobby. It started when Rose was little, and I bought a pumpkin vine for her so that we could grow her own and turn it into a jack-o'-lantern. It turned out so well that the next year, we planted asparagus, which is her favorite vegetable."

"Asparagus?" I echo. "Don't most kids consider that torture?"

Harriet smiles. "Rose has adult tastes, which Beth encourages. Sometimes I wish Rose would dress more like the other kids her age and run around and get dirty. At least she likes to work in the garden with me. After I moved in, Ian and Beth had these beds created for me as a Mother's Day present."

I realize the reason for the waist-high beds when we reach them. Harriet doesn't have to bend over or get down on her knees to garden. Here, the vegetables rise up to meet her.

"What a thoughtful gift," I comment.

I touch my watch again. Two minutes and fourteen seconds. That's how long it took us to get from inside the house to this spot at Harriet's natural pace.

"I think it was actually Beth's idea," Harriet confides. "She's a very considerate woman. Ian typically just gets me a card for Mother's Day."

It seems like a dig at her son. I recall Ian's comment about his mother blaming him for destroying the family, and wonder how deep her resentment goes.

I shift slightly so I can clearly see Harriet's expressions and body language.

"I know Ian and Beth both want Rose to live with them," I begin. "Do you have any thoughts about what the custody arrangement should be?"

Harriet leans over and plucks a dead leaf off a plant. She rolls it between her thumb and index finger, crushing it.

"I think Beth should be given custody," she tells me. "She's a very good mother."

I mask my surprise. Perhaps Harriet's assertion is the product of her generational viewpoint, which usually defaults to mothers as the caretakers for children.

"Ian seems like a devoted father," I offer up mildly.

"He loves Rose, of course he does. But Ian is selfish. He got my ex-husband's looks and charm. Unfortunately, my ex was a serial cheater. Ian also inherited his father's weak character."

Harriet drops the pieces of leaf onto the soil. "Did you know leaves are meant to crumble into the earth and nourish it? Mother Nature knows what she's doing. I explained this to Ian, but he still has his workers come remove them every few days. Appearances are more important than doing the right thing by his land."

Harriet doesn't just blame Ian. She's furious with him.

"If it were me deciding, I'd give Ian ample visitation time with Rose, but Beth should be the day-to-day caregiver," Harriet continues. "Why should Beth be punished when Ian is the one who destroyed our beautiful family?"

Harriet is being remarkably candid, so I move in from a different angle. Ian claims he and Beth weren't truly a couple. I want to know if Ian lied about this, too.

"Were they happy, Ian and Beth?"

"In the beginning, very. Do you know the story of how they met?"

I've read about it, but I say, "I'd love to hear it."

"Ian was twenty-two and working for a landscaping crew that serviced the grounds of Beth's parents' estate in Upperville, Virginia. Beth was a year older and engaged to the son of a family friend. She'd studied at Yale, you know. Anyway, Beth was home that summer planning the wedding. But secretly, she was having doubts. Then one day Ian heard something while he was working in the gardens. A woman crying. He went to investigate, and there was Beth."

It's like a fairy tale: The beautiful heiress, engaged to the wealthy suitor, is rescued from a loveless life by the handsome, kindhearted laborer.

"Then Ian decided he wasn't happy, even though Beth gave him all this." Harriet stretches out her hand to encompass the grounds, her voice rising with emotion. "This beautiful home. This beautiful family. He just threw everything away!"

"Do you think Beth fell out of love with Ian, too?" I ask. "Or was it one-sided?"

"Beth doesn't confide in me. And I don't pry. I know my place."

I glance back at the house. I think I see a flash of movement in the third-story window, like someone ducked away when they saw me turn. But it could just be a trick of the light, or the housekeeper cleaning the upper level.

I wrap my arms around myself. "Is anyone else home now?"

"Beth is working in her office, and Rose is with her," Harriet tells me.

"Is Tina's old room ever in use?" I ask. "Like, as an extra office or something?"

Harriet frowns. "No, no one goes in there. Even when Tina lived there, Rose understood she wasn't allowed to go up to the third level. It was Tina's private space."

An image slams into my mind: Rose, sneaking up behind Tina in her third-floor bedroom on the video.

I glance up at the window again. No one is there.

It's now or never, I tell myself. I may not get this chance again.

I reach into my purse for my cell phone and frown at the screen. It's blank, but I keep it out of Harriet's line of sight. "I'm sorry, it's Judge Morton—she's overseeing this case—and she's trying to reach me," I lie. "I don't know how long this is going to take, so would you mind if we continued chatting later?"

"Of course," Harriet says.

"I'm coming to take Rose to dinner tomorrow night, so I'll see you then." I take a few steps away as I speak.

Then, as if I've just remembered, I pull out the envelope from my purse. "Oh, I have a photograph I took of Rose the other day. I'll just leave it for her in her room before I go."

I continue moving away, putting space between me and Harriet. "I'll see myself out!"

I have two minutes and fourteen seconds before Harriet will make it back into the house—maybe even less if she hurries.

Not nearly enough time for me to search Rose's room.

CHAPTER EIGHTEEN

I touch my watch again, restarting the count as I stride briskly toward the house.

In a stroke of luck, a yard worker fires up a leaf blower. But I caught the shrill tenor of Harriet shouting "Wait!" just before the noise erupted. She doesn't want me anywhere near Rose's room.

Which makes me even more determined to get there.

As soon as I pass through the sliding doors to the kitchen, I bend down and pull off my sneakers, hooking them on my fingertips as I rush to the staircase.

I slip past the housekeeper who is still dusting the living room, but she barely takes notice of me. Her role is to polish and tidy but never call attention to herself—to move about invisibly in this house.

That's what I need to do, too.

I climb the stairs as lightly as possible, but a few moan beneath my weight.

At one point I pause and hold my breath, but I can't hear anyone. When I reach the second floor, my luck holds: All the doors are closed again.

Notes of classical music come from Beth's office. It's loud enough that she and Rose may never know I'm here.

I reach for the cold metal knob of Rose's door, then hesitate. If Rose is inside, I'll likely startle her. But I need to take that risk.

I rap my knuckles as gently as I can against Rose's door, then push it open, holding my breath.

I see a girl on her bed, and my heart leaps into my throat.

Then I realize it's the doll in Rose's image, down to her red hair and scattering of freckles. I step into the room and close the door behind me, shaking off the creepy sense that the doll's eyes are following me.

Rose's room is spotless again, everything perfectly arranged. No books stick out of the rows on her shelf. Her desktop contains only a holder for pencils, a stack of school notebooks, and a whiteboard with an attached marker. Even the pretty little trash can is empty.

I check the nightstand for the book Rose was reading. It's bare, other than a wicker lamp with a frilly shade.

The timer on my Apple Watch hits the one-minute mark.

I hurry to the bookshelf and scan the titles.

Anne of Green Gables isn't there.

Another thirty seconds have elapsed. I peek out Rose's window, which overlooks the backyard, and see Harriet making steady, jerky progress toward the back of the house.

She's almost to the patio.

I yank open her desk drawers, but all I find are odds and ends: a tiny flashlight, a flowered barrette, a package of Post-it Notes. I lift the pillows off her bed and look beneath them. Nothing.

I drop to my knees on the pink-and-cream rug and lift up Rose's bedspread.

Way up near the headboard is a book, leaning upright against the wall.

I wiggle under the bed and pull it out. The title on the dust jacket is *Anne of Green Gables*. I slip it off, wincing as the sharp edge of the thick, glossy jacket slices the pad of my index finger.

Shock sweeps through me.

I read the book's title twice: *The Stranger Beside Me.*

I'm familiar with the book Rose is reading. I've read it myself. But I was in my twenties when I borrowed it from the library, and even then, the subject matter kept me up at night.

No little girl should be reading a book about the serial killer Ted Bundy.

I don't have time to process what I've seen. I pull out my phone and snap a picture before I replace the book jacket. Just as I slide the book back under the bed, I see a tiny drop of my blood has fallen onto the edge of the pages. I try to rub it away, but only succeed in smearing it.

I don't have time to try to clean it. All I can do is replace the book.

I straighten up and peer out the window again, putting my finger in my mouth to clean it and tasting my own coppery blood. I don't see Harriet. She must be making her way through the kitchen now.

I've only got time to check a few spots. They need to be areas the housekeeper wouldn't find and that Rose's parents wouldn't easily stumble across. She's an intelligent girl; she'd choose a good hiding place.

I peer into the closet, searching for the sweater I saw Rose wearing the first time I watched her go to see Dr. Markman. It's draped on a velvet hanger. I feel the pockets gingerly, but they're empty. Other than a pair of mittens, there's nothing in the pockets of the pink coat she wore to Lucille's, either.

Rose's shoes are lined up on a shelf, so small they almost look like they could fit the doll on her bed. Her clothes are hanging neatly. There aren't any boxes or drawers in the closet.

I can't see any other place in this room where she could conceal something.

Then I notice the big velvet jewelry box on Rose's dresser. It looks like an antique—something her grandmother might have passed down.

I open the lid, and a tiny ballerina starts to spin as thin, delicate notes play.

There are a few items in the box—a gold bangle, a necklace with a cross, a ring with a pretty blue stone.

And there's a drawer at the bottom. I slide it open.

Even though I've been expecting to find them, the sight of the objects makes me gasp.

Rose didn't just collect the sharp piece of glass and Lucille's box cutter. She's hiding a small arsenal.

There's also a pocketknife, a shiny shard from a broken mirror, and an ice pick.

I don't let myself think. I go on autopilot, snapping a picture of the contents. As I close the lid, I hear Harriet's voice from downstairs, yelling my name.

I dig into my purse and grab the envelope for Rose, dropping it onto the foot of her bed. I leave a tiny speck of blood on the envelope from my cut finger, but it's too late for me to open it and just put the photo on her bed.

I take one last look to make sure everything else in the room is as I found it, then exit and close the door silently behind me.

I hurry down the stairs, this time not worrying about making noise.

Harriet is just beginning to try to climb the steps. She's breathing hard and leaning heavily on her cane.

"What were you doing up there?" she demands.

I feign innocence, even though my heart must be pounding as hard as hers.

"I left a photo for Rose, like I told you."

Harriet is staring at me intently. I try to conjure a look of innocence, but I'm so shaken I don't know what she sees in my eyes.

She must know it would never take that long for me to merely leave something for Rose.

"I don't feel well. You need to leave," she says.

I step toward the door. "Of course."

I can tell Harriet knows something has happened that has left me shaken.

The loving, protective grandma who whisked Rose away when her parents argued and who claimed Rose was with her when Tina fell shifts slightly. She puts herself between me and the staircase, like a guard.

I have no doubt that if I tried to rush past her to get to Rose's room again, she'd use her injured body to block me.

Waves of anger and fear roll across her face.

I open the door and step out, then bend down and slip on my shoes.

Harriet's voice calls out to me. She doesn't sound angry any longer. Now she's pleading; it's as if she's seeking mercy.

Her words chill me to my core: "She's just a little girl. She needs her family."

CHAPTER NINETEEN

I drive away as fast as I safely can, fleeing the darkness that still feels like it's trying to cling to me. I'm not quite at the gate when an incoming call lights up my Jeep's console. Caller ID shows it's coming from the private school Rose attends.

I shouldn't answer. I'm too shaken to concentrate.

But I've been trying to reach Rose's teacher all week.

I pull over by the gate and put my Jeep in park, letting it ring again while I try to steady my breathing.

"Stella Hudson."

My voice sounds high and tight. I stare at the gate, wondering if the camera is capturing me now. I reassure myself that even if there is one with audio capabilities, my windows are rolled up. They can watch me, but no one can hear me.

"Ms. Hudson, this is Diane Jackson. I'm the principal of Rolling-wood Primary School."

I'd left messages for Rose's teacher, not the principal. She must have passed them up the chain. Still, I go with it, taking my notepad and pen out of my purse as I start to give the principal details about my involvement in the case.

She cuts me off, her voice crisp.

"Rose Barclay was a student here only for a short time. Less than a year. I'm not sure I can be of any help."

My mind snags on the word she used: *was*.

"My understanding is Rose will return to school," I say. Ian and

Beth both told me the homeschooling was temporary; I'm certain of it.

"That is not correct," she tells me. "Rose is no longer a student at Rollingwood. She won't be returning."

"Her parents withdrew her?" I ask.

Silence fills the line. Behind me, the enormous house looms in my rearview mirror.

"Rose was asked to leave. We take violations of our rules very seriously."

It's another enormous lie Ian and Beth conspired to make me believe.

When I first talked to Ian, he acknowledged colluding with Tina. Now he's colluding with his soon-to-be ex-wife. The one he acts like he hates.

My head is spinning. Rose was expelled? "I don't understand."

"I suggest you contact her former school if you're seeking more information."

Rose is only nine. How many schools has she attended in her short life?

I feel a tingle between my shoulder blades, a sixth sense someone is watching me. My hand jerks out and hits the button to make sure my doors are locked.

I whip around and look back in the direction of the house. No one is behind me.

I clear my throat and regain focus. "My job is to get Rose into the best possible environment. That means I need to ask questions that may seem like a violation of her privacy. But the law requires me to do so. I can get a court order to release her records, but it would be simpler for you to tell me. Why was Rose asked to leave?"

She exhales. "Any student bringing a weapon to school faces immediate expulsion."

"A weapon?" I repeat.

"Rose brought a knife to school. Her teacher discovered it in her backpack."

My heart leaps into my throat.

"That's all I can tell you." The principal ends the call.

I think of the way Beth ushered me out of the plastic house during our first meeting. And the grim expression I caught on Ian's face as I studied the vegetable gardens where Rose was supposedly picking tomatoes at the time of Tina's death. Ian and Beth didn't like the idea of me being alone with Rose; I had to negotiate to take her to Lucille's. And Harriet—so warm and welcoming at first—didn't want me anywhere near Rose's bedroom.

The pieces begin to fit together, as Charles promised they would.

This shattered, battling family is united when it comes to the little girl who is obsessed by weapons and who hides a book about a sadistic serial killer beneath her pink comforter.

They are closing ranks around Rose.

CHAPTER TWENTY

Evil isn't merely a word.

It's a tangible, dimensional thing. It slithers through the air, shifting molecules and displacing energy as it considers various hunting grounds. Once it homes in on a target, its malevolent arc of electricity affixes to its prey.

It's easier to sense evil in the darkness. In the warmth of light, our rational minds try to mute our primal brain's desperate warning cry.

Some people appear to be more attuned to the menace linking itself to them than others. Such as the sorority girl in Florida who stepped out of her bedroom late one night to get a drink of water. She felt it, the thing lurking in the shadows. The bone-chilling certainty made her jump back and lock her door. That same night, Ted Bundy rampaged through the sorority house, stealing the lives of two young women and badly injuring two others.

Like Rose Barclay, Bundy was drawn to sharp objects as a child. Once, when his aunt took a nap, he gathered knives from the kitchen and arranged them around her sleeping form.

Did he also read about murderers? I wonder.

I've felt the presence of evil twice in my life. Possibly three times.

Most recently in the plastic house.

And in my early twenties, when my Honda wouldn't start in a nearly deserted shopping mall parking lot. The sun had dipped past the horizon; most of the stores in the mall were closed. As I popped my hood, a man materialized from behind a thick supporting column. He stepped toward me, so close I could see the dark mole between his eyebrows.

"Need a hand?" His voice was friendly. But the aura surrounding him ripped the breath from my lungs.

Time froze as my mind frantically whirled, instinctively calculating physics and risk. The distance to the mall was a hundred yards. My heels and skirt would make it impossible to outrun him. I was near the car hood, and he was by the trunk; if I tried to get inside and honk my horn, he'd be at the door before I could lock it. My purse was on the passenger's seat. It would take too long to grab my phone, which was tucked into an inner pocket.

He knew I was trapped. I could see it in his unblinking eyes.

I could dash around behind my little four-door car and try to keep it between us. But all he'd have to do was duck beneath the windows to conceal his movements while he approached me.

My last, desperate hope—that he really was a Good Samaritan—evaporated when he twisted his head to quickly glance toward the mall.

A roaring noise erupted in my head when I realized what he was doing.

He was checking to make sure no one else was coming.

He took a step closer. His smile widened.

He was savoring my fear. Feasting on it like a delicacy.

Then I heard the distant sound of laughter. Seconds later, three teenagers on skateboards whizzed into the lot, heading in my general direction.

"Wait!" I screamed.

One of them did something with his feet that caused his board to shoot up into the air. He caught it in one hand as his feet stuttered to a stop.

"What's up?" he asked me as his friends came toward us.

The man reached up and made a gesture like he was tipping an imaginary hat to me. Then he turned and evaporated into the night.

When the police arrived, they discovered my car battery had been deliberately disconnected. Then an officer told me something that seared me to my core. Two women who fit my general description had recently been murdered in the area.

Luck, good timing, divine intervention—whatever it was, it disrupted evil's force field that night.

I can't say for sure if I felt its presence a third time, on the night my mother died.

I was so young then, and terror and evil are inexorably linked. Perhaps my mind muddled the two.

This is what I remember: After she ushered me into the closet, my mother opened the front door willingly. I heard the rumble of a man's deep voice. A little later, I thought I heard her protest over the music: "No . . . please." Her voice was soft. She didn't scream or cry out for help. Was that because she didn't want me to burst out of the closet? Perhaps her last act was a breathtakingly loving one, to save my life and sacrifice hers by perpetuating the charade that she was alone.

But now I wonder: Did I truly hear her protest, or did my mind layer imaginary dialogue into my remembrance as a way of comforting me?

The final words I thought I heard her utter could have been a desperate trick by my psyche to convince me she loved me. That she wouldn't have willingly abandoned me.

Maybe the truth is that she eagerly succumbed to the seductive beckon of heroin again, never giving a second thought to her seven-year-old daughter curled up a few feet away.

You can be furious with your mother, Chelsea once told me. *You can love her, and hate her, and desperately miss her too.*

I do, I answer my old therapist in my mind now.

With my father, it's different. I carry a few faded mental snapshots—of him carrying the wiggling bundle that was Bingo into the living room on Christmas morning, and tucking his tongue into a corner of his mouth as he worked on one of his crossword puzzles. But I know there was nothing I—or anyone—could have done to save him. He swerved off a road at dusk and slammed into a tree. Then his beautiful, kind heart stopped beating before the ambulance arrived.

I hate not knowing how my mother died, and if someone killed her by forcing that flow of heroin into her veins.

Of all the ghosts I carry with me, my mother's haunts me most.

The void she left in my life is so deep that I fear if I peer over the edge, I'll tip in and never stop falling.

CHAPTER TWENTY-ONE

I wake up with a scream swelling in my throat.

Someone is breaking into my house.

I leap out of bed, my fingers scrabbling for my iPhone on the nightstand. Blue and red lights pulse through the slats of my blinds, spinning an urgent pattern across the walls.

The tremendous pounding coming from downstairs shakes my home like an earthquake and voices are yelling, "Open the door!"

I dial 9–1–1 and look around wildly. Where can I hide?

Not in the closet. Not in the closet.

An enormous crash tells me they've breached my front door. They're inside now.

There's no lock on my bedroom door. I won't be able to jump out a window in time. It feels like a dream, but I'm wide awake.

"What's your emergency?" the 9–1–1 operator asks.

My throat tightens. For a moment, I'm a child again, unable to speak.

Then I hear a shout from downstairs: "Police!" The blue and red lights mean a cruiser is outside my home.

My legs give out as a rush of relief weakens my body. The police must have scared away the intruder. I slide down to the floor, the phone falling out of my hands, just before two uniformed officers appear in the doorway, guns drawn.

"Is anyone else in the house?" the male officer shouts while the female officer flicks on the overhead light, searing my eyes.

My voice trembles along with my body. But I can speak now. "No . . . no, it's just me."

"Stay put!"

I pick up my phone and tell the operator I'm safe and that the police are already here, then hang up. My phone screen shows it's 2:38 a.m. The classical music I keep on all night is still playing softly through the mini-speaker on my nightstand.

I hear a shout—"Clear!"—and an echoing call from downstairs— "Clear!"

My brain is foggy. I'm in one of Marco's old Georgetown Law T-shirts with a tiny hole in the shoulder, staring up at an officer who reappears in my doorway and puts his gun back in its holster.

The officer kneels down, his deep-set eyes boring into mine.

"Were you screaming for help?" I can smell the acrid trace of cigarette smoke clinging to him.

I shake my head, bewildered. "No. I was sound asleep."

"Could it have been the TV? Or did you have the music on loudly?"

Again, I shake my head. A crackle erupts from his radio, and he silences it by pushing a button.

"What happened?" I ask. My throat is raw and parched. I desperately want a drink of water, but my legs are so weak I know if I tried to stand up, I'd collapse.

"We received a call that a woman was screaming for help inside your residence. We made multiple attempts to get a response before we broke down the door."

My gaze flits to the bottle of over-the-counter sleeping pills on my nightstand. I took one around midnight.

The officer glances over, and I see him clock the pills, too.

"I must have been having a nightmare," I whisper.

I was looking into my mother's empty eyes and feeling her cold skin as I tried to shake her awake when the thunderous sound of the police breaking down my door tore me away from my dream.

The officer straightens up.

"We can help secure your residence for tonight," he tells me. "But you'll need to get your door replaced as soon as possible."

Two hours later, I'm curled on the couch, warming my hands on a mug of coffee.

There will be no more rest for me tonight.

After I pulled on sweatpants and a fleece top and followed the police downstairs, I saw a few neighbors clustered across the street, staring at my house, their exhales forming tiny clouds in the inky night. I have no idea which of them summoned the cops.

My door is barricaded by a heavy armoire now, but cold gusts muscle in through the splintered wood. I'll need to use my back entrance until I can get someone here to fix it.

I'm wrapped in a blanket, my feet encased in fuzzy socks. I can't seem to get warm.

And I can't stop staring at the cardboard box on the coffee table in front of me. My aunt pushed it into my arms when I left her sterile, harsh home the day I turned eighteen. I've kept it in the back of my closet ever since.

This box is all I have left of my family.

My attempts to keep my past locked away are collapsing if I'm screaming in my sleep loudly enough for my neighbors to hear. It isn't hard to figure out why my old terrors are surfacing: A suspicious death, a silent child—the blueprint of my childhood is being drawn all over again. Everything I've held tightly inside for three decades is jarring loose.

The things we try to bury are often the things that need the most sunlight. Chelsea said this in a message on my voice mail after I stopped therapy. Her words felt pushy and strident then. Now I hear compassion in the echo of her voice.

My childhood has been stalking me my entire adult life. Maybe I need to turn around and finally face it.

I reach for the kitchen knife I placed next to the box.

As I slice through the old packing tape, I flash to Lucille making the same motion in her kitchen. In my mind, I begin to flesh out the scene: Rose on the couch, her head swiveling to watch as she began coveting the sharp-bladed box cutter.

Then I force away the image. I have a lot of thinking to do about Rose and the horrifying possibilities surrounding her in the coming days. But these solemn, dark moments are for a different child.

They're for the little girl I used to be.

I reach for the lid, the same sensation sweeping over me that I experienced when I pulled open the drawer of Rose's jewelry box. I both know and fear what I'm going to see.

The item on top is my baby book.

Something pierces my heart as I open the cover and glimpse my mother's pretty cursive.

She captured everything: My first smile at two weeks—*Dad says it's gas, but you and I both know you smiled at me.* My first taste of solid food—*Four bites of rice cereal . . . you ended up spitting most of it out. Our girl has a discerning palate already.* A lock of my hair from my first trim, the tape holding it in place brittle and yellowed with age.

I turn every page, pausing at times to let my fingertips trace her words, my heart cramping. My skin feels as if it has been peeled away; there's nothing buffering my raw nerves.

I stare at a photograph of me tasting my first birthday cake, a look of sheer delight on my face. The chocolate-frosted cake is homemade and slightly lopsided, with my name written on it in pink icing. My mom and dad are flanking me in the photo, both smiling down at me instead of at the camera.

I fold my arms over my stomach and double over. I'm shaking so hard I feel as if I'm going to shatter like a glass bottle dropped on a cement floor.

My mother loved me deeply; I know this much is true.

The question that comes out of my mouth shocks me. Not just because I speak it aloud, but because my voice is so raw and small. It's the voice of a grieving child.

"Why did you leave me?"

CHAPTER TWENTY-TWO

I desperately need to recalibrate my mindset.

As soon as dawn breaks, I lace up my sneakers and go for a punishing four-mile run along the Capital Crescent Trail. A healthy breakfast of blueberries and walnuts mixed into steel-cut oatmeal further centers me. And while I clean my kitchen and do two loads of laundry, I blast my favorite classic rock playlist. By the time I've finished scheduling a contractor to install my new front door, the traumas of my past have been driven back into their compartments—even though the latch holding them no longer feels as secure.

I'm ready to turn my attention to work. My mission has never wavered: I must help my client.

But the kind of help Rose requires may take a different form than I originally anticipated.

Here's what I know about Rose's parents: They love their daughter. And they both lied to project a certain image onto Rose, as if they were superimposing a pleasing hologram over her. They're casting Rose as a victim who was temporarily taken out of school to aid her healing process.

Here's what I know about Harriet Barclay: She's very protective over her granddaughter. And she either unwittingly or deliberately lied about Rose never going into Tina's third-floor quarters. She also provided an alibi for Rose at the time of Tina's death.

There's one other person who has firsthand knowledge about the moments leading up to Tina's death: the friend who was on the phone

with her. I have the feeling Detective Garcia was so forthcoming because she wants me to keep digging. She dangled that tidbit because
she knows I'm in a unique position to get information from Ian and
Beth that the police can't.

Detective Garcia wouldn't give up the name of Tina's friend. But I
know someone who may.

So I text Pete, the boyfriend: Can we talk?

He replies immediately: Why?

I cast the line I hope will reel him in: If you're doing parkour today,
I can meet you at Gateway.

I imagine him staring down at his screen, surprise swelling in him.

I don't give him a chance to ask how I know about his new hobby.
I quickly type: It's my job to investigate people. I'm good at it. And I
want to find out what really happened to Tina.

The clues were all there in Pete's car: the new-looking shoes
without laces, the thin gloves, the T-shirt logo of a guy jumping over
a park bench, and Pete's fresh scrapes and bruises.

I recognized them because one of my former clients took parkour
classes at a gym in Rockville. Once, I watched as he leapt, flipped,
rolled, and jumped over man-made obstacles. But I figured Pete must
be using natural obstacles like flights of stairs, without thick safety
pads or harnesses, given his injuries. And the most popular place for
outdoor parkour in the area is Gateway Park.

My gamble pays off. I don't even have to leave my house to get the
information I need. Pete offers it up willingly a moment later.

Ashley Brown, a twenty-five-year-old Bethesda resident, is the
friend Tina was talking to just before she died.

She's the secret police witness.

CHAPTER TWENTY-THREE

A dull throbbing forms between my temples the moment I step into the brightly lit, cavernous room. Dozens of kids are screaming and shouting and bouncing on what must be fifty connected trampolines that compose the length of a football field.

"Ms. Hudson?"

I pull my eyes away from a little boy who is standing over a bag of spilled popcorn and wailing while his mother soothes him. Ashley Brown stands in front of me, wearing an aggressively cheerful blue-and-red-striped jumpsuit, a round pin that says *Welcome to JUMP!*, and a weary expression on her pretty face.

"Thanks for meeting me, Ashley." I grimace as the cacophony of sounds swells.

Ashley seems immune to it, but she gestures for me to follow her into a side room with a big sign on the door that reads *Party Room One*. She closes the door behind us, sealing out most of the noise. The room is a disaster: Dirty paper plates rim the long, rectangular table, and crumpled napkins litter the floor. Fruit punch juice boxes lie on their side, their sticky red liquid dripping out onto the paper table-cloth. Streaks of blue frosting coat the back of one chair, and a lifeless pink balloon lies spent on a counter. I don't blame the balloon.

"Someone called in sick, so I don't get a break today. But I can talk while I clean up." Ashley begins tossing used party plates and cups into a big trash bag.

I move to the other side of the table and begin to collect debris, too. Partly it's a technique to put myself on Ashley's level; she'll be more likely to open up if I'm acting like her peer. But it's also because I know what it feels like to be young and working in the food service industry and to have to clean up the colossal messes left by others.

"I'm sorry for the loss of your friend," I begin. "I understand you and Tina were close."

Ashley nods as she slides a plate holding an untouched-looking piece of pizza into the bag. "I'd only known her a year, but yeah, Tina was one of my best friends. It's so messed up that she's gone, you know?"

I wait a respectful beat. "Did she ever talk about her job?"

"Sure. We both nannied for rich families in the area; that's how we met. And we both had weird nights off—Sundays and Mondays, since our bosses wanted to have their weekend nights free. So yeah, we talked a lot."

I frown. Pete didn't mention this detail. "You were a nanny, too?"

"Live-in, so I banked all my checks. One easy boy who was in kindergarten. Then, after Tina died, the news got out she was pregnant with Mr. Barclay's baby, and suddenly the mom I work for tells me I shouldn't wear yoga pants around the house. That she wants me to dress more professionally. She watches like a hawk every time her husband is around, trying to see if he's checking me out. Next thing I know, I get my two weeks' notice."

Ashley rolls her eyes, then moves to a tall stack of Domino's boxes on a side table. "Want some pizza?"

I shake my head. "I just ate, but thanks."

She tips two entire pies into the trash, then tosses the boxes into a recycling bin. "When I interviewed here, they acted like it was a perk: *All the pizza you want!* Now I can't even stand the smell of it."

I finish clearing my side of the table and dampen a sponge at the sink in the corner so I can wipe the frosting off the chair. Normally I'd center my questions on the relationship between Rose and her parents. But the focus on my investigation has broadened.

"How did Tina feel about Rose?"

"At first? Things were great. Tina felt sorry for Rose because she didn't have any friends. She'd been bullied at her previous school, so she'd had to transfer to Rollingwood."

I suck in a breath. Is this another cover story created by the Barclays because Rose was expelled from that school, too?

Ashley gets distracted by a blob of what I hope is dried chocolate ice cream on the floor. I toss her the sponge, and she bends down to scrub it away.

"You said it was great at first," I prompt.

"Yeah, Rose adored Tina and vice versa. Then everything changed overnight."

I grow very still, focusing on catching every word.

"It was like Rose turned into a different kid. She'd yell that Tina wasn't her mother. She told Tina to leave and never come back. It was so awful for Tina."

It's hard to imagine Rose yelling. Then I remember how Beth Barclay morphed from a cultured, soft-spoken woman into a wild-eyed shouter when she saw the chef use a glass measuring cup in her kitchen. Ian changed, too, when I first questioned him in his study, his genial facade sliding away like a mask to reveal a grim expression. Maybe the ability to flip moods as easily as turning over the cards in a playing deck is a shared family trait.

"Why did Rose turn on Tina?" I ask.

Ashley straightens up and reaches for a broom to sweep the floor. "We had no idea. Tina couldn't figure out what was wrong. Sometimes Rose would be sweet and hug her, then she'd get cold again and tell Tina to leave her alone, that she hated her."

"When did Rose change?"

Her broom swishes as she considers my question. "Umm . . . maybe a couple weeks before Tina died."

I run the timeline in my head: A flip switched in Rose at about the same time Tina and Ian slept together for the second time. Ian told me it happened in Tina's bedroom—the one Rose liked to sneak into. Could Rose have witnessed her dad and her nanny having sex?

I grab the dustpan in the corner and bend down to capture the pizza crusts and other debris from Ashley's broom; then I toss the contents into the trash bag.

When she speaks again, her voice is weary, and she sounds older. "They used her—Beth and Ian both did. That's what rich people do to people like me and Tina. They hire us to take care of their kids and houses, and they say we're *part of the family*—that's their favorite expression because it makes them seem down-to-earth—but the minute there's trouble, they cut us loose. Now Tina's gone and I'm here. Working for minimum wage plus tips, except most people don't tip."

Ashley was fired because she is young and pretty. She has every right to be bitter.

"I miss Caleb. He's the little boy I used to take care of. I helped him learn how to read. I had a picture he painted up on my refrigerator. And now I'll never see him again."

Ashley dabs her eyes with a clean napkin.

"I'll never see Tina, either. I bought blue hydrangeas every week at first because they were her favorite flower. She loved to pick them in the garden and put them in her room. Then one day something happened and I went to text her, and as soon as I picked up my phone, I realized I'd forgotten she'd died."

Tears glisten in Ashley's big brown eyes.

"I didn't buy hydrangeas last week. She's fading away in my memory."

I don't repeat any of the empty platitudes I heard when my parents died. Instead, I try to acknowledge Ashley's grief by bearing witness to it.

"Isn't that awful? That I'm forgetting?" Her voice breaks on the final word.

I shake my head. "Grief can consume us, so it's a natural protective mechanism to get distracted by other things. Just because you sometimes feel happy or angry or you don't think about Tina as often doesn't mean you are dishonoring her memory. It means you're trying to survive."

Ashley nods. After a moment she resumes her work, removing the soiled, soggy tablecloth and stuffing it into her garbage bag, then squirting cleaner over the surface of the table. I grab a few paper towels and help her wipe it down.

A loudspeaker overhead crackles; then a slightly manic voice blares: "Attention, Jumpers! Emily's party guests, gather in Party Room One for pizza and cake in ten minutes!"

I don't have much longer to get information. Though I can always talk to Ashley later, she's in a raw, revealing state right now. She might not be as open next time. "Pete told me strange things happened to Tina in the house. Did she ever mention that to you?"

Ashley pulls a fresh paper tablecloth out from a cupboard, and I help her spread it over the table. "Oh, yeah." She shudders. "If Tina hadn't been so into Ian, she would've quit and moved out. That house was like Rose—so perfect at first, then all the bad stuff started happening."

"Can you tell me about any specific incidents?"

Ashley looks up and to the left—which people commonly do when recalling a memory. Some researchers believe people who are lying look up and to the right. Of course, anyone who knows this hypothesis can beat the test.

I have no reason to doubt Ashley, but I can never forget what Charles told me when I began my career: Everyone lies.

"It started with little things. Sometimes Tina's stuff went missing. But like, only one of her favorite hoop earrings. As if someone was messing with her, trying to make her wonder if she'd lost it or if it had been taken. Things were a little off in her room—different from how she'd left them. She was sure someone was going through her stuff. And then it got spooky. She swore sometimes late at night she heard her grandpa's voice saying her name. But he died a couple years ago."

"That would unnerve anyone," I comment.

Ashley grabs a stack of paper plates and napkins from the cupboard and begins circling the table, setting down place settings as she moves.

"And this one time Tina was getting ready to go out. She was trying to look hot so she could walk past Ian and make him want her. She tried on two dresses—one black and one red. She sent me selfies of her in both. I told her I liked the black and that's the one she wore."

Ashley is across the table from me now, putting down a plate and napkin in front of the miniature chair at the head of the table. "When Tina came home a few hours later, there was a note on her bed."

The heavy sense of dread that infused me in the house descends, as if its vapory, clutching fingers have followed me here and are wrapping around me. "What did the note say?"

"*You should have worn the red one.*"

My heart stutters. Someone was watching Tina when she thought she was alone in her bedroom.

"Who wrote the note?" I ask.

"It was printed on computer paper, so it could have been anyone."

Ashley puts down another place setting, circling the table. She's coming closer to me.

"Tina thought it might have been Rose. Because Rose used to like to watch her get ready. Tina would give her a dab of lip gloss and do her hair and they'd take selfies. So Tina figured maybe Rose was just watching her and left the note playfully. But it creeped her out. Why type and print it? It felt . . . sinister."

I think about the sense I had at the house that eyes were on me even when I couldn't see anyone.

"Did Tina ask Rose?"

"She planned to. But Rose was acting so hot and cold. She couldn't find the right time . . . You know, I really think Tina would've moved out if it hadn't been for Ian. She hoped he'd leave Beth for her once he found out she was pregnant."

"When was she going to tell Ian about the baby?" I ask.

Ashley moves a step closer to me and sets down another plate. "The day she died. That's what we were talking about—she was going to tell Ian that night and ask him to get divorced. And then, right after she told me her plan, she tripped or fell or . . . someone snuck up and pushed her."

The party room is sparkling clean. The table is set. Through the clear glass door, I see a guy carrying a stack of Domino's boxes heading our way.

I ask one final question.

"Is there anything else that comes to mind—even if it doesn't seem relevant—that you feel like you want to tell me?"

This is the question that often gives people the freedom to mention the detail or bit of intuition they've dismissed. It's amazing how often people save the most relevant pieces of information for the end of my interviews.

"There is one other crazy thing," Ashley says. She has finished setting the table, and she's standing just inches from me. I can smell the spicy notes of her perfume and see the tiny sparkling chip embedded in the light blue polish of one of her fingertips.

"Tina had a feeling Beth might know about the affair. She got the sense Beth was watching her more closely. And Beth started to get on her. Like she said Tina was messing up, picking up Rose at the wrong time from school one day. But Beth never told her about the time change. Then Beth and Ian and Harriet and Rose suddenly decided to go away for the weekend."

Ashley shudders again. "Can you imagine being in that huge house at night? Tina asked me to spend the weekend with her, but I had to work. She was pulling away from Pete because she had fallen in love with Ian. So in the end, she stayed there alone."

I can imagine what that must have felt like for Tina. The creaky floors and dark shadows nibbling at the corners of every room. The hiding places behind heavy furniture and drapes. The sharp, prickly sense that she might not truly be alone, after all. That someone was watching her.

"In the middle of the night, Tina woke up and thought someone was breaking in. She heard men shouting. She completely freaked out. She was about to call 9–1–1 when she realized it was the police at the door."

All the breath whooshes out of my lungs. I'm stunned to my core.

With Ashley's next words, it gets worse.

"Someone called the cops and said they heard a woman screaming for help in the Barclay house at, like, 3 a.m. But no one else was there. Tina said she thought someone wanted to scare her. To let her know how vulnerable she was."

CHAPTER TWENTY-FOUR

It can't be a coincidence.

Someone tried to frighten Tina. Now they may be switching me in as a replacement character in some macabre sequel.

If it wasn't a neighbor who called 9–1–1 to report a woman screaming for help in my house, then who did it?

I plan to file a request for information about the 9–1–1 call, but it could take as long as thirty days for me to receive the report—and even then, it might not have any helpful information. Whoever placed the calls would likely have covered their tracks.

She's brilliant, Gina Markman had said of Rose. Savvy, despite her innocent affect. Rose was able to obtain weapons despite her parents' Herculean efforts to keep them out of her grasp. She got her hands on a book I know her parents wouldn't allow her to read. I need to determine whether she has access to a phone or iPad—potentially one her parents don't know about, too.

I can't completely dismiss Rose, much as I want to. I can't underestimate her.

A chilling thought strikes me: Tina believed someone was in her space, messing with her things.

The other day when I came home, my stereo was turned off.

Electronics malfunction all the time, I remind myself firmly. It was a glitch.

I'm not a naive twenty-six-year-old who is easily spooked. I don't fear ghostly voices or creaks in the night.

Still, I plan to begin regularly checking the locks on my windows—and on my replacement front door, which won't be installed until tomorrow.

I thank Ashley and step out of the party room, into the chaos of a hundred children tearing through the play space. Excited yells ricochet off the walls; high-pitched voices screech shrilly.

It's a universe away from my experience as a child.

Silence was my pain when I was young. Silence was also my punishment.

My aunt believed my muteness was a choice, and her preferred mode of illustrating her dissatisfaction with me was giving me a taste of what she believed was my own medicine.

One afternoon I came home from school on a rainy day and tracked two muddy footsteps onto her freshly mopped kitchen floor before I took off my shoes.

I hurried to the sink to get paper towels to clean them up, but my aunt saw. Two footprints meant she didn't look at me or talk to me for two days.

I was eight years old.

It wasn't the punishment that shook me. It was the satisfied gleam in my aunt's eye when she saw my misdeed. Now she had an excuse to shun me. To show a bit of her hatred for me.

My aunt had no children, but she was married to a quiet, docile man. He wasn't a bad guy. He never touched me in the night or raised a hand to me, but he was cowed by my aunt. Perhaps that was why he took a job as a salesman that required him to travel every week.

To him, I probably seemed like a stray cat she'd brought home. I kept to myself. I flew under the radar. If I cried at first, it was into my pillow. After a while, I stopped crying at all.

I adapted. Learned how to survive in that barren environment.

A few months after my mother's death, my voice came back to me, as swiftly and fluidly as if it had never disappeared at all. I was in a park near my aunt's house, sitting on a curved plastic swing, my hands gripping the chain-links that tethered it to the pole above, when a chocolate Lab dragging his leash ran into the park and stopped directly in front of me, his bubblegum-pink tongue lolling out.

"Hey there," I said instinctively.

It was like a spell had been broken, as if the dog were a magician in disguise. I'd tried to speak so many times before, and I couldn't. Now, with no effort at all, my voice was back. It didn't even sound rusty.

"Huck! Huck, you rascal!" A young woman in jean shorts and a polka-dot shirt ran toward us, sounding out of breath.

I stepped on Huck's leash so he couldn't escape again.

"Thank you so much!" She reached down and scooped up the loop handle.

I opened my mouth, wondering if the spell would hold. It did. The words emerged: "You're welcome."

The woman and Huck left, never knowing how profound our brief interaction was to me.

Even when I could speak again, school didn't get easier.

Kids sense differences and weed out those of us who are different or vulnerable with the calculating cruelty of predators culling the weakest animals from the herd.

I endured that, too. Muscled through with gritted teeth. They never saw me cry.

My tormenters were my training ground.

At some of the bleakest times, I felt as if a guardian angel was watching over me, sending me bright bits of hope. Shortly after my mother's death, I was nominated by one of my old neighbors for a scholarship to attend a two-week-long camp for grieving children, and I was selected to go. The kindness of the counselors didn't fix my pain, especially because I couldn't speak to any of them, but it was a balm to my jagged wounds. And for the rest of elementary school, the school counselor asked me to stay after school on my birthdays. She always had a little cake for me along with a gift—a generous gift certificate to a bookstore, a pretty bracelet, a CD player and a stack of CDs. I kept the CD player hidden in my room and snuck on the headphones at night when I couldn't sleep, finding comfort in music. Those moments felt like buoys, tangible things I could cling to for rest before I pushed off and kept swimming through the dark, turbulent ocean of my young life.

I was let down again and again as a child. But I won't let down Rose—no matter if her family lies and battles me every step of the way.

If Rose is in danger, I will protect her.

If Rose is confused and acting out, I will help steady her.

And if Rose is deeply disturbed—dangerous, even—I will get her help.

My plan for the rest of the day is to go to the grocery store, then take a catnap before I pick up Rose for our waffle dinner so I can begin to see her for who she truly is.

But none of that happens.

The call comes in as I'm driving home from seeing Ashley at the party venue.

"Rose is missing!" Beth's voice is pure panic.

"What happened?" I pull into the far left-hand lane, preparing to make a turn to head toward the Barclay estate.

"Did you pick her up early?" Beth blurts.

"No, I'd never do that without telling you. When did you last see her?"

"She finished her piano lesson with Phillip an hour ago, then went to read in her room. She knows not to run off—"

The Thin Man was at the house before Rose disappeared. Did he say or do something to make her run away?

There's a break in the oncoming traffic. I yank my wheel to the left and speed across the empty lanes.

"Could she be with Harriet? Have you checked to see if she's with the horses?" I ask.

"No, Harriet's here with us. And Rose isn't with the horses; that's the first place we looked."

A mute child has disappeared on the premises where a possible murder occurred.

"Call the police." The words shoot out of me, direct and instinctual.

For the first time, Beth hesitates. Her voice evens out. The modulated Beth is back in control now.

"You see, the police have been here so much recently. If Rose just curled up somewhere and fell asleep . . ."

She's prioritizing appearances over her child's safety. I feel my face burning as I hang up and press harder on the gas pedal.

If I don't hit traffic, I'll be there in less than ten minutes.

I make it in eight and a half.

I don't bother parking in my usual spot by the garage; I pull as close to the house as possible and leap out. I'm in old jeans and a hoodie, and my hair is a little wild from air-drying after my morning run.

But unlike Beth, I'm not at all concerned with appearances right now.

I run toward the house and bang on the front door. Ian yanks it open a moment later, his face anxious.

"I'm here to help look." I don't give him a chance to object. I push past him into the house.

"Did you check Tina's room?"

Ian nods. "She isn't there. I yelled her name loudly just in case she'd fallen asleep. I told her to bang on anything she could see if she was stuck somewhere. I don't know—"

I interrupt him.

"Does Rose have a cell phone?"

"No." He pats his pants pocket. "She borrows mine to play games, but I've got it here."

"Do you have bales of hay in the barn? Places she could tuck into and hide? Any trees she could climb?"

Ian's body slumps. "All of her coats are here. We figured she had to be indoors."

It's about forty-five degrees out, but if Rose has on a few layers and found a cozy spot out of the wind, she'd be comfortable enough.

Ian is already reaching into the closet for a jacket. The sound of Harriet's cane tapping on the floorboards alerts me to her arrival. Harriet glances at me, but her only greeting is a crisp nod.

"She isn't downstairs," Harriet reports. "I looked everywhere again, even behind my shower curtain."

"Stella thinks she may be outside after all." Ian is already walking toward the arched kitchen doorway. "Under a bush, or in a tree. Maybe she made a little spot in the stables."

By now Beth has joined us.

"Stella—thank you for coming."

I don't know how to respond to that, so I don't. We hurry out the back, Harriet bringing up the rear of our group.

The new patio hasn't been laid yet, but the footers have been poured and the earth is level and smooth. There aren't any workers around right now, and I didn't see the housekeeper when I came in. Perhaps she has the day off.

Just as when Tina fell to her death, the house is mostly empty save for the Barclay family.

The sun is sinking lower in the sky. It'll be dusk soon. There are dozens of places for a little girl to hide on the grounds. Every bush and shrub and tree and dark corner offers a possibility.

Ian breaks into a jog, heading toward the stables.

Beth calls out Rose's name again and again, her thin, high voice carrying on the air. She veers off toward the side yard.

I'm trying to catch up with Ian when I feel it again. The skin-prickling sense I'm being watched.

I spin around, expecting to catch Harriet's gaze. But she is following Beth. She isn't looking in my direction.

Then something compels me to glance up, my eyes traveling past the kitchen doors and second-floor hall window.

On the third floor, there's a small figure in the window Tina crashed through. Even though I can't make out her features, I know exactly who it is.

The light is gleaming on her curly red hair.

CHAPTER TWENTY-FIVE

I don't call out for the others or beckon Rose to come to us.

Instinct guides me. It leads me back to the house. I keep my pace even and my movements small, but no one notices I've reversed direction. They're too focused on searching.

I enter the kitchen and make my way to the staircase. I feel as if Rose is summoning me. As if her appearance is a signal that she wants to see me alone.

I hurry up the first flight and turn into the hallway. I don't know which door leads to the attic, so I open two—one for a guest bedroom and the other a bathroom—before I find the correct one.

The attic stairs are cramped and narrow, and the ceiling is so low I have to duck my head. But once I clear the top step, the space opens up.

Beneath the slanted, dark-paneled walls is the queen bed with the blue-and-white quilt I glimpsed in the video Pete sent. There's a tall dresser on the opposite wall, and a reading chair and matching ottoman, nightstand, and knotted rug.

The space is as impersonal as a hotel room. There's no sign a vivacious young woman once lived here.

And no sign of Rose.

For a second, I imagine this space as it must have been: The counter topped with colorful jars of makeup, the closet filled with pretty clothes. A cluster of photos on the bureau. A book splayed open on the nightstand. Perfume scenting the air.

I step into the attached bathroom. The claw-footed bathtub is empty. I call Rose's name softly, then check the big cupboard beneath the sink. I step back into the bedroom and look in the closet, then duck down to peer under the bed.

Everything is scrupulously clean, as if all evidence of Tina has been scrubbed away.

I look around the room again and notice two small doors that blend almost seamlessly into the walls. Only their dark knobs and hinges give away their existence.

I bend down and pull open the first one. It reveals a storage space containing a half dozen suitcases. I lean in to make sure Rose isn't curled up behind one of the bags; then I check behind the second door. It holds a big plastic bin, the kind people use to store holiday decorations or old clothes.

It's big enough to seal a child inside. An involuntary tremor sweeps through me as I reach for the lid.

It's difficult to pry open, but once I do, I see it contains folded towels, floral sheets, a blanket, and a bath mat.

The Barclays must have provided these things for Tina when she moved in. After the police finished their investigation of this room, someone must have packed everything away.

I reach into the bin, feeling around in case there's something else at the bottom. My index finger touches a sharpness, and I yank my hand away. I lift out the pillow and towels to see what jabbed my skin.

It's a single gold hoop earring. Just like the one Ashley mentioned.

I reach down and pick it up. The metal feels warm, as if it has recently been touching someone's skin.

Something about this old, creaky house conjures creepy sensations and thoughts in me. My rational mind battles back; I tell myself my hand is cold, and that's why the metal feels warm.

If Tina simply lost the earring and it was discovered during the cleaning out of her room, why not return it to her mother along with the rest of her things, or simply throw it away? The gold is fake, and so are the little diamond-like crystals scattered on it, so it's not like it was kept because it was valuable. Beth or Harriet would never own something like this, and Rose's ears aren't pierced.

I'm certain it was Tina's.

There's not a single reason I can come up with for why this earring is hidden away in the bottom of a bin.

Unless it was kept as a kind of trophy.

I slide the hoop into my pocket, then replace the contents of the bin and close the door.

I need to go find Rose. But first I hurry to the window overlooking the backyard. I may never get the chance to examine this space again.

The window is about five feet high and perhaps two and a half feet wide. It's set very low—only a foot or so above the floor. Even though sturdy plexiglass now fills the frame and a safety bar has been installed across its center, being near it fills me with deep unease.

I look out the window, then abruptly spin around, trying to mimic what I imagine were Tina's final movements.

What made her violently crash through it?

I pull out my phone and take a video of the area; then I film Tina's bedroom. Only when I've captured the entire space do I make my way downstairs to the second-floor hallway.

Rose's bedroom door is cracked open.

I can't remember if it was like that when I came through the hallway a few minutes ago. I tap on it twice, wait a beat, then push it open.

Déjà vu sweeps over me.

Rose is holding *Anne of Green Gables*. She's in the exact position as when I first met her, down to the way she's resting her wrists on her white wooden desk.

She doesn't acknowledge me—another echo of our initial encounter.

I walk over and crouch down so I'm at her eye level.

"Rose, I'm so glad to see you," I say gently. "I want to help you. Is there anything you can share with me?"

The pencils and school notebooks are still on a corner of her desk along with a small whiteboard and attached marker. Perhaps Rose will write down a message. Or maybe I can ask questions and she can nod or shake her head to provide answers. I'll do anything to foster our communication.

But Rose doesn't lift her eyes from her book.

I quickly glance at it, because now I'm close enough to read the title and author on the page headings.

The Stranger Beside Me has disappeared. The correct novel is back in its dust jacket.

My stomach twists. Does Rose know I came into her room and rifled through her things? I left a spot of blood on her true-crime book as well as the envelope containing the photograph—clear evidence I'd been investigating her private space.

As if she can read my thoughts, Rose closes her book.

She slowly shifts in her chair and meets my eyes.

I can't help it; I instinctively shrink back.

Everything about her appearance and room are like an eerie replica of our first meeting. But there's one staggering difference.

Before, Rose's eyes looked blank.

Now they're burning with anger.

CHAPTER TWENTY-SIX

A moment later, I hear Beth's frantic voice calling from downstairs.

As desperate as I am to communicate with Rose, I can't ignore her mother. I walk into the hallway and call back, "Rose is in her room. I just found her."

Beth must fly up the stairs because she arrives within seconds.

"Rose! We were so worried!" She throws her arms around her daughter. Rose doesn't melt into the embrace, but she appears to accept it.

"Were you up here the whole time?" Beth asks.

Rose nods. It's a version of the truth—Rose was technically upstairs—but she and I both know she wasn't solely in her room.

"I don't know how we missed you!" Beth's relief is visible as she reaches into her pocket for her phone. Her conversation is brief: "She's in her room . . . I have no idea . . . Okay."

Beth hangs up and turns to me.

"How did you find her?" Her tone sharpens midway through her question, turning accusatory. "You were the one who thought she was outside."

I tell a version of the truth, too. "I thought I saw movement in a window, so I came back to check."

Out of the corner of my eye, I catch Rose looking at me. When I meet her gaze, she studies my face. I do the same in return. Her expression is stiff. It's as if the angry girl I glimpsed has drawn down an impenetrable shield, like a storefront owner yanking down a metal security grate.

I hear footsteps downstairs, then Harriet's voice. "Rose?"

Beth reaches out her hand to her daughter. "Come. I'm sure your dad and grandma want to lay eyes on you to make sure you're okay."

Rose shakes her head and gestures to her book.

"You can read in a little bit. It's hard for Grandma to walk up the stairs. Just come down for a minute."

Rose obediently stands up and takes her mother's hand.

Then Beth sends me a clear message. She walks into the hallway and waits for me to exit the bedroom. When I do, she closes the door behind us in a gesture that feels exaggerated.

"We value privacy in our home," Beth says, smiling tightly.

Beth obviously knows I went into Rose's room alone. Harriet must have told her.

I follow Beth and Rose downstairs, as aware of the delicate hoop of metal in my jeans pocket as I would be a sharp pebble in my shoe.

An hour later, I'm sitting across from Rose in a booth at a Waffle House, watching my young client pick up a dark purple crayon and begin the word-search puzzle on her paper place mat.

Getting her here was a near impossibility.

Beth told me Rose needed a quiet evening at home after the stress of the afternoon. When I pointed out that the adults were the only ones who had been stressed, Ian jumped in to protest that things were moving quickly for Rose, and she needed more time to get to know me. I replied that was precisely the point of our dinner.

Finally, after a fair amount of negotiation, I agreed to bring Rose home within ninety minutes. Even then, Harriet again stood by the front door like a sentry, telling Rose in a voice that sounded gruffer than usual that she was looking forward to working with Rose on her Chinese characters as soon as she returned. When we reached my car and I went to help Rose into the backseat, I noticed Harriet was still watching us.

Now I'm finally alone with my client.

It's time to start taking her measure.

"Rose, this menu is huge." I lift up the double-sided, laminated sheet. "Should we get one of everything?"

Rose doesn't lift her head. I study her face, noticing her eyelashes are the same fiery shade of red as her hair.

"I think I'll go for the Nutella waffles. If you've never had it, it's a delicious chocolate hazelnut spread."

Rose's crayon makes several heavy lines on the paper menu, crossing out letters in her puzzle.

The waitress swings by. "Have you ladies decided?"

"I'd love an iced tea." I think about what Ian told me about slipping Rose treats now and then. "How about a root beer, Rose?"

No reaction.

The waiter looks at Rose, then at me, the smile edging away from her face.

"We'll take a root beer," I say. "And could we have one Nutella waffle and one with fresh strawberries?"

"Would you like whipped cream with your waffles?" the waitress asks.

I shrug. "Why not?"

I spend the next few minutes employing different tactics to get Rose's attention. Her affect feels different from when I first met her. Before, she was remote. Now I can feel hostility emanating off her.

No matter what I do or say, I can't get her to look at me. She's bent over her place mat, thickening lines with her crayon until the letters are completely obliterated.

When our drinks and meals are delivered, Rose jerks her place mat out from beneath her waffle so she can continue working on the word search.

I cut a piece of my waffle and offer it to her. It's golden brown and crispy-looking, with melted Nutella dripping off it. "Want some?"

Rose looks up at me for the first time.

She seems to consider my offer, then reaches out her hand. But instead of accepting the piece I've cut for her, she sweeps her arm into her glass of root beer, sending its contents splashing onto the table and into my lap. The glass rolls off the table and crashes to the floor, shattering into a dozen pieces.

The shock of icy liquid makes me gasp and leap up.

A few nearby diners turn to look as the waitress runs over with a handful of napkins.

I mop myself off while the waitress bends down to soak up the puddle of soda on the floor. A busboy arrives a moment later with a broom and dustpan.

"Sorry for the mess," I tell them.

Rose is watching. I can't believe it when I glimpse her expression. A small smile flits across her face.

A beat later my body coils as I realize Rose is surrounded by potential weapons—the shards of glass that hit the floor and the knife at her place setting.

Then I realize there's no way Rose could have gotten another glass dagger. She didn't move from her seat. And her dull silver knife with a slightly serrated blade is still resting on the table.

Of course, she has much sharper implements in her jewelry box. And Rose's coat has pockets. She could have brought something.

She's only a little girl. Harriet's words echo in my mind.

Rose is clearly troubled, but it's my own past and unresolved trauma that makes me feel so unsettled, I tell myself. My jeans are clinging to me, sticky and cold, and I'm glad that the hoop earring is in an inner pocket of my bag now.

I sit down across from Rose again and decide to address the issue head on. Rose may be young, but her intellect is sophisticated. And the truth is, I'm out of other options. "It's obvious you're angry with me, Rose. And maybe you don't completely trust me. But I hope you understand I'm trying to do what's best for you."

Rose puts down her crayon and lifts her head. She stares me directly in the eye.

Ashley's words spring into my mind: *It's like she turned into a different kid*.

Now it's happening again. The polite, shy girl I met only a few days ago has vanished.

Rose looks like she hates me. It's as if a switch has been flipped in her.

She shoves her paper placement toward me. Nearly all of the letters in the puzzle have been covered.

Only a few remain. They're scattered through the puzzle so it takes me a moment to make sense of them.

When I do, a vise squeezes my chest.

Rose has created her own message to me. It's similar to one Tina received a few days before she died.

The letters spell out *GO AWAY*.

CHAPTER TWENTY-SEVEN

I didn't expect to end up at Charles's house tonight.

I intended to stay at home—with my splintered front door and echoes of police footsteps pounding up my staircase—and reinforce my stance, even if only to myself: I won't be scared off this case.

But Charles called a few minutes after I dropped off Rose. As soon as he heard my voice, he knew something was wrong.

When I told him my front door was ruined, he invited me to stay in his guest room.

I hate that it feels like a relief to not be alone tonight. That a nine-year-old girl—one I'm duty-bound to serve—has left me so shaken.

Rose's message feels like an ugly code embedded in two simple words.

I keep seeing her expression in the Waffle House. But not the anger and resentment churning in her eyes. It was the way she smiled at my shock and discomfort when she sent her soda splashing into my lap.

As if she were winning a game I wasn't aware we were playing.

She's like a completely different child from the one I first met.

When I arrive at Charles's stately Tudor in Chevy Chase, Maryland, Charles has a plate of cheese and crackers and two glasses of his best single-malt scotch waiting in the living room.

I sink into the deep sofa opposite the wingback chair Charles favors, tucking my feet under me. The evening has grown chilly, and blue-gold flames dance in the gas fireplace. I sip the scotch, feeling the welcome burn in the back of my throat.

I've been to Charles's home a dozen times before, and even had dinner with him and his wife here, which was a bit uncomfortable due to the obvious emotional distance between them. Their casually elegant home is unchanged: The furniture and drapes and rugs are all done in warm hues and rich textures, and the bookshelves are filled with heavy volumes of law and literature.

Charles's eyes are steady on me, a furrow deepening between his salt-and-pepper brows.

I've talked to Charles about my cases through the years, but never before has he been so invested in one.

I know why. It's because he sees me in Rose.

I thought I did, too.

But I was different as a child. I was terrified, hiding in the shell of my own body. I would have been desperately grateful for someone to help me.

When I open my mouth, the question I've been silently turning over emerges: "Do you think children can be born evil?"

Charles reaches for a cracker and sets a rectangle of cheese atop it. He takes a bite and chews, then dabs his mouth with a napkin.

I know him well enough to understand he isn't delaying or ignoring me. He's thinking deeply. As a judge, he's accustomed to making carefully considered pronouncements. He understands the power of words to shape perceptions.

"In very rare cases, yes," Charles finally says.

"It's like she's two different girls." I wrap my arms around myself, despite the warmth of the fire. "Meek and traumatized, then angry and vindictive. Three girls if you count the Rose I saw on an old video—then she seemed mischievous."

Charles finishes his cracker and takes another sip of scotch. His calm, steady nature soothes my ragged emotions.

"It sounds like you may be considering her a suspect. Am I correct?"

I nod, feeling a sense of shame. As if I've failed Rose.

Kids do kill. It happens. Sometimes accidentally, sometimes deliberately. Years ago in Britain, a ten-year-old girl strangled a small child. And a nine-year-old boy in Illinois was convicted of deliberately setting a fire that killed several family members while they slept in their mobile home.

All along, I've been terrified that I might send Rose to live with a murderer.

Never did I consider that in choosing which parent is awarded primary custody of Rose, I might instead be consigning *them* to that fate.

My mind recoils from the track it's heading down. I don't know Rose well enough yet to make any assumptions.

I fill Charles in on the real reason for Rose's departure from school, and the way she hid the Bundy book. He asks a few questions, and agrees it's too soon to come to any conclusions about whether any of the Barclays are likely to have killed Tina.

Then he seems to sense my need for a conversational shift.

"How closely have you looked at the money in the case?" he asks.

"Only superficially. I confirmed Ian isn't challenging the prenup. Beth gets everything she brought into the marriage, Ian has his company, and they split the proceeds from the sale of the house. Although they may end up taking a loss on the house, I understand."

Charles nods. "And yet, if Ian were awarded full custody of Rose, there would be child support."

He's right. It could be a substantial amount, if Rose maintained her current level of private tutors and activities and vacations. In one case I worked on involving a supremely wealthy DC couple, the wife got no alimony but walked away with $80,000 a month in child support.

I have copies of all the court documents on my laptop, which is in my shoulder bag. I reviewed them at the beginning of this case. But sometimes we need to look at information anew. Given fresh context, situations are like the optical illusion tilt-card books that reveal different images depending on the angle of the page.

"I'm going to look into it more deeply," I tell Charles.

"You're welcome to stay in the guest room until your door is fixed. I'd enjoy the company. And we can continue talking about the case."

An off-note in his voice causes me to pause.

I find myself checking his ring finger. His gold wedding band is still there.

Charles didn't mention how long his wife would be away. And I recall that last month when we had dinner, his wife was visiting one of their sons.

Now I wonder how much time she spends at home. Perhaps with their children gone, there's nothing left to bind them together.

My gaze drifts to the framed family photograph on the glossy wood mantel. I've seen it before, noticing Charles's sons are tall and handsome, like him, and his wife is smiling and elegant. Now I look at it anew, tilting the image in my mind for a fresh perspective. Charles's wife has her arms around their two sons, who look to be in their late teens in the photograph. The three of them are linked together. No one is touching Charles.

I don't know the cause of the rupture in their family. Charles only told me he was a different sort of man when his children were young and he made big mistakes. Big enough that his family never fully forgave him.

Now I wonder: If my mother had lived, would I forgive her for all the trauma she caused me after my father's death?

It's impossible to say, but I suspect that even if she got clean and we forged a new relationship, a permanent scar would remain, forever visible to us both.

I've never before let my mind wander into the possibility of what ruptured Charles's relationship with his family. Somehow it felt disloyal to Charles.

Now I can't help but wonder. Perhaps infidelity was the betrayal.

I catch Charles studying me, and I flush, as if he might have somehow read my mind.

"There's something else I want to look into," I blurt out. And when I say it, it feels both surprising and inevitable. It's the decision I've been moving toward ever since my meeting with Detective Garcia. Maybe

I've been tiptoeing toward it ever since I was a little girl, desperately reaching out to try to shake my mother awake in the grainy dawn light.

"I want to find out more about my mother, and how she died."

Charles's reaction surprises me. He smiles.

I've been on the receiving end of many kinds of Charles's smiles. Pride, when I graduated from college and law school. Joy, when he walked me down the aisle at my wedding.

This one is composed of infinite tenderness.

"You deserve to know," he says softly. "I understand you haven't felt ready for the information before now. But carrying this around your whole life has weighed on you in ways you can't even imagine. Knowing the truth might not make it easier. But it may free you."

It feels as if Charles is giving me his blessing. As if he has been patiently waiting for me to be ready to learn about my past, knowing it will help me move forward.

When Charles wishes me good night, he bends down and kisses me lightly on the forehead.

And I can't help but think that for all of the losses life has dealt us both, it balanced the scales a bit when it gave us each other.

CHAPTER TWENTY-EIGHT

I stay up late into the night, switching my scotch for chamomile tea and moving to the dining room table with my laptop and legal pad as I dig into hundreds of pages of sealed divorce documents.

I know Beth Barclay has money. But I've never looked at how much, since finances aren't an issue of contention in the divorce. I was far more focused on the relationships in play.

Now I pour over Beth's stock reports and bank statements, tallying figures and parsing financial terms. It takes quite a while to decipher the sums. But when I finally come up with the total figure, I lean back in my chair and rub my eyes in disbelief.

Beth isn't merely rich. She's spectacularly wealthy.

Her personal stock portfolio is worth nearly $150 million. As an only child, she's sole heir to her parents' fortune, which would triple her net worth.

Nearly half a billion dollars. That kind of money is incomprehensible to me. It's the sort of sum that sends crowds into frenzied buying of lottery tickets. People have lied, stolen, and killed for far less.

Ian's company made a profit of less than $200,000 last year—a paltry sum by comparison.

I flash to what Ian said the first time I met him: *Business is down.*

Ian's name is tainted. He may be ruined financially, especially if the house sells at a loss. His elite clientele will drop him, just like Ashley was cut loose by her boss.

Ian could end up where he began when he met Beth, as a

paycheck-to-paycheck kind of guy. The private chef and housekeeper and awe-inspiring property will become a distant memory for him.

He seems fine with that. But is he, truly?

The grandfather clock in Charles's living room chimes softly once. It's 11:30. My eyes have grown gritty and my body is heavy. But I can't stop.

Now that I've met Beth and Ian, the terse legal words on my laptop screen leap up and become three-dimensional, as if the two of them are sitting around the dining room table with me, hissing accusations at each other. *Immorality . . . Emotional abandonment . . . Infidelity.*

Neither Beth nor Ian ever accused the other of any form of abuse, or even of having a temper.

Yet both immediately pointed the finger at each other as murder suspects after Tina died. And both walked out of the police station once they were asked about Rose.

Their movements seemed almost . . . choreographed.

By the time the clock strikes a dozen chimes to mark midnight, I've created a diagram of Rose's current schedule.

It feels both busy and empty.

Piano lessons with the Thin Man once a week. Therapy with Dr. Markman for fifty minutes on Tuesday afternoons. Riding lessons once a week. Tutoring with Harriet in core subjects—math, history, science, and English—for fifteen hours per week. Language sessions with a Chinese tutor twice weekly.

But no regular playdates or sleepovers. No group karate classes or soccer teams. No interaction with other children at all.

I review the schedule, my weary eyes snagging on one small detail. I call up the calendar in my laptop, cross-referencing two dates.

My body clenches up when I see the dates overlap.

The Thin Man was at the Barclay home on the day Tina died.

Even though I don't suspect the piano teacher, I want to know his impression of Tina.

She feels elusive to me, like a vapory shape-shifter who was different things to different people.

Pete described her as a victim; Ian, a seductress. Ashley viewed her as a wonderful friend who was deeply in love. Rose apparently saw her alternatingly as an ally and an opponent. In the video I saw, Tina seemed vulnerable and scared.

I wonder what the piano teacher saw.

I circle his name—Phillip—on my legal pad.

A sense of urgency grips me as the grandfather clock softly ticks, reminding me time is passing. That eventually it will run out.

There's one other person I intend to interview soon. Today, even. The Chinese language tutor. According to the schedule, Harriet brings Rose to that session twice a week.

I want to know what the tutor notices about Harriet's relationship with Rose.

She's just a little girl, Harriet told me, a pleading note in her voice, after I discovered the disturbing secrets Rose conceals in her room. *She needs her family.*

Harriet provided Rose with an alibi at the time of Tina's death. She said they were together in the vegetable garden. But Harriet also said Rose never went into the third-floor space.

So Harriet lies to protect Rose, too.

CHAPTER TWENTY-NINE

Fear takes many forms.

It's a great motivator. A powerful deterrent. If a person lives within it for a long time, it can change the contours of their world.

The Thin Man lives in fear.

I see it when I visit him. After he lets me into his ground-floor apartment, he locks the door and tests the knob to make sure it's engaged. He offers me tea, then sets the teapot precisely in the center of the rings on his hot plate, adjusting it by millimeters until he is satisfied. He stirs a spoonful of honey into each mug, swirling it eight precise times. When a car horn sounds on the street outside his building, he flinches.

Music is beauty contained within a rigid structure. Seven letters in the piano's alphabet. Twelve notes. Eighty-eight black and white keys.

It's no wonder he is drawn to it.

Evidence of his passion is everywhere in his small apartment: In the clef-sign sculptures that serve as bookends, the sheet music neatly stacked on his little dining table, and the framed poster of Beethoven hanging on his wall.

A wooden upright piano with a matching bench takes up most of the living area. The remaining space is filled with a reading chair and ottoman and the small round dining table. His kitchen consists of a microwave, hot plate, sink, and hotel-room-sized fridge.

I notice the flower in a bud vase on the windowsill the moment I sit down.

It's a single blue hydrangea. Tina's favorite flower. An informal shrine or a coincidence?

"The tea smells delicious," I tell Phillip as he serves me a mug.

It's hot and good, the honey sweetening the notes of cinnamon and clove. The mug is covered with dancing music notes. It's the sort of thing a student like Rose might give to her piano teacher for the holidays, perhaps with a Starbucks gift card tucked inside.

I wonder what it is like for Phillip to run his long, bony fingers over the glossy keys on the Barclays' Steinway, knowing an instrument of that caliber will always be beyond his reach.

Does he covet it?

Did he also covet Tina, knowing she was beyond his reach?

Phillip sits down across from me at the little table. He's wearing black slacks and a black button-down shirt just as he did the first time I saw him, the clothing hanging on his skeletal frame. Perhaps it's his informal uniform, or perhaps another manifestation of how his fear rules his life, demanding repetition and order.

"Does it taste okay?" he asks in his deep, rich voice. "I blend my own flavors."

I take another sip. It's delicious.

When I tell him so, his face transforms, his eyes lighting up and a shy, appealing smile stretching his skin.

I ask him for the ingredients, and he reels off a dozen types of spices and tea leaves, describing his blending process.

I wonder how often Phillip's clients take an interest in him. Parents like the Barclays would only want to hear about their child's progress and talent. To them, Phillip is probably a type of instrument himself, one designed to make their children even more shiny and accomplished.

"I'm trying to help Rose, and that means I need to understand what the relationships are like in the Barclay house," I begin. "I'd like to know more about Tina, too. And I want to find out if it's possible someone might have wished Tina harm."

Phillip nods and leans forward slightly. His wrists are thin and knobby, and his Adam's apple is prominent.

"A police detective already talked to me. I can tell you what I told her."

I'm surprised at how easy it is. Then it hits me: Phillip is lonely. This contact—my appreciation for his tea, my visit to his home—must be unusual for him. He likely travels to all of his students' homes. I doubt he entertains many guests.

"I've been working with Rose for almost a year, and I've never had a student with so much natural talent. Never. She is extraordinary."

I nod for him to continue.

"Ian and Beth weren't around much at all until recently. I never really saw them interact, just the two of them. Nowadays one or the other will watch a lesson, but we don't chat much before or after."

"And Tina?" I prompt.

"Tina was wonderful," he says, an ache in his voice.

That ache answers my unspoken question.

"She was much friendlier than the Barclays. She'd offer me water or iced tea when I showed up, and she used to stay in the living room and listen while Rose played. I told Tina once that if she ever wanted to try to learn piano, I'd teach her for free. She just laughed and said she was pretty sure she had ten thumbs. Tina had the best laugh. Sometimes I think I can still hear her laughing when I go to the house."

Even though he doesn't seem to mean it in a literal way, my stomach tightens as I recall Ashley telling me Tina sometimes thought she heard her grandfather's voice in the night.

"How did Rose feel about Tina?"

Phillip takes a sip of tea, then wraps his hands around his mug.

"At first they seemed to enjoy each other very much. Then Tina stopped watching our lessons a couple of weeks before she died. I was worried it was something I'd done or said."

He begins swirling his spoon in his mug, the circles even and smooth, never once clinking against the side of the china.

"Then I realized it was because of what happened on the last day Tina watched."

"What happened?" I prompt gently.

"Ian showed up and said he was trying to figure out how to print a document off his phone and needed help." Hurt twists Phillip's face. "And Tina dropped everything and ran to help Ian."

Something doesn't track. "You said Tina never came back to watch a lesson after that?"

Phillip's voice rises slightly, booming through the room, seeming to echo off the walls. "Rose was about to play a Chopin piece for Tina. She'd just finished learning it. And Tina acted like she really wanted to hear it. And then just like that"—Phillip snaps his fingers—"Ian shows up and Tina runs off. She forgot all about Rose."

And she forgot about you, I think. Ian, with his charm and rugged good looks, must be the present-day manifestation of every boy who ever picked on Phillip while he was growing up. No matter what Phillip could offer Tina—free lessons, adoration—he evaporated in her mind as soon as Ian appeared.

I feel a twist of empathy. I identify more with the Phillips of this world than with the Ians.

But I need to get more information about Rose's state of mind, not his.

"How did Rose react when Tina left?"

"She didn't like it at all. I suggested we wait for Tina to come back so she could play for her, but Rose just stood up and slammed down the piano lid."

He winces, as if feeling the pain of the mistreated instrument.

"Rose was that angry?" It would've been hard for me to picture a week ago. But after she swept my drink into my lap, I can see it.

Phillip nods. "She said, from now on, she wouldn't play if Tina was at her lesson. It was like Rose was the adult, the one in charge of making decisions. She banned Tina and that was it. The last time I ever saw Tina."

We talk for a few more minutes, but Phillip doesn't have any other insight. He tells me he left the Barclay home to go to his next lesson around 5 p.m. on the day Tina died—more than an hour before she called Ashley to say she was going to tell Ian about the baby.

Once or twice, I see Phillip's eyes flit to the hydrangea blooming on his windowsill. It's a fresh, pretty note in his plain apartment. Like Tina must have been in his life.

Before I get up to leave, I ask Phillip if he'd mind writing down his tea recipe for me. I feel gratified when he smiles again; then he hurries to get a pen and scrap of paper.

He sees me to his door and I begin to walk toward my Jeep, parked a block down from his building. Then I stop short.

There's a girl coming toward me on the sidewalk.

I rear back. For a split second, I think it's Rose.

Then I realize it's another child. She's a year or two older than Rose and doesn't even look very much like her.

Lack of sleep and stress caused the illusion, I tell myself. Still, I can't help thinking about the message Rose sent me in the restaurant.

I'm not going anywhere, I mentally reply.

CHAPTER THIRTY

I always take the stairs, but that's not the only reason I'm climbing the three flights to the Chinese tutor's apartment. There's no other option.

This low-slung redbrick building in a humble neighborhood in Rockville lacks an elevator. My mind didn't register that detail as significant at first.

I knock on the door of apartment 406, inhaling the scent of spicy curry coming from down the hall, and hear soft footsteps approach. There's a pause I suspect means Mrs. Li is looking out the peephole, then the sound of a safety chain rattling as it disengages from the sliding lock.

The second clue hits me the moment I step over the threshold.

This shabby apartment is studded with shiny pieces of glamour, like a weathered rock flecked with bits of mica that glitter in the sun.

The worn couch faces a big-screen plasma television. On the chipped laminate kitchen counter sits a gleaming Vitamix—the Cadillac of blenders. I inhale and smell eucalyptus, then find the source. A three-wick Nest candle is burning on the coffee table. I know those candles retail for around eighty dollars because I've seen them in stores.

Mrs. Li's place is a puzzle with a missing piece.

She ushers me into the living room and offers me lemonade. When I see she already made a pitcher, I accept.

"It's fresh," she assures me as she clinks ice into a glass. She's maybe five feet if she stands on her tiptoes, with smooth skin and salt-and-pepper hair. I pull my gaze away and scan the living room, taking in the gorgeous glass vase, delicate-looking as a butterfly's wing, on a table next to a photograph in a cheap metal frame.

An antique-looking curio cabinet in the corner has clear panes that reveal treasures inside: a set of wineglasses with goblets for red and more slender bowls for white, a trio of sculptures of horses in glass, a large crystal bowl. The juxtaposition is bewildering.

I'm used to asking probing questions, but I can't think of a graceful way to word the one at the forefront of my mind: How in the world do you afford all these little luxuries?

Mrs. Li hurries over, her movements quick and graceful, and gives me the glass.

It feels heavy and almost regal in my hand.

A sense of déjà vu sweeps over me. This moment is exactly like one I experienced in the Barclays' kitchen, when Beth handed me a glass that was the opposite of what I expected.

It's almost as if the two households switched drinking glasses.

My head swims as I realize it's more than that: This apartment is like a photo-negative of the plastic house.

It's filled with glass objects.

The clues tally in my mind into a realization. It fuels my first question.

"You've been friends with Harriet for a while, right?"

"Yes, for several years. We met shortly after I moved in."

I figure they were friendly enough that when Beth ordered the removal of all glass items from the estate, Harriet sent a few pieces here.

"How did you meet?'

"Harriet lived just down the hall." Mrs. Li points to her left, and I mask my surprise. This is the building without an elevator—my first clue—which meant Harriet struggled to climb the three flights after her knee surgery. It's why Ian and Beth invited her to stay in their lower level.

I start to lower myself onto the sofa.

"No, no, take this chair please. It's more comfortable." She gestures to the recliner.

I move to it and sit down. I need to tread carefully; Mrs. Li is going to be loyal to Harriet.

"It's obvious Harriet adores Rose," I start. "She's a wonderful grandmother."

Mrs. Li nods. "Yes. She loves Rose so much."

I know I'm not going to get anything but praise for Harriet, so I pivot.

"How do you teach Rose Chinese when she can't speak?"

"Right now we focus on written language. Rose is learning characters. She's very smart. She understands so quickly."

"Does Rose ever communicate any information about either of her parents?"

Mrs. Li shakes her head even before I finish. "Never. She's a good girl and she works very hard."

We go around and around for a while longer. I write only a handful of words down on my yellow legal pad: *lesson payments, gifts, loyalty.*

I've seen a lot of hostile witnesses on the stand in court, and Mrs. Li reminds me of the best, the ones who have been well coached by lawyers to avoid giving away anything while appearing cooperative.

Finally I thank Mrs. Li for her time. I don't miss the look of relief that flashes across her face. She can't seem to get me out of there fast enough: Before I've even stood up, she has collected my lemonade glass and is walking toward the kitchen. When I stand to follow, my pen rolls off my legal pad and lands on the wall-to-wall carpet.

I bend down to get it, and as I straighten up, I catch sight of a slim, rectangular object on the floor, directly beneath the chair I was sitting in.

I think I know what it is. But I have to be sure.

I glance at Mrs. Li. She's putting the dishes in the sink. She'll turn around in a few seconds, wondering why I haven't followed her into the kitchen.

I decide to risk it.

I duck down again, fast, and confirm the object is what I thought
I saw: an iPhone.

A white circle for the speaker function on the screen is lit up.
Someone is listening.

It isn't hard to guess who; Harriet has essentially been in the room
with us the entire time.

I straighten up fast, keeping my face neutral. Mrs. Li is still rinsing
our glasses in the sink. She didn't seem to notice me bend down.

Harriet clearly put Mrs. Li up to this so she could gauge the tenor
of my questions. Perhaps she thought she'd get a hint about which
parent I seem to be favoring for custody.

I can use my discovery to my benefit. I can misdirect, lie, and plant
false doubt in Harriet's mind. I can do all of the things the Barclays
have been doing to me.

"Actually, there is one other thing I'd like to talk about. I was de-
bating whether or not to say this, but I think it's important."

Mrs. Li's head whips around. She hurries over to me, as I knew she
would. She doesn't want me far away from the open phone line.

"Beth is a good mother. And Ian seems like such a devoted and
caring father, even though he did hurt his whole family by sleeping
with the nanny."

Mrs. Li looks frozen, as if our conversation has veered wildly off
course—which it has.

But I'm not talking to Mrs. Li now. I'm talking to Harriet, trying
to convince her I'm an ally.

"Rose needs compassion and consistency after Tina's terrible accident," I continue. "That big old attic window—in retrospect, it seems
surprising no one tripped and fell through it before Tina."

My choice of words is precise. Harriet needs to believe I'm convinced
it was an accident. With any luck, she'll convey that information to
Beth and Ian.

But I need to go even further. I'm convinced Harriet alone
knows what happened during those ten or so minutes when Rose

was supposedly picking tomatoes. If she lets down her guard, I may be able to get her to slip and reveal something.

"I need to spend more time with the Barclays before I submit my decision. But I know that Harriet is a wonderful influence. She clearly cares very much for Rose. I hope she stays involved in Rose's life no matter who gets primary custody."

"Harriet would do anything for Rose," Mrs. Li tells me.

That's what I'm worried about, I answer silently.

CHAPTER THIRTY-ONE

I want to give Harriet time to roll my words around in her mind. So even though I'm eager to arrange another visit with the Barclays, I force myself to wait and see if the bait I've dangled catches her.

It would be better if Harriet reaches out to me, deepening the illusion that she is in control.

The company coming to fix my front door isn't due until late afternoon, so I have a pocket of free time. I should go home and try to relax after my late night of work and back-to-back interviews. Lie on the couch, watch TV, order groceries online.

The sorts of things regular people do during their downtime.

The thought makes me feel penned in. Claustrophobic.

Uneasy energy rages through my body. I know from experience mental distraction and physical movement are the only tonic for it.

It's hard for you to sit still, Chelsea observed once. *Have you ever tried meditation?*

Once, I replied honestly. *It was the worst ninety seconds of my life.*

The hard truth is, it wasn't just the issue of whether or not to have children that split apart me and Marco. That was the biggest, most jagged fissure, but we straddled others during the course of our marriage.

On our honeymoon to Thailand, I wanted to tour temples and explore cities, while Marco craved beach time. We compromised and did both, but I was always in the water or going for a jog down the sand or chatting up locals. I knew he wanted me by his side watching the waves, sharing the sense of peace they provided him.

But our atmospheres were so different we couldn't enter each other's orbits.

It was the same way at home. Our workweeks were packed, but Marco liked to have relaxed Sundays: the *New York Times* spread open on the kitchen island, a homemade soup simmering on the stove, a lazy nap. I signed up to run a marathon and spent Sundays as my long training day, running for hours.

Opposites attract. That's what I told myself—and Marco.

He stopped trying to pretend to believe it first.

I miss Marco so much. Since I don't feel comfortable reaching out to him, I do the next best thing. I phone his mother, Angela.

When Angela picks up after the second ring and tells me she's free, a weight is lifted off my shoulders.

I have a reason to keep moving.

Within forty-five minutes, I've swung by home, picked up her seventieth birthday gift and a light jacket since the October chill is setting in, and am standing on the doorstep of her ranch-style house in Silver Spring.

Her front porch is filled with pots of geraniums and fragrant herbs—basil and oregano, thyme and mint—that she moves indoors before the first frost. The furniture is well-worn wicker with flowered cushions, and a little calico with a bell on its collar is curled up on one of the seats. I bend down to pet Cannoli the cat, and when I straighten, Angela is opening the door.

"Stella!" She envelopes me in a hug. I squeeze back, feeling her slender, strong frame. It defies all rules of fairness and logic that despite living on pasta and bread and sweets, Angela maintains the figure of a yogi. With her highlighted blond hair and regular Botox appointments, she could easily pass for a decade younger than her actual age.

She ushers me inside, taking my coat and hanging it over the banister knob before leading me into the kitchen.

"You look wonderful," I tell her. I don't end my sentence with *Mom,* like I normally would.

"And you look thin," Angela replies. She presses her index finger into the space between my eyebrows. It makes me realize how much tension I've been carrying in my face; her touch forces my muscles to relax. "Is it work, or is something else stressing you? Are you dating anyone?"

Her questions are as rapid-fire as bullets. As mothers-in-law go, Angela could be a mixed bag. She melded warm and welcoming with blunt and nosy. It took me a while to forgive her for grilling me on why I didn't want to have children in front of the entire family one Thanksgiving while Marco was out of earshot in the kitchen dishing out pie. When I did—when I accepted her with all her flaws and grew to love her—I knew we'd truly become family.

"I'm not dating anyone special," I tell her honestly. I've learned the best way to get Angela to back off is to deflect her with humor. "How about you? Are you on Tinder yet, cougar?"

She barks out a laugh and reaches into a tin for a handful of cookies. She tucks them into a ziplock bag and shoves them into my hand. It's impossible to visit Angela's house without coming away with food.

"I've got something for you, too." I reach into my big shoulder bag and pull out her wrapped gift. It's a delicate gold necklace with individual round charms engraved with the initials of each of her children.

Angela claps her hands like a delighted kid. "Should I open it now?"

A wave of self-consciousness sweeps over me. "No peeking until your birthday. I hope your dinner is wonderful."

Angela considers me for a moment, and I feel the weight of all that is unsaid between us. For once, she doesn't blurt out her unfiltered thoughts.

"I'm going to pack you up some ziti. No arguments."

"As if." She makes it with homemade noodles and fresh basil.

She opens the refrigerator door, swinging it in my direction. Dozens of photos are tacked up on it with magnets, overlapping like a collage. I've been present at many of the occasions captured in the snapshots— weddings and birthday celebrations, graduations and holidays. I scan the faces of Marco's family, feeling my heart twist.

Then I see it.

A photo of Marco and his new love. She's blond and athletic-looking, with a red bandana tying back her hair and a big smile. She looks perfect for Marco.

All the wind rushes out of me.

Marco looks utterly, completely joyful. His arms are wrapped around his girlfriend, holding her close.

Angela pulls out a big glass pan and closes the refrigerator door, erasing the picture from my view. I'm given a moment of what feels like grace while she busies herself scooping out a big portion and putting it in a container.

By the time she turns to me, I can breathe again.

Still, it's difficult to meet her eyes.

"This looks amazing." I stare down at the baked ziti. "I can't wait to dig into it for dinner."

A second bit of grace is bestowed on me when my cell phone buzzes with an incoming text.

"Shoot, I've got to run. I have a work call in a minute," I lie. "But let's get together for lunch soon."

"I'll cook."

"Obviously. That's why I suggested it."

I kiss her cheek and grab my jacket and hurry out the door. When I reach my Jeep, I slide into the driver's seat and inhale a few shaky breaths.

I read once that we humans are wired to create patterns, even unhealthy ones. The dynamics we learn at a young age, when our brains are the most malleable, are the same ones we seek out as adults. Predictability feels more necessary to us than positive change.

When I was a child, I had a family and lost it.

Now I'm an adult, and I've lost another family.

I take out my phone and scroll to Angela's contact card. I back-space over *Mom* and type in *Angela*.

I do it quickly, like yanking off a Band-Aid.

Then I pull up the text that came in moments ago. Relief pours through me like a drug; a distraction has offered itself.

The text isn't from Harriet, as I'd hoped.

It's from Ian Barclay: Is there any chance we can meet tonight to talk? I'm worried about something.

CHAPTER THIRTY-TWO

If someone peeked into the back of my car, they'd assume I was going on a trip. A carry-on suitcase is wedged into the space, containing everything I need for the different scenarios my job requires.

Sneakers, socks, yoga pants, and a T-shirt in case a client wants to do something athletic. A baseball cap and pack of hair ties for the same reason. A hoodie, light raincoat, and umbrella, because sometimes people open up more easily when we're walking and they don't have to make eye contact. Extra legal pads, pens, and a backup charger for my laptop. A bag of granola bars and Snickers, because my teenage clients are always hungry, and a box of tissues in case they empty the one I keep in my console.

There's one other item in a hard plastic case, in an inner mesh pocket of my suitcase. A sophisticated recording device. It comes with a wireless microphone I can tuck inside my bra, where it'll feed the sound into the device tucked into my purse.

I've never had reason to use it before.

But something tells me I'm going to want to document every word Ian utters tonight, listening to them over and over for clues and telling inflections.

Ian doesn't want to meet at the family estate, which is curious. It seems he doesn't want anyone to hear our conversation—or even know we're having one.

He suggests a wine bar not far from his home.

I counter, saying I'd prefer to meet at a brewery just over the DC line.

It's a huge win for me when he agrees. Our location is critical.

In Maryland, it's illegal for one party in a conversation to record it without the other party's consent. The law is looser in DC. I can secretly document everything Ian says, and it will likely be admissible in court.

I'm a few minutes late because I had to go home to deal with the contractor and get the keys to my new door. I also tucked Angela's ziti into my fridge, squeezed in a quick shower, and changed clothes.

Now I stand in the doorway, shielded by a couple waiting for a table, and watch Ian. He hasn't noticed me yet. He's wearing jeans and a flannel shirt and his work boots, like he's come straight from a job. He's staring at a football game on a silent TV, his body slumped and his face drawn. Two beers are in front of him, their foamy heads grazing the rims of the pint glasses.

Ian may present a different image when he sees me, but this is a glimpse of how he feels: Stressed. Exhausted. His brain and body fried.

The couple moves aside and I step forward, my movement catching Ian's attention. He half-stands, and I join him at the two-top.

He slides one of the beers over to me. "I got you the house special—a Lumpy Dog—but you can order anything you want. The bar was crowded, so I figured . . ."

He lets his sentence trail off. For a moment, I'm wary of accepting the beer. Ian could have done something to it.

But it's true—the bar is busy.

Stress and lack of sleep are making me paranoid.

Ian wouldn't try to harm me here. Not in a public place, with witnesses and a barback who looks like he could be a professional wrestler.

"Thanks." I take a sip and lick the foam off my upper lip. "It's good."

This beer, along with Angela's cookies I gobbled on the drive here, constitute my dinner tonight. I've had worse. But I'm not going to drink more than half. I need to stay sharp. I'm waiting for an opportunity to test Ian.

"Yeah. This is my second. I got here a little early."

"So what's going on?" I ask.

Ian looks down at his hands, seeming to stall, and a flash of anger overtakes me. I'm tired of being lied to and feeling on edge. I hate not knowing if he called me here to perpetuate another smoke screen created by him, Beth, and Harriet.

"I guess it's Hail Mary time." Ian swallows hard. It's a football term, but he is no longer looking at the screen.

"My daughter is changing. It isn't just her being mute, though obviously that's huge. But the doctors say she'll talk again." Ian clears his throat and lifts his eyes to meet mine. "I know Beth and my mom would kill me for saying this, but it's true: Sometimes I feel like I don't know who Rose is anymore."

My gut tightens. Everything around me—the conversations and clank of beer glasses and bursts of laughter—fade away. Ian holds my absolute focus.

"Everyone says Rose is going through a lot, with Tina's death and the divorce," he continues. "And I get it. But the changes in her started a little while before that. I can't put my finger on exactly when."

Ian massages the bridge of his nose, like he's fighting a headache. "You've worked with a lot of kids. Is this normal?"

I give him a nonanswer. "It's hard to say."

Ian reaches into his pocket and pulls out his phone. I have the sense he's about to show me something on it; then he seems to waver. He lays the phone facedown on the table between us, as if his decision is still in limbo.

"Look, I acknowledge I wasn't a great husband. Tina wasn't my first affair. But I'm a good father. No matter what else they say about me, no one can take that away from me."

I'm struck by Ian's need for validation—and his apparent forthrightness. I can't see any universe in which he'd shape the narrative to include affairs that didn't exist.

"Tell me more about what's going on with Rose," I redirect.

He exhales. "I keep finding her up in Tina's room, standing there and staring out that window. When I ask her why, she tunes out. She loves making origami cranes, and it makes me think of them, the way she can fold up into herself."

Ian reaches for his beer and downs a third of it, his Adam's apple sliding down with each gulp.

"I swear I can feel her turmoil. It's palpable. She's scared at times, angry at other times, then she's just . . . blank."

I've witnessed all of those Roses, too.

"What do you think she's scared of?" I ask.

There's no other way to describe it: Ian collapses. His forearms hit the table, and his head curls down as his eyes squeeze shut.

When he finally speaks again, his words carry the hushed weight of a sacred confession.

"What worries me is that maybe she's scared of herself."

The hairs on the back of my neck rise. Ian isn't spinning me or trying to curry favor. He's desperately trying to get help for his daughter.

Ian glances at his phone again, but doesn't touch it. I need to see what's on it.

"I know Rose sees Dr. Markman once a week," I tell him. "I think she needs more help than that. Have you considered intensive therapy for her to try to get to the root of what's really going on?"

Ian nods. "I've suggested it until I'm blue in the face. Dr. Markman tried, too—she thought Rose could benefit from a deeper course of treatment. That's what she called it. But Beth won't do it. She says Rose is messed up because of what *I* did. And that if she gets full custody, the problem will be erased because Rose won't have to see me all that often."

"What about Harriet?" My voice is low and urgent. I'm acutely aware of the hard metal microphone against the soft skin of my chest. "Would your mother be an ally if you told her you needed her help?"

"An ally for *me*?" Ian releases a short, sharp sound that isn't quite a laugh. "No one tells my mother what to do, least of all me. She's adamant that Rose simply needs time and the love of her family. She thinks intensive therapy is a load of crap. My mom has always been that way. If I did something wrong when I was growing up, she'd whack me with a wooden spoon rather than have a conversation about right versus wrong."

Ian glances down at his phone. I follow his gaze.

Turn it over, I silently compel him. But all he does is drink deeply from his glass again, his face drawn and tight.

It hits me: Ian isn't only worried that Rose may be scaring herself. I suspect she's scaring him, too.

So I throw a Hail Mary of my own.

"There's something you're not telling me, Ian."

My words hit their mark; I can see it in the way he flinches.

"Rose is my priority, and I'm duty-bound to serve her. I swear to you, Ian, I will do whatever it takes to help your daughter."

Something that looks like relief floods Ian's eyes. He flips over his phone and enters the pass code.

When he holds it up so we can view the screen together, I recoil.

It's a photo of a redheaded girl—Rose—splayed on the ground, near the spot where Tina landed.

A split second later my mind registers the details and recasts the scene. It isn't Rose. It's the doll from her room, the one that looks like her.

"I caught Rose pushing the doll out of the window Tina fell through," Ian whispers. "She opened the window and wedged her doll under the safety bar and shoved so it fell three stories. Why in the world would a little girl do something like that?"

CHAPTER THIRTY-THREE

There are two wildly divergent possibilities I can think of in answer to Ian's question.

Rose could be trying to process her trauma.

Or she could be reliving the thrill of the experience.

"I don't know why she did it," I tell Ian. "But if Beth and Harriet keep running the show, we may never find out."

Ian swallows the last of his beer. I take another small sip of mine. I'm glad he's had a couple. Alcohol may strip away his ability to mask his natural reactions.

"I need to spend a big chunk of time with Rose," I continue. "I can bring in a fresh perspective. But you'll have to arrange it because I doubt Beth and Harriet will like it."

"I was going to take Rose to the Baltimore aquarium tomorrow."

Ian and I settle on a plan: He won't tell Rose until they're in the car that morning that I'll be meeting them at the aquarium. After a while, Ian will conjure an excuse and peel away, and Rose and I will be alone for much of the day.

It strikes me anew how comfortable Ian is with colluding with different people to throw up blinders about his true actions and intentions. He did it with Tina, Beth, and now me.

Ian's phone buzzes, and he scoops it up and frowns at the screen. His chair makes a scraping sound against the floor as he pushes it back. He stands and nods toward the restrooms. "Excuse me."

His absence gives me the opportunity I've been seeking.

It takes me only a few seconds to set things up. When he returns to the table, my eyes stay riveted on his face.

He doesn't see it for a minute or two. Then he points. "Did you drop an earring?"

The gold hoop I took from Tina's room is next to my glass.

Ian's expression is guileless, his eyes clear and questioning. His tone is casual. Either he's an astonishingly accomplished liar, or he isn't the one who took the earring.

"Must have." I scoop it up and tuck it back into the inner pocket of my shoulder bag.

Ian's phone buzzes again. This time he doesn't look it at. "Sorry, I have to run. Need to get home."

"Everything okay?"

He holds my gaze and nods. "It's nearly Rose's bedtime, and lately that's been hard for her . . ."

"I need to head out, too." I pretend to quickly tap something into my phone, then slide the strap of my bag onto my shoulder.

When we reach the exit to the parking lot, I pause in the doorway and pretend to check my phone. "My Uber is seven minutes away. I'll wait here."

"Mind if I don't wait with you?" Ian runs a hand through his hair. I don't need that signal to tell me he's agitated; it's written all over him.

"Of course. I'll see you soon."

Ian takes off, and I watch through the big glass pane in the door as he climbs into a red pickup truck. As soon as he pulls out of the lot, I race out and jump in my Jeep.

Ian is a master at deception; there's no other way he could have hidden his affair with Tina from the other adults in the house.

I want to see how honest he's being with me right now.

I turn right out of the lot, just as Ian did. At this time of night, the streets aren't busy, and Ian's vehicle has distinctive taillights. It's easy to keep him in my line of sight without getting too close.

I follow as he crosses from DC into Maryland and heads north on

River Road. It's the route that leads to the Barclay estate. Perhaps my intuition is off, and the thread I really should be chasing is what happens with Rose at bedtime.

Then Ian picks up speed. Instead of taking River Road all the way to Potomac, he veers right, onto the Beltway.

I hit the gas and follow, edging closer as we merge onto the four-lane highway. Even at this time of night, there's light traffic on the Inner Loop.

Ian weaves in and out of lanes without signaling, going ten miles above the speed limit. He veers onto I-270 before taking an exit that leads to Gaithersburg.

His route is eerily familiar. I followed this precise path only days ago.

I know Ian's destination even before he makes a right at the next stoplight. But I still can't quite believe it.

This is one of the last places I'd ever expect him to show up.

Luckily there's a grocery store and a drugstore in the strip mall, so the lot isn't completely empty. I park behind a big SUV and kill my headlights.

Ashley exits JUMP! in her blue-and-red uniform. She locks the door behind her. The party place is dark inside now. She must have been cleaning up.

I watch as Ashley climbs into the front seat of Ian's vehicle, as naturally and confidently as if she has done it many times before.

CHAPTER THIRTY-FOUR

Wherever they go, I'm following.

But Ian's car doesn't move. I can't see what's happening inside it, but after less than two minutes, Ashley jumps out. Ian pulls away, his tires squealing.

I've got a few seconds to make a decision: Follow him or stay with her?

I pick Ashley; she seems more likely to give me answers. I step out of my Jeep as she makes her way through the lot, her sneakers soundless against the asphalt. She reaches a blue Nissan with a dented back fender and is unlocking the door when I call her name.

She spins around, her eyes widening.

"Hey." I walk to her side. "I was hoping to catch you."

I can sense her mind churning. She has no idea what I've seen, so she settles on acting innocent.

"I just got off work. Is everything okay?"

I shake my head. "Ashley, come on. I know you texted Ian Barclay and told him to meet you here."

I'm gambling, but it's a calculated one. Ian was flustered by the texts; he cut our drinks short to race over here. It wasn't a scheduled encounter, at least not on Ian's end.

Ashley rears back. "What did he tell you?" Her head whips around as she scans the lot. "Did you call the police?"

I try to mask the fact that her last question throws me. If Ashley and Ian began having an affair after Tina's death—my initial suspicion—I doubt she'd bring up the police. Something else is brewing between the two of them.

"Not yet. I'm giving you a chance to explain first."

Ashley wraps her arms around herself. "Okay, okay. Can we talk in my car, though?"

As I take a step closer to her Nissan, a shiver runs through me. It isn't because I'm chilly.

I don't trust Ashley. I don't trust anyone right now.

And I don't like it that I've begun to doubt some of my instincts. I sipped the beer Ian offered, and now I'm about to get into the car of a near stranger who has pepper spray on the key chain in her hand.

When I first took this case, I identified with Rose. Now my experiences are beginning to replicate Tina's: the police invasion, Rose's alternatingly warm and cold affect toward me, my worry someone has been messing with my stuff. Maybe I *should* be paranoid.

"No," I tell her. "We're going to talk out here. Tell me how this started."

Ashley's voice quavers. "I was never going to do anything with the photo. I just wanted Ian to think I was."

I nod crisply, as if this information isn't new to me. It's amazing how much people will reveal when they assume you're already privy to the details of a situation.

"I need to see it."

Ashley pulls her phone out of her bag and touches the screen, then hands it to me.

I stare down at a selfie of Tina in bed at the Barclay estate. I recognize the blue-and-white quilt and the wood bed frame in the attic. Ian lies next to her, the covers drawn up halfway over his bare, muscular chest. He looks like he's napping. Tina's long hair tumbles over her bare shoulders, covering her breasts. She's smiling.

There's no universe in which there could be an innocent explanation for this picture. The tabloids would go crazy for it. It's the sort of thing that would live forever on the Internet, the first image to appear anytime Ian's name was searched.

"You have to understand, I lost so much when I got fired. I'm making two hundred bucks less every week. I have to pay rent now, too. And I always got a big Christmas bonus, but this year that's not gonna happen . . . I didn't do this just for me. I'm going to split the money with Tina's mom."

So it's blackmail. Ashley is surprising me; I didn't think she had it in her.

I scramble for a question that won't reveal how little I actually know. "You're splitting it half and half?"

Ashley nods vigorously. "Yes. I swear. Tina's mom still lives in the Philippines, and Tina used to send her something every month. I just wanted to do something for her, you know?"

I nod slowly.

"The money won't mean anything to Ian. But it means everything to me."

I'm not so sure about that—Ian can't have a lot of cash floating around—but I pretend to accept it.

Ashley seems to interpret my silence as judgment. She scrambles to tell me more.

"The Barclays are just like the family I used to work for. They always fly first class with their kids, but when we nannies travel with them, they put us back in coach. They spend more on a pair of shoes than they pay us in a month. The only reason they want us to live in is so we're always on call. They want us to be invisible until they need us." Ashley pauses to gulp in a breath. "Ian didn't care about Tina. None of them did. The Barclays didn't even go to her memorial service. She gave the Barclays everything, and now it's like she never existed to them."

She wipes her eyes and sniffs. "So yeah, I guess I just wanted to make them pay."

"How much?" I ask.

"Five thousand. Twice. Once for me and once for Mrs. De la Cruz."

If I told her to return the money, I'm certain she would—especially if I threatened to bring the police into it. Blackmail is a felony.

I step back and gesture toward Ashley's car. "You look cold. You should head home."

Her forehead wrinkles. "What are you going to do?"

Ian didn't even go to Tina's memorial service. None of the Barclays did.

"I'm going to do the same thing the Barclays did to Tina. I'm going to forget all about it."

Relief crashes over Ashley's face as I walk away.

CHAPTER THIRTY-FIVE

I'm not ready to call it a night.

I exit the Beltway at Connecticut Avenue, a main artery that leads into the heart of DC. My city is spectacular on this crisp fall night, with the creamy marble of the Washington Monument soaring into the inky sky, and Lincoln's forever watchful figure anchoring the west end of the National Mall.

I take the parkway that parallels the dark, gleaming Potomac River, heading into Alexandria, Virginia. That's where I grew up.

The neighborhood where my dad, mom, and I lived has evolved, yielding to the hunger of suburban sprawl. Back then, there weren't artisanal coffee shops and wine-tasting bars and apartment buildings with lobbies designed like gorgeous living rooms. It was a neighborhood for working-class folks, with a few parks and empty lots and some single-story homes amid the clumps of town houses.

It's easy to find my way back to ours. The redbrick facade is unchanged, but the door is now painted navy blue and the landscaping is far more elegant. A graceful crepe myrtle stands in the center of the small yard—its slender, pale branches bare for the season—and the lawn is perfectly edged. After we got Bingo, my dad built a simple wooden fence to enclose the backyard, but it has been upgraded, too.

I can almost hear my mother's voice, wafting from the kitchen up to my bedroom: "Stella! Dinner!"

If I didn't answer right away—if I was watching *Double Dare* or playing with Bingo—she'd hurry up the stairs, her footsteps light and quick as a rapid heartbeat.

"There you are!" she'd say, the note of worry in her voice dissolving by the final word.

My mother had significant anxiety. I recognize that now. When her life imploded, she self-medicated, perhaps because help wasn't available to her, or because she didn't know how to get it.

When she died, she was a couple of years older than I am now. Only a few wispy fragments of her remain. The cardboard memory box in my house. Her gentle voice singing John Denver's "Annie's Song" as she put me to bed. Her whispered "No . . . please" on the night she died.

After I went to live with my aunt, I overheard her talking about my mother to her husband, her thin lips pursing as she scrubbed dishes in a sink filled with soapy water.

"Trashy . . . always had the boys chasing her . . . thought she'd just glide through life . . . she was an embarrassment."

I wanted to burst into the room and scream at her: *Stop!*

The protest welled up in my throat, but I couldn't release it.

So I turned and went back to my room. I never defended my mother. Not to my aunt. Not on the night she died, when I could have gotten out of the closet and maybe saved her.

Not even to myself.

I reach for my phone and enter her name into a search engine. Nausea rises in my throat, but I force myself to take deep breaths and look at the results.

I've spent so much time digging into Tina's death. Don't I at least owe my own mother that same effort?

Detective Garcia was right about the deaths of nobodies. My mother merited two lines in the police blotter: *Mary Hudson, 40, found dead of a suspected drug overdose in a Northeast DC apartment. Police urge anyone with information to come forward.*

The detective also told me cold cases never disappear. Files are kept for perpetuity.

I attach the link to an email and address it to Detective Garcia.

She was my mother, I type. *And I'm finally trying to find out what happened that night.*

CHAPTER THIRTY-SIX

I wait just inside the main entrance of the aquarium, scanning the approaching visitors.

Any minute now, she'll arrive.

I feel as wired and uneasy as I did the first time I saw Rose. I have no idea how she'll respond to my presence. At least Ian will bear witness if Rose acts out in an aggressive way.

He's the only Barclay who seems to be holding the possibility in his mind that something could be deeply off with his brilliant, wildly talented, delicate-looking daughter.

A group of schoolkids in matching yellow T-shirts flows around me like a school of fish. They're about the same age as Rose. I think again how peculiar it is that she has virtually no interaction with children.

They'll be impossible to avoid today. I'm going to look for an opportunity to arrange an encounter so I can gauge Rose's reaction.

Ian and Rose show up right on time. Ian smiles and gives a little wave when he sees me. It's impossible to discern Rose's feelings. Her shield is in place.

I bend down to look her in the eyes. "Hi, Rose."

No response.

Ian puts a hand on his daughter's shoulder. "Rose, can you smile at Stella? We're going to have a fun day."

Ian doesn't look at Rose to see if she has followed through on his request. Perhaps he already knows she won't.

"Where should we start?" Ian asks. "The dolphins? Octopi? Sharks?"

Rose shakes her head at each option.

"Touch tank?" Ian guesses.

Rose nods vigorously. We make our way to the exhibit, with Rose and Ian walking slightly ahead.

I study their body language. They stroll side by side, their gait neither hurried nor slow, with Ian reaching out to touch Rose's arm and point out a turtle in an exhibit they pass. At first glance, they look like a typical father and daughter. But despite Ian's striking good looks, Rose is the one who commands the eye. Her posture is as flawless as a ballerina's, and her knee-length plaid skirt and turtleneck sweater that looks like cashmere are far more formal than the jeans and T-shirts other kids wear.

I'm so focused on the Barclays that I don't immediately notice the trio of college-aged women who are following the same path as us. The women edge closer to Rose and Ian, and I have to move aside to avoid getting jostled by them.

The energy surrounding the women feels off; they're huddled together, whispering excitedly, and the blonde in the jean jacket keeps releasing a high-pitched giggle.

We reach the touch tank area, where horseshoe crabs and stingrays move through huge, shallow aquariums filled with salt water.

A staff member tells visitors to rinse their hands if they plan to touch the creatures. Rose and Ian move toward the little sink, but I stay back. I'm watching five people now, including the three women who seem to have no interest in the seawater exhibit.

Ian glances back at me. "The rays can't sting. They're harmless."

I smile. "You two go ahead. I'm good."

The staff member illustrates how to touch the rays with a steady, flat palm, and Rose pulls up the sleeve of her sweater, then extends her hand into the water, watching as a big gray ray approaches.

The women tilt their heads close together, whispering again. The one in the jean jacket lifts her phone and appears to snap a picture.

"It *is* him!" she whispers, this time loudly enough for me to hear. "The daughter has red hair just like his wife."

"Ex-wife," her friend clarifies, and they burst into laughter.

Ian's body language grows rigid. Rose pauses, her hand hovering above the stingray. It glides away before she can touch it.

"You just missed it." Ian's voice is strained. "Try again, sweetie." Rose pulls her hand out of the tank and stands there, her head hung low, her fingertips dripping water onto the floor.

The blond woman lifts her phone again. It's as if Ian and Rose are creatures in an exhibit, too, placed here for her amusement.

Anger rushes into me, as swift and strong as a thunderclap. Not just on behalf of Rose. What I'm about to do is for all the children I've seen turned into pawns in vitriolic divorces. For all the kids who become collateral damage in their parents' lives.

I step forward, inserting myself between the Barclays and the woman just as she takes the picture.

I keep my voice low, but steel runs through it.

"Delete the photos now or I'm calling the police."

Her tone is snide. "For what, taking pictures of the stingrays?"

I keep staring her down. "Show me, then."

Her gaze skitters away. I can sense Rose behind me, taking it all in.

"We can take pictures in public places," one of the blonde's friends pipes up in a snotty tone.

"Correct. However, Section 26 of the Constitution states that a child's best interests are paramount to any matter involving the child. I'm pretty sure your picture is not in the best interest of this child, so it'll be up to the court to decide if this a privacy infringement."

The mouthy woman doesn't have a reply to my bluff.

"Delete it now or I'm calling the cops."

The first woman taps a button on her phone. "Sheesh, fine." I lean closer and watch as the photograph disappears.

"Now empty the trash."

She rolls her eyes, but she does it.

I keep standing there, blocking their view of Rose and Ian, until they leave. The blonde shoots me the finger just before they disappear around the corner.

I give her my brightest smile.

When I turn around, Ian mouths, *Thank you.*

Rose doesn't react, but she puts her hand in the tank again. This time, when the stingray glides toward her, she touches its smooth gray back.

After about ten minutes, Ian squats down to face Rose.

"Honey, I need to peel away and make some work calls. You can spend some time with Stella. I'll be back here to meet you guys for lunch."

Rose looks over at me, and I hold my breath, waiting. Then she nods. I feel a strange sense of triumph, as if I've passed a test.

Still, I'm not letting down my guard. I thought Rose and I had connected at Lucille's, too.

"Where should we go next?" I ask Rose as Ian walks away. I consult the map on the wall and follow his example by listing options: "Jellyfish? The Australia exhibit?" She shakes her head. "How about Shark Alley?"

She nods, and I orient myself before we begin to walk. The aquarium is growing more crowded now that it's mid-morning. I keep an eye out for the trio of women as well as other children. We pass a few going in the opposite direction, but Rose doesn't react. A girl who looks a little older than Rose, however, turns to stare. She could be admiring Rose's distinctive hair or sensing some difference or damage in Rose. It's impossible to say.

Shark Alley is at the far end of the aquarium. While we walk there, Rose occasionally pauses to look at exotic fish or waxy tree frogs. As she lingers to study a harlequin tuskfish, the thin blue light coming from the tank illuminates the soft curve of her cheek, her straight nose, and her ringlets. Rose's profile reminds me of the cameo necklaces that were popular in the nineteenth century.

I don't have a lot of time with her. I need to jump right in. "You must feel so angry sometimes."

She blinks twice—the only signal I've caught her off guard. "Maybe you feel sad and scared, too."

Rose doesn't pull down her shield. She hasn't shut me out.

I do something I've only done with a very few people before, and never a client.

I open up.

"It happened to me, too, Rose. I became mute after my mother died. I couldn't talk for a while. I was seven."

Rose turns to face me. One half of her face is in the light, the other cloaked in shadows.

"I was in survival mode. I didn't trust anyone around me. I'd wake up in the middle of the night and want to cry out for her, but I couldn't."

I can't mask the quaver in my voice. "I felt completely alone, like I was in a tunnel and no one could reach me. But you're not alone, Rose. I don't know what's going on, but I want to help you."

Rose looks at me for another few seconds, then turns and glances back into the aquarium tank. I hope she's letting my words sink in.

After a moment, she continues walking to Shark Alley. A three-story walking ramp with a metal railing zags through the middle of the massive exhibit. The lighting is very dim. All around us are glass walls holding back the creatures in the tank. We're in the center of their world, not the other way around.

Sand tiger sharks and largetooth sawfish glide by, endlessly circling us.

Rose stands in the middle of it all, spellbound.

She watches the sharks. I watch her.

Is there an incremental softening in her? Is she beginning to trust me? I can't say for sure, but I think so.

A few people pass us—a young couple, then a dad with a toddler in a backpack—but Rose is content to stay in place.

"It must feel so strange to not have Tina around," I say softly.

"I remember when my mother died, I couldn't understand it. How could she be here one moment and gone the next?"

Rose turns to face me. She's standing slightly above me on the slanted ramp, which gives her an extra foot of height.

I take a step closer to her before I realize why I'm doing it.

I don't like the illusion that she's almost as big as me.

I've thought about what I would have wanted someone to say to me after my mother died. Now I use those words with Rose. But I temper them to cover all the possibilities.

"The whole world changed for you. Nothing is the same anymore."

Rose is staring intently at me. I feel a hitch in her energy, as if we're linked by a current.

I'm getting through to her. Something I've said struck a nerve.

I'm about to continue probing when a mom and daughter appear above us on the ramp. The girl appears to be only a couple of years younger than Rose, but she looks like another species in her worn jeans and butterfly sweater, with messy hair and a bouncy gait.

The mom has a baby in a front carrier and a diaper bag looped over her shoulder. She's a dozen yards behind. "Olivia, slow down!"

The little girl reaches Rose and blurts out, "What's your name?"

"Hi," I reply. "I'm Stella and this is Rose."

Olivia looks Rose up and down. "How old are you?"

I try to gauge Rose's comfort level. She doesn't appear bothered by the interaction, so I let it play out.

Rose lifts her hands and holds up nine fingers.

"She's nine. Four years older than you, Olivia." The mom looks at Rose for an extra beat, then at me. "We don't want to bother you. Come along, Liv."

I think about how I would've wanted my condition to be explained when I was a kid. "Rose isn't talking right now, but she can hear everything you say." I keep my tone casual, and I don't overexplain. "This is a good spot to watch the sharks, if you want to stay."

The mom smiles easily and sets down her diaper bag with a relieved sigh. "Well, Olivia will talk enough for the both of them."

It's true; Olivia is one of those happy-go-lucky kids who keeps up a steady stream of chatter. She's apple-cheeked and quick to smile.

She tells Rose that sharks never sleep, and it's funny, but I swear I can feel the frustration surge in Rose. She probably wants to tell Oliva that sharks have restful or inactive periods, and the issue is far more complex than most people realize.

Olivia moves closer to Rose and grabs her hand. "Look at my necklace. I got it for my birthday. It has an *O* for Olivia."

Rose tries to pull back, but Olivia grabs her hand again. "You can touch it if you want!" She doesn't give Rose a choice; she pulls her hand to her necklace.

I don't intervene. Rose doesn't need my protection.

"Why don't you talk or smile?" Olivia asks.

Olivia's question isn't aggressive, but I can feel a shift in the atmosphere.

The mom doesn't seem to hear what's going on; her baby has begun to fuss, and she's walking back and forth a few feet away.

"Huh?" Olivia probes.

As if in slow motion, I see Rose reach into the pocket of her sweater.

I lunge toward her.

I know what Rose sometimes keeps in her sweater pockets. I see the flash of something shiny a split second before I grab Rose's arm.

Then I freeze, my hand in midair. It's a silver tube of lip gloss.

Relief pours through me. It seems as if Rose wants to show one of her little treasures to Olivia, perhaps in exchange for seeing the necklace.

Rose twists open the gloss and dabs a bit onto her lips. The vivid red is gaudy against her porcelain skin. I can't imagine Beth letting Rose buy it, or possessing this shade herself. Plus, the brand is cheap, the kind you'd buy in a drugstore, with the fake silver chipping off the tube.

Where did Rose get it?

Then Ashley's words float back into my mind: Tina would some-times put a little lip gloss on Rose when she got ready to go out.

Perhaps Rose took this from Tina's room. It looks like the shade she was wearing in the video Pete sent me.

Did Rose take it as a way to stay close to her nanny? Or as another trophy?

Olivia keeps up her happy chatter. "Can I see it?"

She reaches for the lip gloss, but Rose jerks it away.

The baby is fussing loudly now. His mom bends down awkwardly, reaching into the diaper bag and murmuring something about a pacifier that was just there.

I want to help her—to offer to find the pacifier or hold the baby—but I can't take my eyes off Rose.

I can feel her anger rising; it's palpable.

"No fair! I let you touch my necklace!" Olivia lunges, grabbing for the lip gloss.

Rose throws out her free hand and pushes the little girl.

Olivia staggers back before falling on her behind. She catches her-self before she rolls backward beneath the railing, coming perilously close to tumbling off the edge of the platform.

"Oh, no—honey! Are you okay?" Her mother rushes over, her baby now wailing.

"I'm so sorry—it was—" The words dry up in my throat. It wasn't an accident.

Olivia wouldn't have been seriously hurt if she'd fallen through. The drop is only about two feet.

Still, my heart is in my throat.

"You shouldn't push. That isn't nice," the other mother admon-ishes Rose.

Rose slides the lip gloss back into her pocket and turns her back on us.

The mom takes Olivia's hand and they walk away. Olivia's high voice floats back to us: "I don't like that girl. She's bad."

I know what is going to happen even before I move to look at Rose.

Our fleeting connection is severed.

The shutters have fallen over her eyes. She's unreachable.

CHAPTER THIRTY-SEVEN

The more I get to know Rose, the less I understand her.

I've felt threads of connection to her—strong yet ephemeral as a spider's silk—but each time, the filaments snap so swiftly I question whether they ever existed at all.

Perhaps the connection is a closed circuit, starting and ending with me alone.

After the incident with Olivia, Rose folds into herself, origami-like, until Ian rejoins us. I excuse myself to use the restroom, and when I return, Ian tells me Rose has signaled she has a stomachache and wants to go home.

"Sorry to cut this short. We'll figure out another time soon," he promises.

I watch as they depart, the top of Rose's head barely coming up to Ian's waist, her hand swallowed up in his much bigger one.

I can't stop seeing her on the ramp in Shark Alley. Maybe she did it because she didn't have the words to tell Olivia no. The lip gloss could have special meaning to Rose; it could be her last tangible link to Tina.

But I also can't stop thinking about how Rose's reflex was to push.

I exit the aquarium and wander around the Inner Harbor, looking out at the warships on display in the Patapsco River and watching people under heat lamps dig into piles of Old Bay–steamed crabs. When my stomach growls, I buy a to-go cup of roasted tomato soup from a little deli. It's a gray, chilly day, so I keep walking and sip the hot, savory soup straight out of the container.

I'm about to head back to my car when my phone buzzes. Caller ID reads *Harriet Barclay*.

Hoping she took the bait I cast at Mrs. Li's apartment, I answer quickly.

"Stella, it's Harriet. I hope I'm not disturbing you in the middle of anything important?"

I toss my empty soup container into a recycling bin. "Not at all. I'm just finishing up lunch."

There's a brief hesitation, as if my answer surprised her.

Ian agreed to keep quiet about our encounter. But Harriet has proven herself canny in gathering information. If she expected me to be spending the day with Rose and is disappointed at failing to interrupt our time, she doesn't let on.

"I've been thinking about how our conversation was cut short, and I'm eager to complete it." Harriet is only in her mid-sixties, and despite her physical challenges, she seems robust and energetic. This is the first time I've heard her sound tired. "Things are getting increasingly difficult here. It would be a relief to have some sort of resolution."

"I can meet you in an hour," I tell her.

"Oh—ah, actually, I was thinking a little later. Say 5:30?"

I frown. The time strikes me as oddly specific. "Sure."

"Do you mind coming to the house? My knee acts up when it feels like rain, so it's harder for me to drive."

The October days are short, which means it'll grow dark while I'm inside the house. I've never been at the Barclays' at night before.

"Of course. See you then."

The last time we met, I came armed with a plan: to sneak into Rose's room. Harriet will be prepared for that now.

That doesn't concern me. I already found Rose's hiding place.

What bothers me is my suspicion that this time, Harriet is the one armed with a plan.

★ ★ ★

The sky is heavily layered with clouds when I arrive at the Barclays',
and the air feels damp and swollen. The private road leading to the
estate is illuminated by old-fashioned lanterns, with gas flames flickering within the hurricane globes.

I briefly wonder if the Barclays went to the trouble of replacing the
glass with plastic out here, too. But I doubt it, if their goal is to keep
Rose from amassing more potential weapons.

The tall bases don't have any natural hand- or footholds. They're
impossible for a child to climb without assistance.

When I pull in by the garage to park, I find myself spinning my
steering wheel and turning around my car so it faces the road. My
body is taking steps to enact what my mind is trying to avoid thinking about: I want to be able to get out fast if I need to.

I step out of my car and sling my bag over my shoulder. It's much
lighter than usual. The only work tools I'm bringing today are a clean
legal pad, my favorite pen, and my iPhone.

As I step onto the bottom stair of the porch, a voice floats out of
the far corner.

"Hello, Stella."

Harriet is gently swaying on a wicker swing. A blanket is draped
over her lap, and her polished wooden cane is leaning against the rail.

"Would you mind if we sat out here for a few minutes?" she asks.

"Sure." It's chilly, but I donned a warm coat before I left home. I
pull my fleece gloves out of my pockets and slide my hands into them.

I lower myself into the chair across from hers.

She doesn't immediately speak, so I prompt her. "You mentioned
things were getting increasingly difficult."

"Ian and Beth had a horrible fight last night. I worried it might
become violent."

"Did it?" I interject.

Harriet shakes her head immediately. "They weren't screaming—
well, Beth was a bit, but only at the very end—so I don't think Rose

woke and heard any of it. But they were loud enough for me to over-hear. The subflooring is very thin in this old house, and it was never fixed because that would require tearing up the original wood floors and destroying the historic details. So sounds seep through."

I lean back in my seat. "Why were they fighting?"

"Ian went out, and when he came home, Beth accused him of be-ing with another woman. Apparently they agreed not to date until their divorce is final, to avoid attracting any more media attention."

"How did Ian respond?" I know where Ian went last night, and he *was* with two other women—me and Ashley—but not in the way Beth suspected.

"He denied it, but wouldn't say where he'd been. I tend to believe Beth. Women have a sixth sense about this sort of thing; they know when a man is stepping out. Beth missed it the first time around, with Tina, but I'm sure she's attuned to it now. Once you've been burned, you always know how to look for the clues."

"Clues?" I echo.

"Lust makes men careless. They think we women are foolish; that we're so busy tending to the home and children we don't notice they're suddenly all jittery and possessive about their phones." She gives a smile that looks more like a grimace. "Trust me, I've been there. We women don't get fooled twice."

Harriet gently pushes off with her good leg and the swing begins to move again. "In any case, their argument quickly devolved into who deserved custody of Rose. They accused each other of awful things."

It isn't just her voice that sounds tired. Harriet looks drawn and weary, with the dim light deepening the creases on her face.

"They're so locked in this ugliness they're forgetting about Rose. Ian and Beth were never what you'd call a cuddly couple, but they rarely fought. And I'm worried that the longer this drags on, the worse it'll get. Our family is being destroyed."

"In my experience, things get worse as divorces wear on. No one operates at their highest level when they're wounded and angry." I glance toward the house. "It seems quiet in there now."

Before Harriet can reply, sound pours out of the house, swift and bright as bubbles flowing out of a bottle of uncorked champagne.

Rose is playing the piano. The music sweeps me up in its vibrant, electric current. It's impossible to think a young girl is creating this rapture.

Harriet's face alights with pleasure.

"She's a miracle," Harriet whispers.

She leans her head back against the swing. "This used to be my favorite time of day. I'd sit here and listen to Rose practice and look out at the view. I made sure to give Beth and Ian privacy most nights, but a few times a week I'd join them for dinner and hear about Beth's new fundraiser or the book Rose was reading or Ian's demanding client. Oh, how I miss those times."

After a few moments, Harriet gets to her feet, wobbling a bit until her cane is firmly in her hand. "Come, it's getting too cold. Let's go inside."

I follow her in. I assume we're going to continue talking in a private nook of the house, perhaps in Harriet's basement quarters, which I've never seen.

Harriet leads me toward the kitchen. We pass the living room, but Rose's back—as straight as an ironing board while her fingers perform a frantic dance over the keys—is to me.

Ian and Beth stand side by side next to the kitchen island, like characters in a play waiting to say their lines. They're both staring at me with expectant expressions.

It hits me like a punch: They've been waiting for me.

I've walked into a setup. I'm the only player here who has no idea what's going on.

CHAPTER THIRTY-EIGHT

I address the issue head-on: "Looks like you're planning something. What's up?"

"This might be a bit unorthodox, but we're all in a hurry to finish this process," Beth begins. Her pale hands with slightly red knuckles are wringing together. "We thought you might like to stay for dinner. That way you can spend time with all of us together and reach your conclusions sooner."

I see a green salad in a wooden bowl on the counter, and beside it, a silver dish of dressing. The air smells of roasting potatoes, and five thick filets of salmon are resting on a foil-lined aluminum tray.

I've broken bread with many clients before, but never have I sat down for a civilized dinner with the two opposing parties in an ugly divorce.

No chance am I letting this opportunity slip away. "I'd love to."

I catch Harriet shoot Beth a relieved look. They're colluding again. Perhaps the two of them hatched this plot, then brought in Ian. When I try to catch his gaze, he busies himself brushing marinade over the salmon.

Beth reaches for a clear carafe filled with a ruby-colored liquid.

"Wine, anyone?"

"Just sparkling water for me." Harriet walks to the refrigerator and pulls out a can.

Normally I don't drink on the job, but I want Beth and Ian to be as loose as possible. If I refuse a drink, they might, too.

"I'd love a glass."

Beth opens a cabinet door and takes out three delicate-looking tumblers that match the carafe. She pours a generous serving into each. It feels jarring when I take a sip of the velvety wine and my lips close around the plastic rim of the tumbler.

The music briefly stops, then begins again. This piece is infused with what feels like a deep sorrow.

"*Black Mass*," Beth tells me. "That's the nickname of this piece. Rose just began learning it. It's wonderfully complex."

I suppress a shudder as the notes intensify, seeming to cry out in despair.

"When do you think you'll wrap up your work, Stella?" Harriet asks.

Rose hits a wrong note and pauses, then repeats the section.

"It's difficult to say. The more time I have with all of you, the faster I'll reach my recommendation."

Beth and Harriet exchange another glance. I can't read the subtext.

Ian opens the oven door and checks on the potatoes, then slides in the tray of salmon. He's as skilled at the art of subterfuge as his mother. He told me he was going to make some calls while Rose and I spent time alone at the aquarium. Is it possible he followed us into Shark Alley and witnessed Rose's act of aggression, then filled in Beth and Harriet?

That could explain their sudden pressure. They want me out of the picture as quickly as possible.

"How about giving us a ballpark," Beth prods. "If you have a lot of access to all of us, could you finish in, say, three or four days?"

Police have officially cold-cased the active investigation into Tina's death. I've spoken to the Thin Man, Ashley, Mrs. Li, Detective Garcia, the three adult Barclays, and I've spent some time with Rose. I've gathered some information from Rose's school principal and Pete, and

I've dug deeply into the legal papers and media hits. I've thought about this case to the point of near obsession.

If this were a typical case, I would be getting ready to write up my final report.

But this is no longer a matter of me trying to figure out the best custodial situation for Rose.

I don't trust any of them. They're master illusionists.

"What do you need from us?" Beth asks.

"Honesty," I tell her. "And a little more time."

"Fair enough," she says lightly.

We all fall silent as the music fades away with a mournful, drawn-out chord.

"Rose can play by ear, you know," Harriet tells me. "If she hears a piece just once, she can replicate it. Of course, that's for simpler pieces. The more complex ones require sheet music for her to perform."

"That's incredible," I reply.

All three Barclays are staring at me. Their eyes are like sharp pins driving into me. They're desperate to know what I'm thinking.

"Does Rose know I'm coming for dinner?"

Beth smiles. "Yes. She's very pleased."

I asked for honesty only seconds ago, and I'm pretty sure Beth is already lying to me. Rose has never once been pleased by my appearance.

The dining room is down a narrow hallway off the kitchen. It's a rectangular space with a low ceiling crisscrossed by exposed beams. Dark wainscoting covers the lower half of walls painted a deep maroon, and a heavy metal chandelier is centered over the regal-looking table.

The first thing I notice: This room contains no soft corners—the vibe is like an old-fashioned men's hunt club.

The second: There are no knives at the five place settings.

The baby rosemary potatoes are small enough to eat in a single bite, and the salmon looks tender enough to cut with the edge of fork.

There's focaccia with individual dishes of herbed olive oil for dipping instead of butter. And the salad leaves are torn into pieces no bigger than sand dollars.

Beth brings the plastic pitcher of wine to the table and tops off my glass first, then refills hers and Ian's.

As she finishes pouring, Rose enters the room. I greet her, but her head is low and her affect is wooden again. She's wearing the same outfit she had on at the aquarium, and I wonder if the cherry-colored lip gloss is still buried in her skirt pocket.

"Shall we sit?" Beth suggests.

Harriet immediately claims the middle chair on one side, with Beth and Ian hurrying to flank her. This means Rose and I are left to take the two chairs facing them. It's difficult for me to see Rose without twisting in my seat. I wonder if that was the Barclays' intention, to provide the illusion of proximity.

Behind the three adult Barclays is a large window that showcases the skeletons of giant trees outlined against the darkening sky. Without Rose's music filling the air, every sound is magnified: the scrape of Ian's fork against his plate, Harriet's swallow when she sips her sparkling water, and a light, repetitive bump that I realize is Rose's foot tapping against her chair.

I wonder if her foot is accompanying music she hears in her head, or whether it's a signal she's agitated.

I spear a potato and try to eat it, but my throat closes up. It's an effort to swallow. I can hear echoes of Rose's bleak, anguished music lingering in the air.

Do the others not feel the darkness wafting through this house, snaking into the corners and curling around us like smoke?

"Delicious," Harriet says, indicating the salmon. "Did you use soy sauce in the marinade?"

"A bit," Ian replies.

"I won't have much, then. Soy sauce contains gluten," Beth chimes in.

"Does it?" Ian's voice is indifferent.

Rose is methodically working her way through her plate, her foot steady as a metronome. I can feel the vibrations echoing against my skin. I watch out of the corner of my eye as Rose selects an asparagus tip from her salad. Like everything else about her, her tastes seem far more sophisticated than a typical third-grader's.

"Stella, where did you grow up?" Beth's voice is loud and overly cheery in the cavernous room.

"In the area. I was born in DC and lived in Virginia for a few years. Since then, it's been DC my whole life."

"A native. There aren't many of us around here," Ian notes.

I look down at my salad. Topping the lettuce are a few bright red baby tomatoes. I stare at them, an idea forming in my mind.

I stab one with my fork and hold it up. "Did these come from your garden?"

Harriet shakes her head. "No, it's too cold. The tomatoes are gone by the end of September. The first week of October at the latest."

Rose doesn't move, but I swear I can feel her tighten up next to me, too, as if our nervous systems have linked together. Her foot stops briefly, then starts again, faster now, the metronome only I can hear gaining urgency.

Beth opens her mouth to say something, but I quickly interject. I want to stay on this topic.

"Can you taste the difference in the vegetables you grow here versus the ones you buy at the market, Harriet?"

"Oh, yes," Harriet begins, and I can tell I've hit a subject she's eager to elaborate upon.

Her comparison of the tastes buys me a few seconds to do mental calculations while I nod and pretend to listen: I've already timed how long it takes to rush from the garden to Rose's room; I was able to do it in less than a minute. It wouldn't add many more seconds to the stopwatch to climb one more level to the attic.

"It must be so satisfying to grow your own food," I blurt as soon as

Harriet pauses for a breath. I can't lose this thread; I need to see where it leads.

Harriet beams. I've hit her sweet spot. She can't take full credit for Rose, even though her pride in her granddaughter's accomplishments is palpable.

But the garden is hers alone.

"If you have a green thumb and you're willing to take the time to learn, you'll end up with a very bountiful harvest. We incorporate our produce into our meals, and Rose and I have a deal—whenever we pick vegetables, she digs up a few carrots for Sugar and Tabasco and gives them their treats first."

Taptaptap. Rose's foot is frantic now.

The emotions roiling within her come out in her music, and in the movements of her foot. But they never find release in her voice. They must be building up to a crescendo. If Rose could make a sound now, I'm certain it would be a scream.

Does Rose recognize the massive mistake Harriet just made?

I steal a glance at Rose. Her face is implacable, her gaze focused down at her plate.

Harriet wasn't with Rose the whole time in the minutes surrounding Tina's death. She told me as much.

Rose's routine was to feed carrots to the horses first.

A detail that has always nagged at me explodes in my mind. Who hovers over a mature nine-year-old in a private backyard on a late September afternoon, watching them every single second?

Five or six minutes of distraction is all it would take. The time needed for Harriet to pluck some dead leaves from a few plants, or close her eyes and feel the sunshine on her face, thinking her granddaughter was bringing carrots to the horses.

When Tina landed on the patio, it would have taken Harriet a bit of time to limp over from the garden. She thought it was a tree limb falling; she wouldn't have hurried, and bushes would have obscured her view of Tina. Rose could have flown down two flights of stairs and appeared at her grandmother's side.

Harriet would do anything for Rose, Mrs. Li said.

Even create a false alibi, I think.

I feel the vibration die away. Rose's foot ceases moving. Her symphony is over.

CHAPTER THIRTY-NINE

I barely make it through dinner without succumbing to the urge to bolt. The menace twines greedily around me, as if seeking a new host. It wraps me in a vise so tight I feel nailed to my chair.

No one seems to notice. The adult Barclays are too fixated on Rose.

Once Rose's foot stops tapping, she becomes like a marionette performing prescribed movements: She takes neat, small bites, occasionally dabbing her mouth with her linen napkin. Her elbows never graze the table.

At first her parents and Harriet seem to be trying to excuse Rose's affect with overly cheery exclamations.

Ian: "Rose, you must be so tired!"

Beth: "You had such a busy day, sweetie!"

Harriet: "Maybe you need to go to bed a little early, Rose."

When she doesn't nod or lift her head to meet their eyes, they pivot strategies and appear to try to compensate for her lack of engagement. Harriet and Ian talk energetically, discussing everything from the weather to the origins of the new piece of music Rose is learning to the Halloween decorations Harriet spotted on her recent drive to a doctor's office. Beth joins in the conversation, but she picks at her food and drinks three glasses of wine. With every sip, her hostility seems to tick up, her sentences becoming more clipped and her smiles hardening.

When Ian mentions the new pizza oven in the backyard, praising the taste of the Margherita pie he cooked in it as a test, raw hatred flits across Beth's face. The pizza oven must be a reminder; it exists only because of Tina's death.

Everything in this house must be a reminder.

What will happen when I leave tonight? I shift in my seat, seeking a position that will make my lungs feel less compressed. Perhaps Beth has a stash of wine—boxed, not bottled of course—in her bedroom. I can visualize her sequestering herself, her pale lips stained dark purple by the Cabernet as she leans into the numbing embrace of alcohol. Perhaps she needs it to muffle visions of the excruciating act of betrayal tha ook place just one floor above her.

Rose points to her empty plate and looks at Beth.

"Yes, you may be excused, honey. Why don't you run upstairs and take your bath now?"

Rose carries her plate into the kitchen. I watch her disappear into the hallway, her steps small and even.

I decline the dessert Beth offers—grapes, figs, and cheese—and almost gasp with relief when Ian stands a moment later and begins to clear the table. Harriet insists on taking my plate, even though I don't feel right watching her limping into the kitchen.

"I should head home," I blurt. "I'm sure you all have things to do tonight."

Ian is filling the sink with soapy water, so Beth walks me to the door. I'm desperate to break free from the house. But Beth pauses, her hand on the doorknob, so tantalizingly close to pulling it open. For the first time, I clearly see the pattern on the ivory wallpaper in the hallway. It isn't clusters of flowers, as I'd thought. It's weeping willows.

Weeping willows are a symbol of mourning. They're trees of loss, sorrow, and death.

"Will you be back tomorrow morning, Stella? We're all clearing our schedules to the extent possible to make sure to give you the time you need."

"Yes, how about 10 a.m.?" I pull my eyes back to her.

"I'll need to check with Ian, but that should work."

"Great." Does she not hear it, how strangled my voice has become? Is she taunting me, like a cat that has trapped a mouse, because she senses how desperate I am to get out?

No. It's me; I'm the one with a distorted perception right now.

Finally Beth pulls open the door and bids me goodbye. I want to run, but force myself to walk.

As I head down the porch steps, I suck in lungfuls of the crisp night air. Is it the house itself or the dark energy of one or more of its occupants that instills this deep foreboding in me? Because even though with every passing day it looks more and more as if Rose may not just be *at* the epicenter of whatever is happening—but *is* the epicenter—I will not let myself mentally cement that conclusion.

I need to keep my mind open a little longer. The stakes are too high for a mistake.

And if I become convinced the best way to serve my client is by breaking not only Ian's confidences but also the protocol I've followed in all my previous cases, I'll do it.

But I won't stop fighting for Rose. If this case ends in the way I fear, I'll work to get Rose the best possible help. The Barclays have means. They can afford for Rose to stay inpatient at a place where the caregivers are knowledgeable and kind, where ample time is taken to find the best combinations of medicines, intensive therapy, and cognitive behavioral therapy. There are such places for children who seem beyond hope.

And every once in a while, with massive early intervention, a child manages to emerge and live a productive, healthy life. They are the outliers, but who's to say Rose won't be among them?

It takes an eternity to reach my car, with the wind as my enemy, pushing me back toward the house. When my hand finally grips the cold metal handle, I jump in and engage the locks. The moon is behind a thick cloud cover, as if someone has tucked it in for the night beneath a fluffy comforter, and the tall gas lamps cast golden pools in the inky night that look like floating stepping-stones. I flick on my high beams and force myself to keep the speedometer at a steady twenty miles per hour.

I steal a look in my rearview mirror. Behind me, the Barclay estate is shrouded in shadows, the porch light as insignificant as the flame of a match in the vast blackness surrounding it.

I pull my eyes to the road ahead of me and gasp, slamming on my brakes.

A deer is standing in my path, blinded by the sharp light.

I skid across the road in what seems like slow motion, my mind screaming. I can see everything in that frozen moment: The doe's soft eyes and shiny black nose. Her brown coat and white tail pointing up into the air.

My tires dig for traction on the smooth path. I come to a stop only a few feet from the little doe.

We lock eyes for a second. Then the spell breaks, and she bounds away.

Breathing hard, I reach up and massage my shoulder where the seat belt cut into it.

Tears spill out of my eyes, without sound or warning.

This is what happened to my father. He couldn't stop in time, so he swerved and hit a tree.

I grab a tissue and wipe my face roughly, then push away the images and force myself to keep driving. I do what I can to distract myself, turning up the music and rolling my windows down a few inches, the brace of cold air like a slap.

I'm shaken and wrung out. I should go home, take a hot bath, get some sleep. There's no reason why I can't. I have nothing on my calendar for tonight. Some women would look forward to an open evening stretching out before them, with no demands or obligations.

But the mere thought makes me dizzy with anxiety.

I've tried dating apps before, but I'm not in the right headspace to go on one now. Nor do I feel up to calling a friend or colleague and suggesting a drink. Light conversation is beyond my reach.

The Barclay case demands my absolute focus. I can't do anything but work it through to its conclusion.

I know I should go home.

Yet I find myself steering toward a bar just over the DC line.

I barely touched my wine. I'll have one proper drink, I tell myself. Write up my notes from this evening. Steady my nerves.

I pull into the half-full parking lot ten minutes later. The lights, blare of music, and swell of conversation just inside the bar's door feel like lifelines.

The high-top tables are all full, but the barstools are mostly empty. I claim one by the end closest to the door.

It's chilly out, so I order a whisky and pull my blank legal pad out of my tote bag.

I root around for my Montblanc pen, the one Marco gave me for my birthday a few years ago.

It isn't in the slim, rectangular inner pocket of my bag where I always keep it. It must have fallen out.

I dig around, my fingers grasping. I search every object in my bag: my sunglass case, my wallet, my small makeup bag.

My pen is missing.

There's only one other possible place it could be. And I would never have consciously put it there. Still, I check the second, square inner pocket where I've been storing Tina's hoop earring.

My vision blurs. My breaths come fast and shallow.

I reach into the square pocket again, even though I know my fingers will come up empty. I'm beginning to doubt myself, to wonder if my version of reality is correct. Because this can't be happening.

A few months ago, Tina called the police because she thought an intruder was storming into her home.

After I took Rose as a client, I made the same phone call.

Tina felt as if someone was messing with her things.

So did I, when I came home to discover my music was turned off.

Then Tina said someone took her belongings.

And now my Montblanc pen, the one I've treasured for years and have never misplaced, is gone.

Any of the Barclays could have done it: I left my purse in the kitchen. Ian and Beth were both in there alone at separate times, after they ushered me into the dining room and followed with the platters of food. Harriet also went into the kitchen midway through her meal to get another seltzer. And Rose brought her dish to the sink while we adults remained at the table.

Someone went into my purse tonight. I'm certain of this; I'm not going crazy.

Because my pen isn't the only thing missing from my bag.

Tina's hoop earring is gone, too.

CHAPTER FORTY

When feeling threatened, most people seek out small places. It's a biological response, a genetic inheritance from our Stone Age ancestors. A tiny target has a better chance of being overlooked, or dismissed as not being worth the effort to conquer.

My reaction is the opposite. I can't stand to face the risk of being trapped. As soon as I get home from the bar, I tear through my house, opening every interior door. I flick on lights and turn up my music a few notches, letting Sheryl Crow's voice soar through the air. I take up as much space as possible.

Still, I can't fall asleep for hours. It's as if I'm on watch. Keeping vigil to see if the menace has tracked me here.

Finally, just as the horizon begins to lighten, I drift off.

I awaken a couple of hours later. My eyes feel gritty and my body heavy, but I know there will be no more sleep for me.

I hurry into the shower, blasting my body with alternating cold and hot sprays, trying to chase away my sluggishness.

I towel-dry my hair and slip on old jeans and a black V-neck sweater and my favorite boots—the fashion equivalent of comfort food. I smooth tinted moisturizer over my face, then apply a few swipes of mascara and a bit of lip gloss. I reach for my phone and see that, along with the usual junk, two important messages came in while I was getting ready.

The first is a text from Marco: Heard you stopped by Mom's house. Let's grab a drink soon so I can introduce you to Annie.

Every word is a nail driving into my chest. It's no longer Marco and me. From now on, our encounters will probably always include Annie, the sunny, bandana-wearing blonde who has taken my place in his heart and in his family. I don't want to meet her. It's easier to pretend she doesn't exist. But if I reveal this, I will lose Marco completely.

I don't dwell on that possibility. If I do, I may crawl back into bed.

I decide to answer Marco later and move on to the second message.

It's an email from Detective Garcia, asking if I can swing by her office before 5 p.m. today.

I read the subtext between her terse words. I asked her to provide information about my mother's death. She wouldn't be summoning me unless she had some.

I write back quickly, telling her I'll be there this afternoon.

Then I text Beth, letting her know I'll arrive at 10 a.m. unless the timing no longer works for her.

I slide a piece of whole-grain bread into my toaster, and even though I'm not hungry, I force myself to eat every bite, washing it down with two cups of strong black coffee.

As I rinse my cup and plate, I find myself staring at the knives in the butcher block on my kitchen counter. The sharp, five-inch utility knife would easily fit in my tote bag. I could carry it with me.

I reach toward it, then force my hand to stop.

I can't bring a weapon to the Barclays'. I'm going to be there in the daytime, in a family home. My fear is illogical.

Tina went through this thought process, too. She was going to buy a Taser to protect herself.

I stop my body from preparing for a possibility my mind doesn't want to admit. I force it to pivot away from the knife block.

I pull on my black puffer jacket as I step out into the crisp morning air. It's a crystalline day, and the leaves are beginning to drape themselves in shades of gold and crimson.

The beautiful weather feels incongruous to the emotions swirling inside me. It's too lovely, too pure a day for the world I currently inhabit.

I drive the familiar route to the Barclays' home, stopping at a gas station to fill my tank, and arrive at 10 a.m. sharp. There's a small, tidy *For Sale* sign with the Sotheby's real estate logo driven into the grass by the gate.

I stare at the sign. My understanding was the Barclays were going to wait until their custody dispute was settled to put the house on the market.

It feels as if they're putting another layer of pressure on me.

When I press the button on the security gate, there's no answer. I press it again. Finally a woman's voice flows through the speaker.

After a confused moment in which we talk over each other, I give my name and convey the message that Beth is expecting me.

There's a long hesitation; then the security gate rises. I drive through.

The mares are in the field again, endlessly grazing. A few workers wearing Great Outdoors shirts are working on the grounds, blowing leaves and pruning trees.

The housekeeper I've seen before opens the door when I knock. But instead of welcoming me in, she asks, "Can I help you?"

"Hi, I'm Stella. I'm here to see Beth."

"She's not here."

I frown. I'd assumed we were on for 10, especially given that Beth mentioned everyone was clearing their schedule.

"Are Ian and Rose here? Or Harriet?"

The housekeeper shakes her head.

"Do you know when they'll be back?"

"I'm sorry, I can't say."

I don't know if she means she doesn't know, or whether she has been told she can't reveal that information.

It's a nearly thirty-minute drive home with traffic. I don't want to leave and have to turn around again and head back out here.

I pull my phone out of my tote bag. None of the Barclays have texted or called.

I could ask the housekeeper if I can wait inside, but I don't want to put her in an uncomfortable position. Or maybe it's that I want to spend as little time inside as possible.

I could wait on the front porch, but it's very chilly in the shade. The only other option is my Jeep.

Frustration surges through me. It only takes seconds to send a text. Why didn't Beth reply?

The housekeeper is staring at me expectantly. I can see the conflict playing out on her face. She doesn't want to be rude and shut the door in my face, but cold air is seeping into the house.

"I'll wait out here," I say, my tone softer than my state of mind, because it certainly isn't her fault.

I head to my car and turn on the ignition.

After a few minutes of staring at the bend in the private drive, waiting for one of the Barclays' vehicles to come around it, I grow restless and reach for my phone. I can't do a lot of work on it, but there are some pieces I can tackle.

The earring may no longer be in my purse, but my practice is to document everything. I photographed it the day I discovered it.

I text the picture to Ashley, making sure to crop the background so that it could be any photo I pulled off the Internet. I already know the answer, but I need to be certain: Did Tina's missing earring look like this one?

Her reply pings in a minute later: omg that's it exactly how did u know?

Even though I'm not surprised, my stomach plummets. I type: Can you talk now?

At work but break at 1.

I don't want to wait that long. Maybe Ashley isn't supposed to use her phone at work, but like every other twenty-something on the planet, she probably always keeps it on her and is incapable of ignoring the faint vibration of an incoming text.

I have one more question for Ashley.

I want to look at my notes, but I didn't bring them or my laptop here. I can't recall Ashley's exact words, so I paraphrase.

You mentioned Beth got mad at Tina for messing up. Something about getting a time wrong?

I wait, staring at my phone. But the screen remains blank.

I hear the roar of an engine before the vehicle comes into view.

It's a black Cadillac, strong and imposing. Perfectly polished. It's timeless yet classic—this car could have driven straight out of another era.

I'm not surprised to see Beth behind the wheel. It's exactly the kind of car I'd expect her to own. A moment later, Ian pulls up after her in his red pickup truck with mud-splattered tires.

I step out and raise my hand in greeting.

Beth echoes my gesture. But even from this far away, I see a frown creasing the thin, pale skin of her forehead. She doesn't walk toward me.

Rose and Ian emerge from the truck a second later.

"Hey, Stella!" Ian calls easily.

He takes Rose's hand and leads her to the front door. Beth looks after them, and for a moment, I'm seized with the feeling that she is about to do the same, leaving me out here.

Then she begins to walk toward me.

I meet her halfway.

"Hello, Stella."

Beth doesn't give any indication we had a planned meeting. She offers no apology for being late.

"Good morning. Did you get my text letting you know I'd be here at 10?"

Beth frowns. "How long ago did you send it?"

"Maybe an hour."

Annoyance flickers over her face. "We were with the pediatrician then. I wasn't checking my messages."

Maybe I shouldn't have come here without her confirmation, but still, this inconvenienced me and not her. So why is she acting as if I've done something wrong?

"Is Rose ill?"

Beth folds her arms across her stomach. Instead of answering my question, she offers up an unrelated piece of information.

"When we took Rose to the pediatrician, I got to drive her there and Ian got to drive her home. That's what we're reduced to now—dividing our daughter in half."

Beth somehow appears thinner yet stronger than when I initially met her. As if something is burning within her, both fueling her and consuming her.

"Is Rose ill?" I ask again.

"Rose had a difficult night. She's been having a lot of them lately." The strain in Beth's eyes is apparent, and dark circles stain her pale skin. Nights must be difficult for her, too.

"How does a difficult night manifest for Rose?" I ask.

"She can't seem to stay in bed. We tuck her in and she appears to drift off. But then she sneaks out from under the covers. She sits at her desk and reads. Sometimes she comes and sits outside my bedroom door, or Ian's."

"Was the pediatrician helpful?"

Beth shakes her head. "I'm not going to put my nine-year-old daughter on sleeping pills. We'll try natural remedies."

This concerns me. Rose may very well need much stronger medication than sleeping pills.

"Would you mind if we met later today?" Beth asks. "None of us got much rest last night. Ian stayed with Rose the first part of the evening, and I took over in the middle of the night. She must have slept some, but I confess I'm not quite sure. I know I dozed off, but every time I woke up, her eyes were open."

I shudder, hoping Beth mistakes it for a reaction to the cold.

"I can come back later." I hope Beth doesn't catch the tiny note of relief in my voice. I welcome any reprieve from going in that oppressive house. "But I would like to chat with you for just a few minutes now."

Beth is about as unfiltered as someone like her can be. It may be my best chance to get the truth out of her.

"Fine."

I don't pull any punches. "What was the state of your marriage when Ian had the affair with Tina?"

"Excuse me?" She's clearly furious now.

I repeat my question, keeping my tone neutral.

"I fail to see how this is relevant, Stella."

I need her honesty. So I give her mine.

"I need to know how your version of the story compares with Ian's," I explain. "It may give me insight into his character."

She's clearly wrestling with her thoughts. Maybe she knows that if she tells me they were happily married, it will cast Ian in a worse light. If she lies, she may gain ground in the custody battle.

"You want to know what our marriage was like?" Beth asks. "Ian and I were in separate bedrooms. We hadn't discussed divorce, but our marriage was essentially over by the time he slept with our daughter's nanny in our family home."

Beth's version lines with up Ian's. But she isn't missing a chance to get in a few digs at his character.

"Did you know about the affair before Ian confessed?"

She shakes her head. "The wife is the last to know, right? At times Tina seemed a little giggly around Ian, but I figured she might have a harmless little crush. I never imagined Ian would be irresponsible enough to let it go any farther."

"Is Ian a good father?"

Beth blinks. I can tell she hates this question, too. She appears to choose her words very carefully.

"Ian doesn't always provide the structure a highly sensitive child like Rose needs, but he loves her."

Beth turns to look at the house. "I should go check on her."

"Thank you," I say. "What time should I come back?"

"I'll text you to confirm a time," Beth tells me. There's a note in her voice that feels like a reprimand. She seems to be drilling in a reminder that I didn't wait for her to text me to confirm the timing today.

Is this why I'm being sent away? A subtle form of punishment?

I don't let on that Beth has rattled me. I simply smile and tell her I look forward to hearing from her.

When I reach my car, I see Ashley has texted back.

yeahhh beth got annoyed once when tina went to pick up rose at school . . . beth said she wanted to pick up rose . . . but beth never confirmed it so tina didn't want to take a chance that rose would just be waiting there . . . of course it was all tina's fault.

The ground feels uneven beneath my feet.

I force myself to apply logic and reasoning. Beth's cavalier expectation that others anticipate her wishes without her explicitly stating them is nothing more than a product of the entitlement of her great wealth. She's used to people serving her and tending to her needs.

This latest parallel between my and Tina's experiences isn't an ominous sign.

CHAPTER FORTY-ONE

I have no idea when Beth will summon me back, but I'm not going to hang around and wait.

I don't work for Beth. She's going to have to yield to my timetable now.

I can't bring myself to answer Marco's text and set up drinks with him and Annie. So I email Detective Garcia and let her know I'll be there a little after 11.

I've never been to the Northwest DC police station where Detective Garcia is based, but when I walk in, the building feels familiar. It follows the blueprint of other cop shops I've visited—once to pick up a teenage client who was being held for shoplifting, another time to file a restraining order against a mother who reacted violently to my custody recommendation.

Detective Garcia meets me in the reception area by the long wooden benches that are faded and worn from the weight of the victims and accused who have rested on them through the years.

She wears black slacks and a blazer over a cream-colored blouse. Her long, straight hair is down, and she has on a little makeup.

I find myself wondering about her personal life. There's no wedding ring on her finger, but that could be a defensive technique. Detectives want to obtain information, not give it away, when they're working a case.

She leads me past two uniformed officers manning the front desk
and through the low-partitioned cubicle farm in the open bay. An
intense but muted thrum of energy courses through the air, along
with the scent of fresh brew from an old-school Mr. Coffee. There
are no plants, paintings, or family photos on display. No one wants to
be looking at a photograph of their baby's sweet, gummy smile in this
grim place; every cop I know has a dividing line burrowed deep in
their brain, with work on one side and family on the other.

The detective leads me to her desk in the corner and pulls over an
empty chair.

"How's the case going?" she asks once we're seated.

I don't answer immediately. I can't.

Centered on her neat desk is a single file folder. The name on the
tab is *Mary Hudson*.

My mother.

The decades have faded the typed letters to a soft gray. I'm seized
with a desperate yearning to reach out, to run my fingers over my
mom's name.

The file isn't thick, but whatever it holds is far more than my mind
has allowed me to remember about the night she died.

"Stella?"

I look up. Detective Garcia has registered my hunger for the contents of the file; I see it in the way she casually reaches out and pushes
the file a few inches closer to me. But she keeps two fingers on it.

"I was asking about the Barclay case. How's it going?"

"Oh. I, ah, I can't say much. I hope to reach a custody recommendation before long, but I'm not sure when."

The detective's expression is inscrutable.

"That's too bad."

My eyebrows lift. "What is?"

"That you don't feel comfortable sharing anything. But I understand. Your files are confidential. You wouldn't want to risk anything
by releasing information to me."

As she speaks, she uses those two fingers with the bitten fingernails to pull the folder farther away from me.

I should thank her for her time and stand up and walk out.

But I can't. I'm transfixed by the possibilities the file contains.

I am frantic to know why my mom left me.

If there is something in this file that indicates she didn't intentionally choose drugs over her daughter, that she was forced to inject heroin or harmed in some other way, perhaps I can finally find a bit of peace. Maybe I'll be able to rest at last.

"It's up to you," Detective Garcia says, so softly it's almost a whisper.

My stomach knots as I wrestle with the moral dilemma: Is my stronger fidelity to my young client or to the mother who once loved me?

Is my professional oath more compelling than my loyalty to the family I once had?

Detective Garcia's phone lights up, but she ignores it.

All the other sounds that have been filling my ears—a pair of officers bantering by the coffee machine, a guy shouting something in a hoarse voice in the distance, the sound of a siren wailing—recede.

I have to betray someone.

So I sacrifice Rose.

"The truth is, I think any of them could have done it." I match Detective Garcia's near whisper. "Beth, Ian, Harriet—perhaps Beth and Harriet working together. Even Rose seems like a strong possibility."

Her eyes sharpen. I swear I can feel the hitch in her energy. This revelation doesn't seem to come as a surprise to her.

I've done it. I've stepped over the edge of the precipice.

But Detective Garcia isn't satisfied. I can tell I need to give her more.

"Rose is a troubled girl. The Barclays have walls around her, but I've spoken with her therapist and teachers, and I'm starting to break through them. I can't do my job unless I look into what really happened to Tina, and I've got the access to do it. And when I have a reasonable certainty, you will be the first person I come to."

Detective Garcia nods. She reaches for her cell phone, and I see her scroll down through her contacts.

"Give me your number. I have something to text you."

I recite it and her message lands on my screen. It's a contact card for a man named Samuel Prinze.

"He used to work for the FBI. He knows about troubled kids. Tell him I sent you."

I thank her and she nods. Then she does something that catches me completely off guard.

She stands up.

I'm flooded by the sickening thought that this has all been a trap and she's about to show me out.

Then she says, "Would you mind waiting here? I have to use the bathroom. I'll be back in five minutes."

I nod; I understand the code.

The moment she's out of view, I reach for the folder and open it greedily.

I don't have time to read every page. But I can photograph them. I don't allow myself to react to the words that leap out at me: *Needle marks . . . no ligature marks on neck . . . no defensive wounds . . . Nonverbal girl brought to station . . .*

There's a tox report, and statements by the officers on the scene. I document it all, each click of my phone capturing another piece of evidence.

Then come the photographs.

I swallow hard against the bile rising in my throat and snap picture after picture. My hands are shaking so badly a few of them blur until I steady my forearms against Detective Garcia's desk. I don't let myself think about what I'm seeing; I go on autopilot.

Two drinking glasses with a little light brown liquid in each on the coffee table—*snap.*

My mother's body splayed on the floor—*snap.*

My mother's inner elbow, with old and new needle marks and a dried droplet of blood visible—*snap.*

A close-up of my mother's slack face, her eyes cloudy and unseeing—*snap*.

I finish and close the folder, breathing hard. Panic squeezes me in a vise. I stand up and look around wildly. The two cops by the coffee machine are staring at me now.

I have to get out of here; the walls are collapsing. I stumble on shaky legs back to the reception area, banging my hip against the sharp edge of a table's corner.

I pass Detective Garcia near the entrance. I have no idea what she sees when she looks at me.

She says something, but I can't hear it over the roaring in my head.

I burst outside, gulping in air, blinded by the sharp sunlight.

Then I begin to run.

My heart is going to explode; the contents of my purse are a ticking bomb. My boots pound against sidewalks and through street intersections until some of the adrenaline ebbs from my body. Then I bend over a bush and retch.

When I straighten up, I see I'm not far from the Washington Monument. There's a vendor selling sodas and pretzels and hot dogs a few dozen yards away, and a family—a father, mother, and daughter who looks to be two or three years old—is waiting at the end of the line.

I get in line behind them; I need a bottle of water to rinse my mouth.

I'm shaking and I still haven't caught my breath, but at least I've regained control. Water, home, shower, lunch—I mentally list all the tasks ahead of me, finding comfort in the lack of empty moments.

The mother and father are each holding one of their daughter's hands.

"Swing me!" she yells.

As her parents obey, lifting her off the ground and swaying her a couple of feet forward and back, her delighted little laugh fills my ear.

The mother looks back at me, smiling. "Sorry, she's a maniac."

"Oh, it's great," I tell her.

I look at their linked hands and my mind begins to spin, traveling back in time. It gives me an unexpected gift, one that somehow both shatters and fills my heart. My parents did this with me, too. The long-buried memory is surfacing now, like a silver bubble rising through the depths of dark water. There was a park or field—somewhere with endless green grass—and they each took one of my little hands in theirs and swung me as we walked. I can almost feel the warmth of their palms, and the pure sense of joy I felt.

Tears fill my eyes, and I know they'll overflow before I reach the front of the line.

So I bow my head and turn and walk back toward my car, the sound of the little girl's laughter growing fainter with every step.

CHAPTER FORTY-TWO

I'm on my way home to brush my teeth and grab lunch—something nutritious and comforting, to help steady my body—when Beth calls.

"Stella, I owe you an apology for this morning."

I blink in surprise. Beth had acted as if it was my fault. Now she's taking responsibility. Perhaps she remembered I'm the one who will recommend how much access she has to her daughter following the divorce.

Or maybe Beth is just like Rose: warm one moment, remote the next, and capable of deep anger—which I glimpsed on her face just last night at the dinner table.

"I was wondering if you're free," she continues.

I'm not interested in racing back to the Barclays' this minute. "I'm a little busy now, but I can be there in a couple hours."

"Of course." Beth's tone is conciliatory.

"Will all four of you be there?"

"I don't know Ian's schedule. This is my afternoon with Rose. Harriet will be around. And Ian should be here for dinner. You're welcome to stay, too."

The more time I spend with the Barclays, the quicker I'll finish this job. So even though staying for another dinner is the last thing I want right now, I accept.

I got some valuable information from Harriet last night. Perhaps someone else will slip up tonight.

I head home and take a warm shower, then pull Angela's ziti out of the fridge. Naturally, she gave me a huge portion, so I scoop a quarter of it onto a plate and pop it in the microwave. I sip water and catch up on my emails while Gwen Stefani sings in the background.

First I write to Samuel Prinze, the former FBI agent, telling him Detective Garcia referred me and requesting a meeting. Then I file a brief BIA report on the Barclay case with Judge Cynthia Morton, listing the meetings I've held. Then I print out the documents from my mother's file and staple them together, sliding them into a folder and tucking them in my bag.

When the microwave dings, I bring the ziti to my kitchen island.

I sink heavily onto a stool, my joints aching. I know I'm running myself ragged. Stress, lack of sleep and regular meals, probably a bit of dehydration, too—it isn't a good recipe for peak performance. I make a vow to go to bed early tonight.

I sprinkle some chili flakes onto the savory, delicious-smelling ziti and dig in. The taste is a gateway to the memory of the first time Angela cooked for me.

It happened a month or so after Marco and I moved in together, when he came down with a bad flu. I ran out to the store to pick up juice and NyQuil, and when I returned home, I discovered Angela had commandeered my kitchen.

Homemade chicken noodle soup—even the noodles were scratch— simmered on the stove, and a loaf of bread was rising on my counter. She was grating fresh ginger for some elixir she swore would banish the flu within two days.

I was annoyed. Territorial. This was *my* house. *My* fiancé.

Angela didn't seem to care. My resentment and not-so-subtle comments bounced off her like Teflon.

She left my kitchen immaculate, but I refused to touch her soup or bread on principle.

I inherited the flu a few days later, right when Marco got healthy, as if the illness was a baton he handed off to me.

Marco went back to work, leaving a bottle of orange juice and a box of tissues and some medicine on my nightstand.

I awoke from dozing that first morning to hear someone insistently ringing my doorbell.

When it was clear they weren't going away, I pulled on a robe and headed downstairs.

Angela stood on my doorstep, her arms filled with shopping bags.

"You look terrible," she announced.

She left a couple of hours later, after she'd buttered a warm, crusty slice of fresh bread and heated up a bowl of garlicky soup and delivered it to me on a tray along with her magic elixir.

She was claiming me as one of her own, whether or not I liked it.

It took me a while to get there, but eventually I did like it. I liked it very much.

I put down my fork and reach for my phone. If I ignore Marco's message, it won't be only him I'll lose. I'll lose Angela forever, too.

Texting Marco back isn't the hardest thing I've ever done.

It isn't even the hardest thing I've done today.

I type: I'd love to meet Annie. How's next week look for you guys?

CHAPTER FORTY-THREE

Charles calls as I'm driving back to the Barclays'. He knows me well enough to glean something is wrong by my greeting.

Charles is the only person left in my life I can truly confide in. So I tell him everything—about seeing Detective Garcia, her getting up to go the bathroom, and me photographing the file on my mother.

Almost everything, that is. Because I leave out the part about me trading information on Rose. I don't skip over it because I fear Charles's reaction. Despite his job title, he's one of the least judgmental people I know.

But I don't want to jeopardize his career by making him a party to the knowledge of something legally murky.

"Have you read through your mother's file yet?" Charles's tone is gentle and caring. It's as if he knew I needed him today; like he intuited that he should reach out to me.

"Not yet." I take a deep breath and finish my story, telling him about fleeing the station and getting sick in the bushes.

"Oh, Stella, I am so sorry." Ragged pain threads through his voice; it's a reflection of the emotion I know mine contains. "If you'd like, we can go through the file together. I don't want you to be alone for this."

I briefly close my eyes. "I would love that."

"Then it's settled. The fire will be roaring and I'll open a bottle of something nice. I know this is hard, but it's the right thing, Stella. You deserve to have answers."

"I'll call you as soon as I leave the Barclays'," I promise him.

When I hang up, the heaviness in my body lifts ever so slightly.

As I continue my drive, I pull up information from the files stored in my mind. This morning's encounter makes me want to take a closer look at Beth.

Beth serves on four charity boards, which is as big a commitment as a full-time job. She has no siblings. Beth's mother and father live an hour away in Upperville, Virginia, but aren't involved grandparents.

Beth is a woman devoid of any strong personal connections. I've studied her personal calendar; it was submitted by her lawyer to prove she has ample time to be the sole caregiver of Rose. All of Beth's social events revolve around her charity work.

Perhaps her life once revolved only around Ian. She must have fallen deeply in love with him, given that she broke off her engagement to a blue-blood banker and son of a family friend, blowing everything up to be with Ian. He would have roared into her sterile, well-mannered world, all sex appeal and rugged charm.

Ian described their marriage as a slow drifting apart, like a rowboat whose rope loosens from the dock and rides away on a gentle current.

Today I want to get Beth alone and hear her story of their marriage. I'm curious to compare the two versions and examine the ragged edges that don't overlap.

Because I held back a few pieces of information from Detective Garcia.

I didn't let on that despite Beth and Ian's ugly custody battle, they colluded to deceive me about Beth's supposed fear of glass. It's obvious they created the plastic house to keep potential weapons out of Rose's hands; I can think of no other explanation.

And while this adds even more weight to the dark possibilities swirling around Rose, I can't ignore other scenarios.

Beth and Ian proved they can work together to extinguish messy problems.

Tina was a very messy problem.

And just this morning, Beth engineered my latest parallel with Tina's experience.

It makes me question what else Beth is capable of doing.

★　★　★

When I arrive at the Barclay estate, the now-familiar feeling of dread crashes over me.

The sky is an unbroken swath of cerulean blue, but as I step out of my Jeep, the bite in the wind foretells the barren season ahead, when leaves will wither and creatures will burrow into the earth in a desperate quest for survival.

My old therapist's voice pops into my head, as clear as if she were sitting next to me in the passenger's seat.

You don't give yourself enough credit for how strong you are, Chelsea said to me once.

I'm not that strong, I'd replied as I plucked a tissue from the box beside me and began to shred it.

I disagree.

I'm not sure you're doing your job right. Aren't you supposed to validate everything I say?

She'd smiled, but her tone was serious. *Another child who went through everything you did could have turned out very differently, Stella. Because you survived, you've got the capacity to do tremendous things. You also have a whole lot of trauma we need to process.*

I'd brushed off her words, but she remained dogged in getting her message across. Perhaps she'd already intuited I was one more session away from walking out her door and never coming back.

You're using your pain to propel you to do good in this world, to help other kids. Don't you also deserve help?

I find myself wondering what Chelsea would think if I told her I had obtained the file on my mother. I can't say for sure, but I imagine she would be glad.

I climb the porch steps and ring the doorbell. I wait for nearly a full minute, and am about to ring it again when Beth opens the door.

I take an involuntary step back, my eyes widening.

I can't believe this is the same woman I saw only a few hours ago.

CHAPTER FORTY-FOUR

Beth's skin is drawn and so white it almost looks translucent. Her hair has escaped the neat chignon she wore this morning, with scraggly strands framing her face. She's dressed uncharacteristically sloppily, in a sweatshirt with *Hamilton College* printed in faded letters on the front and a pair of soft-looking black leggings.

"Stella . . . I'm . . . oh, no . . ." She slaps her hand over her mouth and runs down the hall.

I hear water running and then Beth comes into the foyer again.

"Oysters," she croaks. "We had them for lunch, the first time this season . . . they're Rose's favorite. Ian shucked them. A few must have been bad."

Beth leans against the wall, her hands clutching her stomach. There's no way she's faking. Even an Academy Award–winning actress couldn't cause all the color to drain from her face and make herself appear to age a decade in the space of a few hours.

There's another odd detail I register: I'm certain Harriet said Beth studied at Yale. So why is Beth wearing a sweatshirt from another college?

"Is anyone else sick?"

"Ian and Harriet are, too. But Rose seems okay."

An electric charge runs through me. Everyone but Rose got ill from a batch of fresh-shucked oysters in an *R* month, when the mollusks are considered generally safe to eat? It seems statistically improbable.

"I'll spend some time alone with Rose, then," I tell her.

Beth opens her mouth, and I can tell she's about to protest. I don't give her a chance.

"I'm sorry you're all sick. But I've driven out here twice today, and I keep hearing how eager everyone is to wrap up this case. If I don't get some time with Rose, it's going to take me that much longer to write up my report."

Beth squeezes her eyes shut and fights back what appears to be a wave of nausea.

"Fine," she tells me, her voice scratchy. "Harriet's downstairs and Ian is napping on the couch in his office . . . I'll be resting in the family room. If you need anything, call out. One of us will hear you."

The adults are spread out on all three levels of the house. It feels deliberate. Most people, when suffering from an upset stomach, wouldn't choose to rest on an office couch or in a family room with no adjacent bathrooms. The Barclays may be working together, ensuring Rose and I are never too far out of reach.

"Rose is in her bedroom." Beth takes a step forward, as if intending to climb the stairs. She falters, reaching for the wall again to steady herself.

"I know the way. Go get some rest."

I climb the steps, the old wood creaking under my weight. I pass the photographs, still bare in their frames, Rose's steady gaze staring out from each one.

All the doors on the second floor are closed again. I walk to Rose's and gently knock, mindful that Ian is resting only a dozen yards away.

No answer.

I twist the old brass knob and push the door open.

The bed is neatly made, the desk contains its usual tidy objects, and the curtains are pulled back, allowing sunlight to flow through the room.

Rose isn't here. Neither is the doll that looks so much like her. I wonder if Ian got rid of it after Rose pushed it through the attic window.

On top of her bed is a book of poetry by Mary Oliver. It's reading material more suited to an adult, but I have no doubt that Rose understands every nuance—if it actually is Mary Oliver she's reading. I check beneath the jacket, but it isn't concealing a different book.

The next logical place to search for Rose is in the attic. But I don't want to go there immediately. Rose's absence has given me an opportunity.

Beth subtly chastised me for snooping in Rose's room. But now I have an excuse: I'm looking for her.

My intention is that it will take a while to find her.

I close the door, hoping the barrier will provide me a few seconds of warning in case someone approaches. Then I hurry to Rose's jewelry box and slide out the bottom drawer.

All the potential weapons I saw here just days ago—the ice pick and knives and shard of glass—are missing. One of the adult Barclays could have taken them, or Rose could have moved them to a different hiding place after she realized I'd explored her room.

Rose could even be keeping the weapons in her pockets right now.

I walk to the door again and pull it open abruptly. The hall is still empty.

I've already discovered some of Rose's secrets, but this may be my only opportunity to search for Beth's.

I move quietly toward a door and pull it open. It leads to a hall bathroom. I try another door, mentally repeating my cover story in case I'm questioned: *I'm just looking for Rose.*

The lights are off and the heavy raw silk curtains drawn. The decor is done in shades of dove gray and cream, with splashes of sapphire blue in the bed's throw pillows and rug pattern. This room is just like Beth: elegant and restrained, with shadowy parts.

There's a chaise in one corner, an old-fashioned writing desk with a spindly wooden chair, and a long antique bureau topped with framed pictures.

I allot myself sixty seconds to look around; this area is directly above the family room where Beth is now resting. If she hears the floors creaking, she may come investigate.

I hurry into the bathroom and open the medicine cabinet. There's

nothing but over-the-counter drugs—Advil, Neosporin, DayQuil—
and fancy toiletries. The air smells of jasmine and sandalwood, a scent
I recognize from Beth's skin. I trace the source to a tube of Givenchy
lotion in the top drawer of the vanity. For a moment, I wonder where
Beth keeps her perfume.

Then I realize she must have gotten rid of the glass bottles to keep
her daughter from turning them into weapons.

There's a small bottle nestled in the drawer next to the body lotion.
I pick it up and read the label: *Syrup of Ipecac.*

I know exactly what this is; one of the teenage clients I worked for
years ago had a bottle, too. She was suffering from bulimia, and she
bought a bottle at the pharmacy to induce vomiting.

Beth could be keeping it around for the same purpose.

Goose bumps rise on my skin as I consider another possibility. I
found the medicine quickly. If Rose is prone to looking through her
mother's things, she would have, too.

Could Rose have sprinkled a few drops onto the oysters her family
was eating?

I check the bottle. It's open, with about half of its contents used.

I take a quick picture of it and hurry back into the bedroom. I'm
drawn to the photographs on the dresser.

It strikes me immediately: The glass is missing from each frame in
here, too.

I skim the photos: The first one is Rose as an infant, wearing a
long, silky white christening dress that looks like a family heirloom,
her eyes huge in her pale face. Next is Rose on a horse, jumping over
a fence, wearing jodhpurs and a trim black riding jacket, her expression supremely focused. In the middle of the cluster is Rose sitting
upright at the piano, wearing a plaid dress with a lacy collar that looks
even more old-fashioned than her typical garb. She is exhibiting the
rigid, unforgiving posture I glimpsed the other day when I passed by
her as she practiced.

I start to look at the next photograph, of Rose at what looks like
an elementary school graduation ceremony, but something draws my

eye back to the picture of her playing the piano. That photograph is seemingly faded with time.

The piano looks different, too.

I lean in closer.

That's when I realize it isn't Rose at all.

It's Beth.

Beth is a mirror image of her daughter at the same age—not just her features and coloring, but her posture and the angle of her hands above the keyboard. If I hadn't noticed the shape of the piano was different, I might not have spotted the distinction.

I didn't know Beth played the piano. No one has ever mentioned it.

I snap a few photos, then call Rose's name again as insurance in case Beth is creeping up the stairs or Ian is lurking in the hallway.

I've stayed in here longer than a minute. It's time to move on.

I open the door and step out.

My breath catches. Rose's bedroom is wide open. I crane my head and spot her sitting at her desk.

She's staring straight at me.

She knows I've been snooping in her mother's room.

CHAPTER FORTY-FIVE

Perhaps Rose cracked open the door to Beth's room, silently observing me as I explore it. The possibility chills me to my core: Rose slipping inside, creeping a bit closer to me as I studied the photos on the bureau, the rug swallowing the sound of her footsteps behind me.

My mind is whirling, leaping to the worst-case explanation. It's as if I'm being sucked into quicksand, flailing and desperate, every single time I'm in this house. It's impossible for me to think clearly here.

Can Rose sense my fear? I can't see her clearly; she's backlit by the strong sunlight.

I blink rapidly, trying to get rid of the sunspots in my vision.

Rose has caught me off guard too many times. I'm supposed to be the one in charge. But the power dynamic feels like it has shifted in her favor.

I have to tackle this latest issue head-on, before Rose feels as if she's gained the upper hand.

I remind myself to stand tall as I stride into Rose's room. The book of Mary Oliver poetry is spread facedown on her lap. But I have Rose's full attention.

Even without the sun beaming into my eyes, I can't read her expression. I don't know which Rose I'll be meeting today.

Last time I was in her room with her, I squatted down next to her. I wanted to put myself on her level.

Today, that's the last thing I want.

I perch several feet away, sitting on the edge of her bed. Rose is wearing a patterned blue-and-yellow dress with pockets. The folds in the fabric make it impossible to tell whether her pockets are full. I drag my eyes away from them.

"I was looking for you," I tell her. "I thought you might be in your mother's room. Didn't you hear me calling?"

Rose shakes her head, just once.

Still, it's communication.

I hate that I feel grateful for it. It's surreal that this young girl has left me feeling so off-balance and unsure of what she's capable of, especially given that I'm not someone who scares easily. During the course of my work, I've been threatened by more than one parent—I even had to hire a private security company for several months a few years back—and I had one mother jump in my car and drive off when I asked a question she didn't like, leaving me alone in a park at dusk in a sketchy neighborhood without my purse or phone.

Parents act in aggressive ways when they think someone is going to get between them and their kid; it's a feral response.

But this is the first time I've ever felt deeply shaken by a child client.

I look at the slight, oddly formal girl in front of me, and I acknowledge it again: I have no idea what Rose is capable of, or what secrets she holds inside.

But time is against me. So I need to find out.

I walk over to her desk, but I don't watch her face. I keep my eyes on her hands. A cop once told me to do that: If someone pulls out a weapon, you'll see it faster if you're watching their hands.

Rose's hands stay folded on her lap, on top of the facedown book. Her nails are neatly filed, with perfect half-moons at the base.

I reach around her, so close that she could reach up and touch me if she wanted. I grab the whiteboard and blue dry-erase pen, then return to my spot on the bed.

I write: *Do you want to split your time equally between your parents after they divorce? Or is there another arrangement you'd prefer?*

I turn the whiteboard around and hold it up.

I know Rose reads it; I can see her eyes move from left to right.

SARAH PEKKANEN

I extend the board and pen to her.

She doesn't reach for them.

I exhale and print another message directly beneath my first one.

Please answer. Your feelings matter to me.

I hold up the board, giving her ample time to absorb my message; then I offer it to her again.

This time, Rose reaches for it.

I hold my breath as she writes a message of her own. I can't see what it is because of the way she's holding the pad.

Then Rose turns the pad around.

Two words. An eerie echo of her message to me on the restaurant place mat.

GO AWAY.

I reach out, yanking the board away from her, anger flaring in me.

Is she playing with me? Did she do this to Tina, too?

I write six words that I know will spark a reaction in her. I just don't know what kind of reaction. I turn around my pad and watch her face transform as she reads them.

Are you glad Tina went away?

Storms erupt in her eyes.

I can see the emotions roiling her, powerful and turbulent. She's on the verge of losing control. The air between us turns metallic and swollen.

Show me what you're made of, I mentally goad her. *Come at me. Or burst into tears. Tell me your worst secrets. Whatever it is—let me see it.*

She's on the brink. I'm so close to knowing whatever it is she holds deep inside.

Then she pulls herself back.

Rose lifts up her Mary Oliver book, hiding her face from me.

She has turned herself off, as if there's a switch only she can access.

No matter what I say or do, Rose won't look at me again. I plead with her, telling her I need her help in figuring out where she should live, that her opinion is the one that matters most to me. I ask her to take me to meet Sugar and Tabasco. I promise not to ask her any more difficult questions today. I tell her that if she just looks at me, I'll take her to see Lucille and the baby squirrels again.

But she gives me nothing.

It's as if I don't exist.

I wait for what feels like an hour, just sitting on her bed, watching her. At one point I hear a door opening and someone hurrying down the hallway. A moment later a toilet flushes, then the sound of water running through pipes courses through the walls around us. It must be Ian—he's the only other person on this floor—but he doesn't come to check on Rose. Instead, his footsteps sound again, this time less rapidly, as they head back to his office.

Rose doesn't react to any of this. Now and then, she turns a page, the sound a soft whisper in her silent room.

Finally I stand up, completely out of options.

"I'll see you soon," I tell Rose, trying to pretend I have some semblance of control over the situation. But I'm not fooling either of us.

I exit the Barclay house and walk back to my car. I sink into my seat and exhale deeply. Before I turn on the engine, I check my email.

Samuel Prinz has responded, agreeing to my request for a conversation. Judge Morton has written back, too, this time with a request for me. She wants a target date for my report: *Is the end of the week possible?*

I have no idea how to answer her. I am running out of options.

CHAPTER FORTY-SIX

I've never seen a murder room before.

This one is located in the basement of a redbrick rambler in a tidy Silver Spring, Maryland, neighborhood. After my Waze app directed me to turn down this street, I passed a woman pushing a baby in a stroller, a few kids shooting a basketball into a hoop in a driveway, and an old guy in a muscle shirt working on his Chevy.

I'm familiar with this kind of neighborhood; I lived in one when I was young. Working-class families who take pride in the house and yard their hard-earned dollars bought; people who mind their own business yet still look out for one another.

Do any of them know of the horrors contained in this windowless basement?

"I brought a lot of this home with me when I retired," Samuel Prinze tells me.

I came straight here from the Barclays', after Samuel—who told me everyone calls him Sam—said he was free to talk today, and it would be best to do it in person.

Now he leans against the doorframe, arms crossed, watching me take it all in: the old, yellowing newspaper clippings neatly taped to the walls, macabre headlines screaming. Photographs of victims—on a playground, on train tracks, in a bedroom. Mug shots of the perpetrators, the captions revealing their names and ages: A pair of ten-year-old schoolboys who kidnapped and murdered a toddler. A twelve-year-old girl who stabbed her younger brother to death. A fourteen-year-old who killed his mother, then poisoned other family members.

Poison. A vision of Rose taking the syrup of ipecac in Beth's drawer and sprinkling drops into the freshly shucked oysters flits through my mind.

This windowless room is like a tumor deep within the walls of the cozy house Samuel shares with his second wife, where the yeasty aroma of something delicious baking floats through the air and the living room couches are covered in a floral pattern.

I turn away from the wall and face Sam.

He's short statured with close-cropped, receding gray hair, and he still retains the muscular physique of a younger man. Everything about him is tidy: His chinos and blue golf shirt are pressed, his glasses are smudge-free, and his mustache is neatly trimmed.

His workplace is the same: files stacked up in a perfectly straight pile on his desk, a map on the wall with color-coded pins, and index cards covered with clear, blocky handwriting tacked to a bulletin board. There are no extraneous objects here—no jacket slung over the back of his desk chair, no pair of shoes kicked off in the corner, not even a coffee cup half-full of lukewarm liquid.

I think of my own personal tic of not being able to bear leaving dishes in the sink or dirty laundry on the floor, and I get it.

When we're surrounded by danger and uncertainty, it feels important to keep our personal space controlled.

I open my mouth to ask my first question. But the one I'd planned doesn't come out. Instead, I say, "How can you bear looking at this every day?" I gesture not only to the photos of the victims, but to the young killers.

Sam takes a moment to answer. It seems everything he does is considered.

"I don't blame you if you want to look away. But I can't."

His answer is like his workspace: clear and sparse.

Sam gestures that I should take the straight-backed chair in the corner. I do, and he seats himself across from me at his desk chair, wheeling it a bit closer.

He doesn't want pleasantries. He's a cut-to-the-chase guy.

"Everything I'm about to tell you is hypothetical," I begin. "But first I need to ask if you're recording this conversation."

He lifts an eyebrow. "No, I'm not. Are you?"

"No." I shake my head. "Let's say you know of a child who may have violent tendencies."

Sam interrupts. "How violent?"

"Homicidal."

He nods for me to continue, his expression unchanged.

"There's some possible evidence this child could kill—maybe even *has* killed. But you're not certain. Where do you go from there?"

"Does this hypothetical child hurt animals?"

I think of Sugar and Tabasco, and start to shake my head. Then I realize I don't know. When I brought Rose with me to Lucille's, she seemed tender with the squirrels. Of course she knew she was being watched. If she felt the urge to clench her hands tight, squeezing the life out of the fragile little animals she was holding, she wouldn't have shown it to us.

Sam is a man who seems comfortable with silence. He appears to be waiting me out, letting my thought process unspool.

I cast my mind deeper back into that afternoon at Lucille's, bringing the scene into sharper focus. The piece that stood out for me the most was the missing box cutter. Now I examine other moments of our encounter. Rose seemed moved by the different pictures of animals Lucille showed her; the success stories that had come and gone.

But the one she stared at for a particularly long time was a picture of a hawk with an injured wing. The hawk was the only creature in Lucille's album that was badly hurt.

I thought Rose's gaze held compassion. But maybe I projected what I wanted to see.

Perhaps Rose was fascinated by the pain and suffering of this creature. Or, worse, titillated by it.

"I have no evidence she has ever mistreated an animal," I finally say. "But I can't rule it out."

Sam's eyes sharpen beneath his heavy brows at my slip. My hypothetical child now has a pronoun.

I take a breath and look around his murder room again. Even though I sense I can trust Sam, I need to be more careful in my speech.

My eyes are drawn to a brittle-looking newspaper clipping about an eleven-year-old boy who was convicted of first-degree murder for shooting his stepmother in the head while she slept. I lean closer to read the caption. Years later, the child was exonerated. But his life was shattered by what appears to have been a rush to judgment.

The enormity of the responsibility I've undertaken hits me again.

"Two hours a day," Sam tells me, breaking my spiraling thought process. "That's my deal with my wife: I don't stay down here one minute longer. And when I go upstairs, I leave all this behind. I don't want my job to kill another marriage."

I doubt Sam really leaves it behind, but I nod.

"I've spent my career dealing with the same question you must have," he says. "Is evil a natural force in some people, or is it created by man?"

My mouth goes dry. Sam is not a man to be underestimated. He has cut to the crux of the confusing thoughts swirling in my mind.

"What did you conclude?"

He leans forward, steepling his fingertips. "Take two kids who were raised in the same home. They were subject to and witnesses of horrific abuse. Yet they turn out as opposites. One becomes a pattern-breaker and devotes his life to putting away killers. The other remains on the same familiar track, deepening the family legacy of violence and mayhem."

Sam stands up and walks to the far wall of his office. He stands in front of pictures of two boys who look to be about twelve and fourteen, and I realize the example Sam just described to me isn't a hypothetical scenario, either.

I can see it in the faces of the boys: They're both dark-haired and unsmiling. But there's something in the younger one's heavy-lidded eyes that chills me to my bones.

I'm almost unable to pull away my gaze—such is the force of his venomous energy, even through an old photograph.

Then I glance at the older boy and suck in my breath.

I recognize the heavy brows and prominent chin. It's a younger image of the man now standing in front of it—it's Sam as a teenager.

I can tell by Sam's expression he knows I've registered what he shared with me. But he doesn't otherwise acknowledge allowing me to understand such a vital piece of his past.

"I believe evil is a natural force, like a hungry virus, perpetually swirling through the air and seeking places to infiltrate. Most of us bar the door against it." Sam walks back to his chair and sits again. "Others welcome it in."

Sam has lived with a child capable of extreme violence; he told me as much when he called my attention to the picture of his younger brother. And he has spent his entire career trying to counterbalance whatever his brother has already done or will do. He's the opposite side of the coin, the disruptor in his dark family legacy.

I lean forward, eager to soak in whatever he will say next.

"If a child has murdered someone and enjoyed it, he or she will do it again. It's not a question of if. Only when. It could happen in ten years. It could happen tomorrow."

"So there's nothing I can do? I just have to wait and see if the child kills again to know if they're a murderer?"

Sam releases a long exhale. "There is another way to try to find out."

The temperature in the room feels like it has plummeted. I am equal parts desperate and terrified to hear what Sam is about to tell me.

"Think about what triggered the first murder," Sam says softly. The overhead light gleams off his clear glasses, and it's difficult to see his eyes. "A big stressor, perhaps? An enormous life change?"

I think about Tina and Ian's affair, and her secret pregnancy. Rose would have known her world was about to implode if she overheard Tina telling Ashley her plans to reveal the baby's existence to Ian that very night.

"Yes. A huge looming life change could have triggered it."

"If there is another, similar stressor coming up, the child may react in the same way. She may try to get rid of the agent of change."

Tina was the first agent of change—and now she's gone.

Sam's voice grows louder and more urgent. "You've got to pressure this child. That's when people snap. *Make* her snap."

I've spent my career trying to help kids, to ease the pressure and pain they feel.

Now Sam is telling me to do the opposite.

More than that, he's instructing me to set up a scenario in which I position myself as a target. If I do it, I will truly be following the footsteps of Tina during the final weeks of her life.

Because I am the new agent of change.

Above us, a faint beeping sound erupts and is silenced a moment later. There's the clatter of metal that must mean Sam's wife is pulling something out of the oven. Then silence descends again.

"I understand," I tell Sam.

He nods. When he speaks again, I hear a weary, almost despairing edge in his voice. Sam already let me know the toll his work getting into the minds of children who kill has taken on his relationships. But this is the first indication of what his near obsession has cost him; he's a man who has no peace.

"If this is who she is, she will explode under pressure," Sam tells me. "Be very, very careful. Never make the mistake of underestimating her just because she's a child."

CHAPTER FORTY-SEVEN

I drive for miles through the rolling hills of Potomac as my mind sifts through possibilities. I pass farmhouses and gas stations and corn-fields and pumpkin patches. I barely take notice of the natural beauty surrounding me; I'm too focused on running the different scenarios, considering and swapping out elements, whittling down the variables.

Rose is already under intense stress. She no longer goes to school. Her parents are fighting. Her home environment is deeply strained.

But when I issue my report, Rose will face stress and chaos like none she has ever known. She'll be splitting her time between two completely new homes, and she won't get to see either of her parents or her grandmother nearly as much, not to mention her horses. Her whole life will be turned upside down.

If I craft a fake report in such a way to impose maximum stress on Rose and make sure she sees it, it should tip her over the edge.

Sam told me what I need to do. Now I know how to do it.

The reports I write can be anywhere from ten to forty pages, depending on the complexity of the case. I always begin by describing the current custody situation, then detail my observations of the child's health and schooling environment, and finally issue my recommendations.

I use some legal terms in my report, but most of it is written in plain, clear language. My role in the process is fully revealed when my report comes out. In it, I give my unfiltered opinions on how stable, loving, and capable each parent is—and I also detail incidents or con-versations that concern me.

In other words, I pass judgment on parents. And I do it with a lot of muscle behind me.

I start to craft sentences in my mind as I drive: *My strong opinion . . . best interest of the child . . . reintegration into traditional school setting immediately . . . increase therapy to four times per week . . . full custody should be awarded to . . .*

I probably won't see the Barclays for another day or so, since the three adult Barclays are ill—from one kind of food poisoning or another.

I have time to prepare well.

I pass a little vegetable stand and impulsively pull over, my tires kicking up a cloud of brown dirt.

I look through the bins of fall fruits and vegetables, selecting bunches of broccoli and crisp apples and lush leaves of lettuce for a salad. I add a jar of amber honey, thinking Charles might enjoy it with his afternoon tea. When I go to pay the woman running the farm stand, I see buckets of flowers: petunias and roses, big-faced sun-flowers rimmed with gold petals, and groupings of lilies in delicate pinks and oranges.

I reach into a bucket, selecting a bouquet of orange lilies.

"Good choice," the cashier says as she rings me up. "Lilies are my favorite."

"Someone once told me they thrive under difficult conditions."

She nods as she wraps the stems in a sheet of brown paper. "They can withstand heat, cold, they don't need a lot of water to grow . . . That's probably why I like them best."

I pay her and walk back to my car, carefully placing the lilies on the passenger's seat.

I'm going to give them to Charles tonight, along with the bag of farm-fresh food. I'm not sure I've ever told him how much it meant to me when he showed up at my high school graduation with a bouquet of lilies.

I'd only been working for him for a couple of weeks then, rushing to his office as soon as school let out so his receptionist could train me. I was determined to do a great job—the position not only paid well, but it offered health care, two weeks' paid vacation, and sick days. I knew no one else would give a high school senior those kinds of benefits or salary, and I wasn't going to lose this chance. Charles practically had to kick me out of the office at night; I kept finding little things to do that I hoped would make me indispensable, like scanning his files and uploading them to the computer so he could more easily look up his old cases. I even fixed the window by his desk that always stuck, after I asked the shop teacher at school for advice. I found a book that promised to teach me how to type, and I convinced my study hall teacher to let me practice on the library computers. That was my biggest learning curve, but by the time I put on my shiny blue graduation gown and cap, I was proficient at forty-two words per minute.

My uncle was traveling the day of my graduation, and I knew my aunt wouldn't come. I didn't want her to; I'd long ago given up any hope that she would someday soften toward me, or even come to love me. Our intense dislike was mutual by then.

We were called up on stage alphabetically, and even before the *A*s were finished, you could tell who had big families in the audience. Roars would fill the air along with frenzied clapping as beaming students shook the principal's hand and accepted their diplomas.

When it was my turn, I heard a smattering of polite applause. No one chanted my name. There weren't blinding flashes from a dozen cameras.

Then, just as I reached out for my diploma, someone did shout my name, his lone cheer filling the quiet air. I started, then turned toward the audience.

A man in the fourth row was giving me a one-man standing ovation. A huge smile split my face as I recognized Charles. When he caught my eye, he applauded even more loudly. I could see people turning to look at this tall, distinguished man in his dark suit and crisp white shirt.

He waited for me outside the auditorium, his arms filled with orange lilies.

In the card he gave me, he wrote about the tenacity of the flower, and what they endure to bloom.

They remind me of you, Stella.

"I remember that day like it was yesterday," Charles tells me as he fills my goblet, expertly twisting the bottle to avoid drips. He's in his usual wingback chair, and I'm on the living room couch, a tray of olives and hummus and pita bread on the coffee table in front of us. I'd cut up some of the broccoli I brought and added it to the spread, too.

Charles broke out one of his favorite bottles for us tonight, a Cabernet Sauvignon called Silver Ghost. I inhale through my nose before I sip, but I can't pick up the notes of blackberries and violets the wine holds. Still, it tastes delicious and warms my throat and chest.

"Why did you come to my graduation?" I can't believe it has taken me twenty years to pose this question. But when I was a teenager, my trust in people was so broken that Charles's kindness toward me felt as fragile as a bubble, something that could float away and disappear.

Charles sets down his glass and twists to face me directly, his elbows on his knees. His eyes grip mine, and I know he's about to tell me something important.

"When you filled out an application to work for me, you wrote down the phone number of your aunt's house in case I ever needed to get in touch with you."

I nod; this makes sense. I didn't have a cell phone back then, so it would have been the most efficient way to reach me.

"I called once," Charles continued. "I needed to go to court unexpectedly for a client, and I wanted to tell you to take the afternoon off. But you'd already left for school. Your aunt Susan answered the phone."

Even the mention of her name causes me to flinch.

"I asked her to pass along the message. She wasn't aware you had a new job."

I never told my aunt anything. It gave her less ammunition to use against me.

"She asked me why I hired you. It wasn't a kind question, Stella. Not with that tone."

It's the strangest thing, but tears sting my eyes. I thought I was long past caring about anything my aunt did or said, but maybe I'm raw because of what Charles and I are planning to do tonight. I printed out copies of the photographs of the police file on my mother, and my copy of the file is in my shoulder bag by my feet, the very top of the cream-colored manila sticking out. I'm intensely aware of it.

"I asked what she meant, in a tone of my own. But she didn't back off. I'm not going to get into it now, but I ended up hanging up on her in mid-sentence. She wasn't worth my time. Anyway, I knew the day you were graduating because you'd asked to have those hours off work. I figured you deserved to have someone there who cared about you."

Two tears break free and roll down my cheeks, morphing along the way from old pain into new gratitude. I brush them away with my fingertips and take a deep sip of wine while I gather myself.

Charles and I sit together in silence for a moment. Then he asks, "Are you ready to start?"

"Yes." My word comes out as a hoarse croak. I reach for my shoulder bag and pull out the slim manila file that holds fragments of the story of my mother's death. I set it down on the coffee table before us.

I open the cover and stare down at the first page.

CHAPTER FORTY-EIGHT

I'm seven years old, and I'm all alone.

My mother went out earlier tonight, leaving a few lights on and our old television tuned to a staticky game show. She promised she'd be home soon, but she forgot to give me Eskimo kisses before she left. I can hear her going down the hallway, her flip-flops slapping against her heels so rapidly it sounds like she is running away.

I wait for her to remember about the kisses and turn around. But she doesn't.

I check under the bed we share and in the closet of our little one-room efficiency, and no one is hiding. But when it grows dark outside, things look different.

The bedsheets smell sour, and I wish my mother would take them to the laundromat, like we used to do on Saturday mornings, and make them smell like Tide. We haven't been there in months. My mom is always so tired in the morning these days; she asks me to bring her a Coke from the fridge and a frosted Pop-Tart, but even though she used to tell me that sugar would make me hyper, it seems to have the opposite effect on her. She barely moves from the bed to the couch until late afternoon.

I know I should sleep, but noises keep jolting me—the slamming of a door down the hall, a man shouting, a woman rhythmically crying out in what sounds like joy, music from cars that roll by the front of our building, blaring so loudly the walls of the apartment seem to shake.

I stare up at the ceiling with water stains all over it that I try to pretend look like clouds. It grows ink-black outside, and the noises come fewer and farther between, which makes them even more frightening when they do happen. I want to get out of bed and check the little clock on the stove, but I'm too scared to move.

My mom has never stayed out this long before. She doesn't drive because we no longer own a car, so a deer couldn't have jumped in front of her and caused her to crash, like one did to my dad.

But something terrible must've happened. She has never left me alone all night before.

I lie awake for hours, until the sky outside my window turns from black to light gray to blue. Finally I hear a key scraping into the lock. I run into the living room as my mom stumbles inside. Her long hair is tangled, and her makeup is so smudged she looks like she has two black eyes. She's missing a flip-flop, and the sole of that bare foot is covered with filth from the city's streets. Her eyes look strange; it's like she doesn't even see me. Like it didn't matter that she was gone so long.

But she must have seen me because she speaks.

"Could you get me a Coke, baby?"

"Stella?"

Charles's voice rips me out of the past. I take the napkin he passes me and wipe my face.

If a simple notation on a document noting my mother's arrest a few months before her death is enough to plunge me into this terrible memory, what will happen when I examine the photographs of her splayed out on the floor?

I knew my mother had been arrested the night she lost her flip-flop because I heard her telling a friend about the cops who chased her into an alley and caught her. She said she spent the night in a holding cell alongside a few prostitutes.

Now a few of the details from that long-ago night are in front of me in black and white: *Mary Hudson, 40, arrested for possession of heroin.* She was released the next day with a court date scheduled for the following week.

I make a note on my legal pad. I need to get those court records.

If someone bailed out my mother or testified on her behalf—a friend or lover or neighbor—I could try to track them down. Maybe they knew her well enough to give me information about the people who were in my mother's life at that time. They could potentially even lead me to the man who rang our doorbell that final night.

"I can turn to the next page whenever you're ready," Charles tells me.

I'm not ready, my mind cries. *I won't ever be ready.*

I force myself to say, "Go ahead."

The next page is the responding police officers' report, written the morning my mother died. It says paramedics came, which I don't remember. It notes the time of the officers' arrival: 7:06 a.m.

I must have been in the closet for about twelve hours.

I'm able to hold it together as I read the terse report, and I can even get through the autopsy findings by reminding myself it's only words on a page. I note the name of the medical examiner, even though I doubt he'd remember any specific details about a thirty-year-old case. Still, I have to try.

When I take out my phone and bring up the pictures of my mother's body, my stomach bucks and my heart rate explodes. Charles leans forward, and I tilt the screen so he can see them.

"Oh, no, Stella." Anguish fills Charles's voice. Somehow it pulls me back from the brink.

"She didn't—she didn't always look like this," I say haltingly. "She was so pretty. She smiled a lot, and sang to me at bedtime. She used to make me lunches for school and put in a surprise every day: a note or a sticker or a piece of candy."

He shakes his head. "You were so little. It's so damn unfair."

I force myself to look at the pictures again. This is where I need to be my sharpest, to scrutinize the images for clues, even though I'm so dizzy I feel like I'm on the verge of passing out.

I'm the only other person who lived in that apartment. If there's anything unusual in the photographs, I'm the lone person who can identify it.

I don't look at my mother's body. I know that's too much for me to absorb right now. Instead, I take in the other objects in the room, using my fingertips to zoom in on details: The cheap wood coffee table with burn marks and an overflowing ashtray. The ugly couch and big, clunky TV with bunny ears. The brown shag carpet. A memory flash loosens—that carpet always felt a bit stiff and crunchy under my feet.

I study the two glasses on the coffee table, each with an inch or so of watery brown liquid at the bottom. The glasses are close together. Did that mean my mother and her guest were sitting close together, too?

They must have been drinking cheap whisky; my mother couldn't afford anything name-brand. I wonder if the police bothered to fingerprint the glasses.

I can try to track down the responding officers. They may be retired now, but perhaps they'll remember the young, mute girl who opened the apartment door for them, revealing her mother's body on the floor. Maybe there's a bit of information that didn't make it into their report, some seemingly flyaway detail that could unravel the story of what happened that night, now that someone finally cares enough to ask.

"I can't do this anymore now," I whisper to Charles.

I close my eyes and tilt my head back against the couch. Exhaustion descends on me like a powerful wave, pulling me into its undertow. My mind begins to shut down. I feel tears dampening my cheeks, but I can't move.

In the stillness of the night, I hear him whisper, "I'm so sorry, sweetheart."

CHAPTER FORTY-NINE

I wake up the next morning on the couch. Charles has covered me in a soft blue blanket, and there's a pillow tucked beneath my head.

I close my eyes again and lie there, feeling exhausted to my bones. Then I smell fresh coffee.

It gives me the incentive to stand up and shake out the blanket before folding it into a neat rectangle. I hurry upstairs to the guest bathroom and brush my hair and teeth and splash cold water on my face.

A dull throbbing between my temples has me reaching into the medicine cabinet for a bottle of Tylenol. I fill my cupped hands with water, then sip it to wash down two of the white pills.

As I walk downstairs, my stomach growls. I realize I barely ate anything yesterday.

I step into the kitchen in time to see Charles sipping from a mug I gave him, with block letters reading *Let Me Be the Judge of That*. He makes coffee the old-fashioned way; instead of popping pods into a machine, he grinds his own beans. Marco did that, too. It always made our kitchen smell incredible.

"Morning," I say. My voice is husky, so I clear my throat.

"Morning." Charles fills a second mug, adds a splash of oat milk, and hands it to me. He appears to be studying me, as if he is trying to figure out what tone I need from him.

He settles on the correct one. Casual. "How would you like your eggs?"

"Is scrambled in your repertoire?" I joke.

"I think I can manage that."

Sympathy would crush me right now; the only way I can keep functioning is by moving, not feeling.

I scan the kitchen for a task and settle on rinsing and cutting up the strawberries in the clamshell container on the counter as Charles slides two slices of multigrain bread into the toaster.

By the time I've finished with the berries, Charles is turning off the heat below the eggs. He divides them between our plates just as two pieces of browned bread pop up in the toaster.

"You're like a conductor," I tell him. "You timed this all perfectly."

He gives a mock bow, then reaches into the cabinet and pulls out a bottle of multivitamins, shaking two into his hand before passing one to me.

"Do you know a lot of people are deficient in D? I think it's because we avoid sunlight nowadays, which helps our bodies make the vitamin naturally."

That's what we talk about at breakfast: supplements, the weather, and a story in the headlines about a politician who laundered money through his charity.

After a second cup of coffee, we both head out for the day. My grief last night was a rogue wave; it broke over me and churned me around, stealing my breath, making me desperate to claw to the surface. Charles was my buoy.

I know I'm not finished mourning my parents. I may never be. But today I need to move through the present, not the past.

I'm going to go home to write a report that will fill Rose Barclay with fury.

Two hours later, I hit a computer key and watch the pages slide out of my office printer.

There was no way I could ever have made a decision that would have pleased everyone—including Rose. It was far easier to design a false one to inflict maximum stress not just on Rose, but on the whole household. The more pressure that builds in the Barclay home, the better for my twisted purposes.

I clip the pages together, secure them in a manila folder, and write *Barclay* in big block letters near the top with a black Sharpie.

I reach for my shoulder bag and take out the folder containing the documents on my mother, locking it in my top desk drawer. Then I swap the Barclay report into my bag. I tuck a thick paperback book beneath it to prop up the folder until the name just barely clears the edge, visible to anyone who is curious about my belongings.

I need to take care of a few things relating to questions about my mother's death, so I sing along with Miranda Lambert to distract my mind while I write a two-line email to Detective Garcia asking for any documents she can secure related to my mother's court case. Then I google the medical examiner's name. He's still working, and his official email is easy to find, so I craft a brief note to him, too. I can't locate the cops who came to the door of our old apartment, so I write to Detective Garcia again, listing their names and badge numbers and asking if she can track them down.

I don't want to think about what she'll want from me in return for doing all of this.

I've just hit send on my last email when a loud knocking on my front door causes me to lift my head.

I walk downstairs, realizing how vulnerable I am, given the big bay window in the living room is revealing my whereabouts to anyone watching my house.

I almost jump out of my skin when someone bangs against my door again.

"Who is it?" I ask sharply.

"It's me. Lucille."

Relief whooshes through me as I unlock the deadbolt and throw open my door. My favorite neighbor stands on my steps, her kind face creased with worry. Instead of the plate of muffins or handful of fresh mint she usually carries when she stops by to visit, Lucille is holding something else.

A cell phone.

"Come in." I usher her into my living room and get her settled on the couch. The bumpy blue veins on the backs of Lucille's hands look more prominent than usual as she clutches her phone.

"Can I get you some tea?" I offer.

She shakes her head. I'm not imagining it; Lucille looks pale and shaken.

"I got the strangest text message this morning."

My mind flits to scammers who prey on the elderly. I feel a surge of anger. If anyone is trying to mess with Lucille, I'm going to shut them down—fast.

"What did it say?"

"That's the thing. It didn't say anything. It was just a photo."

She holds out the phone to me. I nearly drop it when I see the horrible image on the screen.

It's a dead squirrel, splattered across the road, its body flattened by tires.

"Who sent this to you?" I demand.

Lucille shakes her head. "I don't know." Her distress is palpable. Someone took the thing Lucille loves most—helping injured creatures—and turned it into an ugly weapon against her kind heart.

"Has this person ever contacted you before?"

"Never. This is the first message from that number."

I start to delete it from her screen, then reconsider. "Hang on a second." I race upstairs and grab my cell phone from where it is charging on my desk, then hurry back down and photograph the picture, making sure to capture the phone number that transmitted it. The area code is 240—which links it to Maryland.

"I want to call them," I tell Lucille. "I'll get them talking and let's see if we can pick up any information."

Her forehead wrinkles deepen as she nods.

I enter the digits to call the number back, then hit speakerphone so Lucille can listen in.

A recorded message with a robotic voice comes on the line: "This phone number is not taking calls right now."

Lucille's voice is perplexed. "What does that mean?"

I look up at her, a terrible realization slowly dawning on me.

"What is it, Stella? What's happening?"

Once a client's father got so angry about my recommendation he began calling me, spewing venom into my ear. So I blocked him. But first I researched what kind of message he would get when he tried to call again, and I still remember the precise words.

They are the exact ones we just heard.

"That's a prerecorded message. You get it if someone has blocked your number."

Lucille's hands flutter in the air. "But that doesn't make any sense. The photo was sent to *me*. How would they possibly know *you* might be calling?"

Lucille is a smart woman. I see the realization come into her watery blue eyes a moment later. Emotions play across her face as she spins through the same cycles gripping me: disbelief, anger, fear.

But not shock.

Because I'm pretty sure the reason Lucille came here, directly to me, is because she had an underlying suspicion, one she might not even have been consciously aware of.

Someone would need to know several things in order to facilitate this cruel message: Lucille's phone number. Lucille's caretaking of baby squirrels. My connection to Lucille. And my phone number.

Very few people have my number; it isn't listed. But I always give it out to clients.

Which means the Barclays have it.

But the only member of the Barclay family who knows of my connection to Lucille is Rose.

Ian told me Rose didn't have a phone. But if she has access to a secret one, that could explain not only this message, but also the police's middle-of-the-night arrival at my home, since it's possible to text 9–1–1.

"Do you think that little girl could have done this? How could she get my number to text me?"

I use my phone to google Lucille's name and address. Her phone number pops right up.

I flip my phone around so she can see the screen. "These are the waters kids swim in now. They can find out all kinds of things with a few clicks."

"If it's that little girl . . ." Lucille swallows hard and looks down at her hands. Then she stares up at me and I see something I don't expect. A kind of fierceness.

"She needs help, Stella. Kids don't do this sort of thing unless there is something seriously wrong at home."

I don't challenge Lucille's assertion, even though I'm not sure I believe kids are fully a product of their home life and upbringing.

Instead, I say, "I promise I will do everything I can to get help for her."

"I know you will." Lucille stands up. "I should get back home."

I grab a light jacket out of the closet by my front door so I can accompany her down the street.

Lucille still looks shaken, so I reach for her arm to keep her from falling as she navigates down my steep front steps.

As I do so, a question flits through my brain.

If Rose deliberately pushed Tina to her death—and if she *enjoyed* doing it—then why would she be suffering from traumatic mutism?

A possible answer arrives like a thunderbolt, shaking me to my core.

Unless she isn't.

CHAPTER FIFTY

Fury is more menacing when it glides beneath a seemingly placid sur-face. People who can control their rage, spiraling it out and yanking it back like a whip, are far more unsettling to me than someone who erupts in the heat of the moment.

When a fit of rage sweeps over most of us, our minds don't seem to be guiding us. Only after the fiery heat of the emotion passes do we even seem to register that it gripped us. Depending on the circum-stances, we may feel remorse, embarrassment, or satisfaction.

But when wrath is a choice, and the mind works in sync with the body's physiology, calculating and planning when and where to unleash it?

It's utterly terrifying.

I wonder which kind of rage my fake report will provoke.

It's 2 p.m., a little over twenty-four hours since I last came to the Bar-clay estate. Beth called this morning shortly after I walked Lucille home to let me know everyone had recovered from their food poisoning.

"It's going to be a while before any of us will want to eat seafood again," she'd said.

I couldn't resist coming back with, "Except Rose, of course. Her oysters were fine. It's so strange how everyone got sick except her."

Beth hesitated, as if she was parsing my underlying meaning. I didn't rush to fill the gap with an explanation or soften my comment. I *want* Beth to be unnerved. It isn't just my fake report that will signal a huge shift in tone. I'm going to arrive in a new persona when I visit today, too.

Finally Beth broke the silence, her voice a few degrees chillier. "Yes, well, we'd like to invite you over. I have a board meeting tonight, but everyone will be home today."

When I arrive, I see the *For Sale* sign still by the gate, the smiling face of the Realtor pictured beneath her company logo. As always, the grounds are a gorgeous swath of green rimmed by graceful trees. Fall has begun to tint the leaves in hues of yellow and orange.

The moment Beth opens the door and lets me in, I feel it again. The dark undercurrent beneath the smooth unrippled surface; the thing I can't yet identify.

"You look like you're feeling better." I smile at Beth and don't wait for an invitation to take off my long, light wool coat. "Mind if I hang this in the closet?"

My affect today needs to be strong. The impression I want to convey is that I'm certain of my path, that closure is near.

"Of course. Please, let me." Beth reaches for my coat. While she hangs it up, I take a few steps forward and peer into the living room.

Harriet is sitting on the stiff-looking couch, a needle and thread in hand, mending the pocket of a purple sweater that must belong to Rose, given how small it is.

"Nice to see you, Harriet!" I give her a cheerful wave.

"Stella, I'm so sorry about yesterday." Harriet sets down the sweater and her sewing items and reaches for her cane.

I raise my palm to her. "Don't get up. I'm going to talk to Beth for a few minutes, then I need to see Rose alone."

Harriet seems to instantly pick up on the impression I'm trying to convey—that I'm no longer here as an observer because I've stepped into an authority role.

I don't imagine it; a tangible arc of energy sparks between Harriet and Beth as they glance at each other. Their polite smiles slide away, revealing something underneath I can't quite put my finger on. But I know this for sure: They don't want me alone with Rose.

They've *never* wanted me alone with Rose.

My gaze drifts to the little sweater. Rose is a calm, contained child. I can't see her being careless with her clothes, or leaping around on a jungle gym and accidentally ripping her pocket.

But a sharp item, like a knife, could easily cause a tear if it were tucked into the soft fabric.

Harriet is no longer looking at me. She's staring at my big shoulder bag. The Barclay name is peeking out over the top.

I allow her a long, tantalizing moment to stare at my fake report; then I reach out and touch Beth's forearm. I don't imagine it; she flinches slightly. Does she not like being touched, or is she so on edge that a tiny surprise jolts her?

"Why don't we chat privately in the kitchen, Beth? Then I'd like Rose to show me the horses. I know how important they are to her. After that, Harriet, I'm hoping you and I can talk in your living area. It's important for me to get a sense of Rose's current environment, and I've never seen the lower level of this house."

"Certainly," Harriet replies. "I'll wait here until you're ready."

I don't really want to talk to Beth alone in the kitchen. But everyone in the household has an excuse to go there: a drink of water, a snack, a need to wash one's hands. Just as important, the big plexiglass doors leading from the kitchen to the patio afford a good view of the backyard, so when Rose and I go to look at the horses and I leave my bag on the island, anyone who is interested in monitoring my whereabouts will be able to watch me coming and going.

Whoever is itching to look through my belongings will have an excellent opportunity to do so.

Instead of waiting for Beth to walk to the kitchen, I lead the way there. I set down my bag on the island and give my shoulder a little rub with my opposite hand, as if I'm relieved to be free of the weight of the straps.

Beth is wearing an A-line black skirt and sweater that are so simple and elegant they must have cost a fortune. She has on low heels and a few pieces of understated gold jewelry. I bet she owns only one pair of jeans, and they're tucked away in the back of her closet. She's a lovely woman, but she is so repressed and controlled that she lacks even an ounce of charisma.

"May I offer you anything, Stella?" Beth asks.

Her words are so formal. *She's* so formal, just like her daughter.

Just like her daughter. The words reverberate in my mind, tugging at the corners of my consciousness. The simple phrase has set my synapses firing, alerting me to pay attention to them.

I mentally list the ways Beth and Rose are similar. They look very much alike—so much so that when Beth was a child, she and Rose could've passed for identical twins.

Both play the piano.

They seem old-fashioned. They both come across as aloof at times. Despite growing up in the DC metro area and living here most of her life, Beth doesn't have any close friends.

Neither does Rose.

Beth doesn't even seem to have any good friends from college, which is when many people form lifelong bonds—

My train of thought screeches to a halt.

There's another similarity, one I didn't catalog as significant at first.

Rose left her prestigious school recently.

Is it possible Beth did the same?

I'd assumed Beth transferred from Hamilton College to Yale. But what if it was the opposite?

Most people don't transfer *out* of Yale, the crème de la crème of the Ivy League. So why would Beth leave to go to a non–Ivy League college, if that's what happened?

"Stella, are you all right?" Beth is staring at me.

"Perfectly fine." I smile at her. "And no, I don't need anything to drink. I know how eager you are for me to wrap up my work, and I'm glad to tell you that I've formed my conclusions. I need to submit my report to the court on Friday, so I can't share my recommendations with you, but I did want you to be aware that you'll learn of them soon."

I give that a moment to sink in. I step slightly away from my bag, leaving it on the counter, gaping slightly open.

Beth loses some of the color in her face. She must be terrified of what my report might say.

I move toward my bag again and casually lay my hand on it. And then it happens—Beth's eyes track my movement. I see it in her face, the exact moment she spots the folder with her family's name on top.

I don't give her long to take it in. "I'd like to talk to Ian for a minute before I see Rose. Would you like to go get him, or should I do it?"

Beth swallows. For a moment, I almost feel bad for her. She was pummeled by a violent physical illness yesterday, and now I can see she's mentally overwrought.

Then I remind myself of the sinewy strength in her arms. Beth didn't go to Tina's funeral. Out of anger and embarrassment over Ian and Tina's affair? Or something more sinister?

"I'll . . . Excuse me, I'll go get him. He's in his office."

Beth hurries away, and a few moments later, Ian walks in.

It takes Ian a little longer to notice the file; I have to reach into my purse for a tissue and pretend to sneeze to get him to notice the folder.

But when he sees it, Ian's reaction is the most unsettling of all.

He doesn't blanch, or flinch, or exhibit keen interest. Whatever he feels, it's gliding far below the surface.

CHAPTER FIFTY-ONE

I make sure Rose and I spend a good twenty minutes with the horses. My sham report is several pages long; the Barclays need time to read it. Perhaps one of them will photograph it so they can study my words, letting them sear into their brain.

Rose runs a dandy brush over Tabasco while I watch. Her strokes seem gentle, and the horse appears to enjoy the grooming. I don't attempt to engage Rose in any kind of communication. That's not why I'm here today. I merely lean back against the side of the stall, smelling the slightly sweet scent of bales of hay, listening as Tabasco occasionally exhales noisily through his nostrils.

I know Rose saw my folder before we left the kitchen—her eyes went to my bag as soon as she entered the room. I wonder if that's a sign she was the one who took my pen and Tina's earring. Perhaps Rose's heightened awareness of my belongings is an indicator of her culpability.

When Rose and I make our way back into the kitchen, the room is empty. I immediately look to the blocky island with the cement countertop. My bag is just where I left it.

A rhythmic tapping sound alerts me to Harriet's approach.

"Hello, ladies." Harriet leans on her cane as she pauses in the doorway. "Did you have a nice visit with the mares?"

"It was wonderful," I answer. "Rose gave Tabasco a brushing."

"She's so good with them. Horses bond to people, you know, and those two have chosen Rose."

I don't reply. Instead, I turn to Rose. "I'm going to talk to your grandma for a while downstairs now."

Then something happens I don't anticipate.

Harriet steps deeper into the kitchen and presses a panel. It draws back and reveals the open maw of the elevator. She walks inside, clearly expecting me to follow.

How could I have forgotten about the elevator when I asked to see Harriet's living quarters?

I always take the stairs. Even when it means climbing the six flights to Dr. Markman's office.

Being confined is my Achilles' heel. Claustrophobia took root in me, fast and deep, right after I spent the night in a too-small space while the life ebbed out of my mother only yards away.

"Stella?" Harriet's voice seems to echo in my brain.

I can't let anything distract from all I've set into play. I walk into the elevator so Rose will be alone with my folder.

Harriet presses a button and the door slides shut. The elevator gives a little jerk, then makes a grinding noise as it begins to descend.

It's just one floor down, I remind myself.

But I'm hyperventilating. Sweat forms under my arms and on my face.

"A lot of people get uncomfortable in elevators," Harriet says soothingly. She must see my distress.

My throat is too pinched to answer; I can't get enough air in this small container.

"We're just about there," Harriet tells me. "A few seconds more. Tell me, Stella, have you ever seen a horse up close before?"

Her words infiltrate the cloud of my terror. Somehow Harriet is doing the one thing capable of easing the grip of my panic: She is distracting my mind.

"Yes—a client—had a horse—Pacino."

"How old was that client, Stella?"

Whatever else she has done, and whatever she may be doing now, this one thing is true: In this moment, Harriet is my ally.

My panic is on the verge of tipping into a full-blown attack. Harriet's questions are keeping it hovering behind that line.

"Fourteen," I gasp.

The elevator stops. The door slides open, agonizingly slowly.

I squeeze out the moment the gap is big enough, desperately sucking in air.

"Are you okay?" Harriet is peering at me.

I nod, but it takes a minute for my heart to stop fluttering.

"Sorry about that," I finally say. My legs feel weak, but my mind is now clear again. I resist the urge to sit down. I have to press on. "So this is your place?"

"At least until the house is sold," Harriet replies.

This is not the dark, cramped basement I expected. It's above ground, with lots of windows to let in air and light. Unlike the rest of the house, which is chopped up into dozens of rooms, this space is mostly open, with just a few support beams in place. The floor is covered by a soft gray carpet, and lush plants are grouped by the windows, sunshine spilling over their vivid green leaves. There's a yellow couch, a big recliner with a matching ottoman, and several bookshelves filled with hardback volumes. Nestled in a corner is an artfully designed kitchenette, with a copper teakettle resting on the stove and a bowl of dewy red grapes decorating the counter.

I walk over to the bookshelves. Harriet leans toward mysteries and historical nonfiction.

"Beth knows I love to read, so she got me a subscription to Book of the Month for my birthday," Harriet tells me. "I go through two books a week."

I hear footsteps above us in the kitchen, starting and stopping as someone moves around. Harriet is right; the old bones of this house don't provide a lot of cushioning or soundproofing. You can hear everything down here.

I wish I could see everything, too. Right now, at this very second, someone could be looking through my report, their fury mounting.

Despite the air and space, I'm not comfortable in the basement. It isn't just a remnant of the panic I felt in the elevator. The thick, suppressive current that pervades this house flows down here, too.

When I can't stand to be here for another minute, I thank Harriet for showing me around. She takes the hint and leads me past her bedroom to the spiral staircase that is tucked away in a far corner near a storage room.

"I'll meet you upstairs," she tells me. Then she turns and walks to the elevator.

As she does, I hear something that makes the hair on the back of my neck stand up.

I swear it's a girl's voice saying "Hi!"

I spin around, expecting to see Rose standing behind me. But the space is empty.

"Rose?" I call out, my voice shaking.

Harriet turns around to face me, a puzzled look on her face. "Rose isn't down here, Stella."

I heard Rose say "Hi!" Didn't I?

I keep looking around, expecting to see her pop out from behind a piece of furniture, smiling that same grin she showed me at the Waffle House.

Harriet resumes limping toward the elevator, and I hurry up the spiral staircase, the metal clanging beneath my steps, and find myself in yet another room I haven't seen before. It holds a deep purple velvet couch and matching chairs, with thick curtains covering the windows. It has the feel of an extraneous space, a room that is never actually used. Could Rose have been up here, leaning over the staircase, uttering that one word?

It's possible. Her voice was like the first beep from a smoke detector, impossible to locate with just that single reference point. It could have originated anywhere.

Or it could have been my imagination layering my worst fear onto a different kind of sound.

I keep turning around, scanning my surroundings. Every inch of me feels exposed.

It hits me like a thunderclap: This happened to Tina, **too**.

Eerie voices called to her in this house, too. Ashley told me Tina heard her grandpa saying her name in the night.

I make my way to the kitchen in time to see Harriet stepping off the elevator. No one else is around. My eyes go instantly to my bag. It's exactly where I left it, with the Barclay name still peeking over the top. I reach for it and hook it over my shoulder.

"Please tell everyone I thank them for their time today."

Harriet's eyebrows lift. "Are you leaving already?"

I nod, trying to remember the lines I'd planned. "But this isn't the last time you'll see me. I'll make sure I have the chance to say goodbye to Rose."

Harriet seems to fumble for words. "It's hard to believe this is over."

"Almost," I reply.

Then I walk to the front door and step out onto the porch.

I make my way to my car quickly, feeling the skin-tingling sense that someone is watching me.

No matter what else is going on in this plastic house, I know this for sure: Every single member of the Barclay family has had the opportunity to snoop through my folder.

Someone would have been tempted. Someone would have been desperate to know what I'd written.

Someone is going to erupt.

CHAPTER FIFTY-TWO

SUPERIOR COURT OF MONTGOMERY COUNTY, MD
FAMILY COURT
Domestic Relations Branch

ELIZABETH BARCLAY,	)	
	)	
Plaintiff,	)	Case no. DRB 1014
	)	Judge Cynthia Morton
v.	)	
	)	
IAN BARCLAY,	)	
	)	
Defendant.	)	

BEST INTEREST ATTORNEY'S REPORT

Stella Hudson, Best Interest Attorney (BIA) of the minor child Rose Barclay, hereby submits this report to inform the Court regarding Rose's status and to make recommendations regarding Rose's best interests.

Rose Barclay is a 9-year-old girl who is the only child of her parents, Elizabeth "Beth" Barclay and Ian Barclay. On September 26 of this year, Ms. Barclay filed for divorce and asked the Court to grant her sole legal and physical custody of Rose. Two days later, on September 28, Mr. Barclay filed an answer to the complaint and requested he be granted sole legal and physical custody of Rose.

CUSTODY/VISITATION

After hearing testimony from both parties, who said they were "separated in place" and intended to reside in the same residence in Potomac, Maryland, until this matter is decided, this Honorable Court entered an Order on October 2 of this year, providing that the defendant and complainant each get an equal amount of time with Rose until a final judgment is rendered.

Undersigned counsel was appointed in this matter on October 8. Undersigned counsel was not able to communicate with Rose privately about her feelings on the ongoing custody case, given Rose's diagnosis of traumatic mutism. However, this BIA has had the opportunity to spend time with Rose and to observe her in the presence of both of her parents as well as her paternal grandmother, Harriet Barclay. This BIA has spoken to Mr. and Ms. Barclay, as well as Harriet Barclay, outside of Rose's presence, to further understand the dynamics of this case. Additionally, this BIA has interviewed Rose's therapist and piano and Chinese-language teachers.

This BIA visited with Rose first with her mother present. Rose presents as a traumatized, occasionally angry child who is extremely intelligent but has trouble controlling her emotions. During this BIA's brief initial visit with Rose, she noticed Rose appeared comfortable in the presence of her mother, but did not seem particularly warm or affectionate to Ms. Barclay, which could indicate a fracture in their bonding.

By contrast, Rose appeared to be more engaged with her father during several occasions this BIA witnessed. It was clear Rose likes spending time with her father, which is apparent through her relaxed body language and her frequent smiles when he is present.

The BIA visited Mr. Barclay in his home office for their first interview. Mr. Barclay and undersigned counsel talked for some time while Rose was present in another area of the house. The BIA found Mr. Barclay to be very open as he expressed remorse for his brief affair with the family's nanny, Tina de la Cruz. Mr. Barclay explained he and Ms. Barclay have been essentially separated in place for several years, which is why he sought consensual companionship outside the marriage. Unlike Ms. Barclay, who appeared to consider her words carefully before speaking, Mr. Barclay presented as uncalculating and forthright.

Undersigned counsel was advised Harriet Barclay is home-schooling Rose following Rose's withdrawal from her private school. When this BIA met with Harriet near the garden that she cultivates on the grounds of the family home, Harriet was candid about her viewpoints. Harriet expressed concerns she wanted to make clear to this BIA about Rose's custody. Harriet feels that Ms. Barclay should be granted full custody, with Mr. Barclay getting visitation rights. However, Harriet's rationale for this point of view is that Mr. Barclay cheated on Ms. Barclay and he is therefore "selfish." She acknowledged Mr. Barclay is a good father but appears to be angry with him for "breaking up the family," and therefore it is this BIA's opinion that Harriet's support of Ms. Barclay as the custodial parent is offered more as punishment for her son rather than a true consideration of what would be best for Rose's well-being.

During this BIA's time with Rose, the little girl was unable to communicate her custody wishes, so a determination of the best and most nurturing environment is left to this BIA.

HEALTH

Rose is reportedly in good physical health. Her emotional state is far more fraught. Rose appears to be angry, withdrawn, and even vindictive at times. When this BIA took Rose out to a Waffle House for her favorite meal, Rose knocked a glass of soda into this BIA's lap in a move that appeared deliberate. Although Ms. Barclay told this BIA Rose had been withdrawn from the Rollingwood Primary School because of the stress currently on the family, this BIA learned this was untrue. The principal of Rollingwood told this BIA Rose had been expelled for bringing a knife to school. While this incident could be a manifestation of the anger Rose feels because of the divorce, and is simply an episode of "acting out," this BIA is deeply concerned about Rose's mental health. Although Rose attends therapy once per week, there does not appear to be any other effort to address her emotional issues.

EDUCATION

It is the understanding of this BIA that the Barclays intend for Rose to continue to be homeschooled by Harriet, with supplemental piano and Chinese lessons, for the foreseeable future. However, this BIA believes this is not in the best interest of the minor child. Rose has no interaction with children her age and is missing out on critical social and emotional development due to her sequestration.

RECOMMENDATIONS

Given the information available to the BIA and the interviews with Ms. Barclay, Mr. Barclay, Harriet Barclay, Rose's former school principal, and Rose's therapist, it is clear that Rose is a child who is bonded to her father and greatly enjoys spending time with him. Rose also seems to love her mother. Unfortunately, undersigned counsel is not of the belief it is in Rose's best interest at this time to divide her time between her parents. Ms. Barclay and Mr. Barclay have very different ideas and philosophies on child-rearing, and it is likely that based on these differences, shared legal custody may not be in Rose's best interest in the long term.

This BIA believes the ideal custody schedule would be for Rose to live with her father full-time and for her mother to have visitation with Rose two afternoons per week immediately after school, from 3:30 p.m. to 7:30 p.m. and every Saturday from 9 a.m. to 7 p.m. Rose should also be able to see her horses during those time, presuming her horses remain with her mother.

Rose does not appear to be particularly bonded to her grandmother Harriet Barclay, but given that they currently spend a lot of time together, this BIA recommends that Rose be visited by her grandmother once per week for a duration of no more than two hours.

This BIA also recommends that Rose's individual therapy sessions be increased immediately. Rose has undergone a tremendous deal of stress recently and needs intensive help. This BIA suggests Rose attend therapy four times per week, and would recommend that the therapist provide regular updates to the court and to both parents in case this schedule needs to be increased.

This BIA also recommends that Rose be enrolled in a full-time school as soon as possible, and that the school be one designed for children with special emotional needs. Based on the uncertainty of her living situation and the upheaval from the divorce and death of her nanny, Rose needs to return to an environment where she can broaden her connections to other children and her teachers. Rose should also be closely monitored at school given her history of bringing a knife to school, and her angry outburst at the Waffle House that could have resulted in this BIA being injured. It is this BIA's opinion that Rose desperately needs early and swift intervention, as well as the speediest possible resolution to the custody dispute.

> Respectfully submitted,
> Stella Hudson
> Bar No. MD92871502

CHAPTER FIFTY-THREE

Is someone growing angry, their emotions swirling into a frenzied peak?

They are good at concealing it; they can slip on a mask when necessary.

I've set everything up to tip them over the edge. Now all I have to do is wait and see how they respond.

I can still hear the echo of Rose saying "Hi!" in a faint, faraway voice, but the passage of time is lessening my certainty that it really happened. I was tilted off-kilter, as I am every time I go into the Barclay home. Could it have been something else—a snippet of a video Ian was watching on his phone in the kitchen seeping through the thin floorboards, or a hiss from a radiator, gearing up for the colder weather ahead?

Maybe my mind was playing tricks on me.

I force myself to go to the grocery store to pass some time. I rarely cook, but I like to have the ingredients for smoothies and sandwiches on hand. More critically, I'm nearly out of coffee.

When my phone rings as I'm selecting bananas, I park my cart and snatch it up.

"Stella, are you home?" Detective Garcia asks.

It's a strange question to lead with.

"No, but I'm ten minutes away," I tell her. "Why?"

"I'm in your neighborhood. Thought I could pop by."

I've never given Detective Garcia my address, but I'm sure that's not the only piece of information she has dug up on me.

I start to abandon my cart and walk toward the exit. "I'll see you in a few." Then I spin around and look at the bag of dark-roast beans I just ground, nestled in the baby seat like the precious cargo it is. "Actually, make it fifteen minutes."

"Nice place," Detective Garcia tells me as she follows me into the kitchen. "You live here alone?"

"Why am I pretty sure you already know the answer to that?" I set down my groceries on the counter and take out the big bottle of green juice I use as my smoothie base, putting it on an empty shelf in my refrigerator.

"Isn't it going to be lonely in there all by itself?" Detective Garcia's voice is teasing. She's showing me a side of herself I've never seen. "Your fridge is as bad as mine. At least I buy lettuce and stuff and stick it in the bin until it rots."

"I have lettuce! It's organic, so it probably rots faster." I pull a clamshell container of arugula out of my shopping bag and hold it up like a trophy.

I can't believe how comfortable I am with her in my kitchen; Detective Garcia's presence is washing away the aftereffects of my disturbing visit to the Barclays'. Despite the fact that we met under strange circumstances and I barely know her, joking around with her in my kitchen feels like the most normal thing that has happened to me in a while.

Instead of a dark suit, Detective Garcia is wearing jeans and a red V-neck sweater that looks great against her golden-brown skin. Her hair is down again, long and shining. I've met a lot of cops through work, and I know they always carry their guns, even when they're off duty. But I can't see where Detective Garcia would hide one in her slim-fit jeans, unless it's in an ankle holster.

"You need a better lock on that window," Detective Garcia tells me, gesturing to the one above my sink.

"You think?" I put a new one on myself after Marco moved out.

"All someone needs is a flat-head screwdriver and they can get through in about ninety seconds."

"They'll also need a ladder," I point out. The window is ten feet above ground.

Detective Garcia looks at me—*really* looks at me—and I see intensity burning in her dark eyes. Her playfulness has vanished.

"So you think you're safe because rapists are lazy? None of your neighbors are ever going to leave out a ladder when they're doing lawn work or cleaning the gutters? Spend the damn five bucks and buy a pin for the corner of that window."

All the laughter and ease has been sucked out of the room. There's a beat of silence as the tension peaks, then begins to dissipate.

She closes her eyes briefly, and when she opens them, the intensity is gone.

"I used to work SVU."

That's all she needs to say by way of explanation. SVU handles sexual assault cases.

"I'll buy a pin," I tell her. "I mean it."

I pull the coffee out of my bag and spoon some into the built-in filter of my machine. I take two mugs down from the counter and put one in front of Detective Garcia.

She slides onto a counter stool as I fill the machine's reservoir with filtered water from the tap inside my fridge. I get the sense she's taking in everything in my kitchen—from the sad little plant that looked much better when Marco was its caretaker to the stack of mail I need to go through that's piled in a basket by my toaster.

I also catch her studying me.

A flush rises to my cheeks. I turn around so she doesn't see it, feeling an unaccustomed swooping in my stomach.

It takes me a moment to identify what it is: excitement.

I can't deny it: Detective Garcia is very attractive.

But I've been around beautiful women before. This feels different.

I've never been attracted to women. My emotions have been all over the place recently; this is just the latest manifestation, I tell myself.

By the time the last drop of coffee falls, my cheeks feel cool again. I fill our mugs and sit down on the stool next to hers, swiveling my body so I'm facing her.

"I found your mother's old court files," she tells me.

"That was fast."

She shrugs. "I pulled a few strings. Now you've got me wondering if it's a homicide. I like puzzles."

She came here to show me the court folder. I'm going to find out more about my mother's final months.

"I didn't mean for that to sound insensitive. Hazard of the job." Detective Garcia is peering at me, her forehead creased.

"No, you didn't, it's just hard to remember those times," I assure her. I don't even think about it; I instinctively reach out and touch her hand.

As soon as I feel her skin, an electric jolt travels all the way up my arm.

I jerk my hand back. I have no idea what's going on.

Is she affected, too? I can't tell. She's trained to have a poker face. Maybe she's uncomfortable that I'm sitting so close to her and that I just touched her. She could be uninterested in women romantically. Or she could have someone at home.

Get a grip, I tell myself.

"Do you have the files with you, or are they electronic?" I blurt out to cover my unease.

"I printed the documents." She juts her chin toward her bag.

She must want information from me before she shares them. That's how this works.

"I still don't know if any of the Barclays killed Tina," I begin. "But I'm following some loose threads. Beth Barclay attended both Yale and Hamilton College, but I'm not sure of the order. I'm wondering if there's something in her past that the family covered up, some reason she had to leave Yale. And Harriet, the grandma. She's so tough on Ian. She doesn't think he should get custody. I'm starting to wonder if maybe she thinks Ian pushed Tina, and that's why she wants to keep him away from Rose."

I take a sip of coffee. "But the biggest open box is Rose. There's something about her that's really off—she switches moods so fast."

"Look, that's not why I came here. I mean, I'm glad you told me. But the reason I came is to ask if you really want to be the one to dig into what happened to your mother."

I feel my eyebrows lift. "Who else is there?"

Detective Garcia takes a long drink of coffee, then sets down her mug. "Me."

"I can't ask you to do that."

"You didn't. I offered."

"Why?"

"I saw the look on your face when you ran out of the precinct last time."

She came all the way out to my house to offer to help because she knows it's painful for me? I can't read too much into this. She could have an agenda I'm not even aware of, some sort of quid pro quo I'll discover later.

"And I told you, I like puzzles," Detective Garcia says.

"Thanks. But I think I need to do it." I hesitate. "The stuff you saw—the court records and autopsy report—my mom wasn't always like that. That wasn't the real her."

Detective Garcia nods. She reaches for her bag and pulls out a few folded pieces of paper. "That's all there is."

She drains her mug and stands up. I find myself feeling disappointed. She's leaving, and I don't want her to.

"I can look into that Yale thing for you," she offers.

"That would be great," I tell her.

"Let me know how it goes."

"Yeah, I'm hoping to get more info on the Barclays very soon."

"No, I meant—your mom. You can talk to me about what you find if you want."

I carry our mugs to the sink so I can gather myself before I answer her. As I pass behind her, I smell a trace of light citrus. Maybe her shampoo, or a lingering hint of her perfume.

What's happening is a little disorienting, like being told your eyes are actually gray when you've always thought they were light blue.

But Detective Garcia plays everything cool. I have no idea if her interest is purely professional or if there's something else mixed in. If it is, maybe that's what I'm responding to: her interest in me.

"Thanks," I tell her.

I walk to the front door and open it—I can see her assessing the locks on it as I do—and she steps out. I watch as she walks down the steps. When she reaches the last one, she turns around and gives me a smile.

I've always been a sucker for a nice smile. Hers is a knockout.

When I close the door and go back to the kitchen, I see she left me something on the counter. A business card.

Her work numbers are listed. And next to it, in blue ink, is a handwritten number for her personal cell phone.

CHAPTER FIFTY-FOUR

I know exactly where I need to be when I read the court records on my mother. I'm just ashamed I haven't gone there in so long.

The sun is shining brightly as it drifts down toward the western horizon, but the air is chilly enough that I grab a jacket on my way out the door. I drive along Wisconsin Avenue, crossing from DC into Maryland, and stop at Trader Joe's, where there's always a small selection of plants. I choose one with orange blooms. Orange was my mother's favorite color and my father's favorite fruit. They had a little joke about that—I can almost hear the husky timbre of my father's voice and my mother's higher, crisper one responding—but the precise words of that inside family joke is forever lost to me.

I carefully place the plant on the passenger's side floor mat and continue driving. Tall buildings and packed traffic lanes yield to tracts of land and spread-out houses as the cityscape recedes in my rearview mirror. A few miles deeper into the suburbs, ornate metal gates that remind me of the ones sealing off the Barclay estate signal I've arrived at my destination.

The acres that compose the cemetery are filled with neat rows of headstones. Curving stone pathways wind through the grass, and beneath oak and maple trees are small benches. All the attempts to make the grounds look serene and welcoming can't disguise what this is: a place steeped in sorrow.

I park and reach for the plant, then step out. There doesn't seem to be anyone else around other than a white-haired man in the distance walking along one of the paths, his head bent low.

My mother didn't have a funeral—I'm not sure who would have wanted to come, except me—but my aunt did one good thing: She ensured my mother was buried next to my father. I wonder if my aunt did this because at some point, she actually cared about her sister—maybe when they were both little girls, before my aunt's jealousy and bitterness poisoned her from the inside out.

It's a short walk to my parents' headstones. I find my way easily, even though I haven't been here in years, passing trees that are weeping yellow and red leaves.

I stand in front of the small twin pillars, staring at the words etched on them.

Daniel Stewart Hudson, loving husband and father.

Mary Grace Hudson, loving wife and mother.

My legs feel so weak they're threatening to collapse under me. I sink down onto the grass.

Memories drift through my mind like a series of frames from old videos: My father using a knotted piece of rope to play tug-of-war with Bingo. My mother putting her feet on my dad's lap while she stroked my hair, the three of us cozily snuggled together on the couch. My dad tossing me over his shoulder as he carried me to bed.

Tears stream down my cheeks as I wrap my arms around myself.

Somehow I both fear and crave this solitude. Isolation is a sunken pit always trying to lure me in, promising me the paradox of comforting familiarity and despair.

I reach into my pocket for a tissue and wipe my face and blow my nose. Then I pull the two folded sheets of paper out of my bag.

The story contained in the terse, legal terms begins to take shape as I read.

My mother was arrested late at night with a small amount of heroin in her possession—enough for a single dose. She appeared intoxicated, was verbally belligerent, and tried to flee when two officers approached her. She was arrested and used her one phone call to reach her lawyer. He negotiated her release the next morning.

The name of her lawyer is lightly underlined, like someone took a pencil and skimmed its point beneath his name.

I see the name, but it doesn't register for a second. It feels like my brain is glitching.

Then it slams into my consciousness: Charles Q. Huxley, counsel for the defendant.

My body jerks backward and I drop the pages as my mind struggles to process the familiar name.

Charles.

The world is tipping off its axis; nothing makes sense anymore. I knew Charles was a defense attorney long before he became a judge. But how is it possible that he defended *my mother*?

My vision blurs. The tombstones seem to be swirling around me.

I can't comprehend this. But there's no way it's a mistake. The proof is right there, in black and white. It has been for decades, just waiting for me to discover it.

Charles must have known exactly who I was when we met. The one adult who I thought had never let me down has been lying to me for my entire life.

"No!" I scream a futile protest into the wind.

The unimaginable is now my reality.

I drop my head into my hands as nausea roils through me.

When I lift my head, the sheets of papers I dropped are starting to flutter away on a breeze. I lunge forward and grab them.

Did I imagine this? I stare down at the name again. His name is still there: Charles Q. Huxley. The Q is for Quince. It's a family name.

There can't be two defense lawyers who worked in the DC area during that time with the same unusual name. It's him. My Charles.

My whole body is trembling.

Charles has always represented stability and integrity to me. How could he do this?

I can't wrap my mind around it. Charles knew my mother. He was in her life when I was a little girl, a decade before he came into the restaurant where I worked.

My thoughts splinter in a dozen directions and rearrange themselves, like the colorful shards in a kaleidoscope.

It can't be a coincidence; Charles has a formidable memory. He would have noted the similarities of my last name and the details of my story that lined up with his encounters with my mom. If we'd met by accident, he surely would have told me.

Which means the briefcase of money that brought us together wasn't serendipitous, either. The realization lands like a sucker punch, stealing my breath.

Charles must have planted it for me to find. He wanted an excuse to meet me, to pull me into his life.

It's another huge deception from the man I trusted most.

A sharp caw causes my head to jerk up. A flock of birds is flying overhead, their wings beating, as if they're frantic to get away from something.

My body is in fight-or-flight mode, too; but I force myself to stay. To think.

Because there's something else swirling in the kaleidoscope, a particular shard I need to examine.

The person who came to the door on the night my mother died was a man. He had a very deep voice—like Charles.

Could it have been Charles, the man I consider a second father?

What has he done to my life?

I don't know how long I sit there. My hands and toes grow numb, matching my insides, as the sun sinks deeper into the sky. At some point a woman walks by and says something to me—maybe "Are you okay?"—but I don't answer, and after a brief hesitation she moves on.

A ringing sound finally pulls me into the present moment. My cell phone is jangling. I almost ignore it; then I fumble through my bag and close my fingers around the hard case.

Even before I see his name on the screen, I sense it's Charles.

"I was just checking in to see how you're doing."

"I'm fine."

"I can hear in your voice that you're not. I know this process is painful, Stella."

His gentle tone almost rips away the armor I'm erecting over myself. But I recover quickly.

I'm not going to have this conversation on the phone with Charles.

I want to see his face when I confront him with the information Detective Garcia gave me.

I've met a lot of liars in my life. I thought I was good at sussing them out. But Charles is in a league of his own.

Now I need to do whatever I can to fool him. The element of surprise is the only weapon I have.

"You're right." I exhale. "It's harder than I thought. I could use a drink. Are you free?"

"Absolutely. Would you like to come over or meet somewhere?"

"I'll come to you." I stand up and start walking toward my car. "See you soon."

CHAPTER FIFTY-FIVE

Lies gather force when the stakes rise.

Everyone fibs—by pretending to remember someone's name, or to get out of a dinner invitation—but those untruths are rooted in a desire to spare another's feelings or avoid an awkward moment. They're white lies. Generally harmless.

Here in DC, lies are as ubiquitous as pollen in the spring air. They're spread to undermine someone in power, or to elevate one's own prospects. Sometimes the lies are debunked. Other times they're so ingrained in the public consciousness they might as well be truth.

The most determined liar of all is someone who is fighting for their life. They'll say anything, pretend to be anyone.

The one thing these different types of lies have in common is the end game: They serve a purpose. They benefit the liar.

None of this holds true for people who lie simply for the thrill of lying.

Which type is Charles? I wonder.

He pours a healthy splash of red into a goblet and passes it to me, then serves himself.

My anger is a hot coal burning in my gut. And yet when I notice how old his hands appear—they're bony, with a few brown spots on the back—my heart contracts with something that still feels like love.

Looking into Charles's eyes is impossible.

How could he look into mine for all of these years?

I don't know how to start this conversation. So, I'm a little shocked when Charles does it for me.

"I know you needed a break last night. But I'm wondering if you're ready to go through any papers together now?" he asks.

I nod and set down my wineglass. I haven't taken a single sip. I want my brain to be crystal clear for this conversation.

I reach into my bag and pull out the slightly crumpled sheets from Detective Garcia.

I set them down on the coffee table in front of Charles and wait while he takes his reading glasses out of his breast pocket and smooths out the papers.

What happens next will be one of the pivot points in my life, a moment when everything changes—just like when I first walked into my aunt's house with a suitcase in my hand, or when Marco turned to me, tears in his eyes, and twisted off his wedding band.

The silence in the room crashes down on me as Charles reads.

Just when I think I can't bear the tension any longer, he lifts his head. If I thought he looked old before, now he has aged a decade in the space of minutes.

All my fury and pain funnel into a single word that explodes out of me like a bullet: "Why?"

"Why was I your mother's lawyer?"

I can't believe he's so calm. But maybe he has always known this conversation would come. He's had years to prepare for it, unlike me.

"The most important thing for you to know is that I love you like a daught—"

I cut him off. "Did you know she was my mother all along?"

He nods and I violently recoil.

"How *could* you!"

"Please, Stella, let me explain?"

I want to upend the coffee table and run out of his house. But a bigger part of me is desperate for this to be some sort of complicated misunderstanding that Charles will magically put to right with his words.

So I gesture for him to continue.

He inhales deeply. "I became your mother's lawyer the first time she got arrested for public intoxication. Those charges were dropped. We talked about what she'd—what both of you—had been through. I felt for her. I told her to call me whenever she needed help."

It all sounds so honorable. When did it become twisted and deceptive?

"We became friends. And this is something I never told you, but"—he hesitates and squeezes his eyes shut briefly—"I also used back then."

"You used heroin?" It's a staggering confession; Charles has never hinted at this.

"I never shot up, but I smoked it. I've told you I was a different kind of man back then."

"Were you an addict, too?"

He shakes his head. "I got lucky. It didn't grab hold of me that way. Maybe if I'd kept using, I'd have spiraled, but I only did it a dozen or so times."

A dozen or so times. I probably shouldn't be so stunned; people are capable of all kinds of things. Everyone holds a bit of darkness inside. And clearly I never knew Charles as well as I thought.

"Your mom kept telling me she wanted to turn her life around. But then she'd use again. She called me when she was arrested and held in jail overnight." He gestures to the papers and shakes his head. "She was determined to sober up after that."

I can't believe it's Charles who is revealing the details of my mother's last days. That he was with her, privy to her mindset.

My anger and shock are temporarily snuffed out by my yearning to know.

"Were you there the night she—" My voice is hoarse.

He swallows. "She called me. She was feeling the itch badly.

Something had happened that reminded her of your dad. So yes, I came over the night she died."

Charles reaches into his pocket for a handkerchief and wipes his eyes.

I should be crying, too, but I can't. I feel completely hollow inside.

"I could see the kind of woman she truly was, Stella. The pain was just too big for her; it was consuming her. I tried to talk her through it that night. And then something happened."

I hold my breath.

"I put my arms around her and she leaned into me. I could feel how much she was yearning for someone to hold her. And the truth is, I was yearning for it just as much. Then I tried to kiss her."

Charles's voice breaks. "She told me no. She said she couldn't be with another man, not given how much she still loved your father."

No . . . please. I didn't imagine those words I heard from inside the closet. But they didn't mean what I thought; no one was forcing her to do drugs.

Her protest was a tribute to my father. To the family we once had.

"My pride was hurt. My marriage was— Well, that's no excuse. I stood up and apologized and then I left."

I can barely speak. It's almost like I'm seven again, my throat sealing up around the words I desperately need to voice: "What happened after you left?"

Charles drops his head into his hands. Then he lifts it and looks at me with red-rimmed eyes.

"I've thought about this for more hours than I can count. I represented a fair number of addicts back then, and they were incredibly capable when it came to securing a fix. Even those who were determined to give it up. Some of them kept a bit of drugs around almost as a security blanket when they were trying to get clean, so that the giving up wasn't as terrifying. The cops let me into your old apartment a few days after she died. I found a couple of small bags taped to the back of the toilet. I think she must have used one of them when I left that night."

My mother chose the comfort of heroin as her last act. No one made her do it.

I begin to tremble.

Charles's face collapses into grief. "I blame myself. Maybe it tipped her over the edge when I tried to kiss her—but it wasn't just physical, Stella. Your mother's heart was so beautiful, and she was so vulnerable. I imagined we could be together. I thought I could fall in love with her, help her get clean for good. But she never felt that way about me. I think I made her realize she might never feel that way about anyone again. It was too much for her."

Instead of coming to get me in the closet and holding on to me, she chose the embrace of oblivion.

Charles reaches out to touch my hand. I jerk it away.

"There's more you haven't told me. You set me up with that briefcase."

"Stella, I couldn't save your mom. So I began trying to save you."

My head swims. "What do you mean?"

"I didn't know you were in that closet. I was aware your mother had a child, but I guess I assumed she had some childcare arrangement. *I didn't even think about you.* I can never forgive myself for that. If I'd known you were there . . . But when I found out, I couldn't *stop* thinking about you."

His voice is ragged now, his breath coming faster.

"I tried to watch over you as best as I could."

My voice is tinny, as if it's coming from far away. "I don't understand. How did you watch over me?"

Charles's words rush out, as if he has held them inside for so long they're bursting forth from the accumulated pressure.

"I tried to do little things to make your life better. I arranged for you to go to the grief camp—"

"Wait, that was *you*? I thought it was a neighbor."

"I told the camp to tell you a neighbor nominated you. I did everything anonymously. But sometimes I'd watch you walk home from school so I could lay eyes on you and make sure you looked okay."

I blink rapidly. "You did everything anonymously? What else did you do?"

Then it clicks. I answer before he can. "Those birthday gifts from my school counselor. You arranged that."

Of course he did. What school counselor would spend so much time and money creating a birthday celebration for one particular student unless she was just the proxy for someone else?

Charles nods. "I've been trying to save you for your whole life, Stella."

I bend forward and rest my forehead on my knees. I'm so dizzy I feel like I'm going to pass out.

"That's why I left an old briefcase in the deli. I figured you'd either take the money—most people would have—or it would give me an excuse to get to know you."

My mind is so overloaded it takes me a minute to process what he's really saying. "You set me up. None of this was real."

"No, no, please don't say that. I only wanted to help you, Stella. And as soon as I got to know you, I grew to love you. I swear it."

I lift my head, but I can't bring myself to look at him, so I stare down at my feet.

"Why didn't you tell me? You had so many opportunities . . ."

"I couldn't." His voice is ragged. "At first I told myself you were too young, and then, as time built up, it seemed like I'd missed my chance. I pretended it didn't matter how our lives had come together. I told myself you needed me as much as I needed you. I also thought you weren't ready before now to know more about your mother and how she died. Was I wrong?"

I can't answer him. We sit in silence for another few moments. Finally I force myself to look at him. He is intensely familiar yet completely foreign—like my Charles has been replaced by an identical twin with nearly identical DNA but a different soul.

"I know this is a lot for you. But there's more I need to tell you."

I lift my palm to him. My brain feels battered, as if someone has been shaking me and making it bang around in my skull. It can't absorb anything else.

"Stella—"

Before Charles can continue, my phone rings.

I instinctively glance at it on the coffee table and feel my eyes widen. A scream rises in my throat.

This is impossible.

The name caller ID shows flashing on the screen is *Tina de la Cruz*.

CHAPTER FIFTY-SIX

I answer the phone and hear the kind of rapid, jagged breaths that signal terror.

The hair rises on the back of my neck. "Who is this?" I whisper.

No answer. Just breathing.

Logic asserts itself, taking control: Tina is dead. Her phone went missing the day she died. Someone must have it.

"Pete?" I guess. "Beth?"

More frantic breathing.

"Rose, is this you?"

The line cuts off.

"Who was it?" Charles asks. "What's happening?"

I fight to establish a clear train of thought. Right after I took Rose to Lucille's, I gave her my business card and let her know if someone called and I heard breathing, I would know it was her. I would come right away.

Whatever bomb my report set in the Barclay home must be on the verge of detonating. Is Rose calling me because she's scared of what someone might do? Or is she terrified of what *she* might do?

Of course, this could be a trap. And racing to the Barclays' right now, in my current state of mind, may not be the smartest move.

But there is still a chance Rose is innocent. If she's in danger, I have to save her.

You're the only one who can.

The words Charles spoke to me at the Italian restaurant when he was trying to persuade me to take this case roar back into my mind.

Charles lied to me about so many things. But that one line might be the most important truth he has ever uttered.

"Stella? Is everything okay?"

I look at Charles. His pallor is gray, and when he reaches out a hand to pick up his wineglass, it's shaking so badly the ruby-colored liquid sloshes around in the goblet.

I haven't even begun to sort out the emotions he ignited in me with his decades-long deception. But I can't bring myself to speak harshly to him.

"I think that was Rose," I say.

My phone rings again: *Tina de la Cruz.*

This time when I answer, instead of breathing, I hear slightly muffled voices—as if the person holding the phone is a little distance away from a conversation.

"We can say Rose is sick and can't see anyone."

It's Beth's voice. But who is she talking to?

I listen intently, my body curving around the phone.

"Stella would never believe—"

The rest of Harriet's sentence is obliterated by a clanking noise, as if someone in the Barclay home roughly placed a pan on a stove burner.

"What are we going to do, keep Rose bubble-wrapped for the rest of her life?" Ian's voice is so loud I flinch. He must be closest to the phone—plus, he's yelling. "Hidden away from the world?"

Harriet replies in a placating murmur; I can barely make out the words. "Not for the rest of her life. Just for a little while, just until she's better."

Rose could be anywhere—crouched just outside the kitchen door or even concealed in the elevator.

I miss the first bit of Harriet's next sentence, but I catch the gist of what she's saying: ". . . can't see Dr. Markman if Rose has a chronic illness that keeps her housebound . . . We'll find another therapist who comes to us, someone a bit more low-key." Harriet's voice is clear and calm; she's guiding the conversation. Steering Ian and Beth toward a conclusion. "How can Stella possibly dictate the schooling if Rose has a serious medical condition?"

"I can't believe it's come to this." Beth's voice is so raw and bitter I almost don't recognize it. "So we call off the divorce?"

"In name only," Harriet soothes. "It's the safest course for a little while."

Harriet's voice is louder now, as if the person holding the phone is creeping closer to her. "You and Ian can still live separately. We'll turn the shed into a guesthouse for him as quickly as we can. I'll continue to homeschool Rose for the time being. I'm not sure how much power Stella will have once we cancel the divorce, but it's best to have Rose being chronically ill as a backup."

The Barclays must have all read my report. Now they're forming a counteroffensive.

Are they actually planning to give Rose something to make her too ill to attend school? Or will they just find a physician who will say whatever they tell him to?

A hundred and fifty million dollars can buy just about anything— including the word of a corrupt doctor and therapist. That kind of money can entice the wrong kind of people into becoming puppets.

Rose is cunning. Sophisticated. Brilliant. She could have used Tina's cell phone to summon the police to my place in the middle of the night, and to text the disturbing photograph to Lucille.

But I can't see any way she could have set up this conversation.

Rose wanted me to hear of the adults' plans to make her even more isolated. She needed me to be prepared for Beth and Ian to cancel their divorce.

Rose must have kept Tina's phone, just like she kept her lip gloss.

Do not underestimate her, Samuel Prinze warned me as we stood in his murder room surrounded by pictures of child killers.

"I think we need to start giving Rose a little Valium," Harriet says this as if it's the most natural thing in the word to suggest drugging a little girl. "Just until all this is sorted out. It'll keep her calm and peaceful. And if the court orders any kind of evaluation, Rose won't be able to participate."

"That's crazy," Ian replies.

"She's trying to protect Rose!" Beth snaps. "That's all Harriet has been doing all along! If not for Harriet, things could be very bad for Rose!"

"A small dose," Harriet repeats. "It's perfectly harmless. I've researched it. We can start tonight so that Rose finally gets some sleep—so we can all sleep."

"This is insane." Ian's protest is weaker now. The fight is going out of him; he knows he's outnumbered. I sense he's going to capitulate soon.

The voices grow fainter and more muffled. Rose must be moving away, carrying the phone with her. Then the line cuts off.

Rose is finally trying to reach out to me. And I promised her that if she needed me, I'd be there.

The adults in her life are planning to drug her and keep her apart from the rest of the world.

I think about myself as a child, the isolation and fear that were my constant companions. How will I be able to live with myself if I consign another little girl to that?

I've leapt to my feet and am heading toward the door before my mind registers that I've made a decision.

CHAPTER FIFTY-SEVEN

"Where are you going?" Charles hurries after me.

"That was Rose calling on Tina's old phone. She needs me."

"Will you come back tonight to finish talking?"

I grab my puffer coat from the closet as I reply, "I don't think so, no."

His shoulders slump. Normally I'd hug him goodbye, but my arms refuse to move from my sides.

We stand there for a painful beat; then he reaches for the front door and opens it. "Let's talk again soon" is all he says as I walk out.

I look back at him as I jump into my Jeep. He's still standing in the doorway, his face drawn. I want to leap back out and run to him and tell him we'll be okay, that we'll get through this. But I can't bring myself to do it.

Instead, I turn my face away, toward the road in front of me, and press down on the gas.

At this very moment, Harriet could be handing Rose a pill and a glass of water, telling her it's a new vitamin. I'm about twenty minutes away—more if there's traffic. How long does it take Valium to grip hold of your system? I wonder.

I know a big enough dose could turn Rose into a temporary zombie. It can cause memory loss, intense drowsiness, and muscle weakness.

I'm desperate to call Rose back, but it isn't safe. If the adults are nearby, any noise could alert them to the existence of her secret phone.

My speedometer inches up above the speed limit as my hands grip the steering wheel tightly.

Everything else that has exploded into my world recently—Charles's confession, and the electric link I felt to Detective Garcia—recedes. All I see is Rose, alone in her room in that eerie, heavy house, while the adults conspire about how to seal her away.

I run a yellow light, pass a slow-moving truck, and make an illegal right turn on red, shaving precious minutes off my journey. I reach the gates to the Barclay estate in record time.

They're wide open. Did Rose do this so I'd be able to get in?

Or is someone else expecting me?

I yank my wheel to the right, pulling to the side of the road, and reach for my cell phone. There's no way I'm going into that house without a safety net.

"Stella?" Charles's voice is filled with hope. "I'm so glad you—"

I cut him off. "I can't talk long. But I need you to do something for me. I'm at the Barclays' now and I'm going to see Rose. I'll call you when I'm leaving."

"How long will you be there?"

"An hour at most. But if you don't hear from me, I need you to call this number and tell Detective Garcia what's going on." I recite the cell number from Detective Garcia's card, then tuck it back in my wallet.

"Stella, are you in danger?"

I hesitate, then I remind myself I'm not like Tina, despite the parallels of our experience. My guard is up; no one is going to catch me unaware. "Nothing's going to happen to me," I assure Charles.

"Then why—"

I cut him off again. "I'm sorry, Charles, but I have to go. Talk to you in an hour."

I hang up and resume driving along the paved private road, following the flickering gas hurricane lanterns. It's barely 6:30, but dusk has bruised the sky a dark purple. My pulse quickens when I curve around the path and see the hulking silhouette of the Barclay home looming in the distance.

I back into my usual parking spot, feeling the familiar clenching of my muscles. Blood rushes through my veins, roaring between my ears.

My rational mind can tell me I'm safe. My animal brain wants me out of here.

I step out of my car and walk toward the house.

"Hey!"

I spin around, my heart leaping into my throat. Ian steps out of the shadows next to the garage.

"What are you doing?" Surprise sharpens my tone.

"Um . . . I was just going to ask you that."

Ian wears jeans and a canvas L.L.Bean–style jacket. His posture is unthreatening, and he's holding a small bag by the handle. At first glance, he looks like a guy who's heading out to the local pub. Then I see the dark circles under his eyes, the shirttail hanging out from beneath his coat, and the fatigue dragging down his features.

"I need to see Rose."

Ian rocks back on his heels. "She may be asleep already."

"This early?"

He looks down. "Yeah."

At the sound of the front door opening and quickly closing, we both turn. Beth is hurrying down the front porch stairs, her long camel-colored coat floating out behind her, talking on her cell phone.

". . . tell them not to start without me. I can't—"

She catches sight of me and her eyes widen. "I'll call you back," she says into the phone.

She walks toward Ian and me, a smile stretching across her face, but it looks staged. Beth is far more put together than Ian with her sleekly styled hair and slim black pantsuit beneath her coat, but the tension radiating off her is palpable.

"Stella, what a surprise."

"I need to see Rose. It's important."

Beth glances at Ian. I can't read the unspoken message between them.

"It's a bit late for an unannounced visit, isn't it?"

I'm not in the mood for her passive-aggressiveness.

"It doesn't seem to be too late for you both to be heading out. And isn't Rose's bedtime 8 p.m.?"

Beth's phone begins to ring. She glances down at it, then looks back at me. "Rose doesn't feel well. She went to bed early."

"I won't stay long. I just need to see her so I can add a final assessment to my report, saying she's safe and healthy as of twenty-four hours within my filing. I can wait as long as I need to. Perhaps she'll wake up in a bit. And if not, I can peek in her bedroom and lay eyes on her and we'll be done."

Beth's face tightens. "Give me a moment."

She whirls around and hurries back up the porch steps. What's she going to do? I wonder. Warn Harriet of my arrival and make sure Rose is zonked out, probably.

I look back at Ian. "Are you heading out for the night, too?"

He shrugs. "For a couple hours."

"Where are you going?"

Instead of answering, he lifts up the object in his hand, and I see it's a small, soft-sided cooler.

He smiles sheepishly, like a boy caught doing something naughty. "Sometimes when it gets to be too much around here, I walk to the end of the property and have a few beers. I made a little fire pit there last year. Dragged in the stones, set up a camp chair. It's a nice place to sit and be alone. I can show you if you like. It's about a third of a mile away." He points behind the house.

It feels like an odd invitation. Before I can reply, Beth steps back out onto the porch. Whatever transpired while she was inside appears to have calmed her down. She descends the stairs more slowly than before, then addresses me.

"Rose is asleep, and I'm heading to a board meeting, but Harriet is home. You're welcome to talk to her for a few moments and then peek in on Rose if she doesn't wake up."

It'll be easier to get to Rose with just one gatekeeper instead of three. And if Rose heard the plan about the Valium, maybe she outsmarted everyone and spit it out, or hid it in a pocket. Rose is good at hiding things.

If she knows I'm in the house, maybe Rose will find a way to evade detection, silently slip through the shadowy house, and find me.

I thank Beth and walk toward the house.

For someone who seemed to be in such a hurry, Beth isn't moving. I can feel her and Ian watching me as I climb the porch stairs and knock on the door.

Even though Harriet had advance notice of my arrival, it takes her a full minute to answer.

"Stella, please come in."

Whereas Beth was a little icy and Ian a touch too friendly, Harriet strikes the middle ground. She's neither warm nor aloof. She seems almost businesslike, similar to a busy store clerk conducting a sales transaction.

I look back over my shoulder. Beth and Ian are stock-still. They're cloaked in shadows; I can't see their expressions.

I could still change my mind. I could get to my car and drive off and call Detective Garcia.

But what would happen then? Detective Garcia might show up here, but a phone call with someone breathing on the other end of the line isn't cause for a search warrant. She would leave.

And Rose would know I'd let her down, just like all of the other adults in her world.

That feeling is all too familiar to me right now.

A little girl is alone inside this strange, creepy house, waiting for me to help her.

If she's wrestling with a darkness inside of her—if that's what is truly scaring her—then the fact that she reached out to me may mean she's still within the boundaries of being able to be saved.

And if someone else is scaring her, it's equally important that I save her.

The other possibility—that Rose lured me here for another purpose—is one I can't ignore.

I need to be prepared for anything.

I step forward, into the house.

Harriet closes the door, sealing me inside.

CHAPTER FIFTY-EIGHT

The house is utterly silent.

There's no ambient noise—no piano music, construction clanks, roaring leaf blowers, or creaking of floors as people move about.

I can't hear anything but my pulse thudding between my ears.

"Would you care for some tea?" Harriet offers. She wears a blue sweatsuit, and her short gray curls are brushed back from her face, as if she has been settling in for a relaxing night at home.

There's no way I'm eating or drinking anything one of the Barclays prepares. "I'm fine, thanks. I just need to see Rose."

Harriet nods. "Let's give her another few minutes and see if she wakes up. She may just be taking a nap. If she isn't up soon, I'll bring you to her room."

She's stalling. Trying to delay until the Valium kicks in?

"I need to see her *now*." Maybe Harriet senses I'm going to do whatever it takes to win this power struggle because after a brief hesitation, she nods again.

"Very well."

She gestures toward the stairs. "Would you mind following close behind me? I'm a bit awkward on the stairs since my accident."

"You don't need to come with me. I'd actually prefer to go alone."

Harriet responds quickly, like she was anticipating this: "I promised Beth I'd be present when you interacted with Rose, since this isn't a scheduled visit and Rose isn't feeling well."

Her cane taps as she makes her way to the grand staircase. I stay close behind her, as instructed, as she steps up with her right leg, then turns her left leg sideways and drags her foot up to the first step. She repeats the process, clutching the banister with her right hand and bearing down on her cane with her left.

Halfway up, she pauses. "Just give me a moment to catch my breath."

I don't feel the slightest bit guilty for making her take this trek. Harriet is the one who came up with the idea of drugging Rose.

At the sound of a muffled thump from downstairs, I turn around fast. But my view is limited; I can't see anyone.

My mind scrambles to reassure me: The noise was probably just the restless old house settling, or maybe Ian ducking in to grab a blanket or bag of chips. Plus, I'm still wearing my jacket and my phone is in its pocket. And Charles knows where I am. He'll call the police in about fifty minutes if he doesn't hear from me.

I crane my head, listening hard, but I don't hear anything else.

We continue making slow progress, passing the pictures of Rose staring out at us from glassless frames.

We finally reach the landing, and Harriet limps down the second-floor hallway. All of the doors on this level are closed, as usual, and it's very dim, with just a faint light filtering up from downstairs. It seems cruel to leave a child alone on this dark floor at night. It's as if they've already begun to tuck Rose away from the world.

Harriet pauses at Rose's door and gently knocks, then twists the knob and pushes the door open.

She gestures for me to look inside.

It takes a moment for my eyes to adjust, but when they do, I see Rose is beneath the covers, her hair splayed out on her pillowcase. She appears to be asleep.

I take another step into the room, hoping she knows I'm here and that she'll send me some kind of signal.

"Rose?" I whisper softly.

She doesn't move.

Harriet frowns and puts a finger to her lips. She leans very close to me: "I told you she was sick."

I recoil; the warm breath from her whisper felt like it slipped down my ear canal and wormed into my brain.

I wait for another few moments, but Rose doesn't move. I can't even hear her breathing.

Harriet touches my arm, and I suppress the urge to shake her off. She gestures for me to step into the hallway so she can close the door. I back up, keeping my gaze fixed on Rose.

At the very last second, while the door is only a couple of feet open and closing fast, Rose's eyelids fly open, the whites of her eyes gleaming in the night.

She looks directly at me.

CHAPTER FIFTY-NINE

Harriet doesn't react; I'm pretty sure she didn't notice.

"Now it's time for the journey back down. I'd appreciate it if you would stay close in front of me this time, just in case."

My mind whips through different scenarios: If I tell Harriet I want to take her up on her offer of tea, I can slip upstairs while she's in the kitchen. Or perhaps Rose is plotting on her own; maybe she'll come to me.

"Stella?" Harriet moves closer to me, reaching out like she's going to touch me again.

"That's fine," I say quickly.

Harriet gives me her cane and I step in front of her. She turns to face the banister, holding on to it with both hands. She leads with her right foot, then slides her left foot down to the same step before repeating the process.

We make our slow, laborious way downstairs. By the time we reach the first floor, Harriet is breathing hard.

"Mind if we sit in the living room?" I ask before Harriet can show me to the door. "To be honest, I've had a long day and I need to rest for a moment, too."

Harriet's expression is strained as she settles into a chair by the piano.

I take the hard, formal couch so my back is to a wall, tucking my hand into my pocket to reassure myself my phone is still there.

I need to distract Harriet. Disarm her. Buy time until Rose and I can find a way to each other. So I start talking fast.

"Thank you for taking me upstairs. I know how difficult it was. Now I can file my recommendation with the court. But I was wondering if we could chat for a few moments, just informally."

Beth and Harriet and Ian have hatched a plot to circumvent my report. They'll probably have Ian's work crew here first thing tomorrow, transforming the two-story shed into his new living quarters. Beth will withdraw her divorce petition. And I'll be completely powerless to help Rose, or even ever see her again.

I make a split-second decision to lean into the plot they're hatching. Maybe Harriet will say something I can bring to the judge and use as evidence of what the Barclays are doing. I can't legally record her, but I can be a reputable witness.

"I noticed Beth and Ian seemed to be on much better terms tonight when I saw them outside," I say casually.

Harriet leans forward, her eyes brightening.

"I noticed the same thing. Before they left, I actually heard them laughing in the kitchen."

I raise my eyebrows. "Do you think that's because they know a resolution is coming soon, and they'll be able to proceed with the divorce?"

Harriet shakes her head. "I can't believe I'm saying this, but I actually think it's the opposite. Beth and Ian and I all had a long talk earlier. They've been so caught up in the heat of the moment they lost sight of what's important. Now they're finally putting Rose first."

Anger surges through me; no one in this family is putting Rose first. It's a struggle to keep my face neutral.

"That's wonderful. But—what does that mean for Beth and Ian going forward? Do you actually think a reconciliation is possible?"

A smile spreads across Harriet's face as she nods. "Wouldn't that be wonderful?

"An ugly divorce is so terrible for families," she continues. "Believe me, I went through one myself when Ian was a boy, and it scarred me so deeply I never dated anyone seriously again. I tried to shield Ian from the worst of his father's actions, but he was badly affected. How could he not be when his father was sleeping with our next-door neighbor's wife? That may be why Ian acted out with Tina; he was replicating old patterns he learned from his male role model. Ian is finally beginning to take responsibility for what he did to this family."

She leans closer to me. "So yes, I do think there's a real possibility Ian and Beth may try to reconcile."

A noise comes from overhead. Is it the creak of a door opening? Rose may be creeping out into the hallway. But I can't listen for more clues because Harriet may hear them, too.

I blurt out the first thing that comes to mind: "It might be hard for Beth to trust Ian again, but I think trust can be earned."

"Absolutely." Harriet is beaming now. "I think it's safe to say Ian won't be straying outside of the marriage again, if Beth gives him a second chance. It will take some time, but in the end, they'll both realize how important this family is, and how hard it would be to go through life alone."

I hear what sounds like a footstep overhead. Rose needs to be quieter; she's making too much noise.

I keep babbling. "And of course, you're the one who told me that women don't get burned twice if they know how to look for the clues. What was it you said? When a guy's acting strange about his cell phone . . ."

An electric bolt tears through my body.

I stare at Harriet, feeling my eyes widen as my mind reels back to just a few nights ago, when Harriet swayed on the porch swing and described one of the signs of a cheater.

They're suddenly all jittery and possessive about their phones.

That's the detail that just electrified me, commanding me to pay attention.

Something isn't adding up.

Because Harriet's husband cheated when Ian was a boy—more than thirty years ago. Cell phones weren't common back then. They certainly weren't used for instant messaging and selfie transmissions, like they are today. So why did Harriet reference this particular clue?

Maybe it's something she saw on television or read in a book.

But it didn't sound that way. There was a bitter edge to her tone that felt deeply personal.

"Stella?" Harriet peers at me. "You've gone a bit pale. Would you like some water?"

I nod and try to smile, but it feels as plastic as this house.

Another memory slides into my brain, like a jagged shard fitting into place as I reassemble a shattered vase.

I've never been with a guy who acted strangely around his cell phone in the way Harriet described. But I *know* one who does: Ian. He even told me so.

The very first time I met him, Ian described sitting at the dinner table and asking his daughter if she wanted more green beans as his cell phone buzzed against the table, alerting him to an incoming selfie of Tina in lingerie.

Rose and Beth and Harriet would all have had the opportunity to gauge Ian's reaction when he picked up his phone and glimpsed the picture.

Beth might not have known how to look for the clue.

But Harriet already told me she did. She'd been burned once by her husband, and her family was destroyed. She would have noticed Ian and Beth's slow drifting apart. She'd be on high alert for further signs of trouble.

Even Phillip the piano teacher remarked on how quickly Tina dropped everything to rush to Ian's side. Surely Harriet, with her heightened awareness of these sorts of situations, would have noticed Tina's longing glances at Ian and her eagerness to be with him.

"I could use something to drink myself," Harriet says, reaching for her cane and heaving herself to her feet.

I stand up, too, and slide my hand into my coat pocket again, closing my fingers around my phone.

There's another important element, one I hadn't considered before: Sounds travel between floors in this house.

And Ian and Tina shared their first kiss in the kitchen, directly above Harriet's living space.

My mind is diving into the thick, hard knot at the center of the problem I've been trying to solve, feeling it finally begin to loosen.

If Harriet was aware of Ian's affair with Tina, and if family is so desperately important to her, why wouldn't she have done something to put an end to it?

My mouth dries up as three words float into my mind:

Unless she did.

"Maybe a little Chardonnay instead of water would hit the spot," Harriet says. "Perhaps you'd like some, too, Stella?"

My throat is so dry it's tough to release the words "Sounds good."

Her slow limp to the kitchen will buy me more time to work the knot.

"After you." Harriet is standing by her chair, gesturing for me to lead the way to the kitchen.

The shortest path between me and the kitchen would require me to skirt the inside of the coffee table and pass very close to Harriet.

My instincts are screaming at me not to go anywhere near her.

So I walk to the other end of the coffee table, taking a wide arc around the room, watching Harriet the whole time out of the side of my eye.

Harriet is staring at me. I can't read her expression. But something in her eyes is changing.

"Wine sounds perfect," I say loudly, hoping my voice will carry to Rose and alert her that we're moving to the kitchen.

The shattered pieces are assembling quickly now. I know what to do, just as Charles promised I would.

I need to get Rose out of this house as fast as I can.

I've finally identified the source of the dark energy that permeates this house. I felt it when her whisper snaked deep into my ear like a curl of gray smoke. It's always present because *she* is always present.

It comes from Harriet.

Harriet pretended to be Rose's alibi during the time of Tina's death.

But I think Harriet was actually using Rose as her alibi.

CHAPTER SIXTY

I don't like Harriet walking behind me, out of my line of vision.

At least the tapping of her cane against the floor provides a reference point. I don't release the breath I'm holding until I reach the kitchen and duck to the side of the open doorway.

"Normally I don't drink alcohol unless it's a special occasion, but this feels like one." Harriet's voice enters the room a moment before she does.

"What do you mean?"

"Talking about Ian and Beth's possible reconciliation put me in a festive mood. I'm hoping Beth will withdraw her divorce petition soon."

Harriet's hand is in the pouch of her sweatshirt. She's holding something—a bulky object. A gun?

I glance around the kitchen. There are no butcher blocks of knives. No heavy glass bottle of olive oil on the counter, or big crystal vase of flowers on the island. Nothing I can use to defend myself.

Harriet is still standing between me and the doorway. Her genial mask is peeling away, revealing what lies beneath it: desperation.

She takes a step closer to me. I instinctively back up, keeping about three feet between us. "Oh, Stella. When did you figure it out?"

"Figure what out?"

"Don't pretend. Something changed in the living room. I slipped up, didn't I?"

If Rose is nearby, she needs to hear the truth. She has to know I believe in her. That I finally see what has been going on.

I can't sacrifice her ever again.

So I say it loudly: "I know you killed Tina."

Harriet's eyes fill with what looks like true anguish. "No, no, it was an accident. I didn't even lay a hand on her. But I was there, up in the attic, when she went through the window."

"If you knew Tina's death was an accident, why didn't you just say so?"

She shakes her head. "Who would have believed me? And there were . . . well, extenuating circumstances. I could easily have ended up in prison for the rest of my life. And now it's gotten even messier. I can't let you go to the police and tell them what you know. It won't end well for me. Beth and Ian and Rose will all hate me. I'll lose my family forever."

Harriet takes a forward step, and I match it with another backward one.

"Why did you have to come here tonight, Stella? This was so close to being over."

I've made a terrible mistake; I forgot to keep looking at her hands.

Her right hand rises, pointing a blocky piece of metal that resembles a gun at my chest.

With her left hand, she raises her cane. For a moment, I think she's going to jab me with it. Maybe I can wrest it from her grasp, I think frantically. It'll be hard for her to move around without it.

But Harriet uses the tip of her cane to poke the panel next to me.

It slides open, revealing the elevator.

"I have a special bottle of wine Beth gave me for my birthday. I'd like for us to drink it tonight."

Bile rises in my throat. I can't go in that tiny space again.

I shake my head. "No."

Rose must be aware that Harriet was absent during the minutes surrounding Tina's fall. That was why her leg desperately tapped at the dinner table.

But I failed my young client. I didn't heed her wordless clue.

"What is that thing?" I'm stalling, desperate to stay out of the tiny, claustrophobia-inducing place.

"Did you know you can buy Tasers online and have them shipped to you?"

Pete told me Tina wanted to buy one. Perhaps that's how Harriet got the idea.

"I'll give you to the count of three and then I'm going to fire this thing. I watched some videos on what happens. You may lose control of your bladder. You'll probably collapse. Then I'll drag you into the elevator. But please don't make me do it."

If I do as Harriet says, we'll be tucked together in a confined space. Maybe I can turn my worst fear into an advantage. I could lunge at her, wrestling the Taser out of her grasp. Or I could kick her bad knee.

"One."

I'm wearing my light puffer jacket. It's unzipped, leaving my chest exposed, but if I use it like a shield, it might dull the effects of the Taser even if Harriet gets off a shot at me.

Rose is waiting for me to help her. If I don't come through for her, she'll be consigned to a life under Harriet's reign.

"Two."

I take a step toward the elevator. The moment Harriet crosses the threshold after me, I'm going to spin around and fight.

I step into the elevator. The walls seem to buckle as my vision blurs. I dig my nails into my palms as hard as I can, the sharp burst of pain briefly distracting my brain.

I take one more step, feeling my legs weaken as terror saps my body's strength.

A low roaring noise fills my ears, signaling a panic attack is imminent.

I force myself to listen for the tap of Harriet's cane to alert me to her whereabouts. Once she's inside, I'll whip around.

I hear the tapping.

I start to spin around. Then a tremendous shock explodes, seeming to originate inside my body. My legs give out. I can't move or think. I can't even breathe.

CHAPTER SIXTY-ONE

"Stella?" Harriet's voice sounds like it is coming from far away.

My ears are ringing and my muscles feel like jelly.

But the dominant thought in my mind is clear: I have to find a way to save Rose.

From the very first day I glimpsed her on a busy street corner, my deepest fear was that she'd desperately need me, and I'd fail her.

You're the only one who can help her.

My senses reignite. I become aware of the hard elevator floor beneath my cheek. I smell chemical traces of cleaning products the housekeeper must have mopped in here. The sharp ammonia scent clears some of the dullness from my mind.

I don't know why Harriet is taking me into the basement, but it isn't to retrieve a bottle of wine.

A grinding noise signals the elevator door is sliding shut. We're beginning our descent into the bowels of the house.

"Are you awake?" Harriet's voice is very close now. She's in the elevator, looming above me. "I saw you turning around and I had to zap you. I know it hurt."

I keep my eyes shut, knowing the element of surprise is the only thing I have going for me.

The elevator lurches as we begin to sink down.

My insides no longer feel like they're convulsing. But I'm not strong enough to fight yet.

Charles won't summon the police for at least thirty or forty minutes. He may be too late.

But Rose has Tina's phone. She could text 9–1–1. Perhaps Rose can use her whiteboard to write a message to the police when they come to the door. My car is still outside, evidence I'm in the house. Maybe Rose was listening from a hiding spot and has *already* summoned the police.

All I need to do is stay alive until someone gets here—or until I can get Rose out.

I feel a jab on my thigh. Harriet is poking me with the tip of her cane.

"If I have to drag you out of here, I'm going to need to zap you again to make sure you're really unconscious," Harriet warns me.

She jabs me again, harder.

But now I'm ready for it.

My eyes fly open as my hands spring up and I grab the end of the cane.

I don't try to wrestle it away from Harriet. She'd expect that. Instead, I yank the cane toward me, then suddenly reverse my arm's motion and thrust the cane backward and up, as hard as I can. The curved handle smashes into the middle of Harriet's face.

Blood spurts from her nose as she staggers back, leaning against the wall of the elevator. She releases her grip on the cane and puts a hand to her face, but she keeps hold of the Taser.

The pain must be explosive; her eyes are probably watering. With any luck her vision is temporarily compromised.

She begins to lift the Taser and point it at me just as the panel door slides open.

She's probably expecting me to leap to my feet and run. Instead, I crawl.

I scuttle out on my hands and knees, moving as fast as I can, still holding on to Harriet's cane.

By the time I'm a dozen yards away from the elevator, my legs feel steady enough to carry my weight. I run to the spiral staircase tucked past the storage room and grip the thin metal banister as I begin to climb.

I don't hear anything behind me. Harriet is likely taking the elevator back up to the main level, or maybe she's checking to see if I'm hiding in her living room or bedroom. She'll have to move more slowly than usual until she finds a makeshift cane. Rose and I might have time to get to my car before Harriet reaches the front hallway.

My lungs still haven't recovered from the volt of electricity; they feel as if they're being shredded as I force myself to move faster, hauling myself to the top of the stairs. I cut through the strange, sterile room with the purple couch and heavy curtains, then head toward the main hallway.

"Rose!" I yell. My voice is thready, but for once, this old house is my ally. Noise travels through its thin floors; she should be able to hear me. "Hurry! Run to the front door! We need to get out of here!"

I reach into my pocket for my phone as I wait for her to run to me.

But there's no response.

And my phone is missing.

Harriet must have grabbed it when I passed out.

"Rose!" I scream again, my voice echoing in the stillness.

Nothing.

If Rose won't come to me, I'll have to find her. I hurry to the staircase and grab the banister, heaving myself up the steps as fast as I can. I reach the landing and turn toward Rose's bedroom.

Her door is closed. I fling it open.

At first I don't see her; the room is too dark. Then I spot her sitting in her chair in the corner, rocking back and forth, her arms wrapped around her knees. She's wearing a thin white nightgown and her feet are bare.

If I'd seen her like this two days ago, I'd have thought she looked creepy.

Now all I see is a terrified little girl.

I run to her and kneel down on the rug, looking up at her.

"Rose, I know Harriet is doing bad things. I'm so sorry I didn't figure it out before. But I need you to trust me now. We're going to get your parents and go to the police."

Rose is completely still for a breath and I fear I'm too late, that she has retreated so far inside herself she can't come back out.

Her expression is wooden. I misinterpreted that look before. I thought it meant Rose was deliberately pulling down a shield. Now I know it means she's shutting down because she feels too much.

Then her lashes flutter and she seems to see me for the first time.

What comes into her eyes breaks my heart.

It's hope.

Of all the sides of Rose I've seen, I've never once glimpsed her looking hopeful.

I grab her hand. "Come on!"

We run into the hallway and head for the stairs. Just before I reach the top step, I lean over the banister to see if Harriet is coming. All the breath whooshes out of my lungs.

Harriet is hurrying around the corner of the landing, her Taser in hand.

I can't believe what I'm seeing.

She's practically *running.*

Harriet clearly doesn't need a cane. She has been faking all along. Which means she has been able to move around the house swiftly and quietly whenever she wants.

Harriet climbs the first step, using her supposedly bad leg. Her nose is still bleeding, leaving a trail of tiny red splatters in the hallway.

"This way!" I hiss at Rose, still holding her hand as we run toward the other end of the hallway. I pause halfway there and close the door to Rose's bedroom as quietly as I can, hoping Harriet will search that space first and buy us time. Then I yank open the door leading to the stairs up to Tina's old room.

"Do you have a hiding place up here?" I whisper to Rose as we begin to tiptoe up the steps.

She nods.

"I want you to get in there and wait until you hear your mother or father or me calling for you. Don't come out for anyone else, okay?"

She nods again.

Her hand feels so soft and tiny in mine. I don't know why or how things changed between us, but she trusts me now.

"Show me your hiding place," I whisper when we reach Tina's old quarters.

Rose walks a few feet away from me and presses the wall. A built-in door pops open, revealing a space the size of a tiny closet. I never noticed it before because there are no hinges or knob on the outside. On the floor is a phone in a shimmering pink case with a picture of Tina blowing a kiss as a screensaver. My heart leaps at the sight of it; Rose can summon help.

I hear a slamming sound right below us. Harriet is searching for us. She'll be here soon.

I bend down and look Rose in the eye. "I know Harriet was in the attic when Tina died. You have to tell your parents. They'll believe you. They'll keep Harriet away from you."

As soon as I say it, I realize it may not be true. Harriet has already planted doubt in Ian's and Beth's minds, convincing them their daughter could be disturbed. Harriet will spin whatever Rose says as further evidence Rose is unhinged.

"No matter what you hear, don't come out until your mom or dad or I call for you, okay?"

Rose's eyes are huge as she looks up at me and nods.

There's another slamming sound, closer this time. Harriet is coming.

"Make sure Tina's phone is on silent mode, then use it to text 9–1–1. Tell them everything Harriet did. And write it down for Dr. Markman, too. Make sure you find a way to tell her. Send her a letter if you have to."

I hear the door to the attic creak open. I've only got a few seconds.

"Don't make a noise." I close the door, making Rose disappear.

Nausea fills my throat. A child is sealed in a closet, hidden away—

just like I was so many years ago. And when I stepped back out, the whole world was upside down.

"Stella? I know you're up here."

Harriet is almost upon me.

If I fail in my effort to protect Rose—if she steps out of the closet to find me on the floor, immobilized by the Taser, or, worse yet, gone forever—Harriet will rule her life. She'll keep Rose away from anyone who would believe or help her.

The sustained trauma may be too great for Rose to endure.

I've got nothing but a wooden cane, while Harriet is armed with a Taser.

I slip across the room so I'm standing as far away from the secret closet as possible. I don't want Harriet to see the thin seam outlining the door or hear any sound Rose inadvertently makes. I zip up my coat as a final layer of protection.

Harriet appears at the top of the stairs, blood streaking the lower half of her face and her powder-blue top.

"There you are!" she cries.

CHAPTER SIXTY-TWO

The symmetrical pattern of Harriet's footsteps sounds alien. There's no tapping of her cane to signal her arrival.

The enormity of her subterfuge is staggering. Harriet faked an injury for years. What was her endgame?

I grip the wooden cane, testing its weight.

"Beth and Ian will see your blood!" I blurt. "You won't be able to clean everything up. They'll know something happened here."

Harriet grimaces. "Why did you have to hit me? You're making it worse for Rose."

"If you touch her—"

"I would never!" Harriet sounds almost indignant. "She's my granddaughter. I think what happened is she threw her book across the room when I told her she needed to stop reading and go to sleep. She didn't mean to hit me in the face with it."

Harriet is twisting and shaping the narrative, manipulating Ian and Beth into fearing the worst about their daughter. She made me fear it, too.

"Where is Rose?" Harriet asks. "She's not in her room. Is she hiding up here?"

"I have no idea."

"I'll find her." Harriet shrugs.

"Why did you pretend to have a limp?" I blurt, hoping to give Rose time to follow my instructions and text the police.

"Have you ever worked a blue-collar job, Stella? Do you know how soul-killing it is to scrub someone else's filthy bathroom and lug a heavy vacuum cleaner up and down the stairs all day, then come home to a lonely dinner in front of the TV? When I had knee surgery and Beth invited me to move in during my recovery, it was like stepping into a dream. Fresh-squeezed orange juice and coffee delivered to me on a tray by the housekeeper every morning. The gardens, the horses, the views. And best of all, the family dinners."

Her voice takes on a yearning quality. "At night Rose would play the piano while the chef whipped up something delicious, and then we'd all sit around the table together. I'd been alone since Ian's father left. I didn't know how worn-out and lonely I was until I came here. And I knew when I recovered from surgery, Beth would send me back to my apartment. So I just . . . didn't recover."

Harriet takes another step forward. My back is pressed against the wall. There's nowhere to run.

"You knew Ian and Tina were having an affair." I shout this so Rose can hear every word. "You were furious Tina was trying to break up Ian and Beth's marriage because if they got divorced, you'd go back to having nothing! You pushed Tina out that window!"

I want Rose to know that even if her grandmother has tried to convince Rose her reality is false, I see the truth.

"That's where you're wrong," Harriet tells me. "I didn't know Tina was home. She'd said she was going out. I snuck up to her room to do something else, and I heard her on the phone telling her friend she was pregnant. But I already told you I didn't lay a hand on her."

Harriet adjusts the angle of her Taser, aiming it at my chest. "I need you to walk downstairs. I'll be right behind you."

"How can you do this to your granddaughter?" I yell. "You used her to deflect suspicion away from you!"

Harriet's voice breaks as she says, "I know this is a tough time for Rose. I feel terribly about that. But once this is all over, she'll go back to school and she won't need any more medicine. Can't you see why I had to do it? A few short months of Rose's life being upended, versus me spending the rest of my years in a jail cell because of an accident.

It wasn't supposed to get this complicated, Stella. We'd almost made it through."

Behind Harriet, the closet door silently glides open.

"What you did to Rose is unforgivable," I fire back at Harriet.

"I didn't mean for any of this to happen! I was only trying to make Tina quit!" Tears fill Harriet's eyes. Her voice quavers. "No one was supposed to die! I'm doing everything I can to keep this family to-gether!"

Rose is creeping up behind Harriet, her bare feet silent against the rug.

"What are you going to do to me?" I shout, trying to cover any noise Rose might make. *Run downstairs!* I silently urge her.

"I can't let you go. Maybe you had a terrible accident while you were here. Beth and Ian could come home to find you on the grounds."

My blood runs cold. "Beth and Ian would never believe it was an accident."

"Yes, they would. And they'll help cover it up if they think Rose inadvertently caused it. They're fiercely loving parents, Stella, and they will do anything to protect their daughter. Once you're out of the pic-ture, we can continue on as a family. Rose will be fine, I won't go to jail, and after a little while, everything will go back to the way it was."

Get away, Rose! I want to scream it, but I can't.

I can no longer help her. I am completely powerless to do any-thing.

But Rose isn't.

In the next moment, she transforms. Her eyes blaze, and her small, thin body vibrates with palpable rage as she begins to run. She stretches out both arms in front of her and slams into Harriet, pushing in a furious, desperate gesture—exactly the way I used to imagine she pushed Tina through the third-story window.

Harriet stumbles forward, falling heavily to her knees.

The Taser's needlelike prongs shoot past me as the weapon slips out of her hands.

I've got a split second to decide: I can dive for the Taser, but Harriet might reach it first. Or I can get to Rose.

It's not even a choice. I run toward Rose, still holding the cane, yelling, "Downstairs!"

As we scramble to the second level, I gasp out, "Your dad is back by the edge of the property. Look for his bonfire when we get outside!"

If the Taser slams into my back, I'll go down, but at least Rose will have a chance. I've got on my jacket and Rose is wearing only a thin nightgown; I can't let her get hit. She might not survive it.

We've just made it to the dark, shadowy second-floor hallway when I hear Harriet thundering down the attic stairs.

We sprint down the hallway and arc around to the next staircase. I stumble on the first step but catch myself before I crash into Rose.

When we reach the bottom step, I grab Rose's shoulders and steer her toward the kitchen. Ian is only a third of a mile or so away. All we need is a few minutes to make it to him.

We sprint through the kitchen, past the trail of blood coming from the elevator.

I waste precious seconds unlocking the back door as I hear Harriet's heavy footsteps enter the kitchen. It feels like she's almost upon us, the dark current she carries wrapping around us and trying to suck us back into her grasp, when the latch yields and we burst through the door, leaving it open behind us.

The cold, crisp air hits my face like a slap. Rose is like a ghost just ahead of me, flying across the patio in her white nightgown. She crosses the spot belonging to another ghost—the place where Tina's broken body once lay.

Rose must have known what happened all along.

Even if Rose was in the barn when Harriet snuck inside and pushed Tina, she would have heard Tina land on the patio. She must have seen Harriet coming from *inside* the house.

Rose has been living inside a nightmare.

My lungs are aching; it's hard to take deep breaths. I keep expecting to feel an electric surge zapping the back of my head; I try to avoid moving in a straight line so I won't be hit.

The crescent moon provides dim light, but Rose's nightgown stands out like a plume of white smoke. Harriet could use it to track us. I search for cover: The raised vegetable beds are too low, but there are big trees a bit farther back as well as full, leafy bushes.

We're much faster than Harriet. We're going to get away.

Then Rose crumples, as abruptly as if someone swept out her legs from beneath her.

I skid to a stop and bend down and see her holding her foot, silent tears streaming down her face. The end of a small twig is buried in her skin, just beneath her toes.

I don't try to pull it out. I just scoop Rose up and feel her arms wrap around my neck. Her cheeks are wet with silent tears.

"I've got you, Rose," I whisper as she leans her head against my shoulder.

My jacket and pants are black, and my hair is dark. Harriet probably can't see me, and now that I'm blocking Rose's nightgown, she'll have to track us by sound alone.

But I'm losing ground. My legs feel heavy and uncoordinated, as if I'm struggling through quicksand. The weight of the child in my arms, my lack of familiarity with the grounds, my limited vision in the darkness—it's all slowing me down.

I hear a crashing sound behind me. Is Harriet getting closer?

"Help!" I scream, hoping the sound carries to Ian.

I stumble on a big rock, nearly falling and dropping Rose. The sickening realization hits me: Harriet may reach us before I reach Ian.

A bit ahead and to my right is a full, squat bush. I veer toward it as quietly as I can and duck behind it, dropping Rose beneath it. "Stay here," I whisper. "I'll come back for you."

I sprint away from the bush, not worrying about staying quiet now. I want to make noise to keep Harriet's attention on me.

I look back and spot Harriet a dozen or so yards behind me. I scream for Ian again, then see what I've been looking for: a thick-trunked tree in the distance.

I don't know if Ian heard me, or how far away he is. He might not even be at the bonfire anymore; he could have changed his mind and gone to a bar.

I can't catch my breath; my lungs are on fire. I dart past the tree, then double back and tuck myself behind it, gasping.

I hear Harriet coming toward me, branches snapping beneath her shoes, her breathing loud and strained.

I lift up the cane like a baseball bat and hold my breath, my lungs struggling for air. I can't give away my location.

My heart frantically pounds. I close my eyes and channel every ounce of concentration I have into tracking the sound of her footsteps. She's maybe ten yards away. Then eight.

I'm desperate for oxygen; my battered body needs it right now. But I can't breathe; she might hear me.

Five yards.

I open my eyes, my lungs screaming.

Then I jump out from behind the tree, swinging the cane in a broad, powerful arc, aiming to connect with her skull.

But I'm a split second too early; the cane doesn't quite reach Harriet.

As the cane whizzes through empty air, Harriet reverses course. Her arms flail in a reverse arc as she thrusts herself backward to avoid the blow.

In that frozen moment, I see an echo of Tina making the same motion.

I finally know exactly how Tina died.

Harriet snuck up to Tina's room when she was certain everyone in the house was occupied and Rose was with the horses. She was planning to do something to unnerve Tina as part of her campaign to get Tina to move out. Instead, she overheard Tina telling Ashley about the pregnancy.

Harriet lost control; Tina was about to destroy the family. Harriet lifted her cane, making some small noise that alerted Tina—or maybe

Tina sensed the energy shifting behind her, turning threatening. When Tina spun around to see Harriet swinging, Tina leapt backward to avoid the stinging blow, not thinking about the thin old window directly behind her.

Harriet didn't intend to kill Tina—but she's right, who would have believed her?

"Ian, help!" I scream again.

I hear Ian's voice in the distance, shouting something.

"Harriet has a Taser!" I yell. "She killed Tina! Call the police!"

I don't wait to see what he does. I veer to my left and reverse course, zagging through the trees. My strength is coming back now, my feet light and nearly soundless as my eyes sweep the landscape, searching for the bush that hides Rose.

I see a wispy white beacon in the darkness, almost as if the moon has beamed down a glowing circle to guide me. It's Rose, huddled in a shivering ball, her face streaked with tears.

I scoop her up as if she weighs no more than a feather.

I say the words I yearned to hear when I was a child. The best words I could ever utter to her. "You're safe."

CHAPTER SIXTY-THREE

I don't let go of Rose even after I run back into the house. I carry her with me as I lock the back door and search for a landline phone. I find it tucked behind a fruit bowl on the counter.

I dial 9–1–1 and gasp out the Barclays' address, telling them Tina de la Cruz's death wasn't an accident.

"Harriet Barclay tried to hit Tina with her cane and Tina fell through the window," I say, knowing I'm on a recorded line. "And I think Harriet was going to kill me tonight."

When I hear a loud bang on the kitchen door, I recoil as if it's a gunshot. But I don't let go of Rose.

Instead, my grip on her tightens as I twist, putting my body between her and any danger.

"I've got you," I promise her as I set down the phone receiver, keeping the 9–1–1 line open. "I won't let anyone hurt you."

Ian is standing there, his features twisted in worry and confusion.

I run toward the door, my hand reaching for the lock. Then, limping up out of the darkness behind him, I see Harriet.

She isn't wielding her Taser now. She's using a stick as a makeshift cane, and blood still stains her face and powder-blue sweatshirt. She looks like an injured, feeble grandma; she's superimposed that persona over herself like a Halloween costume.

"What's happening?" Ian shouts, his voice slightly muffled by the plexiglass. "Stella, what's going on?"

I point behind him. He swivels and sees Harriet. Her lips move as she begins to spin a story, filling Ian's ears, using her formidable cunning and deception.

She speaks too softly for me to hear, but Ian is listening intently to her.

Does he believe her? Is Harriet convincing him *I'm* the one who is a threat to Rose?

"Don't listen to her!" I shout. "She's lying! She lied about everything!"

"Please, Ian . . ." Harriet's voice lowers as she leans closer to her son.

"Harriet is responsible for Tina's death!" I scream, trying to drown out her words. "And she's been pinning it on Rose!"

Harriet shakes her head sorrowfully.

"Rose, honey? Come over here and let us in," Harriet calls.

Ian looks back and forth from me to Harriet. I can see it in his eyes; he doesn't know who to believe. She's his mother; he's only known me for a short time. How could she do the horrible things I'm accusing her of?

Then he does something that makes my heart stutter. He reaches into his pocket and pulls out his keys.

I back away, keeping my eyes on Harriet.

Ian fits a key into the lock, the small scraping noise magnified by the silence.

Rose lifts her head. For the first time ever, I hear her make a noise.

She releases a wail—high-pitched and keening. It goes on and on, seeming to spiral up out of her very soul. She's pointing at Harriet through the layer of plexiglass and shrieking as if she's seen the devil.

Ian stares at Rose, his eyes widening. Then he follows the direction of Rose's finger and turns to look at Harriet.

"Stop it, Rose! You just need some rest!" Harriet yells. "Ian, let me in and I'll put her to bed!"

Rose's shriek intensifies. She is in the throes of primal terror. And there's no mistaking the source: She's still staring straight at Harriet, who is rattling the door, trying to get in.

"No, Mom!" Ian shouts. "Wait!" But Harriet doesn't stop. She roughly bumps Ian aside and wrestles with the key in the lock.

Ian forces himself back in front of the door, shoving Harriet away. Then he opens the back door, yanks the key out, jumps inside, and slams and locks the door, sealing Harriet outside.

Rose's shriek subsides. Her breath comes in loud, hiccuppy gulps as she collapses against me.

"What's going on?" Ian shouts. His head jerks as he spots the blood on the floor by the elevator. He looks at Rose, scanning her for an injury, his arms reaching out for her. "Who hurt you, Rose? Stella or Harriet? Can you point to who it is?"

"It's Harriet's blood, not Rose's," I tell him. "I hit her with her cane after she used a Taser on me."

He stares at me, stunned. "My mother did what?"

I say the words he needs to hear: "Your mother was responsible for Tina's death. And she doesn't need a cane because her knee is fine."

He shakes his head. "No, no, that isn't possible. My mother didn't kill Tina. None of this is possible. Her knee is bad; she can't even make it up to the attic. She saw two surgeons after her operation failed."

"Did you ever hear her diagnosis firsthand from a doctor? Or did you just believe what Harriet told you?"

Ian falls silent, his widening eyes telling me the answer.

"Rose never hurt anyone, least of all Tina," I say. "But Harriet made everyone think she might have in order to deflect suspicion from herself."

Ian staggers forward and grabs the edge of the island. His face turns pale.

I see the comprehension hammer into him. He knows every word I've said is true; he heard it in Rose's scream.

In the distance, I hear approaching sirens.

Rose's breaths are steady and warm against my collarbone now. Her breathing slows until it matches mine, our systems syncing with each other's.

CHAPTER SIXTY-FOUR

Time blurs. The house fills with cops, summoned by Rose's text from Tina's phone and my subsequent 9–1–1 call. Beth comes flying through the front door, her eyes huge and frantic, shouting Rose's name.

I'm in the middle of giving my statement to the police, but I pause and peek into the living room to take in the sight of Beth and Ian hugging Rose between them.

For the first time, they look like a family.

When I've finished, I join them, feeling light-headed from exhaustion. Rose is sandwiched between Ian and Beth on the couch, and I've taken the chair Harriet claimed earlier tonight. I'm aware that on some level, even though I know Harriet was handcuffed and taken to a police precinct, I've positioned myself between Rose and the entry point to the room. It's hard to take my eyes off my young client.

I feel as if I've never truly seen her before.

Beth and Ian each have an arm around Rose, sheltering her within their joint embrace. Rose is asleep, her head leaning on her mother's shoulder, the cut on her foot covered by a thick Band-Aid.

I've recounted all the details of my involvement with the case to the police, starting with my first day and going through my final encounter with Harriet.

But I didn't reveal I'd begun to suspect Rose. I never want those words in an official record—one the tabloids might spread and distort, scattering seeds of doubt in the public's mind about whether Harriet was actually taking the fall for Rose.

"I can't believe my mother did all of those things." Ian's voice is tight and low. "And you think Rose knew she was in the attic with Tina all along?"

I nod. "That's why Harriet wanted to keep Rose isolated."

"Rose must have been so scared." Beth shudders and bends her head to gently kiss Rose's hair. "She couldn't sleep, she was gathering weapons to protect herself . . . and Harriet made us think Rose killed Tina, either accidentally or on purpose. She told us Rose came running out of the house after Tina fell. Who could blame that on a little girl?"

Ian's face reddens in anger. "Rose hid that knife in her backpack because she was alone with Harriet on the drive to and from school and she was terrified. But my mother twisted everything. She made me start to doubt my daughter's sanity."

I look at Beth. She wears the same expression as Ian: anger mixed with guilt and shame. "You never had a phobia of glass."

"No." She lowers her eyes. "We were desperate. Rose kept collecting weapons, and when we got rid of all the knives in the house, she began breaking glass and hiding jagged pieces under her bed or beneath the car seats, so we got rid of the glass, too . . . We did everything we could think of to make Rose stop. She seemed so different after Tina died. And Harriet kept telling us even young kids can get locked up if they're convicted of murder. I thought maybe Rose was with Tina and there was an accident, but I knew it could be portrayed as something else if anyone found out . . . Her entire life would be destroyed. We talked to Rose and told her that if she was up in the attic when Tina fell, we wouldn't be mad at her, she just needed to let us know what happened."

Tears roll down her cheeks. "Rose knew we suspected her. That we were a little scared of what she might do next. She must have felt so alone. What did we do to her?"

I tell them they aren't to blame—and that a few days ago I considered grabbing a knife and tucking it into my purse in case I needed to defend myself, yet I had been unable to see that's exactly what Rose was doing, too.

Ian is still trying to make sense of everything; he's tilting old images in his mind and gaining new perspectives. "Remember how she threw her doll out of the attic?" Ian looks at me, his eyes widening. "Do you think Rose was checking to see if Harriet could push her out the window even with the bar over it?"

"She could have been," I say. "Rose could also have been trying to figure out exactly what happened to Tina. Rose is very smart; she was trying to make sense of things. She wanted to understand Harriet and how someone who'd done something so evil could camouflage it from the people who knew her well."

The book *The Stranger Beside Me* explores that exact theme. That was why Rose was reading it.

I missed that clue, too.

Behind me, I hear Charles calling my name. I twist around, and he rushes toward me, relief filling his face.

"You didn't call within an hour," he cries. "I phoned the number you gave me and told the detective who answered to come here and then I kept calling you. But you didn't answer . . ."

He looks as dapper as always in his blue blazer and khaki slacks, but his shoes are mismatched—one black loafer and one brown—as if he threw them on while he ran out the door, intent on getting here in case I needed help.

I see the full force of it in his face, the fear and worry he has carried on my behalf. Not just tonight, but for most of my life.

A bit of the hardness in my heart toward him softens.

I stand up, feeling a deep ache in my chest, and walk to him. I hesitate, then hug him. "I'm okay," I tell Charles.

It isn't the complete truth, but it's close enough for now.

As I pull away from him, I see Detective Garcia standing by the front door. She's wearing a leather jacket and jeans. It's a good look on her.

Our eyes lock.

"You've had quite a night," she says calmly. "How are you feeling? Any injuries?"

"A few bruises, but nothing major."

"I'd like to get you checked out. Being Tased is no joke. Mind coming with me? I've got an EMT waiting outside."

A warmth spreads through my stomach. She may just be doing her job, but I like it that she seems to care.

"Go ahead," Charles tells me. "I'll wait for you here."

Detective Garcia crosses her arms, and the sleeves of her jacket ride up. I blink because I can't believe what I've just seen.

On her inner wrist is a small tattoo of an eagle, its wings spread in flight.

I don't believe in signs, but I can't help but think of the eagle statue in the mediator's office that promised hope.

I choose my next words carefully. Because even though I don't believe in signs, I do believe in taking chances.

"I don't mind going with you at all," I say.

And I swear I see it: a little movement at the corner of her lips, quick as the flutter of wings, that tells me she understands exactly what I mean. And more than that, she likes it.

A MONTH LATER

CHAPTER SIXTY-FIVE

This house feels so different. Glass is everywhere: in the globes composing the hallway chandelier, in the decorative mirror by the entryway, and in the drinkware on the coffee table in front of us.

The suffocating undercurrent—that desperate, cloying sense of doom—must have trailed Harriet to her jail cell. The air here feels bright and clean, smelling faintly of lemons.

I sit on a blue sectional couch in the family room across from Beth and Ian, studying them. Beth wears black slacks and a silky beige top, and her makeup is subdued and elegant. Diamonds glitter on her earlobes. Ian is in worn jeans and a green fleece jacket, with stubble covering his jaw and neck.

You have to look very closely to see the change in them. But their eyes tell the story of everything they've been through.

Their eyes look like shattered glass now.

"I let Harriet convince me to drug my daughter. What kind of mother am I?" Beth asks.

I'm about to answer when Ian leans in closer to his soon-to-be ex-wife.

"A good one," he says firmly.

I give it a moment so his words can sink in.

"Rose outsmarted Harriet. She never swallowed the Valium," I add. But I know Beth is worried about more than that.

"My report was completely false." I've told her this before, but she needs to hear it again. "If I had to write one now, I'd recommend joint custody. Fifty-fifty. But I like the way you've arranged things even better."

Over the past few weeks, all of the Barclays have revealed sides of themselves I didn't know existed.

It began with Beth. She purchased a beautiful—but not old or opulent—home in a nearby neighborhood in Potomac. It was a lightning-quick transaction since she made an all-cash offer and the house was move-in ready.

Then Beth did something extraordinary. She purchased a second home in the same neighborhood for Ian, just two blocks away.

"Rose needs both of us in her life as much as possible now," Beth explained. "This way, she can see us every day."

Beth's home, where we are now gathered, is surrounded by four acres, with a fenced pasture and barn for Sugar and Tabasco. She hired specialty movers to transport Rose's beloved piano here, too. Even before he moved into his new home, Ian brought in his work crew and installed a bright blue slide that leads from a corner of Rose's bedroom into the room he's turning into a little art studio for her. He also went to an animal shelter and adopted a skinny dog that reminds me a bit of Bingo.

They're fiercely devoted parents. Harriet was right about that.

"Stella, the irony is when Rose read your fake report, she realized you were the only one trying to get her away from Harriet. Rose desperately wanted to go back to school. She couldn't bear to live with Harriet any longer. That's why she finally reached out to you for help." Ian grimaces. "God, when I think about the things my mother did . . ."

I'd figured at least one of the Barclays would be unable to resist pulling the manila folder out of my purse as it sat unattended in the kitchen. It was a little surprising to learn they'd *all* done it.

My report may have been a sham, but Ian and Beth are adhering to one of the recommendations in it: Rose sees Dr. Markman four times a week. Bit by bit, Rose's story is emerging.

Harriet was constantly whispering into Rose's ear, swirling the little girl's mind into a hot, rancid stew. She didn't want Rose to trust me—and potentially confide in me—so she convinced Rose that I was going to take her away from both of her parents. Harriet even found an old news story about a BIA who brought in child protective services because she believed a young girl with divorcing parents was better off in foster care. Harriet presented it as evidence I was planning to do the same to Rose. That's why Rose acted like she hated me at times and wanted me to go away.

Harriet also knew if Beth and Ian thought I was growing suspicious of Rose, they'd do anything to get me out of their lives and save their daughter—even call off their divorce.

So she deliberately pretended to slip up by telling me Rose never went into the attic, realizing I'd believe she was covering for Rose. She also summoned police to my house in the middle of the night, took things from my purse—the police found my Montblanc pen in her bedroom—and spiked the oysters Ian and Beth ate to make them ill and feigned illness herself so that I'd be even warier of Rose.

Harriet knew the harder I looked at Rose, the less I'd see Harriet's culpability—and the quicker Ian and Beth would close ranks around their family.

But with Harriet gone, and the truth known, and her parents behaving as a team, Rose is finally in a safe place where she can begin to heal.

"Does Rose know I'm coming today?" I ask.

Beth nods. "She went to give Sugar and Tabasco some carrots and peppermints. I'm trying not to hover over her because Dr. Markman said it's important to not let my anxiety and guilt affect how I treat Rose. She's right there, in the barn."

Beth gestures through the bay window to the simple wood barn fifty or so yards from the house.

"Want to go to see her?" Ian asks.

"I'd love to." I stand up, and Beth and Ian do the same.

We walk through the kitchen and step through the back door. It's a brisk, windy November day, but the sun is brilliant in the clear blue sky. There's an apple tree in the backyard, and next door I see a wooden play structure. It gives me hope that Rose will make a friend in her new neighborhood.

Rose is grooming Sugar with her dandy brush as I approach the barn. She's so small she barely comes up to the top of her horse's leg, but she stretches her arm high overhead, doing her best to brush any dust from her horse's coat.

"You go ahead, Stella," Ian says. "We'll wait here."

"We don't trust many people around our daughter these days," Beth adds. "You wouldn't believe how carefully we checked out her new school and teachers. But you, Stella, we trust completely."

I nod at them, feeling a swell of emotion in my throat.

I walk closer to Rose, watching her work. Her hand stops brushing Sugar as she seems to sense my presence.

She turns around slowly, and when she sees me, the brush falls out of her hand to the ground.

"Hi, Rose," I say softly.

I leave the next move to her. I know Rose has a long road ahead of her. She'll be in therapy for years. I keep in touch with some of my former clients, but I don't know if she'll want to be one of them.

She stares at me, seemingly frozen, and I wonder if I'm an unwelcome reminder of all she has been through.

Then Rose begins to run to me, her hair a brilliant flame beneath the sunlight.

I bend down and stretch out my arms, feeling my heart soar.

When Rose reaches me, I scoop her up and feel her arms wrap around my neck, just as they did on the night we fought Harriet together. When we saved each other.

Her breath, smelling sweetly of peppermints, brushes my cheek. And for the first time, Rose speaks to me.

I'll carry her words in my heart forever.

"Thank you," she whispers.

CHAPTER SIXTY-SIX

There's one other trip I need to make today. I stacked the two visits on purpose. They're the yin and yang of my life right now, like the counterbalancing symbols in the mediator's office.

Seeing the Barclays brought me hope.

Seeing Charles makes my insides feel pinched.

The bright afternoon sun has slid away, dissolving into pink and violet clouds on the horizon by the time I stand at his door. He lives here alone; I know that now. He told me his wife is moving in with her sister. Their marriage has been over for decades. They're finally formalizing it.

During my divorce, Charles was the one who held me up. He called every few days and took me to dinner on Sunday nights. He was a counselor, father, and best friend.

He buoyed me through the years in so many other ways. I've been remembering more of the moments I considered gifts from a guardian angel, which I guess, in a way, they were. The helpful, age-appropriate books on grieving and resilience that found their way into my hands throughout my childhood and teenage years. The twenty-dollar bills I came across—four separate times—while walking home from elementary school. The pretty little apartment with the unbelievably low rent that became available near Charles's office a few weeks after I started working for him.

All of this was by Charles's invisible design.

He opens the door, wearing a button-down cardigan and tan slacks, his silver hair combed and his face freshly shaven.

"Stella."

That's all he says, just my name, but he infuses it with hope and sorrow, too.

He has laid everything out in his living room: the tray of olives and nuts and cheeses on a platter, the matching iced teas. The glasses are close together on the coffee table, just as they were on the night he shared a drink with my mother before she overdosed.

"How are you?" he asks, taking his usual chair.

"It's been quite a month," I reply as I sit on the couch facing him.

It was Detective Garcia who told me everything, after I came to the precinct to answer a few lingering questions on the Barclay case. She laid out the information quickly and clearly, like a surgeon making a precise and vital cut; then she walked me to my Jeep and waited until she was certain I was able to safely drive myself home.

It's why I haven't seen Charles recently: I needed time to get myself in the right headspace.

"And Rose is doing well?" he asks.

"She likes her new school and her teacher. It's a small Montessori. They have a gerbil and a betta fish in the classroom, which makes her happy."

"That's wonderful. And she's talking normally?"

"Normally for her—which means she speaks with the vocabulary and poise of an adult."

Charles takes a sip of his iced tea, but I don't carry the conversation.

He clears his throat and sets down his glass. "Stella, when we last talked . . . there was more I wanted to say."

I feel like I'm strapped into a roller coaster soaring up to a distant, dizzying peak. It's too late now; I can't stop the gears from grinding into motion.

Whatever happens next could forever change our relationship. I see it in the halting cadence of Charles's words, and the pallor of his face.

He clasps his hands together, like he's praying. Maybe he is, because he's silent for a long moment. Then he just says it.

"I wasn't assigned randomly to be your mother's lawyer. I took the case because I knew her before she ever got arrested."

The same rush of light-headedness I experienced when Detective Garcia first told me this information hits me again, but it's not as intense. I'm thankful she prepared me.

I swallow hard and force myself to keep looking into Charles's eyes.

He reaches a trembling hand toward me across the table, then withdraws it.

It's hard to breathe. I hope he makes the next cut fast, even though speed won't make it hurt any less.

"I was there the night your father died, too."

I drop my face into my hands and let my tears fall. It's hard to know how to feel; I wasn't sure if Charles would be honest with me. I didn't know how we'd go forward if he wasn't.

And I'm not sure how we go forward now, either.

All along, I thought the biggest unopened question in my life was what happened to my mother.

But the real secret was what happened to my father.

There was a deer in the road on the night my father died; that part of the story my mother told me was true. But there was also another car involved, driven by Charles.

I didn't know that critical piece of the story until Detective Garcia told me she'd been digging through old information to help me learn more about my mother and noticed Charles's name on the police report of my father's death. She reminded me that I'd given Charles as a reference when I first called her about the Barclay case. His name had jumped out at her when she read the file on my mother—it was her pencil that drew a light line beneath it. And when she saw he was present at my father's accident, she immediately reached for the phone and called me.

I've reconstructed what happened from the old reports she let me read: It was dark out that night. The road held a sharp turn. My father was in a rush to get home from work. Charles was, too. Their cars headed into the turn from opposite directions, each very close to the middle yellow dividing line. They nearly collided, and my father overcorrected and almost lost control of his Chevy. He might have made it, but a dozen yards ahead of him, a deer was taking a tentative step into his lane. My dad jerked the wheel to avoid it, still wrestling for control of his old Chevy. He slammed into a tree and died instantly.

Two other drivers who witnessed the crash debated whether either—or both—cars were speeding, and whether either vehicle crossed the center line just before the drivers nearly collided.

I read the witness statements; no clear answers emerged. But one thing stood out: Charles had alcohol in his system. He was under the legal limit, but just barely.

In the end, no charges were filed. No one was found at fault.

A thousand elements played a part in the death of my father: the sharply curved road with its blind spots, the moonless dark of night, the deer's halting step onto the asphalt road. And even before that, countless micro-decisions led to the fatal moment: The three scotches Charles had enjoyed with another attorney to celebrate the conclusion of a big case. Charles and my father leaving work and getting into their cars at the precise moment they each did. The red and green traffic lights they hit or sailed through. The weight of their feet against their respective gas pedals. Their collision course was set by all of these variables.

"After I saw your dad's car crash, I jumped out of my car and ran to help him. But he was already gone, Stella. I am so, so sorry."

We sit in silence together until I raise my face to him. I see tears running down his cheeks, too.

He looks so scared. I know he's terrified I'll walk out his door and never talk to him again. That he'll lose the only family he has left.

"Did my mother know all this?"

"Yes," he says instantly. "I reached out to her shortly after your father's accident. We met at a coffee shop, and I answered all her questions truthfully. I told her that your father died instantly, that he didn't suffer. I also asked her to call me if she ever needed anything. We became—well, not exactly friends—but we were bonded somehow. We kept in touch. That's how I became her lawyer."

I nod. It was my mother's decision to tell me my father swerved to avoid a deer—to truncate the story into something more manageable for my young mind. Or perhaps that's the conclusion she herself reached, that no one was responsible, that it was nothing more than a horrible accident. The kind that tears apart more lives than the one it first claimed.

"After the night your father died—well, things went a little off course for me. I did my job, but not much else. I'd come home and walk straight to the liquor cabinet and pour myself something. I'd fill my glass all night long, even though that was the very thing I couldn't stop thinking about: Maybe if I hadn't had that third strong scotch, I would've done something differently, and your father would still be alive."

Charles's breathing takes on a strained quality.

"After a while I started to dabble in other drugs. It was easy to get them—half my clients were dealing. I tried whatever I could: Valium, coke, speed, heroin. Thankfully OxyContin wasn't around then or I would've been on it. That one might have done me in. And then, after your mom died . . . I stopped cold turkey—everything but the drinking, and I scaled that way back. My family had given up on me. I didn't have much to live for, Stella. But I thought if I could just save you . . ."

A thousand elements played a part in my mother's death, too: her decision to tape a bag of heroin to the back of the toilet, the kiss from Charles, and the fact that I stayed obediently in the closet instead of opening the door like Rose did when I was in trouble. And even before that, there was the choice she made to walk into a certain corner deli at the exact same moment as my father, and to start talking to him as they waited for their sandwiches. My parents' collision course was set by as many variables as there are points of light in the sky.

"I knew you would learn the truth when you were ready, and I vowed to be honest with you when you came to me with questions. I know I don't have the right to ask for your forgiveness, Stella. I've deceived you for so long."

"You did," I tell him.

He hangs his head, pain sweeping over his features.

I quickly say, "No, that's not what I meant."

I wait until he looks back up at me. I want him to know this; it may be the second most important thing I'll ever tell him.

"You did save me."

I stand up and reach out my arms, and in an instant, he's there, hugging me tightly. This time, I'm the one whispering into his ear. And I tell him the first, most important thing. "I could never hate you. I love you too much for that."

CHAPTER SIXTY-SEVEN

"How'd it go with Charles?" she asks.

I look across the high-top bar table at Detective Natalia Garcia. She came to meet me straight from work, and I'm guessing by the way she keeps nibbling at her thumbnail that something happened today she isn't easily able to shake off. A troubling new case, maybe.

I wait while the waiter delivers our drinks—a whisky on the rocks for her and a Malbec for me—before answering.

"I was surprised by how easy it felt to forgive him. I can understand why Charles did what he did. He thought if he could just save me . . . Not that it would erase everything that happened, but—" I'm fumbling for the words to explain.

"I get it," she interjects. "He did the wrong things for the right reasons. Most important, his heart was always in the right place."

She sums it up so simply and accurately. It feels good to be understood.

I take a sip of wine, feeling its warmth all the way down into my stomach. Adele's rich, soulful voice is playing over the speakers, and the votive light on our table casts a golden glow over Natalia's tan skin. I can't imagine wanting to be anywhere else.

"Do you think Harriet's going to get out of jail while she's still alive?" I ask.

"Probably," Natalia says. "She's taking a plea, but I doubt she'll serve more than ten to fifteen years. She could have a decade of freedom after that."

Rose will be a young adult by then. She'll be in control of what kind of relationship she has with Harriet—if any.

If it were me, I'd cut Harriet out of my life forever. Harriet's cunning, born of desperation, was breathtaking: After she discovered Tina and Ian slept together for the first time, she tried to turn Rose against Tina, figuring that might make Tina quit. Harriet told Rose about the affair and said Tina was planning to live with Ian and become her new mother. Rose could see Tina liked Ian too much; she couldn't discount Harriet's stories. That's why Rose was so conflicted; she really did alternately love and hate and fear Tina.

When Tina didn't leave, Harriet stepped up her campaign. Police found her secret stash of electronics: She hid mini-cameras in Tina's room to monitor Tina and Ian's trysts and gauge the seriousness of the affair. That led to the creepy note telling Tina she should have worn the red dress.

Harriet also hid a tiny tracker in Rose's coat when I took Rose to Lucille's. When Harriet saw the photograph of Rose cuddling the baby squirrel, she made Rose look especially disturbed by texting the roadkill photo to Lucille.

"I just lost you," Natalia says. "What were you thinking about?"

I slowly twirl my wineglass by the stem.

"I thought I heard Rose say something once when I was with Harriet. It turns out Harriet had downloaded an old video of Rose waving at the camera and saying 'Hi' and she played it when I was in the basement to make me think Rose was choosing not to talk."

"That would be a natural assumption," Natalia tells me.

But I know better. I remember what it was like when people didn't believe I couldn't talk.

"That old Frank Sinatra song must have really freaked out Tina," Natalia says, referring to another recording found on Harriet's phone: a snip of the Frank Sinatra song "Tina." Harriet told police she played it through the air duct that led into the attic late at night to terrify Tina.

"Harriet did everything she could think of to drive Tina out. But when she realized Tina was pregnant, she lost control." I shake my head. "Did she really think Rose would just go back to normal after a few months, like nothing happened?"

"Harriet will pay for that." Natalia's shoulders square, like she's getting ready for a fight. I think about what Charles told me when he was urging me to take the Barclay case—that I haven't gotten jaded. Natalia hasn't, either. She takes on cases involving the worst things human beings can do to one another. She runs straight into the storm. I wonder what makes her tick.

"I found out why Beth left Yale, too," she tells me.

"Oh, yeah?"

"She was a little shy and different from other girls, like her daughter. There was an incident with a boyfriend—they were together one night, and he invited a couple of his buddies in to watch without Beth knowing. Word spread around campus. He was expelled and she decided to leave, too."

There's a parallel between Rose and Beth here, too—but not the one I feared. Rose truly was bullied at the school she attended before Rollingwood, which is why she left.

"How is Rose doing?" she asks.

"Better," I tell her. "I'm going to her piano recital next month."

She takes a sip of her whisky. "Are you going to break your rule again and work with more young kids?"

I look down at my hands. "I don't know. They're tough. Sometimes they distort their own realities. Other times people deliberately do it for them."

"Is that the only reason why they're tough for you?"

She wants to know what makes me tick, too.

"It's easier for me to work with older kids. They've got more agency, you know?" She deserves my full honesty. "And obviously I didn't have the greatest childhood, so . . ."

I see it in her expression, her recognition of a counterpart in me. Silence stretches between us for a beat, but it isn't uncomfortable.

"I get it," she interjects. "The thing is, people like us—we want to go back in time and change things for ourselves. We can't. But when we help other people . . . well, it doesn't fix us. But for a little while, every time I close a case and I've gotten some justice for a victim, I get this feeling of—"

"Peace."

"Exactly."

Our eyes lock and I feel a little dizzy.

"So what do you do for fun on the weekends?" she asks.

"Well, on Saturday I'm going out for a drink with my ex-husband and his new girlfriend."

She smiles, full on. I feel it all the way down to my toes. "Sounds interesting."

The question flows out of me, like it's the most natural thing in the world. "Want to join us?"

I see it again: the corners of her mouth fluttering. Her answer is perfect.

"It's a date."

She leans across the small round table, very close to me. "Remember that time in my office when I told you I like puzzles?"

I nod; her proximity takes my breath away.

She leans a few inches closer and kisses me lightly. Her lips taste of whisky and feel like a promise.

"You're a puzzle," she whispers.

CHAPTER SIXTY-EIGHT

I don't know how I'll feel when the door opens and I glimpse her face.

I could turn around right now and walk away. I could claim I'm overbooked—that I have too many cases vying for my time.

But then I'd be lying to myself.

I shake out my hands and do a few neck rolls, trying to force some looseness into my body. Then I close my eyes and think of the new touchstone in my life, the one that gives me strength and shapes my new determination: Rose's arms around my neck, and her whispered *thank you* in my ear.

I grab the brass knocker and rap it twice.

The office door opens, and there she is, her hair shorter than when I last saw her but her expression as welcoming as I remember.

"Hi, Stella."

My old therapist, Chelsea, steps to the side, clearing the way for me to enter her office.

I take a deep breath and walk in.

ACKNOWLEDGMENTS

My gratitude to my wonderful friend Jamie Desjardins, who not only told me about her job as a BIA—which ignited the spark for this novel—but also throws amazing book parties for me.

Jennifer Enderlin, my cherished and indefatigable editor, joined me in brainstorming plot twists early on and had her hand in everything from choosing the title to the cover. Jen, I adore working with you and look forward to many more books together. I'm also deeply grateful to the rest of the smart, hardworking, and fun team who now feel like my family at St. Martin's Press, including publicist Katie Bassel, marketing gurus Erica Martirano and Brant Janeway, and Robert Allen, Jeff Dodes, Marta Fleming, Olga Grlic, Tracey Guest, Sarah La Cotti, Christina Lopez, Kim Ludlam, Kerry Nordling, Erik Platt, Gisela Ramos, Sally Richardson, Lisa Senz, Michael Storrings, Tom Thompson, and Dori Weintraub. A special shout-out to the stellar audio team of Guy Oldfield, Mary Beth Roche, Emily Dyer, and Drew Kilman.

My thanks to my fantastic team at William Morris Endeavor, especially my literary agent, Margaret Riley King, and my film agents Hilary Zaitz Michael and Sylvie Rabineau, foreign rights director Tracy Fisher, and Celia Rogers, Jack Nielson, and David Rafailovich-Sokolov. My gratitude also to entertainment lawyer Darren Trattner and to Robin Budd.

Laurie Prinz, thanks for being an early reader and smart critiquer, all-around sounding board, and inspiration. My gratitude to the readers who improved my first draft: Jamie Desjardins, Suzy Wagner, John Pekkanen, Lynn Pekkanen, Ben Pekkanen, and Tammi Hogan. And to the friends and family who buoyed me while I wrote it, especially Rachel Baker, Laura Hillenbrand, Amy and Chris Smith, Cathy Hines, Lucinda Eagle, and Robert and Saadia Pekkanen. And Alex Finlay—I hope we have many more years of authorly walks, talks, and book events together.

Big thanks to Suzy Wagner and Karlee Rockstroh for helping me up my social media game, and to Chelsea Schneiders for winning the Hope for Henry auction to buy a character's name. And to eagle-eyed Roger Aarons for always reading my pages and catching the quirky errors that might otherwise slip by.

To my sons, Jackson, Will, and Dylan—you three inspire me every day. I couldn't love you more.

And finally, to all the Bookstagrammers, social media friends, librarians, booksellers, and readers—a high point of my day is interacting with you on Instagram and Facebook. I want to hear what you think about *House of Glass*. Please tag me so we can connect!

ABOUT THE AUTHOR

Kristina Sherk

Sarah Pekkanen is the number-one *New York Times* bestselling coauthor of four novels of suspense, including *The Golden Couple,* and the solo author of the thrillers *Gone Tonight* and *House of Glass.* She is also the solo author of eight international bestselling women's fiction books and is an award-winning former journalist. She serves as US ambassador for RRSA India and works hands-on in India to rescue street dogs. She lives just outside of Washington, DC, with her family.